NORTH BEACH

In memory
of Don Douglass

NORTH BEACH

John T. D.

A NOVEL BY **MILES ARCENEAUX**

North Beach

Library of Congress Cataloging in Publication Data:
Arceneaux, Miles
North Beach / Miles Arceneaux
1. Title. 2. Fiction. 3. Mystery. 4 Suspense
-
First Edition: October 2015
978-0-9968797-1-2

Printed in the United States of America
Written by Brent Douglass, John T. Davis and James R. Dennis
Designed by Lana Rigsby, Thomas Hull, and Carmen Garza

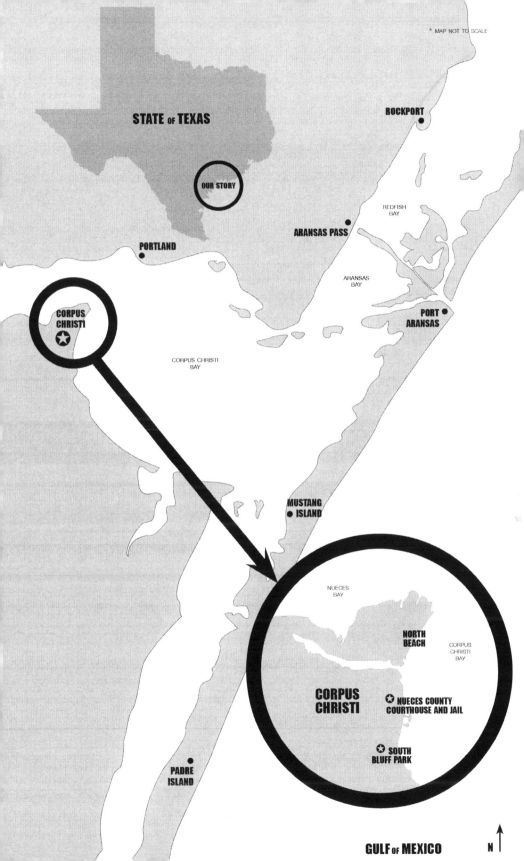

* MAP NOT TO SCALE

STATE of TEXAS

OUR STORY

ROCKPORT

PORTLAND

ARANSAS PASS

REDFISH BAY

ARANSAS BAY

CORPUS CHRISTI

CORPUS CHRISTI BAY

PORT ARANSAS

MUSTANG ISLAND

NUECES BAY

NORTH BEACH

CORPUS CHRISTI BAY

CORPUS CHRISTI

NUECES COUNTY COURTHOUSE AND JAIL

SOUTH BLUFF PARK

PADRE ISLAND

GULF of MEXICO

N

This novel is a work of fiction. Names, characters, businesses, places, and events were either made up or used in a fictitious manner. However, some old-timers might recognize semi-famous personalities like Billy Boomerang and Bill the Beachcomber (both now deceased). We are fortunate that the Texas Gulf Coast has provided us with such an inexhaustible supply of local color.

Corpus Christians may also remember some of the local landmarks we used in our story: Pick's, Snapka's, the Ship Ahoy restaurant, the Municipal Auditorium, the Thunderbird Drive-In Theater, Lichtenstein's Department Store. Most are gone now, but one landmark in particular, is not. From the elevated freeway in downtown Corpus Christi, you can see the once stately Nueces County Courthouse & Jail crumbling and rotting away. Attempts to save the historic building have stalled and largely failed— a symbol of the city's dysfunctional politics these last fifty years.

North Beach, the one-mile-long strip of land underneath and alongside the Harbor Bridge, is trying to make a comeback, inspired by its glory days in the '30s, '40s, and early '50s. The seedy bars, flophouses, and curio shops that came after were mostly bulldozed and have been replaced by the Texas State Aquarium, the *USS Lexington,* and a growing collection of family-friendly hotels and restaurants. One nostalgic business owner even brought back a working replica of the old amusement park Ferris wheel. *North Beach* has a certain affection for the strip's bad old days. If Charlie ever went back and got that tattoo, he ain't telling.

— MILES ARCENEAUX

CHAPTER 01

JULY 1962

I lifted my head off the dock and checked the red and white bobber floating limply on the surface of Redfish Bay, and then went back to watching a parade of billowy white clouds glide across the sky. It was a lazy summer afternoon and, with any luck, nothing was biting. I didn't want to mess with reeling in a fish anyway.

Though you couldn't really call what I was doing fishing. For one thing, I was using a beginner's rig that some kid left lying on the dock earlier that day—a little Zebco spincaster with a plastic float and a piece of hotdog still stuck on the hook. I put it to use mainly out of boredom, but also, I admit it, to get out of some work. While I pretended to fish, my brother, Johnny, and our friend Pete Lopez were filleting sea trout at the cleaning table and taking issue with my idleness.

"*Oye*, Johnny, what's the deal with your brother? He always this worthless?"

"Naw, man, sometimes he's even worse. You oughta see him on the shrimp boat. He's either eating, sleeping, or jerking off."

"Liar," I said, giving the fishing line an experimental shake. "Sometimes I'm fishin'." Inside the bait house, I could hear the Beach

Boys' "Surfin' Safari" playing on my crappy little transistor radio. It seemed like the AM station in Corpus played it two or three times every hour. It was the perfect soundtrack to my fifteenth summer. "I'd get up and help, but you guys are hogging the table."

"The way I see it," Pete continued, "since we're doing all the work, we should take half his pay."

"Ha. I'd like to see you try."

Pete shook his head melodramatically. "Man, what a loafer."

A jerk on the line prompted me to check my bobber again. The float jiggled a bit and then stopped—probably a piggy perch picking at my bait. Maybe a blue crab. I considered reeling in but decided it wasn't really worth the trouble. I sat up and watched my two co-workers expertly fillet the last of the guests' afternoon catch.

Pete was a lot shorter than Johnny, but the sun had baked them both the same shade of brown. Running around shirtless and in cut-offs all summer, Johnny and I almost could've passed for Pete's younger and much taller Mexican brothers. Except that Pete wore a slick, jet-black pompadour, while Johnny and I had disheveled, sun-bleached hair.

"You guys hurry up," I said. "We're gonna have to hustle if we want to catch any waves before supper."

Johnny flipped a fish head at me with his fillet knife. "Whatever you say, loafer. Why don't you make yourself useful and get our boards ready?"

My brother and I usually spent June out in the Gulf of Mexico working on one of our dad's trawlers, so we hardly saw land for an entire month, but shrimping season was closed in July and August for conservation purposes. This was fine with us, as we were inclined to goof off as much as possible during summer.

Our dad thought different, of course, so he sent us to work at our Uncle Rupert's fish camp on Ransom Island. With a name like that, it sounds like a perfect hideout for pirates, and it kind of was—a weather-beaten collection of buildings and characters on a little hook-shaped island across the water from Aransas Pass. The operation consisted of a big dancehall and restaurant, a cluster of cabins for fishermen and duck hunters, and a string of charter fishing skiffs. Pete lived in Corpus Christi, but for the last couple of summers he'd worked with us on Ransom Island. The three of us bunked together in the bait house. We were at the beck and call of Rupert Sweetwater, my uncle and the Kingfish, you might say, of the lodge.

Our job at the fish camp was nothing but one glamorous task after another—from minor boat repair, to outfitting the daily fishing charters, to K.P. in the restaurant and dancehall. We also cleaned the customers' catch, which we thought we'd just about wrapped up until Rupert's brother Flavius walked up and dropped a heavy stringer of gafftops onto the fish-cleaning table. Our normally cranky uncle had a wide grin on his face, which was never a good sign.

"Here's a present for you boys. The Pattons want to eat these beauties for supper tonight."

"They want to eat gafftop?" asked Johnny. He used his knife to poke at one of the ugly dirty-grey fish. The gafftopsail was a type of catfish, so named for a sail-like fin that hung off its long dorsal spine—the fin spike was sharp enough to puncture a foot or a hand clean through. It was also absolutely the slimiest fish found in the Gulf Coast waters. Local anglers called them "tourist trout." We called 'em "snot rockets."

Pete looked at the stringer and frowned. "How 'bout we give 'em some of these trout fillets instead?"

"Or better yet," Johnny added, "have Miz Leona fry up some of those fish sticks she keeps in the freezer? They're already breaded and everything. I bet the Pattons'll never know the difference. Aren't they from Odessa?"

"Abilene," Flavius answered. "And they want what they caught them-selves . . . cleaned and skinned. You numbskulls stop bellyaching and do your job. Charlie, get your ass up off the dock and help 'em!"

The job was nasty business, but the three of us crowded around the table and began working quickly and with purpose. A stiff west wind meant there might be decent waves at Bob Hall Pier that afternoon. While we hurried to finish, Flavius sat on the doorstep of the bait house watching us work, smoking cigarettes, and scowling.

I scraped a pile of fish guts into the bay and pushed one of the gafftops towards Pete. "Come on, 'Lightning.' Let's see if you can live up to your name."

Earlier, we had been discussing the "ring" names we'd adopt if we became professional fighters. I had decided on Charlie "Sweet Dreams" Sweetwater, while Pete had chosen "Lightning" Pete Lopez. My brother said fans would someday know him as "The Gulf Coast Gladiator."

When we mentioned our nicknames to Flavius, he snorted. "Ring names? How 'bout the 'Gulf Coast Goobers?'" He glared at us and then shook his head.

Flavius glared a lot, and at pretty much everyone. My grandmother had saddled him with the name Flavius Octavius Sweetwater when he was born, and he'd been angry about it ever since. To make matters worse, he was a head shorter than his three brothers and had flaming red hair that stuck out in all directions. The chip on his shoulder was legendary. Though he was only about five-foot nothin', he'd been a brawler of a flyweight in his day, fighting in informal smokers and at the bottom of the card at arenas up and down the Coastal Bend, one time even as far away as Little Rock. But these days he just brawled for fun with anyone who looked at him wrong.

"How 'bout y'all win a few more amateur matches before ya start puffin' your chests out and talkin' about goin' pro?" he said, shaking his head. "Ring names . . . . Gawd almighty."

We were quiet after that and continued to work on the gafftops. It never paid to argue with Uncle Flavius. We weren't really serious about the ring names. At least not me and Johnny. We already knew we wouldn't box for a living, just like, deep down, we knew we wouldn't follow in our dad's footsteps and become shrimpers, either. But Flavius insisted that any nephew of his was going to be schooled in the sweet science, so we had no choice but to learn to box. Our dad, Dublin "Dubber" Sweetwater, hoped it would keep us mostly out of trouble, although we still managed to find our share.

Johnny had turned sixteen the previous October, old enough to enter last year's Golden Gloves tournament as a sub-novice. He won three bouts and was runner-up in his division. My sixteenth birthday wasn't for another eight months, *after* the amateur tournaments were over, so I'd yet to have an official fight and that bugged the heck out of me. I was aching to test myself in a real boxing match.

Pete Lopez, on the other hand, had been state flyweight champion two years running, and did well in Nationals, too. Everyone believed Pete had a legitimate shot at a pro career. But Flavius still treated him like a rank amateur, either to keep him from getting a big head, or maybe out of envy. When my uncle was in Golden Gloves, he never advanced past Regionals, mainly because he could never get past Dick Menchaca, a terrific fighter who went on to became the U.S. Army champ during World War II.

"Soon as you boys clean those fish, Rupe wants you to hose out the slime in the boat. Them gafftops really boogered 'em up. After that, I expect y'all to get your butts to the gym for a workout."

When we didn't answer, he gave us his laser stare. "The gym. You savvy?"

"Yes, sir," we mumbled.

"And if you're thinking of skipping out, don't. 'Cause I'll sure as hell hear about it."

So much for our afternoon beach plans.

We delivered the fish to the kitchen, and while we waited for the ferry to take us to Aransas Pass, Miz Leona, Shady's colored cook, fixed us peanut butter sandwiches to tide us over until supper. She handed me two.

"You need ta put some meat on those bones, Charlie. I'm afraid a strong breeze might carry you off one day."

"I eat all the time, Miz Leona. Nothing sticks."

"Well, it will, honey, it will. Believe it or not, I was skinnier than you when I was your age. Now look at me."

I resisted the urge to look too close. Leona was as big and stout as a smokehouse, and probably could've gone eight rounds with Floyd Patterson.

We heard the ferry approaching, so we grabbed our sandwiches and started for the landing. As we loped off, I heard Leona calling to me.

"Oh, Charlie! I forgot to give you this."

To my horror, she was holding a dog-eared copy of *Playboy* magazine, the May issue.

"The maids found it inside your pillowcase in the bait house."

"It must be someone else's," I said, flushing red. I could already hear Pete and Johnny sniggering behind my back.

She raised an eyebrow and nodded. "Uh-huh. So you want me to throw it out?"

I shuffled over with as much dignity as I could muster and grabbed the magazine.

As humiliating as it was to be busted by Leona, it wasn't half as bad as climbing into the car with Johnny and Pete. They made it worse by keeping silent at first, until they couldn't hold back any longer and burst out laughing.

"*Órale*, Charlie. I didn't know you were starting a library inside your pillowcase."

"Screw you, Pete. I hid it there so you wouldn't steal it."

"You kidding me, *cabrón*? I wouldn't touch it. All the pages are stuck together."

"All the pages with pictures, anyway," Johnny laughed.

They kept ribbing me until, thank goodness, the ferry rumbled up to the landing and dropped the ramp. I'm not sure why I was so embarrassed about the stupid magazine. This new obsession I had with girls had kind of taken me by surprise. Last year they were barely on my radar, and now they were all I could think about. Seemingly overnight, my interests had switched from Batman and Superman to the Playmate of the Month. Females had become a thrilling source of mystery and desire, competing mightily with sports and fishing for my attention.

Some of my other new diversions were less confusing: surfing, for instance, and surf music, and, for the first time in my life, my very own automobile. Well, officially it was my brother's—a rusty four-door Jeep wagon with a V-6 engine and re-covered bench seats. But because I helped fix it up and sprung for half the gas, he let me drive it around some, and I always had first dibs on the front seat. The old wood-paneled wagon greatly expanded our range and gave us more liberty than we'd ever known. We spent most of our free time fishing up and down the coast, surfing the mushy waves on Mustang Island, and driving around looking for girls.

I figured that when high school rolled around, things would get harder. Johnny would be starting quarterback on the Rockport Pirates football team, and I knew if I didn't make varsity I'd never hear the end of it. My brother was already a big wheel at the school, and having Sweetwater as a last name came with certain expectations in our little town. Being cool was almost a full time job in itself.

But in the meantime, boxing.

CHAPTER 02

We drove the twenty-odd miles from Aransas Pass to Corpus Christi and parked in front of a one-story stucco building with cast bronze numbers and letters set over the door:

★ **1936** ★

CENTENNIAL · MUSEUM

I was pretty sure that Stubby Hunsacker had the only boxing gym in Texas housed in a former museum. It was one of many buildings and monuments erected in 1936 by patriotic committees throughout the state to celebrate our century of independence from Mexico. But once the raucous, yearlong party was over, most of them stood neglected and woefully short of maintenance funds. The Centennial Museum was no exception.

The museum was only four blocks from the bay, so it deteriorated rapidly in the exposed tropical setting. When civic attention shifted to the Nazi/Jap menace, the city council gladly leased the small, un-adorned art deco building to Stubby and named the Corpus Christi Police Department as official sponsors of the gym's Golden Gloves amateur boxing program. The program would "help keep juvenile delin-quents off the street," proclaimed the mayor.

I suppose it did keep some petty hoodlums and would-be criminals busy for a few hours a day, especially if Stubby decided to take a kid under his wing. He'd transformed some of the sorriest street punks in the area into first-rate amateur boxers. Stubby had a big heart, but he didn't put up with any bullshit, and he insisted on a rigid decorum at his gym. Signs declared that there be "No loud talk or bad talk," and you were commanded to "Respect the property of others." Anybody caught drinking, smoking, or spitting anywhere near the building was treated to a week scrubbing out the gym toilet before he was allowed back in the ring or on the bags.

But once you crossed the threshold, the gym seemed anything but decorous. Your nose was assaulted by a funky stew of canvas, sweat, moldy plaster, and dirty socks. Nothing quite smells like a gym in South Texas in the summertime. Soft light filtered through the dirty, barred windows, and industrial floor fans labored to circu-late damp air around a room only sixty feet long by forty feet wide. Over the noise of the fans, you could hear the rhythmic thumping of the speed bags, the clanging of the free weights, skip ropes popping the floor, and the thuds and grunts of guys working the heavy bags.

I stood at the entrance and lingered, letting my senses adjust to the intense heat and noise—I always took a moment to soak it all in.

"Heads up, Charlie," I heard Pete say.

Out of the corner of my eye I saw a medicine ball hurtling toward me like a Whitey Ford heater. I tried to duck, but the heavy sand-filled ball caught me on the side of the head and sent me crashing into the wall. I slumped to the floor and saw Naco Flores, a half-witted, one-armed Mexican kid who worked at the gym, double over in laughter. Johnny and Pete were laughing, too.

Pete leaned over me. "You want an eight-count, Charlie?"

I waved him off. "Leave me alone."

I struggled to my feet, and Johnny handed me my gym bag. "You okay?"

"Why does that crazy kid always mess with *me?*" I asked, rubbing my temple.

"Because he likes you."

I heard Stubby's voice from across the gym. "Sweetwater! Stop playing grabass and get dressed."

Stubby cut Naco Flores a lot of slack inside his gym. Probably because he was mentally slow and, according to Pete, went home at night to a squalid shack and an abusive, alcoholic mother. The kid practically lived at the gym. Even though he was younger, smaller, and skinnier than me, he could catapult those medicine balls with punishing accuracy and had put me on my butt more than once.

There was no dressing room to speak of, just an area at the back of the building defined by a narrow row of benches and a wall of rusty wire baskets used for stowing street clothes. A long portable chalkboard provided some privacy. As we walked by the chalkboard, Stubby was erasing MARINER 1 from the USA side of the ledger. SPACE RACE had been written in big block letters above a line that bisected the board: one column tallying successful space missions by the USA, and the other listing successful missions by the Russians. I saw that the US was up seven to six.

"What happened to the Mariner, Mr. Hunsacker?" asked Johnny.

"Went off course. Blew up." Stubby took every sort of competition seriously, and after President Kennedy threw down the gauntlet and announced to the world that we would put a man on the moon by the end of the decade, he'd been especially invested in this one.

"But it looks like we're still winning."

Stubby grunted and shifted the cigar stub to the other side of his mouth. "Won't be if we keep blowing up our own rockets."

According to the dates on the chalkboard, Russia took an early lead with the Sputnik, Luna, and Vostock missions, but the good guys—that would be us—made a strong recovery with the Mercury program and then pulled ahead after the latest earth orbits by John Glenn and, three months later, Scott Carpenter.

Pete pointed to an early Russian mission involving a dog named Laika. "It counts if they send up a dog?"

"They send up dogs. We send up monkeys. Same difference."

Stubby tossed the chalk into the wooden chalk tray and faced us, hands on hips; he resembled a garden gnome when he stood like this. Most other times, he reminded me of the heavy cast iron bulldog he kept on his desk and used as a paperweight, given to him, he'd told us, by Mickey "Toy Bulldog" Walker, a champion middleweight in the twenties and thirties.

"After you boys warm up, I want three rounds of shadow boxing, five minutes on the speed bag, and ten on the heavy bag, and then I want you to pair up and work the mitts. After that, check back with me."

We dressed out and started our calisthenics. While the three of us were on the floor doing crunches, we saw Karl McDevitt walk through the door, trailed by his squirrely little friend Boyd Parker. Karl was a rough-looking white kid, six-foot three inches tall and weighing close to two hundred pounds. There was no fat on the guy, and he wore tight T-shirts to show off his muscles and tattoos. Naco was squatting near the entrance holding a medicine ball under his arm and attempting to pick up a second one when Karl shoved him to the ground with his foot.

"Freak," he said, kicking the medicine balls away.

Pete shook his head. "I hate that guy."

"He's a coward," said Johnny. "Watch him. He'll always look around to make sure Stubby's not watching before he jacks with somebody."

"How old is he, anyway?" I asked. "He looks thirty."

"He dropped out of high school, so I'm not sure," Pete huffed between crunches. "Twenty-one maybe? But I heard he still lives with his mom."

Karl glared at us as he walked by. "Ladies," he said.

I never understood why Stubby allowed Karl in the gym. Thought he could turn him around, I guess. Johnny and I could have told Stubby it wasn't working.

We continued our workout and were soon drenched with sweat. The air in the gym felt like Jell-O pudding. Midway through our bag work we stopped, along with every other boxer in the gym, to watch Jesse Martel spar a few rounds with a big farmboy from Mathis. Jesse was Cuban and went by the ring name of *El Rey Feo*, the Ugly King, but at the gym we called him *Feo* for short, a name he answered to good-naturedly. He was only twenty-five, but he had a sad, rough-hewn face that could have belonged to an old man. A short neck made his head seem exceptionally large, and his flattened nose, deep-set eyes, and bushy eyebrows gave him a menacing, almost savage appearance. Which was why his big toothy smile and gentle demeanor outside the ring was so disarming. He and I had become pretty good friends, despite our differences in age, background, and skin color.

Stubby was Jesse's manager, preparing him for his first professional match in January—a welterweight bout against a mid-ranked boxer who was nearing the end of his career. Everyone agreed that Jesse could've started higher up the ladder—heck, we believed he'd be welterweight champ within three years—but Stubby wanted to bring him along slow and smart. He cared about his fighters and was particularly fond of Jesse.

With the slower sparring partner, Jesse mostly worked on his footwork, circling his opponent like a dancer, moving diagonally forward to jab but never overcommitting, unleashing rapid flurries even when he was going backwards. He claimed he learned his footwork after watching a kangaroo box a man in Cuba, a story I found hard to believe but had fun trying to picture. Stubby insisted that heavyweight Cassius Clay picked up his fancy footwork after watching Jesse box at the 1959 Pan-American Games in Chicago.

"*Vaya*, look at that, will you?" said Pete. "He moves like a flyweight."

"Makes that Mathis boy look like a tree stump," Johnny added.

I was searching for an open viewing spot at the edge of the ring platform, when I happened to glance back at the dressing area and saw Karl McDevitt's feet under the blackboard. Suspicious, I hurried over and found him rifling through my pants pockets. I grabbed him by the shoulder. "Hey, man! What do you think you're doing?"

Karl stood up and pushed my hand away. "Nothing. Buzz off, dickface."

He moved away and I checked my wallet. The cash was gone. "I had sixteen bucks in my billfold. Give it back!" When I seized his arm, he spun around and grabbed my neck, pinning me against the wall.

"You touch me again and I'm gonna *hurt* you."

"You stole my money," I said through clenched teeth. Even with both hands, I couldn't loosen the chokehold he had on my neck.

"And I say I didn't, you little shitheel."

Karl pulled back his fist and it occurred to me that we were hidden from view behind Stubby's oversized blackboard. I waited for the blow. Through watery eyes, I saw Johnny step into the dressing area. He grabbed Karl's arm and jerked him backwards before I got slugged.

Karl turned around, furious. "Come on, you sumbitch," he snarled at Johnny, and the two of them began shoving each other and trading a few punches. The blackboard fell to the ground with a crash, and every head in the gym turned to the sound. Stubby quickly jumped between Karl and Johnny, roughly pushing them apart.

"What's this about?" he yelled.

"I caught him stealing money out of my billfold," I said, pointing at Karl.

Karl's scowl moved from Johnny to me. "You're a liar. I saw you messing with *my* billfold, and then your chickenshit brother snuck up and jumped me from behind." He tried to reach around Stubby to shove Johnny.

Johnny took a step toward Karl. "To keep you from sucker punching a kid half your size. You think you're pretty tough, don't you? Picking on a tenth grader?"

I may have been skinny, but I was almost as tall as Johnny and only a year and a half younger, but I kept my mouth shut. This didn't seem like the time to nitpick. Karl McDevitt scared the hell out of me.

"Anybody accuses me of stealing is begging for an ass-kicking," said Karl.

"Enough!" said Stubby. "McDevitt, empty your pockets."

"I didn't take nobody's money. He's lying."

"Empty 'em."

Karl hesitated and then reached into his pocket, producing a switchblade, a pack of Luckies, a motorcycle key, and five dollars. "I earned that money cuttin' grass. If you don't believe me you can ask my mom."

"Keep going," Stubby ordered. "Back pockets too."

Karl narrowed his eyes at Stubby. "That's it."

Stubby sighed. I think he knew Karl had more money in his jeans, but for some reason he didn't press him to continue. "Boys, you know the rules. I've gotta ask the three of you to leave . . . for fighting outside the ring."

I started to protest, but Johnny spoke first. "Why can't we settle it *inside* the ring?" he asked. "Me and Karl."

Karl huffed. "I'd mop the floor with you, punk." He had more than three years, forty pounds, and an inch in height on my brother.

"Let's find out," Johnny answered.

Stubby chomped on his cigar and deliberated. I saw him look over at Jesse Martel, who had his arms resting on the ropes, watching the drama from inside the ring. Jesse nodded his head just a fraction.

"Okay," said Stubby. "Three rounds, standard rules. But if I see one of you hotheads hit below the belt, head butt, or throw an elbow, the fight's over and you're both going home. Got it?"

They both nodded.

"Go put on the gloves."

Pete and I helped Johnny wrap his hands and lace his boxing gloves. "You scared?" I asked him.

Johnny smiled nervously. "Piece of cake."

"I've seen this guy fight before, 'mano," said Pete. "He's a brawler and a dirty fighter, but he's slow on his feet. He's gonna come out like a pissed-off bull, so just keep away from him 'til he runs out of steam."

Johnny smiled again, but sort of distantly.

"Anything I can get you?" I asked. Somehow the whole thing seemed like it was my fault.

"Got an axe handle?"

Boyd Parker helped Karl put on his fight gear, then opened the ropes so his older friend could climb through. Stubby was standing in the middle of the ring with his hands on his hips. He looked at Jesse Martel. "Work the bell, will ya, Jesse? Three rounds, three-minutes each."

Jesse said okay and moved to the brass bell mounted on a support post.

As Pete predicted, Karl came out like a madman, throwing wild punches and haymakers, almost tripping over himself as he pursued Johnny around the ring. Johnny landed a few jabs, but mostly he just kept out of range or covered up. Karl's dark eyes were wild with rage, but Johnny kept his cool. Me, I would have been scared shitless. The bell clanged, ending the round, and Karl threw a late punch that Johnny seemed to know was coming. He ducked easily underneath it.

Stubby stood on his tiptoes and got in Karl's face. "I don't want to see any more of that crap, son."

Two minutes into the second round, Karl became so winded we could all hear him wheezing, and Johnny moved in and connected with a series of jabs and counter punches, each one landing squarely on his opponent's nose. After that round, Karl sat heavily on his corner stool and hung his head. A trickle of blood had appeared under his nostril and Stubby came over to examine him.

In the opposing corner, Pete wiped Johnny's face with a towel. "You bust open his nose and Stubby's gonna stop the fight. Karl's leaving himself open ten different ways. Avoid his nose. Pick your punches."

Johnny nodded and waited patiently for the bell. When it dinged, he proceeded to batter Karl with one flurry of punches after another: crosses, hooks, uppercuts, body shots, each blow taking its toll. An exhausted Karl was helpless against the onslaught. He looked like a clumsy heavy bag swinging from a hook as Johnny pounded away.

Two and a half minutes into the third round, Stubby stepped in. "Okay, that's enough."

Jesse entered the ring to help separate the two fighters.

"Now, I want you two to shake hands," said Stubby, pulling the boxers toward him.

Johnny held out his glove but Karl batted it away and spun around to leave the ring. He must have been dazed from the beating he'd just received because he ran smack into Jesse, who he shoved in anger. "Get out of the way, nigger," he snarled and took a wild swing at Jesse's head.

Jesse easily deflected the punch and wrapped Karl up in a bear hug, pinning both his arms to his side. "Take it easy, man."

"Let me go, goddamnit!"

Jesse let go and Karl climbed out of the ring. Everyone in the gym watched him remove his gloves and throw them to the ground. Stubby climbed out of the ring, too, and approached him as he dressed. "Don't do this, McDevitt. You walk out like this and you're not coming back. You hear me?"

"Fuck you," said Karl, walking toward the exit. "Fuck all you cocksuckers."

A moment later, we heard his motorcycle roar away down Tancahua Street. Karl's little buddy, Boyd Parker, left too, probably afraid he'd get picked on if he stayed.

A few of us began whacking Johnny on the back, congratulating him for whipping Karl's ass, but Stubby told us to lay off.

"Get your butts back to work," he yelled. "There ain't nothin' to celebrate."

Stubby seemed saddened by what had happened, and later I said something about it to Jesse.

"Stubby never want to lose a kid," he said. "And that Karl . . . he is lost for sure."

"He's no good, Feo. He's a thief and a liar. And he's a dirty fighter."

Jesse nodded. *"De veras,"* he said softly. *"Es una mala hierba."*

I looked at him. "What?"

"He's a bad weed, you know?"

"I think so."

"It means he's bad through and through." Jesse punched me lightly on the shoulder. "Don' you look so worried, Flaco. He won't bother you no more. He's afraid of your brother now."

———

CHAPTER 03

Johnny, Pete, and I returned to Ransom Island and were given another load of chores to do before dinner. After we'd finished the work, we slouched on our barstools inside the main building of Uncle Rupert's Shady Boat and Leisure Club oasis. The tin-roofed, cedar-planked dancehall/restaurant/bar was populated by a couple of dozen sunburnt fishermen drinking beer and telling lies.

We waited impatiently for our supper and responded to Rupert's checklist as best we could. We were so tired and hungry we could barely hold up our heads.

"Cleaned the boats?"

"Done," said Johnny.

"They're tied down good?"

"Tied down good," answered Pete.

"Put away the fishing tackle?"

"Check." Johnny again.

"Scrub the toilets in the bait shop?"

Pete and Johnny looked at me, the low man on the totem pole who got the worst jobs. "Check."

"Inboards *and* Outboards?" My uncle's catchy names for the ladies' and men's rooms.

I sighed. "Yes, sir."

"For God's sake, Rupe," said Cecil Shoat from the other side of the horseshoe-shaped bar. "Those boys may starve to death before you get through that checklist."

Sitting next to Cecil, Gideon "Giddyup" Dodson sipped on a Falstaff and nodded his head in agreement. "We'd surely die of thirst if we had to play Twenty Questions every time we wanted a beer."

Cecil and Giddyup had been Shady's regulars for years. They practically regarded themselves as co-owners. Cecil craned his neck toward the bar entrance. "I wonder who that is scratching at the door?"

Giddyup shrugged. "Why don't you go check, Cecil?"

Tired as we were, we turned and watched Cecil amble over to the screen door and peer out onto the porch. He returned to the bar and sat down, expressionless.

"Well, who was it?" asked Pete.

"Aw, nobody. Just you boys' asses finally draggin' in from work."

Giddyup erupted into laughter and spit beer all over the bar top. Cecil and Giddyup could entertain each other for hours. The stupider the joke, the harder they laughed.

Rupert's wife, Vita, backed through the double-swing door balancing three platters filled with meatloaf, mashed potatoes, and green peas. Half a loaf of white bread was stacked on top.

"What's so funny?" she asked. Vita was Rupert's third wife. Not every woman was cut out for life on Ransom Island, but she seemed to take it all in stride.

"Just having a little fun with the boys," Rupert answered, still chuckling.

"You shouldn't pick on 'em when they're hungry, baby." She shouldered Rupert out of the way and set the food in front of us. "They might turn on you."

We attacked the food with about as much grace as a sounder of feral hogs.

"Look at them boys go," laughed Cecil. "Careful you don't lose a hand, Vita."

Within minutes, we were mopping the plate with our bread. Vita smiled. "Seconds?"

All three of us answered in the affirmative.

We finished another plate and were rewarded with three slabs of apple pie à la mode, courtesy of Leona. She came into the bar to watch us eat it.

"Miz Leona," said Johnny, "This pie is so good it makes me wanna slap my brother."

I looked up quickly to make sure Johnny wasn't speaking literally.

"You better slap him while you can," she answered. "'Cause he's gonna be big as you 'fore long, and then he'll be doing the slappin'."

"Maybe." Johnny smiled and punched me on the arm. "Maybe not."

Flavius walked into the bar, followed by Zachariah Yates. I liked Zach. His daddy had been born into slavery and then migrated to South Texas after the Civil War. According to Zach, his dad had been a natural born-horseman and an expert roper. Zach took after his old man and grew up cowboying, working his way up to top hand at the Salt Creek Ranch on nearby Matagorda Island. I had no idea how old he was, but he'd told us stories about taking Teddy Roosevelt on a javelina hunt along the Nueces River, long before Teddy became President or even before he made his charge up San Juan Hill in the Spanish-American War. Zach had been a fixture at Shady's my entire life.

Flavius patted Johnny roughly on the back. "Hey, champ. I heard through the grapevine you cleaned Karl McDevitt's plow this afternoon."

"We had a disagreement. Stubby made us settle it in the ring."

Cecil, Giddyup, and Juan Ezekiel Estrada, another Shady's regular, demanded more details. Pete was only too glad to tell the story, in his rushed, animated way.

"Karl McDevitt, huh?" said Rupert, after Pete finished. "Seems like you boys have mentioned him before. Big kid, idn't he? Troublemaker?"

"Big troublemaker," said Juan. "Last year he got arrested for shootin' porpoises with a .22 over on North Beach. Killed a pair of them that was swimming by the Rincon Point pier."

"That really happen, Juan?" asked Vita, leaning her elbows on the bar. "Or is it some gossip you picked up in town?" Juan Estrada was notorious for repeating questionable stories and was not above stretching them for dramatic effect. Juan was Anglo, despite his latino name, and lived on an old engineless Chris-Craft he claimed once belonged to a famous gangster. He had slicked-back, dirty blond hair and a biography that seemed to change with every telling. Like Mark Twain, Juan seemed to value the truth so highly that he used it sparingly.

"No, it really happened," Juan answered, eyes wide with sincerity. "Jack Kearney said he heard it from Bill Coxwell, who heard it from a friend of one of the cops who patrols the beach."

Vita shook her head. "Straight from the horse's mouth."

"Well, it wouldn't surprise me," said Cecil. "My nephew went to school with Karl McDevitt, at least until Karl dropped out. Every school has a bully, but my nephew said he was the worst kind. Not just mean, but mean out of spite, like he enjoyed it, was the way he put it."

"Well, today *my* nephew took that bully down a notch," said Flavius proudly. "Didn't you, Johnny?"

Johnny raked his fork tines through the melted ice cream on his plate. "It wasn't that big a deal. And Charlie's still out sixteen dollars."

Flavius reached over and poked me in the breastbone. "You always gonna let your big brother fight your fights for you? One of these days you'll have to stand up for yourself."

I felt my face redden with embarrassment. I opened my mouth to respond but nothing came out.

Vita shot a disapproving glance at Flavius. "That's your answer for everything, isn't it? Punch first and think later?"

"It's always worked for me."

"That other boy is practically a grown man," Vita continued. "And Charlie's still a child."

I felt my face redden even more. Since we'd left the gym, I'd been plenty upset about the episode with Karl, embarrassed that I hadn't taken up for myself and embarrassed that I'd damned near peed in my pants at the thought of tangling with him. And now, in front of everyone, Flavius was calling me a chicken, and Vita was practically making me out to be an infant.

Vita continued to berate Flavius. "There are other things you could teach these boys besides how to beat somebody up. There's more to being a man than that."

Flavius narrowed his eyes at Vita. He and Vita had got into it before, and she was as unlikely to back down as he was.

"What kind of beer you want, brother?" asked Rupert, the peacemaker, positioning himself between the two of them.

"You know what kind of beer I drink."

Rupert pulled a can of Schlitz out of the cooler, punched a hole in the top with a church key, and handed the beer to his hot-tempered brother. Vita made a sort of "harrumph" sound and went out onto the covered porch to smoke a cigarette.

"So, how's Jesse's training coming along?" Rupert asked, redirecting the conversation.

"He looks good," answered Johnny. "Today he sparred with some big bohunk from Mathis and ran circles around him. I don't think the other guy landed a punch."

Pete nodded vigorously. "Jesse told me afterwards that the other guy had deceptive speed—he was slower than he looked."

Rupert laughed appreciatively. "I'll have to remember that one."

"Except Jesse said it in Spanish," Pete added.

Cecil tilted his head inquisitively. "He speaks Spanish?"

Pete nodded. "Of course he does."

"But he's colored, isn't he?"

"Yeah, and he's from Cuba."

"Oh. So he's a colored communist, then." Cecil seemed to regard this as something exotic, kind of like a jackalope or a mermaid.

Since the US embargo of Cuba began that spring, the local newspapers had pretty much painted anything Cuban, up to and including rum-and-Cokes, as an evil tool of the Soviets, although I hadn't paid much attention to all the fuss.

"No, I don't think he's a communist," Pete answered. "Jesse's never mentioned politics, now that I think of it."

Zach felt compelled to comment. "I didn't know there was such a thing as Spanish-speaking colored folk."

"Well, dang, Zach. I didn't know there was such a thing as a colored cowboy until I met you," said Giddyup Dodson.

"That shows how much you know about cowboying," said Vita, who had rejoined the group.

Giddyup, despite his self-appointed nickname, boasted only two and half years on a West Texas dude ranch to support his cowboy credentials, while Zach had been the real thing. Now Gideon Dodson sold vacation bungalows to snowbirds flocking to Aransas and San Patricio counties. He still liked to dress up like Gene Autry, though.

"Sure, Zach," said Rupert. "There's lots of Negroes on those Caribbean Islands. In Brazil, too. I read about 'em in *National Geographic*. They were brought there from Africa to work on the sugar plantations mostly, kind of like they were brought over here to work in the cotton fields."

"But Jesse Martel, he's a free man, idn't he?" asked Zach.

Rupert nodded. "Same as you and me."

That seemed to satisfy Zach. "Don't that beat all. A Spanish-speaking colored man. I might have to watch that man box sometime. When does he fight, Johnny?"

"December first, at the Municipal Auditorium."

"Same place Johnny and Pete will be having their Golden Gloves bouts come January," added Flavius proudly.

"What about Charlie?" asked Zach.

Flavius grunted. "He's too young . . . and obviously not ready."

Johnny shook his head and smiled. "According to the rule book he may be too young, but trust me, he's plenty ready." He put his arm around my shoulder. "Right, Sweet Dreams?"

I didn't answer. I was imagining my fist in Uncle Flavius's big mouth.

——

When we came to the gym the following afternoon, Karl McDevitt was back, but this time he'd brought his mom.

Mavis McDevitt was a fearsome creature. She was petite and trim, but carried herself with a confident, almost aggressive bearing. She'd apparently run Karl's no-count daddy off long ago. Or maybe she'd just devoured him. She had sharp features and a yellow-blond bouffant that was so lacquered with hairspray it looked like a plastic Halloween wig. Presently, she was berating Stubby, using a lit cigarette to emphasize her points.

When we walked up, Karl leaned down and whispered in her ear. She turned and studied us. "Which one accused you of stealing?" she asked her son, glaring at the three of us with equal malice.

"That one," said Karl, pointing at me, "He's the liar."

She wagged her finger at me. "Sonny, you need to tell everyone here that you made a mistake . . . that you told a lie."

"I wasn't lying."

She pursed her lips and turned back to Stubby, who stood with his arms folded across his chest, chewing furiously on his cigar. "Some kid loses his lunch money and you immediately come down on *my* boy. You humiliate him by making him empty his pockets, finding nothing, by the way, and then you set three experienced fighters on him."

"Three fighters?" Stubby said incredulously. "Mrs. McDevitt, what are you talking about?"

"Karl told me what happened. First those two brothers ganged up on my son, and then you made him fight that coon over there." She motioned to Jesse Martel, who sat on the edge of the boxing platform, watching impassively.

"Jesse had nothing to do with it," said Stubby, struggling to control his temper. "All he did was time the rounds."

"Mr. Hunsacker . . . ."

Another man walked up—a lanky man with a pale, droopy sort of face. His thin hair was parted way to the side. I hadn't noticed him earlier. He cleared his throat.

"Mr. Hunsacker, the police department expects you to run this gym fairly, and not to play favorites."

Stubby shook his head. "The CCPD sponsors the Golden Gloves program, Sergeant Radcliff, not the gym, and my gym has its own rules." Stubby pointed to a placard posted on the wall that read "GYM RULES." There were ten of them. "The third one says respect the property of others, and the one after that says no fighting outside the ring. Karl broke both those rules, not to mention the ones about using bad language and showing good sportsmanship at all times."

"Well, it doesn't sound like there's proof Karl stole anything," Radcliff continued. "And to be honest, I don't think it's fair or responsible to throw a boy into the ring against a professional fighter who's at least ten years older."

Stubby's face turned red. "I told you Sergeant, Jesse didn't lay a hand on Karl. Just ask him. Ask anyone here."

"Oh, that's just great," said Mavis, turning to Radcliff. "Who are you going to believe, Harley? My son or that commie nigger over there?"

"Watch your language," said Stubby icily.

The sergeant continued. "Look, Hunsacker. You operate this program under the auspices of the city. It's not your private club. We sponsor it to give these kids something to do and to keep them off the street and out of trouble. We allow everyone,"—he cast a sideways glance at Jesse—"and anyone, to participate. So we expect you to do the same."

"Tell him he needs to apologize to my son, Harley," Mavis demanded.

Radcliff sighed and shrugged his shoulders, looking at Stubby like it was the most reasonable suggestion in the world. "I'd say that's a pretty fair request, don't you think, Mr. Hunsacker?"

"This is my boxing program," said Stubby, his face still red. "Golden Gloves is part of it, but otherwise I run the gym as I see fit." He pointed to the rule board again. "I'm going to send a copy of that list over to your precinct chief, and one to the mayor, and they can look it over and tell me which rules get to be ignored and which don't. Until then, I'm standing by my decision."

Mavis started ranting again, but Stubby ignored her and went into his office and slammed the door. Radcliff whispered something into her ear, his hand resting familiarly on her shoulder. She nodded and picked up her purse. As they walked out, she flipped her cigarette toward me and my brother. It landed at our feet. Karl turned around before he went through the door and gave us the finger.

"Jesus, what assholes," Pete murmured.

"Did she call that cop Harley?" Johnny asked.

Pete and I laughed. "Suits him," said Pete.

"Anyway, forget them," said Johnny. "Let's get started on our workout. If we hurry, we can catch a movie at the Thunderbird Drive-In tonight."

"What's playing?" asked Pete.

Johnny put his finger to his temple, trying to recall the selections on the theater marquee. "There's *Hatari!*—that John Wayne movie about catching wild animals in Africa, and the other one's about brainwashed commie assassins, or something like that. Sinatra's in it."

Pete and I looked at each other and wrinkled our noses. A skinny Eye-talian crooner versus the Duke? "*Hatari!*" we said simultaneously.

The movie was so good we came back and watched it again the next night.

CHAPTER 04

I fell in love with Carmen Delfín the first time I laid eyes on her. It had to be love because I'd never felt anything else like it.

She was sitting on a bench outside Stubby's office, reading aloud to Naco Flores. As they bent over an old issue of *Ring* magazine, the only publication Stubby kept in the gym, I was pretty sure I'd never seen Naco so still and serene. And I was certain I'd never seen a girl as beautiful as this one.

When I walked by the bench I knelt down, pretending to tie my shoe, and I heard Naco ask her a question in Spanish. She answered him patiently in the same clipped Spanish I'd heard Jesse Martel use. She began to read aloud again but stopped when Naco looked up and flashed his big buck-toothed smile at me.

"Charlie!" He looked around reflexively for a medicine ball.

"Hey, Naco."

The girl frowned. Somehow it made her even more attractive. "His name is Diego."

"Diego," I repeated. "I guess I didn't know that."

"Well, now you do. The other name is offensive."

That I did know, although I wasn't sure why it was offensive. I think it had something to do with being low-class and uneducated.

Anyway, I'd never heard Naco called by any other name. "Are you a friend of . . . Diego's?"

"We just met."

I stood awkwardly in front of her as she looked me over. Though she seemed about my age, her voice was low and throaty, a woman's voice, and her English was as fluent as her Spanish.

A beat later she nodded her head toward Stubby's office. "I'm here to see my uncle."

Through the office window, I saw Stubby Hunsacker and Jesse Martel talking to a short, portly man in a brown tailored suit and open-collared shirt. The man had a long cigar in his hand, which he waved around emphatically when he talked.

"I guess I don't know your uncle."

"No?" she answered, turning a magazine page for Naco. "That's funny. You see him almost every day."

She spoke patiently to me, as if I were a bit dim. She was tall and fair-skinned, with a sculpted face and long blonde hair she'd pulled back in a high ponytail. Her eyes were a dark shade of blue I'd never seen before, and they were very direct. "I didn't know Stubby had a niece," I said.

"I'm *Jesse's* niece."

I opened my mouth to tell her that now I was *really* confused, but she held her finger to her lips to shut me up, and then placed her ear to the wall behind her. Something the men were talking about had caught her attention. Stubby's office walls were paper thin, and I eavesdropped along with her.

I heard Jesse tell the fat man, very bluntly, that Stubby Hunsacker was his manager and he wasn't interested in changing their current arrangement. Stubby opened the door for the man, who stood up and gazed long and hard at the pair. He set his Panama hat on his head and wagged his cigar at them again. "I'll give you two some time to think about it."

"We already did," Stubby answered.

The stranger forced a smile and pulled a couple of cigars out of his coat. He stuffed them into Stubby's shirt pocket. "I'll tell my boss you're thinkin' about it."

"You never got around to tellin' us who your boss was," Stubby said.

"A boxing fan," he answered, "with an eye for talent." He looked at Jesse. "He could take you to the top, boy. Make you a whole lotta dough. More than you could ever pull down here." He looked around the shabby gym and gave a dismissive snort.

Stubby and Jesse stood quietly, their arms crossed, until the man walked out.

He tipped his hat at Carmen and walked through the gym like he owned it, trailing cigar smoke all the way to the exit.

Jesse came out of the office next, his eyes troubled. When he saw me, his expression brightened. "Hey, Charlie, *que bola?*"

"*Hola,* Feo," I said as we shook hands. "Who was that?"

"Ah, some promoter from Miami." He watched the man until he left the building, and then he looked at me and smiled. "Hey, I see you met my niece. Pretty girl, no?"

"Kind of . . . ." His niece raised her eyebrows as I fumbled for words. "What I mean is, we only kind of met. I still don't know her name."

Jesse put a big arm on my shoulder. "Charlie, this is Carmen Delfín. She is the most beautiful ballet dancer in the whole city, and one day, in the whole worl'. *De veras, mi Carmelita chiquita?*"

Carmen got up and kissed her uncle affectionately on the cheek. I stood there awkwardly and listened to them chat in Spanish, unable to understand or contribute to the conversation. Carmen said something that made Jesse laugh and look at me.

"Sorry, Charlie," he said. "She ask me why you call me 'Feo.' This is the firs' time she comes to the boxing gym, and she don' know the customs, you know? I tol' her we all have nicknames here." He winked at me. "I also tol' her you're a pretty good guy."

"What's your nickname?" she asked me pointedly.

"I don't have one." I wasn't about to tell her the ring name I'd come up with.

"It's *Flaco,*" said Jesse. "Tha's what some of us call him."

Carmen looked me up and down, and I felt a little like an emaciated stray. *Flaco* meant "skinny" in Spanish. That much I did know.

Naco Flores raised his head from his magazine, his eyes wide. "Flaco… and Naco," he said with wonder, giving the names a test run. "Naco and Flaco!" He laughed hysterically at the rhyme he'd made and then skipped away, repeating his new mantra. "Flaco and Naco! Naco and Flaco!" I looked at Carmen and raised my hands in a shrug. *Don't look at me.*

Stubby came out of his office wearing an angry expression, still upset, I guessed, about the guy in the brown suit. "Flores! Did you pick up those medicine balls like I asked you?"

Naco answered "yes," but I could see about six of them lying around the gym.

Then Stubby's attention turned to me "Why are you still in your street clothes, Sweetwater? Get your gear on." He turned to go back into his office.

"Mr. Hunsacker." I cleared my throat nervously. "I um . . . . "

He stopped and turned around, deep furrows forming on his brow. I felt like I was speaking to one of the rock heads on Easter Island.

"What is it, Sweetwater? Spit it out."

"I came to tell you that we're going out of town this week . . . on vacation."

Stubby chomped down hard on his cigar stub. "Going where?" he asked. "And who's *we?*"

I hesitated, and then decided to be aboveboard about it.

"Me, Johnny, and Pete thought we'd go camping on Padre Island . . . before, ahh, football practice starts next week."

"You, Johnny, and Pete," he said, fixing me with a baleful stare. "The other two sent you in here to speak for them?"

"I um . . . I drew the short straw." I heard Jesse muffle a laugh.

Stubby marched to the front door, and I could see him scanning the street for our Jeep, and then I heard him yell at Johnny and Pete to get their butts out of the car and account for themselves. He went out to meet them.

"Is it fun camping in the sand?" I heard the girl of my dreams ask behind me. She sounded skeptical.

She sat with her long legs crossed, her back straight, and her hands folded on her knee. "We like it," I answered. Jesse had moved away to talk to another boxer, so it was just the two of us.

"It must be . . . gritty. Where, exactly, do you go?"

"We start in Port A and then drive south until there are no more tire tracks in the sand. Our camp is pretty much the middle of nowhere."

"It sounds so adventurous." She stood up, smoothed her skirt, and smiled. "Maybe I'll meet you down there." Which I took to mean, *Not in a million years.*

"Sure," I said. I stood there awkwardly while she continued to watch me. "Is Feo really your uncle?" I finally asked.

"*Jesse* . . . is married to my mother's sister, my aunt. She still lives in Havana."

"So, does that mean you're from—"

"From Cuba? Yes, I was born there. And, yes, there are blonde-haired, blue-eyed Cubans, if you were going to ask."

I wouldn't have asked, even though I wanted to. I knew next to nothing about Cuba, except that the politicians were always hollering about Castro. And Jesse didn't talk about his native land that much. He talked about his wife and kid, but never about politics.

"Your Spanish is very good." It was the only thing I could think of to say.

"Thanks. And your English is very good. Almost as if you were born here."

I blinked stupidly, feeling distinctly like an idiot. Stubby entered the gym with a roguish gleam in his eye, his cigar at a jaunty angle. "I'll be seeing you in a few weeks," he said to me. "And *very* early, at that. Enjoy your holiday."

"Goodbye, Charlie." Carmen offered her hand, which I took. "It was very nice talking to you."

I think I muttered something in response, or maybe I just stood there with a head full of nothin' until she asked me for her hand back. I walked away, flustered, and then I was almost knocked down by a medicine ball that hit me right between the shoulder blades.

"Naco and Flaco!" I could hear Naco's laughter all the way to the curb.

When I climbed into the car, Johnny and Pete looked crestfallen.

"Smooth move, Ex-Lax," Pete mumbled.

"What did Stubby say?" I asked.

Johnny looked over his sunglasses at me. "He said that once we get back from our 'vacation,' he expects us to come in every day to train."

"But football practice starts next week, and then school two weeks after that. When the hell does he expect us to come in?"

Johnny turned around and looked at me. "He wants us here *before* school."

"Shit." I slumped down in the back seat. Pete continued to glare at me from the front. "Don't mad dog me, Pete. You don't have to drive thirty miles to get here." Pete attended high school in Corpus and lived less than a mile from the gym.

"No, but now *I* have to come to the gym before school *and* after."

"Well, it's not my fault," I protested. "Stubby got into it with some outta town guy who wants to manage Feo. He was pissed off long before I mentioned any vacation."

Johnny put the Jeep in gear. "No it's not your fault. I say let's worry about that stuff later . . . because right now," he turned around and smiled, "we've got bait, rods, a week's worth of food, and a big-ass cooler of ice-cold beer in the back of the wagon. I say let's end this summer right."

Pete and I couldn't have agreed more. "Hey! Baby," by Bruce Channel came on the radio, and we sang along at the top of our lungs as we cruised down Ocean Drive towards the North Padre Island Causeway. "Hey . . . hey, baby . . ." we crooned, "I wanna know, oh, oh . . . if you'll be my girl." As I sang, off key, I thought of Carmen Delfín.

Girl of my dreams.

━━━━

CHAPTER 05

The Padre Island seashore is a deserted, otherworldly ribbon of sand and surf that begins south of Port Aransas and stretches a hundred miles down to the Mexican border. It is uninhabited, untouched, and completely wild. Our kind of place. And it was timeless—if we'd driven up on a gang of man-eating Karankawa Indians chasing some poor shipwrecked Spanish conquistador, we wouldn't have been the least surprised.

The government was turning it into a national park in a couple of months, and that gave our trip sort of an outlaw flavor. We fancied ourselves the last of the wild Indians, ruthless pirates, or swash-buckling cattle barons to roam the barrier island. This time next year, there'd be nothing but sunburned tourists and park rangers. We vowed to make the most of it.

We topped off our gas tank in Port A and drove south along the water's edge for almost three hours, getting bogged down only once in the soft sand near Big Shell. Late that afternoon, we reached The Wart—our name for the Sweetwater beach camp.

The Wart was made from two old junkyard school buses butted together end-to-end and buried up to the axles. My dad and uncles dropped the vehicles there before the war, and each year the yellow paint faded a shade lighter, and the rusting buses settled a few more inches into the sand. Eventually, the Wart would disappear underground or be uprooted by a hurricane and swept away. But until then, our gypsy camp offered us a dry and relatively clean space for cooking and sleeping. A twenty-foot well provided water fresh enough for washing up.

After we'd unloaded the Jeep, Johnny pulled a church key out of his pocket and punched holes in three beer cans. He handed them around and raised his can to the sun setting over the Laguna Madre. "Bless this beer to the nourishment of our bodies."

"And us to thy service," I added.

We all took long swigs. "Amen," we chanted in unison.

Before it got full dark, we dug a pit and made a driftwood fire next to the camp. For supper, we wrapped sliced potatoes, onions, and cobs of corn in tinfoil and then buried them in the coals. Later, we threw thick steaks on a makeshift grill and then feasted under a waxing moon and a bright spray of stars. A sea turtle, dragging herself out of the surf to lay her eggs on the beach, regarded us with stoic indignation and gave us a wide berth.

We sat by the fire in our canvas chairs late into the night, kneading our bare toes into the sand, swapping stories, and toasting to our bright futures. We talked about sports, friends, movies . . . and girls, of course, but only in general terms. Especially me, since I didn't have much specific knowledge about the subject. I kept Carmen, and my thoughts of her, to myself.

The following day, we rigged up our rods and spent the morning waist deep in the surf, fishing the gut between the second and third sandbars. Mostly we were silent, absorbed in our angling, somewhat mesmerized by the rhythmic crash and boom of the surf. Occasionally, Pete would belt out one of the Mexican *corridos* his grandpa had taught him. We didn't understand a word of the songs, and to be honest, we weren't sure Pete did either, because we'd never really heard him speak Spanish before. But he had a strong tenor voice and the songs blended well with the music of the surf.

That night, after we'd eaten, we stripped naked and seined past the gulf breakers to get bait for the next day. Johnny, the strongest swimmer, swam the end of the hundred-foot net all the way to the third sand bar, and then the three of us hauled it up to the beach, just beyond the swash. We emptied the contents onto the sand and watched a shimmering constellation of white shrimp, skipjacks, crabs, mullet, pinfish, and pogies pour out of the net—popping and flipping like mad. It was hypnotic, and as alien-looking as any sci-fi movie at the Thunderbird Drive-In. We sorted through our catch, and then Johnny swam the seine out for one more drag. As we were pulling in our haul, a five-foot tarpon deftly leapt over the encircling net, its iridescent scales reflecting the light of the moon.

The week progressed in much the same way: breakfast, fishing, swimming, lunch—followed by a nap, fishing, exploring the dunes, more fishing, beer, dinner, more beer. Each day seemed better than the one before, and we told ourselves it couldn't get any better than this. And then, unexpectedly, it did.

Johnny was the first to spot the truck driving toward us on the packed sand. As it approached, we watched it apprehensively and with some irritation. We didn't want anyone to intrude on our private retreat. We were pirates, by God, laying low at our beach hide-away—wild, free, living off the land (and a jumbo cooler of beer, soda pop, and Oscar Mayer wieners).

"*Ave María Purísima!*" said Pete, as the truck drew near. "I think my dreams have been answered."

A brand new Chevy C-10 pickup pulled to a stop beside us. Carmen Delfín, her windblown hair wrapped in a blue bandana, leaned out of the passenger window and smiled. "Hello, boys. I hope we're not inter-rupting your little wilderness adventure."

Two girls sat next to Carmen in the cab, all three of them, we noticed, wearing bikinis. The driver killed the engine, and Johnny, Pete, and I stood there with our mouths open.

Johnny was the first to recover from the pleasant shock of the unlikely visitors. "Welcome to Camp Cabeza de Vaca," he said, with a sweeping bow. "We were expecting you."

"Were you?" teased Carmen. "It didn't look like it when we drove up."

The other two girls looked similar in age to Carmen, high school seniors, I guessed. Their bodies were lean and muscular, like Carmen's, which made me think that they might be dancers, too. I noticed three suitcases in the bed of the truck.

"Why are you here?" I stammered. "And how did you know where to find us?"

Pete shot me a look of disbelief that said, *Who the hell cares?*

"You told me," answered Carmen. "Remember? At the gym?"

When I didn't respond, Johnny jumped in. "And we're so glad you came. Park your truck over there by the bus and we'll help you unload your gear. Y'all are staying for dinner, aren't you? We're having fresh-caught trout tonight. Hope you have reservations."

"We have lots of them," said Carmen, winking at me. One of the girls nudged Carmen in the ribs. "Oh, sorry. Boys . . . this is Veronica, and Rachel."

The two girls smiled and continued to study us carefully. We studied them back. Veronica had light brown hair that flipped up at her neckline. Rachel, the driver and shortest of the trio, wore her dark hair in sort of a curly bob style.

Johnny stepped forward. "Johnny Sweetwater is my name, and this is Mr. Pete Lopez."

"Nice ride," said Pete, nodding at the truck. The baby blue pickup had chrome as bright as tarpon scales. Even though it was streaked with salt and dusted with sand from the long drive, it seemed almost like a mirage on the desolate beach.

"Rachel's dad owns a car dealership," Carmen explained.

"He let us use the truck so we could visit colleges," Veronica added. "We were on our way to Austin to see UT. I guess we missed a turn."

Johnny nodded. "Sure. It's easy to do."

The other girl, Rachel, lifted her chin at me. "Who's this one?"

Johnny put his hand on my bare shoulder. "*This* one . . . is my little brother, Charlie."

When everyone looked at me, I felt like a snot-nosed kid, just tagging along, hoping they'd include me in whatever big-kid fun they were planning. Thankfully, Carmen made that feeling go away.

"It's great to see you again, Charlie," she said, looking only at me, "And thanks for telling me about this place. It's beautiful, like you said. I hope you don't mind that we came."

Unable to speak, I shook my head no. The wind lifted her blonde hair as she turned to inspect the Gulf. Even the squawky seagulls shut up, for once. She looked like a figure you'd mount to the prow of a ship.

"Then I guess we'll stay for awhile," she said brightly.

The girls went to park the truck and stow their suitcases in the bus. When they were out of earshot, Pete elbowed my arm. "*Híjole*, Charlie! You're a regular Casanova. Not bad, for a sophomore. By the way, I got dibs on Rachel."

Johnny laughed. "Maybe . . . if that's how it plays out. I think the only girl who's made her choice is Carmen, and she's the prettiest one of all. It's obvious she only has eyes for young Charlie here."

It had seemed that way to me, too, and I was so excited I didn't know whether to bury my head in the sand, run as fast as I could toward Mexico, or let out a wolf howl. So I kept my trap shut and looked down at my feet, which were sinking deeper into the sand with each successive wave. *Be cool,* I implored myself. *Don't say anything stupid.*

The girls helped us gather more wood for the fire, and then we made room at the table for six. We dined on sea trout, canned beans, and s'mores. With beer for every course. "Our wine cellar is a little limited," said Pete by way of apology.

After dinner, Johnny tuned his battery-operated radio to a border-blasting AM station in Ciudad Acuña. We listened to Wolfman Jack play a long string of Motown hits and dirty-bop blues, and the six of us danced until we were glistening with sweat. By danced, I mean we boys thrashed around in the sand, doing variations of the Twist, while the girls did tricky little coordinated bits of rhythmic business with their feet and hips and hair.

When the radio batteries finally died, we all cooled off in the surf, and then Johnny and Pete paired off with Veronica and Rachel and went their separate ways. Carmen and I walked north along the beach, talking and, on the way back, holding hands. When we reached the campsite, everyone was still gone, so we reclined against a big driftwood log near the fire embers, which glowed and pulsated in the pit.

I heard Carmen giggle beside me. "My mother would kill me if she'd seen me dancing like that."

"She's not a fan of soul music?" I asked.

"For her, Tchaikovsky is soul music."

"She likes classical?"

"She likes music for ballet. She is, or rather *was,* a prima ballerina when she was younger. She was a principal dancer with the American Ballet in New York and performed all over the world. Now she runs the ballet academy in Corpus Christi."

"I didn't know Corpus had a ballet academy."

"Unfortunately, you've got lots of company. South Texas is not exactly the center of the ballet universe. People around here think a *jeté* is one of those long stone piers you build out into the water."

"Then why did she come here?"

"Ah, that's more complicated." She turned onto her side and looked at me. "It was love, of course . . . *el amor impetuoso*."

"*El* what?"

"Impetuous love. It's the title of a little book of poetry my dad gave me when I was young. Anyway, *el amor* makes us do crazy things sometimes."

"I guess it does," I replied, like I knew what I was talking about. "So, your dad was a um, a *ballerino*?"

Carmen laughed. "You can just say male ballet dancer. No, he was in the Navy, stationed at the Brooklyn Navy Yard in New York. My mom was dancing with the American Ballet Company during that same time. One weekend he saw her perform at the Met. Said it was love at first sight. He brought her roses after every performance until she finally agreed to see him. Anyway, they got married and I was born nine months later. Closer to eight months, but don't ever mention that in front of her."

"How in the world did you end up in Texas?"

"My dad was relocated to the naval base in Guantanamo shortly after they were married. I was actually born in Cuba, in Havana. But when I was ten, the Navy transferred us again, to Corpus Christi. Then, two years later, they sent him to a base in Guam. He went. We stayed. My mother won't speak his name to this day."

I lay still and let this sink in. I wasn't even sure where Guam was. "So your parents are divorced?"

"Yeah. Things started to fall apart between them after we moved to Texas. I remember a lot of yelling."

"Well, I'm glad *you* stayed."

"I am, too." She scooted closer to me and laid her head on my shoulder.

"Is your dad still in the Navy?" I asked.

"'Once a sailor, always a sailor,' he used to say. I think he's in Italy. He sends me something interesting every year on my birthday and at Christmas. Last year I received a box of chocolate-covered espresso beans from Naples. I found out there's a naval base near there."

"But you never see him?"

"Not since he left. But I'd like to get to know him better. After I finish high school I plan to find him, and then maybe I'll live in Europe for awhile. Who knows?"

"Well, I've noticed you're pretty good at finding people."

She laughed. "Yes, I am. So, tell me about your family."

"Our story's not as interesting as yours."

"All family stories are interesting."

"Okay. My dad's a shrimper. Johnny you've met. My mother passed away when I was young."

"Sorry about your mom." I could feel her watching me in the firelight.

"Thanks. I barely remember her. I think it was hardest on our dad."

Our fingers had been sort of loosely entwined while we talked, but then she took my hand more firmly.

"Uncle Jesse tells me you two are pretty good friends."

"He's a swell guy. And a terrific boxer." I was going to add that he also treated me like an adult, but thought better of drawing attention to my age. Maybe Carmen didn't know I was only fifteen.

"You know that his wife and child are still in Cuba?"

"Yeah. He said it's gonna be difficult for them to leave there."

"Yeah, Castro took care of that, the son-of-a-bitch."

I was mildly shocked to hear her curse, but then again, almost everything about her surprised me. I poked at the fire a bit, and we watched bright sparks float up into the blackness. I changed the subject to something that had been bugging me. "Carmen, that fat man that was in the office with Stubby and Jesse the other day at the gym? Do you know him?"

"Jesse said he represents a promoter in Miami who saw him box in the Pan-Am Games. I guess he was impressed. He wants to sponsor Jesse's pro fights. Has some big-time manager all picked out for him."

"No wonder Stubby was pissed."

"My mother said those Florida promoters are all *mafiosos*. That they'll use Jesse up and then dump him on the street when he stops making them money. Jesse agrees."

"Apparently, so does Stubby Hunsacker."

"Yeah. Him, too. That old man's an odd duck, but Jesse seems to trust him."

"Yeah. Stubby's alright, and he's definitely in Jesse's corner. Feo is smart to listen to him."

"My uncle's a good judge of character. He likes *you* doesn't he?"

I started to say something, but Carmen leaned over and kissed me, maybe the most pleasant sensation I'd ever had up to that point in my life. We kissed some more, and then she kicked her leg over and straddled me, working her knees into the sand. Her long hair caressed my face and her breathing quickened as we kissed and touched each other.

While my hands roamed, I tried to process the myriad sensations coursing through my mind and body. I couldn't believe this was happening.

"Carmen?" I whispered.

"Yes?"

"I've never. . . I'm kind of new at this."

"So am I."

"I didn't bring a—"

"Don't worry. They have a pill now. Rachel got them for me."

We fumbled over each other's bodies, clueless about our moves, but steadily abandoning our inhibitions.

"You're trembling," I said.

"Is that normal?"

"I don't know. But I think I am, too."

Suddenly she leaned up. "Shhh. Someone's coming."

She was right. I could hear Pete and Rachel talking as they walked up from the surf.

Carmen laughed softly and sat up next to me, quickly adjusting her bikini top back to its proper place. "Charlie . . . ," she began hesitantly. "This is . . . unusual for me. Especially with someone I've just met. I'm not even sure why I did it."

"*El amor impetuoso,*" I said, butchering the Spanish.

She laughed again and then leaned over and kissed me. "Well said, *Flaco*. You're a quick learner." She stood up and pulled my arm. "Get up. *Levántate!* Let's go for a midnight swim."

CHAPTER 06

The girls insisted we hang a bed sheet to separate the bus into his-and-her sleeping quarters—to preserve the illusion of propriety, I suppose. The next morning, I was in my bunk gazing out the window at a flock of white pelicans that glided effortlessly over the surface of the water. They seemed to float on an invisible air cushion that propelled them over the ocean swells. So graceful in the sky, but when one spotted a fish it came down like a sack of bricks.

I was the first person awake, alone with my thoughts. I lay there wondering about the troubling dreams I'd had—dreams of rejection, inadequacy, insecurity. And there were other kinds of dreams, too, mostly dealing with what had almost happened between me and Carmen, and what I hoped might happen yet.

Carmen was more than two years older than I was, off-the-charts beautiful, and so damn self-assured. What had happened between us the night before seemed like fantasy, and way too good to be true. Would she regret it? Act like it never happened? Pat me on the head and send me back down to the minors—namely the girls in my sophomore class in Rockport?

In the end, I decided to do what all Sweetwater men do when confronted by the challenge of understanding females—I decided to stop thinking about it and find something purposeful to do, which at that moment meant stepping outside to take a pee. My head was a little foggy from the beer I drank the night before. Johnny called the malady "bulkhead."

I found a gap in the sand dunes and began emptying my bladder. About fifty yards north of me, I spied a coyote trotting along the swash line, stopping occasionally to sniff at organic flotsam that had washed ashore. The coyote stopped abruptly and raised its head in alarm, focused on an object out of my view. He began to lope away when a brown object swooped out of the sky, narrowly missing his head. He broke into a dead run and the spinning object rose again and began to circle back. At first, I thought it was a small hawk defending its nest, but when I moved a few feet over to watch it fly away, I realized the object wasn't a bird after all. It dropped down and I was shocked to see a man on the beach reach up and grab it out of the air. The man had broad shoulders, a narrow waist, and an Aussie-style hat on his head, one side of the brim pinned up to the crown.

I banged on the bus next to Johnny's bunk. "Somebody's here," I said.

Pete and Johnny struggled into their salt-stiff cut-offs, and we walked out to meet the stranger.

"Mornin'," the man said cheerfully when we approached. We muttered "good morning," in return and checked out our unlikely visitor. He was about Pete's height but had the look of a body builder, with oversized muscles popping out of his thighs, arms, and pecs.

"Nice bivouac," he said, pointing at the Wart.

"Nice boomerang," Johnny replied, nodding at the crescent of polished wood resting in the man's hand.

"Thanks. Made it myself. It's kind of a hobby of mine." He stepped forward with an open hand. "My name's William McMahon, but people call me Billy . . . Billy Boomerang."

We shook his hand and introduced ourselves. Pete commented on the elaborate shark's tooth necklace hanging around his neck.

"That's my other hobby," said Billy. "Shark hunting. Early this morning I caught a ten-footer. Got the jaw soaking in a bucket if you want to see it."

We looked up the beach and noticed a low-slung Jeep in the hazy distance, and then we studied the wayfarer some more. The barrier islands had always attracted oddball characters. I wasn't sure whether the Gulf washed them ashore or if they'd been driven to the edge of the sea because they didn't fit in anywhere else. But still—this guy was too much. He spoke with a grating Yankee accent that didn't jibe with the outback bush outfit he wore. And who the hell carried around a boomerang? It made for an odd combination.

"You almost beaned that coyote a minute a go," I said.

He held up the polished wooden throwing stick. "Yeah, he was too fast for me, though."

Without warning, he reared back and launched the boomerang seaward. It dipped low, almost clipping the top of a wave, then swooped upward and circled back in a graceful arc. It flew back to Billy like a well-trained raptor.

The girls walked up, sleepy-eyed but curious, drawn to the impromptu boomerang exhibition. I got the feeling this wasn't the first time Billy Boomerang had used the trick to attract the girls.

"Nifty," said Veronica. "Are you from Australia?"

Billy flashed a bright smile. "Nope, not from Down Under . . . but from up north, New Jersey to be exact."

He laughed, as if being from New Jersey was a funny joke.

"I discovered Padre Island while doing a four-year haul with the Coast Guard back in the early fifties."

"I think I've seen you before," said Rachel. "On South Padre Island. It was over Spring Break."

Since the *Gidget* beach party films had hit the theaters, college kids had been flocking to South Padre for an annual bash. I hadn't been there yet, but I'd heard it could get wilder than an acre of snakes. It didn't surprise me to hear that Rachel had made the trip; I'd already figured her for the wildest of the three girls. Apparently, her car dealership-owning dad gave her free rein, and she took full advantage of it.

Billy smiled at Rachel. "Yeah? You probably did. I live in Port Isabel," he pointed to the southwest with his chin, "and I spend a lot of time on South Padre. My favorite place in the world."

"What are you doing up here then?" asked Pete. I think he was a little miffed about Billy Boomerang crashing our party.

"What Pete means," Johnny added amicably, "is how did you get across the Mansfield Cut?"

"It's a funny thing," said Billy. "I've driven my rig the forty miles from Port Isabel up to the Mansfield Cut about a hundred times, and I often wondered what it was like on North Padre Island. Yesterday I woke up and decided to give it a look. Fished all night off the Bob Hall Pier, and then, before the sun came up, began following this beach south."

"What's the verdict?" asked Veronica.

"Well . . . ." He pretended to think about it. "One side's as beautiful as the other, but I have to say, the girls are a lot prettier on the north end." Billy flashed the girls a bright smile.

They smiled back, in spite of themselves.

"Listen," he said, taking a more serious tone. "There's some bad weather coming this way. You might wanna think about heading back, if you weren't going to already. I was just getting ready to turn around myself."

"Bad weather? You mean, like a hurricane?" Johnny asked with concern. "Did you hear something on the radio?"

"I don't have a radio. But trust me, it'll be a big storm. Maybe a hurricane. I don't know yet."

"How do you know about this bad weather?" Pete asked suspiciously.

Billy tapped his temple with a forefinger. "I saw it in a dream." When he noted the look on our faces, he nodded his head gravely. "I'm serious, fellas. I dream about these storms before they arrive. It's a gift from above," he said, pointing to the heavens.

We were waiting for him to laugh at his own joke, but we saw that he *was* serious.

"I saw Carla before it ever entered the Gulf of Mexico," he continued. "In my dream it was clear as a bell. I saw which direction it was going, how big it was, everything."

I looked out at the Gulf. Last year's Hurricane Carla was one of the most vicious storms ever to hit the Texas coast, with top wind gusts of 175 mph. Every community from Port Aransas to Sabine Pass was damaged, and it just about flattened Port Lavaca and Port O'Connor. But today, the sky was clear and there was only a whisper of a breeze. Beyond the gentle breakers, the undisturbed water stretched to the horizon.

"Well, we'll sure keep your dream in mind," Johnny said earnestly. "In the meantime, can we offer you a beer or something, Mr. Boomerang?"

The girls struggled to keep from giggling.

"We're out," said Pete, acting like he was the camp gatekeeper. "We drank it all last night."

"Oh, I don't drink," Billy answered, "but thank you all the same. Anyway, I better be getting back." He put his hand to the brim of his hat and gave an elaborate farewell to the girls, then pumped our hands once more. "Don't forget about what I said," he reminded us. "I got tangled up with Audrey in '57 when I was in the Coasties. I warned the captain she was coming, but he wouldn't listen. We survived that storm, thank the Lord, and even rescued a crew from a disabled freighter. I don't have to tell you that hurricanes are dangerous business."

He walked away with his chest out, moving in the stiff, awkward manner of bodybuilders. When he was out of earshot, Johnny said, "I wonder what the Coast Guard captain said when Seaman McMahon informed him about the killer storm he'd seen in his dreams?"

We all laughed. "What a crackpot," said Pete.

"I thought he was cute," said Rachel.

"So what do you think, Charlie?" Carmen asked. "Is there a storm coming?" She affectionately put her arm around my waist, and my pulse quickened. I hadn't been sure until that moment that she'd even acknowledge me after last night, and here she was acting like my *girlfriend*.

I saw that everyone was waiting for me to answer, so I wet my finger and held it up to the breeze, shutting my eyes tight and pretending to deliberate. When I opened my eyes, I pronounced that Pete was probably right; Billy Boomerang was a crackpot. Everyone laughed again, but in the back of my mind I wondered if there was anything, anything at all, to his unlikely forecast. If there was, our dad would need a lot of help to secure his vessels and prepare for the storm. Hurricane Carla caught us unprepared last summer. It blew the roof off our house and sank one of Dad's best shrimp boats, the *Jenny Jill*. Shrimp boats were his life and livelihood; losing one was like a knife in the gut. If there was so much as a tropical disturbance brewing out there, he'd expect us to be by his side and ready to jump into action.

Johnny must have been thinking the same thing. "We probably need to start back anyway," he said.

Pete looked at him in dismay. "What? Why?" I saw that he and Rachel were holding hands.

Veronica sighed. "I *did* promise my mom I'd be back today." Although the way she said it, the promise seemed as breakable as a sand dollar.

"We'll make up a story," Rachel offered.

Pete nodded, like it was the best idea he'd ever heard. "Yeah. You can tell her you had to help an Australian find his boomerang."

Rachel giggled as if he'd told a dirty joke. That girl was a pistol. Pete was gonna have his hands full when we got back to civilization.

"What's your vote, Charlie?" asked Johnny.

I took a deep breath and looked toward the Gulf, stalling for time. Pete would throw a fit if I voted to go. Carmen put her lips to my ear and whispered, "It's okay if we go back, Carlito."

Her endorsement sealed the deal for me. "I have a motto," I told the group. "When the beer is gone, it's time to go home."

Before Pete could protest, Johnny seconded my suggestion. "I agree. Always leave when you're having fun. That's a good motto, or is it a maxim? I never can remember."

Johnny and I walked toward the truck, ahead of the girls. Pete jogged up behind us. "That's not your motto, *cabrón,*" he whispered to Johnny. "Your motto is exactly the opposite of that. You're always the last to leave a good party." He fell in step and looked at us with resignation. "You two are worried about not being around to help your old man if there's a storm, aren't you?"

Johnny put his arm around him. "You're pretty smart for a flyweight, Pete."

Pete shrugged off the arm. "Dipshit. I was really making progress with Rachel, too."

"It wouldn't have worked out," said Johnny.

"No? Why? Because she's a rich white girl and I'm a North-side Mexican?" Pete was getting his dander up.

"No, man. Didn't you notice? She lost interest in you once she realized Billy Boomerang was almost an inch taller than you."

Pete shoved Johnny, who tripped over my leg and fell down in the sand, causing me to fall on top of my brother. Pete gave some kind of Mexican rebel yell and dog piled on top of the both of us. The girls squealed with delight and ran over and jumped onto the pile of bodies for good measure. We rolled around in the sand laughing hysterically.

It had been a great beach trip. Maybe the best one ever.

CHAPTER 07

Billy Boomerang was right about a storm coming, and we were right about our dad being anxious about it.

"Out lollygagging on Padre Island," he scolded, "with a hurricane forming in the Gulf. No phone, no radio . . . no way to contact you. No more sense than God gave a pissant."

It was a funny thing about our dad. When he was in full-on "DAD" mode, like now, he didn't dick around. He was The Man, our ranking parent and authority figure. But he'd always lived in his head a lot, even before our mom died, and he was often away for weeks at a time, even when he was home. Sometimes I thought of him less as Dad than as a Dubber, a semi-absentee big brother.

But he could still work harder, and longer, than anyone I'd ever known. For the next few days we worked nonstop, until we were stumble-drunk with fatigue: tying down boats, battening hatches, screwing sheets of plywood over doors and windows, stowing everything that could be blown or washed away.

And while Dublin Sweetwater and sons prepared for the Armageddon of storms, the rest of the townsfolk kept an eye on their television sets, waiting to see if "Flossie" would grow beyond a Category One storm and if her erratic path would swing in our direction. Sweating our asses off in the August heat and humidity, we watched people drive by our house in their air-conditioned cars. They stared, pointed, and shook their heads. Why go to so much trouble if the storm might peter out or head to Mexico? There was still lots of time, they told themselves.

I'd learned that most coastal residents were fatalists. They figured a storm would grow, or it would fall apart; it would hit 'em, or it would go somewhere else. What the hell could they do about it?

Our dad, however, had become pessimistic and superstitious, and storms always energized him and filled him with a grim sense of resolve. He believed a storm's chance of hitting him was directly proportional to his level of preparedness. If he did nothing, he'd be slammed for sure. When Hurricane Carla caught us with our pants down last year, it validated his theory, at least in his mind.

So people drove by our house, curious, amused, and generally unconcerned about the weather. To be truthful, people drove by our house and stared even when we weren't swarming around it like carpenter ants. This was because we lived in a concrete geodesic dome that looked like it belonged on the set of a science fiction movie.

The house sat alone at the end of Water Street in south Rockport, at the edge of the bay. It had been designed and constructed by a retired physics professor from the Midwest, who created the odd-looking concrete monolith because he was bored and had lots of money, and also to prove that it could be done. The result was a structure that was solid as a granite boulder but was also damp, awkward, and had acoustics so wacky that a conversation in my bedroom could clearly be heard on the other side of the house. Little round portholes provided the only interior light.

After the physics professor died, the house was vacant for many years, an architectural oddity that made the Chamber of Commerce list of "interesting and unusual" things to see in the area. When Dad saw it, he admired its indestructability above all else, and said we'd be safe from attacks both meteorological and military. So, after Carla, he bought the house for a song and soon occupied the space as intractably as a hermit crab taking up residence in an abandoned shell.

Nobody in town was surprised by this. Sadly, neither were Johnny and I. In an area known for its colorful characters, our dad was beginning to stand out. He was becoming, in his low-key way, as eccentric as his brothers. We, the next generation, began to fear what might be in store for us as the years passed.

It hadn't always been that way, but after our mother died, our dad found refuge from his crushing grief by working excessively. The off-months, when shrimping season was closed, were when he was most unpredictable. Sometimes he would get down in the dumps and the mood would last for weeks at a time. Occasionally, he would break from his daily grind and go on epic bouts of drinking. But even then, he was never abusive, at least not in a physical way.

We were told he was quite proud of our accomplishments in school and sports. If he wasn't out in the Gulf, he never missed a home game, though he didn't always let us know he'd been there. And when our little experiments in anarchy blew up— he'd bailed us out of trouble more than once—he always had our backs, at least until we got back home.

Despite our laborious preparation (or perhaps because of it), Hurricane Flossie was eventually downgraded to a tropical storm and brought nothing more than high tides, gale force winds, and about eight inches of rain to the largely uninhabited counties south of Baffin Bay—almost exactly, we noted, where we'd run into Billy Boomerang. After three days of backbreaking work, my brother and I were almost disappointed the storm had missed us. We finished taking down the last of the plywood just in time for football practice— two-a-days—and the misery began all over again.

When the first week of two-a-days was over, we spent Saturday limping around the house cursing the football gods. I would've liked to have seen Carmen, but she was attending a ballet workshop in New York that week. It was just as well. My football "workshops" didn't leave me with much in the tank at the end of the day, anyway.

On Sunday, my brother and I decided to treat ourselves to a steak at the Eat-A-Bite restaurant on Peoples Street in Corpus. As we drove through South Bluff, Johnny suggested we stop by the gym to see if Pete was there; maybe he'd want to join us for lunch.

"If Stubby sees us, he might make us work out," I cautioned.

"Naw, he said we didn't have to start coming in until school starts."

"Yeah, but still . . . ."

"If he lights on us, we can tell him we're on our way to church. Stubby still wants to stay right with Jesus, I think."

We entered the gym and I saw a medicine ball on the floor near the front door. I picked it up quickly and surveyed the room, searching for Naco Flores. Instead, I saw Pete Lopez working on the speed bag in the back corner of the building. The bag was almost invisible it was moving so fast.

"You up for some lunch, Pete?" asked Johnny.

Pete gave the bag one final pop. "Yeah, I'm starving. You guys hear about what happened?"

"What?" we both asked at once.

"Somebody broke into the gym last night and stole a bunch of stuff."

Johnny looked around the shabby room. "No shit? What did they steal? What's there *to* steal?"

"A radio, a little TV, some Cokes and other junk. Not that much, now that I think of it. But they made a real mess of Stubby's office."

We looked through the office window and saw Stubby and Jesse talking inside. Pete continued. "They turned over his desk and the file cabinets, and worst of all, they broke those pictures he had on the wall."

"Even the autographed one of Joe Louis?" I asked. Stubby had acted as a referee in Louis' title bout against Max Schmeling in 1938. The Brown Bomber had signed the photo "To my friend, Stubby, fair but firm."

"That one they took," said Pete. "Stubby's in a crappy mood right now, so you guys might want to steer clear."

But it was too late. Stubby glanced up and saw us, and then stuck his head out the door before we could escape. "Shit," Johnny muttered.

"Johnny Sweetwater," he barked. "Get your gear on. I want you to spar with Jesse today."

Johnny and I looked at each other with wide eyes.

"*Válgame Dios!*" Pete exclaimed. "You got any last words for me or your brother before you die?"

Johnny shrugged and tried to act cool, but he had to be shaking in his high-tops. "To my brother Charlie," he said solemnly, "I give my *Playboy* magazines, my fishing tackle, and the Jeep. Pete, I'm giving you my best suit from third grade. You've grown enough that it'll probably fit you now."

"*Besa mi culo,*" Pete replied. When Johnny trotted off to change clothes, I heard Pete grumble, "I was kind of hoping he'd give me the Jeep."

Johnny warmed up, and then, as we were taping his hands, Jesse walked over and squatted next to him. "Hey, Juanito," he said smiling. "You okay to spar with me?"

"Sure, Feo. If Stubby thinks it's alright . . . ."

"It was my idea, not Stubby's," he said, patting Johnny on the knee. "Don' worry. It'll be okay, man."

"I just don't wanna hurt you, that's all," Johnny answered with forced humor.

Jesse laughed his big booming laugh and then looked Johnny in the eye. "Look, this guy I'm fightin' in December, he has a long reach and he knows how to throw a jab. You got an even longer reach and throw a pretty good jab, too. Don' be afraid to lemme see 'em, man."

"Okay, Feo."

"Okay."

Stubby made Johnny put on headgear and then he yelled "Box!" and the two fighters began waltzing around the ring. Of course, everyone in the gym had crowded around to watch the high school kid spar with the next middleweight champion. Naco pushed in next to me and watched with rare attentiveness. He normally ignored the boxing action in the ring, preferring to focus on his own peculiar interests.

Johnny must have been scared, because he came out kinda wild and somehow popped Jesse in the mouth with a very solid right cross. Jesse smiled, spit out some blood and nodded in appreciation. For the duration of the sparring rounds, Jesse controlled the tempo. We noticed he never really tried to connect with full force, or it would've been the ballgame. Johnny gamely tried to land some of the punches that Stubby suggested, but Jesse was just too damn fast.

"More combinations, Johnny. Throw those jabs faster," Stubby shouted. "You be the aggressor. Show him something now."

But Jesse dodged, deflected, and stepped away from almost every punch Johnny threw at him. Not all of them, though. Johnny had a very effective jab, just like Jesse said, and several times he slipped one inside and caught Jesse in the face. All in all, it was a commendable performance by my brother, and he seemed to give his opponent a pretty good workout. Jesse said as much after they'd both removed their gloves.

"Good job," he said. "Bes' challenge I had since Stubby brought in that heavyweight from Houston las' spring."

Johnny looked up wearily. He hadn't thrown that many punches in a long time. "Thanks, Feo," he said.

When Jesse walked off, I asked him what it felt like, boxing El Rey Feo.

"Hard to hit," he answered. "But when I did, it was like hitting concrete. I can barely lift my arms."

Later, I invited Jesse to join us for a late lunch at the Eat-A-Bite. He gave me a puzzled expression.

"Maybe tha's not such a good idea, Charlie."

I started to ask why, and then I realized how stupid I was. Johnny walked over and looked at us. "What?" he said.

Jesse whacked me on the back affably. "Your brother is bein' a good guy, tha's all."

"I asked him to come to lunch with us," I said sheepishly.

Johnny thought about it a second and then looked at the clock. "Good idea! That is, if they're not already closed. The Eat-A-Bite shuts down early on Sunday, but I'm sure Snodgrass, the owner, will fix us a plate to go, at least. As many times as we've run fresh shrimp over to him from Dad's boats?"

Eventually we convinced Jesse to go with us, and as we were heading for the truck, Pete grabbed Johnny by the arm. "Are you crazy, man? This town only started lettin' Mexicans eat at the white restaurants two years ago."

"Snodgrass is a good guy," Johnny answered. "He's friends with my Uncle Rupert."

We pulled up to the Eat-A-Bite and Johnny killed the engine. Before we could get out, he told us to wait while he checked to see if the diner was closed. Through the restaurant's front window, I could see him leaning over the cashier's counter talking to Mr. Snodgrass, who turned around and studied the three of us sitting in the Jeep. A moment later, Johnny stuck his head out the door and beckoned us inside.

It had taken me a minute to figure out Johnny's plan. If Snodgrass said no dice to serving Jesse, Johnny could come back to the truck and say the restaurant was closed, and everybody would save face. But Mr. Snodgrass apparently had no problem with integrated dining, so the first part, getting in the door, was pretty easy.

Ten stools and a long counter fronted a fry grill on one side of the restaurant, and on the other side, a half-dozen booths were lined against the wall. Two guys who looked like dockworkers sat at the end of the counter, drinking coffee. Across the floor, a group of businessmen occupied one booth, and a couple of elderly women sat at another.

Everyone stared at us when we walked in. Mr. Snodgrass tilted his head toward the stools at the opposite end of the counter from the dockworkers, indicating where he wanted us to sit. As soon as we sat down, the two elderly ladies got up, paid their bill, and walked out in a huff. Mr. Snodgrass took their money, but otherwise completely ignored them.

The cook's name was Franklin, and he was almost as black as Jesse. He looked over at his boss and then approached us, wiping his hands on a towel. "What can I get you?" he asked nervously, alternating glances between us, Mr. Snodgrass, and the men at the other end of the counter.

Johnny spoke first. "Franklin, we're hungry. You got any of those ribeyes left?"

"Yessir, I think we do."

"Well, that's what I want, and a Coke float from the soda fountain."

Pete slapped down his menu. "That sounds good. I'll have the same."

"Ditto," I said.

Franklin stopped in front of Jesse and their eyes met. I could tell they both recognized how serious this was. Jesse was sitting at a lunch counter with white men. Breaking race barriers in Texas was ballsy, high-stakes business. For one thing, it was illegal. I watched them weigh the risk and reward implied in this simple act—one man taking another man's order at a public restaurant.

"You, sir?" asked Franklin.

"Guess I'll have the same," said Jesse.

Our Coke floats arrived, and the two guys from the other end of the counter stood up and walked over. One of them jingled some loose change in his hand. The other one had sideburns shaped like cowboy boots running down his jaw. We tried to act nonchalant, sipping on our sodas and acting like the four of us were regular customers at the Eat-A-Bite, but the tension was so thick I found I was unable to swallow. I'd never felt the shame of segregation as intensely as I did at that moment, sitting next to my friend Jesse at the Eat-A-Bite counter. I wondered if he felt that way all the time.

"Boxers, right?" asked the bigger of the two men.

"We are," Johnny answered warily. "Golden Gloves."

"Thought so," he said, nodding. "But you," he pointed a calloused finger at Jesse. "You fought the Naval Base champion last year at the Coliseum, am I right?"

"Tha' was me," said Jesse.

"You whipped that boy pretty good. Hell of an exhibition. And you . . . ." this time he pointed at Pete. "You won the Gloves tournament. Bantam weight."

"Flyweight," Pete corrected.

"Y'all still boxing?"

"Still boxing," answered Jesse.

The guy looked at Jesse and Pete and nodded slowly. "Well, good luck to you both." He walked away jingling his handful of change.

Sideburns winked at us as he walked by. "See y'all at the fights," he said, and gave us a stained, chipped-tooth smile that reminded me of the chain on a chainsaw.

The bell on the door rang them out. Franklin, the fry cook, had a stunned expression on his face like *Did that just happen?* On the other side of the counter, the four of us looked at each other in disbelief, and then we started chuckling.

"You just never know, do you?" Pete said in wonder.

"Boxing fans," said Johnny. "God bless 'em."

Mr. Snodgrass looked up from his perch behind the cash register. "I figured they might cut you some slack once they recognized Jesse."

Pete elbowed Johnny in the arm. "I guess your fights didn't impress Moneybags all that much, 'cause he didn't mention you, did he?"

"No," laughed Jesse. "I don' think none of 'em did."

We continued ribbing Johnny until our steaks came, each one pooled in butter, with sides of fried potatoes and lima beans, and on a separate plate, a big wedge of iceberg lettuce covered with Thousand Island dressing. As we ate our food, we talked about the vandalism at the gym. The South Bluff area was pretty rough and getting rougher every year, and after awhile, we decided it could have been just about any juvenile delinquent in the neighborhood. There were plenty to go around.

"Hated to see Stubby lose that Joe Louis photo, though," I said.

Pete dug a dollop of vanilla ice cream out of his Coke float and sucked it off his spoon. "I guess that's why he was in such a bad mood all day. You were in that office with him for an hour, Feo, before you sparred with Johnny. He seemed upset about something else, too. What's he sore about?"

Jesse fingered his straw. "We're gettin' a lotta pressure from those promoters in Miami," he answered after a pause. "Stubby really hates thos' guys."

"Why is that, Feo?" asked Johnny. "Aren't there a bunch of successful pro boxers outta Miami? Seems like it might be something you'd consider."

"Carmen says all the Miami promoters are *mafiosos*," I said.

"My niece is prob'ly right, Charlie."

"So, what's the story with these wiseguys?" asked Pete. "They sure put their prizefighters in some big money fights. Is that such a bad thing?"

Jesse looked at Pete with sad eyes. "Soon you are going pro, Pete. And you need to find a team that takes care of *you*. Not themselves, not their boss, nobody but *you*." Jesse's voice was rising. "Wrong manager, wrong trainer, wrong promoter—they can ruin a fighter." He pounded his fist on the counter. "*Ruin* him, you understan' me, Pete? And they'll ruin you too, if you let 'em. Sell off fifty percent of you to ten different guys. Then you wind up owin' *them* money."

We sat in startled silence. We'd never heard Jesse speak that way. Franklin came over and took our plates, looking at Jesse like he was pushing his luck with an outburst like that. We quietly sipped our sodas.

A moment later, Jesse turned to us. "Lemme tell you guys a story. You ever hear of Benny Paret? He's a welterweight fighter."

Pete's eyes got big. "Two-time welterweight champ, *Kid* Paret?"

"Yes, Benny, "Kid" Paret."

"He's that Cuban boxer that Emile Griffith killed in the ring last March," said Johnny.

Pete nodded solemnly. "I watched the fight on TV. In fact, I think the whole country watched Paret get beat to death that night."

I watched it, too. And I would never forget the black-and-white TV images of the defeated fighter, tangled in the ropes, insensible at that point, getting pummeled again and again by Griffith—at least twenty-four consecutive punches to his unprotected face and head. The announcer kept screaming, "Are they going to stop it? Will somebody stop it?" But Paret just hung there, limp and defenseless, his eyes hammered shut, his brain swelling, already slipping into a coma. It was a horrible thing to see.

"Did you know him, Feo?" I asked.

Jesse nodded. "We fought each other many times in Cuba when we were growing up. He was the same age as me, but he went pro when he was young, barely seventeen years. I tol' him 'Wha's your hurry, Benny? There's plenty of time. Le's go pro together.'" Jesse shrugged. "But Benny was impatient. He left and went to Havana, and after that, to Miami. Everyone want a piece of him. And the team he got was no good. They gave very bad advice."

"What kind of bad advice?" I asked.

"Like they schedule his fights too close together. He fought twelve times in 1957, if you can believe it. Most years it was ten fights, and agains' tough guys, too." He shook his head in disgust. "And like matchin' him against Gene Fulmer."

"I remember that fight," said Pete. "Fulmer was a beast. A big, brawling middleweight."

"Benny shouldn' have taken that fight. He had jus' defended his title in a hard fifteen-round match against Emile, and then two months later, they sen' him against Fulmer, who was above his weight class. Benny got beat up very bad in that fight. Very bad. I think it shoulda been his last fight, to tell you the truth. When you get hurt like that, the body needs time to recover, you know? But three months later, those *payasos* from Miami had him fightin' Griffith again, to defend his title. They might as well've push him in front of a bus."

"And he died in the ring," said Johnny.

Jesse's eyes clouded over. "Yeah. He died in the ring." We were silent for a moment, each of us staring into our soda glass, remembering the fight, until Jesse continued. "He made it harder on himself by calling Griffith a *maricón* before the fight."

Pete looked up. "He really called him that?"

"What does *maricón* mean?" I asked.

"It's like a girly boy," said Pete. "A homo. It's the worst thing you can call someone in boxing. No wonder Griffith went so crazy."

"Benny was a good guy," Jesse continued, "but he always had a smart mouth. He was tryin' to get inside Emile's head. Anyway, after Benny died, his wife and kid never saw one penny from tha' fight. An' you know wha' Benny's manager said? He said, 'I guess I have to go find a new boy.'" Jesse took a deep breath. "Mr. Hunsacker may not be a big-time manager from Miami, but he would never le' that happen to me." He looked at Pete, "or to you, either, Pete."

CHAPTER 08

By the end of two-a-days, I had earned a first-string spot on the Rockport Pirate varsity. Peer pressure probably had something to do with it; Johnny was the starting quarterback, of course, and probably the best player on the team. If I wound up riding the bench, I'd probably feel like I had a big scarlet "L" painted across my head for "Loser." Anyway, I managed to beat out a pimply-faced senior who was fast as the dickens but couldn't catch a football if you dipped it in pine tar.

After the last practice, my brother and I were dog-tired when we drove back to the house, but otherwise feeling pretty good about ourselves. Outwardly, we pretended that being studs on the high school football team wasn't *that* big a deal. But football is king in Texas, and despite our well-practiced indifference, we were excited about the prospects for our team. There was a good chance we'd win district if we could somehow get past the Port Lavaca Sandcrabs. Last year they'd whipped our butts by three touchdowns. Johnny had been knocked out cold in the second quarter when a homicidal cornerback blitzed into our backfield and blindsided him. My brother was itching for some payback.

When we pulled up to the house, we were surprised to find Carmen parked out front, sitting behind the wheel of her mom's

Nash Rambler. Johnny whistled. "Well whaddaya know? Did you know she was coming by?"

I shook my head no, and somehow found the wherewithal to keep from leaping out of the moving car and bounding up to her like a puppy.

"Hey, Carmen," I said. "You're back."

She pushed her sunglasses onto the crown of her head and smiled at me. "Hi, Charlie. I am. I was just admiring your house."

I turned to the concrete mushroom we called home and shrugged. "My dad had a bad experience with a hurricane. He overreacted a little bit."

"It looks very . . . safe."

"That's one way to describe it."

Johnny walked up to the car and he and Carmen traded oblique kisses on both cheeks, a Latino custom I'd observed before. Why the hell hadn't I thought of it?

"As usual, it's a surprise to see you," Johnny said with a grin. "There's just no telling where you'll show up."

"I came by to see Charlie. By the way, Veronica says hello."

"Yeah? Well, tell her hello back."

"I will, but I think she'd like it if you told her yourself."

"Okay, I will." Johnny stood there smiling and nodding until he noticed Carmen looking past him and straight at me. He took the hint and went inside the house.

"I came to invite you to dinner," she said to me after he was gone. "My mother wants to meet you."

"She wants to meet *me?*"

"Yes. Between Jesse and me, I think your name came up one too many times in our house. She insisted on an audience with you."

I didn't like the sound of that. "An audience?"

"Maybe that's too strong a word, but only a little. My mother is very . . ." Carmen thought for a moment, "traditional."

"Well, in that case, I would be *delighted* to join y'all for dinner." I presented Carmen with a short bow. "Should I wear a suit?" I joked.

"That would be a nice touch."

I realized she was serious. "Okay, a suit it is." I had only one J.C. Penney's suit, which I'd worn on rare visits to church. I hoped the damn thing still fit. A pair of dress shoes was stuffed back in my closet someplace.

"Tomorrow night, seven o'clock?"

"I'll be there, with bells on . . . and a necktie."

After a pause, I asked her if she wanted to come inside.

"Thanks, but I've got to run." She started the car and then handed me a slip of paper with her address on it.

I glanced at the Corpus Christi address—Cole Street, only a few blocks from the Bay—and then took Johnny's lead and leaned into the car to do the peck-on-the-cheek thing. But Carmen held my head with both hands and gave me full-out kiss on the lips.

"See you tomorrow," she said.

I stood in the driveway and waved goodbye as she drove off. I had been invited to dinner at Carmen's house. "Hot-diggity, dog-diggity, boom!" Perry Como's corny song played inside my head. I had an official date with Carmen Delfín. How bad could it be, meeting her mother?

—

Johnny loaned me the Jeep on Saturday night, even though technically, at fifteen, I wasn't supposed to drive without adult supervision. But Dad was out in the Gulf shrimping, and he never paid much attention to that particular law anyway. In his mind, if you were big enough to buy a car, fix it up, and pay for the gas, you were big enough to drive it. At Johnny's suggestion, I walked to the bayfront behind our house and cut a bunch of fresh flowers to take with me.

"If you want to stay in the game with Carmen, you've got to win over her mother," he counseled. "Remember not to pick your nose. And act confident, like, you know, a grown-up. If you get in trouble, just ask yourself, 'What would my big brother do?'" He straightened my tie and brushed a hair off my shoulder. "Although I suspect you and Carmen might've gotten to know each other pretty good out on Padre."

I must have blushed a little because Johnny patted me on the back. "Don't worry, brother man," he said. "Your secret's safe with me. It's bad form to kiss and tell, especially with a girl like Carmen."

Carmen lived in a modest two-bedroom house in the Six Points area in Corpus. The house was freshly painted and fronted by a well-tended yard with roses, hibiscus, and a tidy St. Augustine lawn. Tucked into a corner of the backyard was the one-room cottage where Jesse stayed. The location was ideal for him; it was a short distance from the running path along the bay and an easy jog to Hunsacker's Gym. I glanced at myself in the rearview mirror and tried unsuccessfully to push the surfer-cut bangs off my forehead. "Here goes nothing," I muttered. After two knocks, Carmen answered the door.

"You're right on time," she said, rewarding me with a quick kiss on the cheek.

"You look lovely, Carmen." And so she did, wearing a sleeveless, scoop-neck dress that showed off her dancer's figure. I held out the flowers. "I brought these."

"Oh, thank you. They're very nice. Now," she took a turn at trying to brush back my hair, "are you ready for this, *Flaco?*"

"Ready as I'll ever be."

"Good. Come on in."

I stood inside the doorway while Carmen went to tell her mother I'd arrived. The house was kind of fussy, with doilies and glass figurines on the end tables, and a Persian rug covering the living room floor. The main wall had a mosaic of framed ballet playbills: *Swan Lake, Giselle, Sleeping Beauty, The Nutcracker,* with subtitles in French, Russian, Spanish, and English. I knew less about ballet than I did nuclear physics, but I did recognize the name "Alisa Delfín" on all of the posters. She had been a star, just as Carmen said, and had danced in theaters all over the world.

Carmen walked into the room holding her mom by the hand. Seeing her mother's perfect posture, I automatically straightened my back. She was an elegant woman, no longer the young prima ballerina pictured on the playbills, but still very beautiful. She must have been in her mid-forties, with an erect figure and a long, aristocratic nose. She raised an eyebrow at the fistful of wilting morning glories I'd brought for her daughter. It crossed my mind that in Cuba, these particular flowers might be horribly inappropriate, representing something awful like death or infidelity. Maybe they were considered a common weed there.

"Mrs. Delfín, my name is Charlie Sweetwater," I blurted, "and I'm real glad to meet you." I thrust out my hand to shake, and I felt a little bit like I was trying to sell her a smoked turkey leg from the carnival.

"*Encantada,*" she said, finally taking my hand and giving it a cursory shake. I stood by awkwardly and resisted the urge to check and see if I'd left my fly unbuttoned.

"Mother," said Carmen. "Charlie knows *Tío* Jesse from the gymnasium."

"Yes, so you said. Mr. Sweetwater, do you aspire to become a professional boxer like my brother-in-law? Or do you have other ambitions?"

"I'm studying my options."

"Of course. You are still so very young."

For a moment I thought she was going to pat me on the head like I was a precocious little boy, but instead, she grabbed me firmly by the arm and escorted me to the back door. "Come," she said. "Let's say hello to Jesse and Ramón."

I looked back at Carmen, who gave me a weak smile, like I hadn't completely failed the first impression test, but that the result was less than satisfactory. And who was Ramón?

Jesse and a lean Hispanic man wearing a sports jacket and a collared white shirt were standing on the brick patio smoking cigars. Carmen's mother opened the back door for me and, as soon as she caught Jesse's eye, left me standing alone on the porch.

"Charlie!" Jesse called jovially. "I am happy to see you, man. Come meet my new friend, Ramón Cruz."

I shook hands with Ramón, and a wide smile appeared beneath his bushy mustache. "Jesse was just telling me about you," he said. "He says you are a good friend."

I noted the guy's thick accent "I'm his biggest fan."

Ramón laughed and reached into his coat pocket. "Would you like a Cuban cigar? They say they are the best in the world."

I glanced at Jesse for a cue. The only cigar I'd ever smoked was a flavored Swisher Sweet cigarillo, and halfway through it I turned green and threw up. Jesse gave me a brief nod of consent.

"Sure," I said. Anything to seem older than I was. He used a small implement to clip the end off the cigar, and then he handed it to me, along with a gold-plated Zippo lighter. I lit the stogie and took an experimental puff, hoping not to choke. It was surprisingly smooth.

"I was just telling Jesse how I am visiting Camaguey on business when I meet his *suegro,* Ernesto, at the hotel bar."

I looked at Jesse for some help.

"Camaguey is a town in Cuba," Jesse said, smiling. "*Suegro* . . . it mean brother-in-law."

Ramón continued. "So Ernesto mentions to me that his sister lives in Corpus Christi, and I say *coño!* I travel there on business sometimes. Well, the next thing I know, he is telling me all about Doña Delfín and Jesse. Can you believe it?"

I said no, I couldn't believe it.

"Anyway, that night we drink about a dozen *mojitos,* and before I leave, Ernesto gives me Doña Delfín and Jesse's address and makes me promise to look them up the next time I am in Texas."

I nodded my head stupidly. That was a lot of information to absorb in a short time. Who was Doña Delfín and what the hell was a *mojito*?

"What business are you in, Mr. Cruz?" I asked, trying to make adult conversation.

"Agriculture," he said.

"And you're from Cuba?"

Ramón's smile widened a bit, and he observed me more carefully. "No, I am from Mexico."

The man's face was angular and deeply tanned, and even though he had a winning smile, there was something about his eyes that was unsettling, although I couldn't say exactly what. Maybe it was how intensely they fixed onto whatever they were looking at.

"Ramón arrive from Mexico City this afternoon," Jesse explained, "and he came here to say hello and to pass along news from my family. So of course, Alisa invite him to have dinner with us."

"Mrs. Delfín?"

"Yes, but call her *Doña* Delfín if you wanna score some points," Jesse said with a wink.

"So, is Ernesto married to Doña Delfín's sister?" I asked, still hazy about the familial connection. Maybe it was the cigar, which was making me feel a little woozy.

Jesse laughed. "No, Ernesto is Alisa's brother, and I am married to Isabella, their youngest sister. By the way . . ." He lowered his voice, "Delfín is Alisa's maiden name. We don' mention the ex-husband's name in this house. Is complicated, you know?" He grinned and placed his arm around my shoulder. "Come. Let's have a beer. I promise not to tell Stubby."

I listened to them talk about Jesse's in-laws, and about Camaguey, until Carmen called us in for dinner. On the way to the house, I stashed the cigar in a flowerpot, so it wouldn't completely ruin my appetite.

The table was set with formal place settings, with way too many spoons and forks for my comfort. Jesse and Doña Delfín sat at each end of the table, and Carmen and I sat opposite Ramón. The conversation was polite, and the dinner seemed to be going fairly well at the beginning. After a few innocuous questions directed at me regarding where I lived and what my family did for a living, they began talking about ballet. Apparently, Ramón was a big fan, and effusive in his praise of Doña Delfín and her international career. Carmen's mother was visibly pleased to hear it.

Later in the dinner, the conversation moved to politics, and they began speaking Spanish. I was able to make out the names "Fidel" and "Kennedy," but otherwise, I sat there like a bump on a log, twirling a dessert spoon. Carmen listened intently, and even jumped in a couple of times with her own comments, until she realized I had been exiled from the discussion. "I think we should speak English," she announced, "so Charlie can participate, too."

Oh no.

"*Por supuesto!* We apologize, Charlie," said Jesse. "It is very rude of us. We are talkin' about Cuba, and how everythin' is changin'."

"What do you think?" asked Ramón. "I am interested to hear the American perspective."

The question was so general, I didn't have a clue how to answer, but everyone was looking at me so I gave it a shot. "I heard Castro wants to meet Elvis."

I swore I remembered reading that somewhere.

Everyone laughed at me except Carmen.

"What did I tell you about American kids?" Dona Delfín said to Ramón. "They are absolutely *oblivious.*"

Ramón said something in Spanish, and Dona Delfín laughed again. Jesse looked away, embarrassed for me, it seemed.

"Leave him alone," Carmen said defensively. "What did any of *you* know about politics when you were teenagers?" She looked fiercely at her mother. "You thought only of ballet," and then to Jesse, "and you boxing." Lastly, she stared pointedly at Ramón. "What was it with you, Mr. Cruz? Soccer? Baseball?"

"Carmen, *basta!*" her mother snapped. "Mr. Cruz is our guest."

"So is Charlie," she answered.

"It's okay, Doña," Ramón said soothingly. "I suppose I love baseball the best."

"So, you played baseball, huh? Were you any good?" I was trying to be friendly, but I don't think Ramón took it that way. He turned to me with a smile that had no warmth in it.

"I didn't have much time for it, unfortunately. When I was your age, I was shining the shoes of rich *Americanos* in front of their fancy hotels."

We locked eyes and I refused to blink first. I was a little taken aback by the "rich *Americanos*" jab. What had I ever done to this guy? There was something slippery about Ramón that I hadn't liked from the moment I saw him. I may have been ignorant of world affairs, but

I'd been around enough bullshit artists to smell a lie. Shady's, and the characters it attracted, had been a real-world classroom for me. If Ramón was a Mexican businessman, I was Martian.

"Mamá," Carmen said quietly. "I think Charlie and I will go out for awhile. If it's okay with you," she added tersely.

Doña Delfín seemed to bristle at this, but then she forced a smile and reluctantly assented. "Don't stay out too late."

Carmen scooted her chair back and stood up. I did the same. "It was a pleasure, Mr. Cruz," she said stiffly to Ramón.

"Likewise," Ramón answered, rising from his chair and making a little bow.

I leaned over and we shook hands, both of us gripping hard, and then I thanked Carmen's mother for the dinner and told Jesse I'd see him at the gym.

Carmen and I walked out without speaking. After I'd started the car, I looked at her. "Where to?"

"You said your dad was out of town?"

"He's in the Gulf, working."

"And your brother?"

"He went to a double feature at the picture show."

"So maybe we can go to your house?"

"It's over a half hour away. Your mother said for you to be home early."

"Don't worry about my mother. Start driving. On the way, I'll tell you all about *la gloriosa revolución Cubana*," she said sarcastically.

While we were in the car, she gave me a crash course on recent Cuban history: from the pre-Castro corruption, to the guerrillas in the mountains; from the triumphant rebel march into Havana, to the brutal crackdown that followed; and from the island's cozying up to Russia, to the disastrous Bay of Pigs invasion earlier that spring. It didn't seem to me that Carmen thought the revolution all that glorious or even all that revolutionary. She concluded her summary at my house.

"So basically, you've traded one dictator for another," I said. We were sitting on the sofa in our circular living room.

"Basically."

"And I guess Fidel Castro's not an Elvis fan?"

She laughed. "I doubt it. Last year he actually *banned* rock and roll. He said it was 'imperialist' music."

"And what about this Ramón guy?"

"I've known him as long as you have. I saw him this evening for the first time."

"He seems passionate about the Cuban Revolution."

"Everyone is passionate about the Revolution. But enough of politics." She leaned over and kissed me. "Do you have any music? Something soft?"

I hopped up as casually as I could and put a Johnny Mathis record on the turntable.

"Good choice," she said. A shy smile appeared on her face. "Charlie, are you sure we're alone?"

I nodded my head, trying to hide my growing excitement.

"Good." She crooked her finger and beckoned me over. "Turn down the lights and come over here. Let's you and me be *oblivious* for awhile."

We started kissing, and it got pretty steamy on the couch. Eventually things progressed, and we began to remove our clothes, watching each other closely and with frank curiosity as we undressed. It was the first time I'd ever seen a woman's naked body, a live version, anyway, and I gaped in wonder at the sight.

"Charlie, you're staring."

"I can't help it," I said. "You're . . . you're beautiful."

Carmen giggled but made no attempt to cover herself. Nor did I.

"What now?" she asked. "I don't know the steps to this dance."

"I don't either. We'll both follow."

We laid down on the couch, where she guided me gently with her hands, letting me know with her breathing when I was doing something right. We took our time exploring each other's body, and when it finally happened, when we finally came together, it was quick and liberating.

I had anticipated and dreamed of this for a long time. But with Carmen, it was different from what I'd imagined. Better. Sweeter. Our hearts were pounding and we were painted in sweat. Moonlight filtered through the portholes in the walls.

Carmen smiled up at me. "So that's what it's like," she said.

"That's what it's like."

"Being a virgin is overrated."

I rested my forehead against hers. "Boy, is it ever."

CHAPTER 09

September rolled around, which meant that football kicked into high gear throughout the state. Ball squads, coaches, marching bands, cheerleaders, and booster clubs welcomed the new season with renewed hope that this might just be their year. I was caught up in the excitement, too. I'd dreamed of putting on the green and white uniform of the Rockport-Fulton Pirates since I was old enough to pick up a football.

That wasn't the only reason I was walking around feeling ten feet tall. Carmen Delfín had ushered me into a bigger world where colors were a little sharper and sensations were a little keener. At practice, the coach saw me grinning distantly at nothing in particular and told me I'd better knuckle down and get my game face on or I was gonna get my ass handed to me come game time. Yessir, Coach, I said. And then the grin was back.

Our first game was against the Kingsville Brahmas. They were small but scrappy, and had a scrambling quarterback who gave us fits the first two quarters. He was so quick he left a string of hapless defenders lying on the ground in his wake. The Brahmas were up 15–0 at halftime, and our coach was fit to be tied. In the locker room, he shattered three pieces of chalk as he spelled out our blunders with Xs and Os on the blackboard.

"You boys better grow some hair on your peaches right quick," he thundered, "or I'm gonna send you pantywaists home and suit up the marching band instead! Now get out there and hit somebody!"

We managed to pull it together in the second half. Our defense stiffened, and on offense we finally remembered how to execute the plays we'd worked on for the last thirty practices. Johnny was responsible for three straight touchdowns. The first score came early in the third quarter, when he scampered forty-six yards on an end sweep. In the fourth quarter, he tossed two touchdown passes—the last one a jump ball thrown to me in the corner of the end zone. It helped that my defender was five inches shorter than me. Small and scrappy only gets you so far. Anyway, we ended up on top, 28–15.

After the game, we shook hands with the team we'd just defeated and then knelt around our coach for the team prayer, where he thanked Jesus Christ, our Lord and Savior, for rewarding us with a victory. I doubt that Jesus had anything to do with our win that night, but if he did, he might have reconsidered had he followed Johnny and me around after the game. We got into trouble, of course, and since Dad was out in the Gulf, Rupert had to drive over from Ransom Island to bail us out of jail after we'd been charged with "criminal mischief." The two female mannequins we'd wedged into the claws of the big blue crab sculpture on top of Delmar's Grill (HOME OF DOROTHY'S FAMOUS CRAB CAKES) did not amuse Delmar, Dorothy, or the Rockport Police, although we thought the mangled, life-size dummies added drama to the local landmark. The police report mentioned that alcohol might have been involved.

We asked Rupert if he could somehow forget to tell our dad about the incident.

"Hell, no," he said. "But if he gets too wound up, you might ask him how he managed to get a live alligator into the trunk of the school principal's car back in '36." (We did.) "Maybe then he'll go easier on you." (He didn't.)

—

Starting the following week, Monday, through Thursday, our schedule required us to wake up ridiculously early and drive to Corpus for our boxing workouts. Not only did Stubby Hunsacker follow through on his promise to make us train before school, he even drove to Rockport to get buy-in from our dad and the football coach. The coach asked only that we skip training on Friday so we could rest up for the Friday night game, and also on Saturday, so our bodies had a chance to heal *after* the game. Still mad after our blue crab art project, our dad pushed for seven pre-dawn practices a week. Mercifully, Stubby said four was enough. Pete got a reprieve from the early morning sessions, the lucky bastard, and was allowed to double up on his afternoon training.

The drive from our house to the gym in Corpus Christi took forty minutes. On the first Monday, we showed up for our workout at 5:30 a.m., bleary-eyed but on time. As we pulled up to the gym, we were surprised to see another car parked alongside Stubby's old Chrysler. It had Florida plates, I noticed.

It was mostly dark inside the building, but a light was on in the office. The desk lamp illuminated three men: Stubby was in his chair, another man sat on the corner of his desk, examining the cast iron bulldog paperweight Stubby kept there, and a big fellow stood directly behind Stubby. We walked toward the office unnoticed in the darkness.

"What do we do?" I whispered to Johnny. I thought maybe the men were boxing promoters there to discuss Jesse's upcoming fight. But there was something unsettling about the two strangers who crowded the old man in his office so early in the morning. Shadows obscured their faces, and the big man had one of his hands on Stubby's shoulder.

"I don't know," Johnny answered. "Do you know those guys?"

"Maybe the short one. I can't tell from here."

The man sitting on the desk put down the paperweight and, without prelude, backhanded Stubby across the face while the other, bigger man, pushed him down in his seat.

"Hey!" Johnny shouted.

The men looked up, surprised, and then the shorter man rushed through the door and peered into the darkness until he spotted us. "You kids get the hell out of here!" he yelled. "The gym's closed."

It was the same heavyset guy who had visited Stubby before. The *mafioso*.

"What are you doing to Mr. Hunsacker?" Johnny yelled back.

"None of your business. I said get out of here!"

"Screw you!" Johnny answered.

This seemed to enrage the man, and he strode toward us all bowed up like he intended to throw us out himself. Johnny and I bolted in opposite directions, and the guy went after Johnny first. When he caught him, he wrenched his arm behind his back in a way that made Johnny groan and drop to his knees. "What'd I say, kid? Huh? I told you to scram."

Seeing my brother writhe in pain, I rushed the guy and planted my shoulder under his rib cage. We crashed to the ground and I leapt on top of him, trying to pin his arms, but he was much stronger than I was, and quicker than I would've expected for such a stocky guy. And, unfortunately for me, he knew what he was doing. Next thing I knew, he was on top of *me,* with one hand pressing on my chest and the other boxing my ears.

Next it was Johnny's turn to throw himself at the man. The two of them rolled across the floor and then sprang up and started throwing punches at each other. Johnny was doing okay until the guy maneuvered him against the edge of the boxing platform and shoved his head backwards into the ropes. I jumped in again and tried to pull him off my brother. Then something viselike grabbed me under the arm and tossed me aside like I was weightless. Soon after, Johnny landed beside me in a heap. Lying on the concrete floor panting, we heard a gravely laugh from the big guy.

"For Christ's sake, Walter," said a deep voice. "Quit fucking around with these kids and let's finish what we came here to do."

Walter straightened his shirt and tie and swiped his hand across his lips. He noticed blood on the back of his hand. "Goddamn punks bloodied my lip."

The big guy laughed again. "I'll get one of 'em and you get the other," he said. "That is, if you think you can handle it."

They jerked us up and were shoving us toward the door when the overhead lights came on in the gym. Stubby stood by the door with one hand on the light switch and the other clutching a little double-barreled derringer.

"Let 'em go," he said, pointing the gun at the men.

They released us, and the short one, Walter, smiled. "That's not real smart, Hunsacker."

"Maybe I don't like a couple of palookas coming into my gym, threatening me, and then roughing up two of my kids."

The big guy wasn't smiling anymore, and I saw him open and close his hands like he was aching to set them loose. Walter exhaled loudly. "You're a feisty little fucker, I'll give you that, Hunsacker. But you know how this is gonna turn out in the end, don't ya?"

Stubby continued scowling at the two guys. "Get out of my gym."

Walter shrugged. "Whatever you say, pal. You got the gun. I'll just get my hat."

"Forget the hat."

Walter paused and turned around slowly. "Don't push it, old man. I'm not leaving without my hat."

Stubby fired a shot into the air and all of us jumped. Bits of plaster fell down from the ceiling. "You're leaving now."

Stubby kept the gun on them while they walked out the door, and then he watched them until they got into their car and drove out of sight.

"You boys okay?" he asked. His cheek was still inflamed by the blow he'd received.

"We're fine," Johnny answered. "Who *were* those guys?"

Stubby took a deep breath. "Just some jokers from out of town. Forget about it, okay?"

"I saw one of 'em here last month," I said. "It's about Jesse, isn't it?"

Stubby turned to me and planted his hands on his hips. "What do you know about it?"

"I know that *mafiosos* in Miami want Jesse to work for them . . . but he doesn't want to."

Stubby blinked and cocked his head.

"The walls to your office are really thin," I explained. "I heard you and Feo talking to the fat guy . . . Walter . . . last month."

He stared at me a moment longer and then sighed. "Listen, I don't want either one of you to say a word about this to Jesse. He's got his training to concentrate on. He doesn't need to be worrying about anything else. We clear on that?"

Johnny and I both nodded.

"Not one word," he repeated.

"Okay, Mr. Hunsacker," Johnny answered. "But . . . do you think they'll come back?"

"Naw. Now that they know I won't roll over, they'll find another fighter. There's others out there that are ripe for the pickin'. Unfortunately." Stubby began walking away and then said over his shoulder, "You boys get your gear on. None of this means you get to skip your workout."

Johnny and I looked at each other, both of us thinking the same thing: this problem with Miami, it wasn't over. The two thugs Stubby just pulled a gun on didn't seem like the types to forget something like that, or to work for a boss who would.

———

CHAPTER 10

Carmen kept mentioning she wanted to meet my family. I warned her
to be careful what she wished for, but she wouldn't let it go. So on the
following Saturday, against my better judgment, I agreed to take her to
Ransom Island, where she was sure to be exposed to all the Sweetwater
charm she could stand. I admit I'd been putting it off, telling her I was
waiting for Dad to sail in from the Bay of Campeche. But when he finally
returned, and Rupert and Vita invited us over for a Hawaiian-style luau
to celebrate the end of summer, there was no backing out of it. Rupert
and Vita encouraged me and Johnny to bring our friends. "The more
the merrier," they said. I hoped that the confusion of a big party would
provide plenty of escape options if things got out of hand.

I suggested that Carmen invite Rachel and Veronica.

"Do I really need reinforcements?" she asked.

"It might help. Besides, it would make Pete and Johnny very happy."

The plan was to pick up the girls at the ballet studio after their workout
or practice, or whatever they called it, and then we would ride together
to Ransom Island. The dance studio operated in a windowless, one-story
building on Everhart Road, between a dry cleaners and a five-and-dime
store. But inside the drab building, the studio was filled with bright light,
mirrors, and polished wood floors. Through a long interior viewing

window, we saw rows of dancers in elastic tights leaping and twirling across the floor, dancing to classical music played by a pianist tucked back in the corner. Doña Delfín walked imperiously around the room, shouting instructions to the dancers.

"Man, oh, man," Pete whispered, his nose pressed up against the glass. "Get a load of all those hot-looking chicks."

Johnny poked Pete in the back. "Don't be a dipstick, Pete. What you're looking at is fine art."

"'It's fine alright, '*mano.*"

Carmen danced toward us with a wave of ballerinas, her movements both fluid and controlled at the same time. When the line reached the window, she smiled and waved at me. I noticed Veronica and Rachel in the class as well.

"Check it out," said Pete. "A dude."

A slender guy in black tights and a sleeveless shirt advanced across the floor, executing an arching leap that made my end zone catch seem like a frog's hop.

"All those beautiful females, and he's probably a fairy," Pete said.

Johnny thumped Pete's ear. "Or maybe he's not, and this is the best-kept secret on the coast. One guy, twenty-five girls. Did you ever think of that, Einstein?"

When Doña Delfín saw us, she walked to the window and jerked the cord on the blinds. They fell with a resounding pop.

"Way to go, Pete," said Johnny.

"What'd *I* do?"

"You were practically slobbering on the glass."

We sat awkwardly in the hallway as a procession of moms entered the studio, holding the hands of their kiddy ballerinas in their kiddy ballerina tutus. They all stared at us like we were convicts on a chain gang.

"Maybe we should wait outside," I suggested.

We went next door to the five-and-dime and rummaged through the fishing tackle and cheap paperbacks. A half-hour later, the girls walked out of the studio in shorts and blouses, with their dance bags slung over their shoulders. Veronica and Rachel hopped into the Jeep straight away. I held the car door for Carmen, who almost made it inside but stopped short when her mother called to her from the studio entrance.

Carmen sighed. "*Ay, Dios mío.* This will only take a second."

I watched the two women argue, with Doña Delfín speaking in Spanish and Carmen answering back in English. It was an odd exchange, but I gathered that Ms. Delfín absolutely did not want her daughter to go with us to the party—or go anywhere, for that matter, with me.

The argument ended when Carmen put her hands over her ears and walked away. "Let's go," she said, climbing into the car. I stood holding the door, wondering if I should try to say something reassuring and responsible to her mother, something to ease her misgivings about me, whatever they were. Carmen's mother must have read my mind—she glared at me and shook her head.

"You stay out of this," she said. Then, to her daughter, "*Ay, hija!* No seas tonta. Don't fall for the very first boy who brings you flowers."

"You mean, like you did?" Carmen snapped.

Carmen's mother stiffened her jaw. "*No cometas el mismo error.* You are better than that." Which I took to mean, better than me.

Carmen pulled me toward her. "Get in the car."

"*No te vayas con este . . . palurdo!*" Doña Delfín continued.

I gave the mother a helpless *what am I supposed to do?* look and then scooted in next to Carmen.

"Go!" she yelled.

Johnny hit the gas, the tires spun on the pavement as we peeled out, reinforcing Doña Delfín's impression of us as wild-ass delinquents from across the tracks. All of us were silent for a few blocks until Johnny turned to Carmen and asked her if she was sure she didn't want to go back.

"Keep driving," she answered.

Later, as the small town of Aransas Pass materialized out of the heat haze, I asked Carmen the meaning of *palurdo*.

"Forget what my mother says. She's not mad at you. She doesn't even know you."

"What is she mad at?"

"Everything. Let's not talk about it, okay? Let's talk about your family."

"We can't wait to meet them," said Veronica, anxious to lighten the tension.

"Yeah. What are they like?" asked Rachel.

Johnny glanced at me in the rear view mirror. He was looking at me as if to say, *this was your idea, not mine.*

"They're mad, too," I said, "but in another way."

—

The Ransom Island Bridge had been torn down a few years back to provide a more convenient route for barge traffic on the Intracoastal Canal. Now patrons of Shady's had to catch a small ferry to visit their favorite fish camp and watering hole. We drove onto the ferry and the attendant chocked our wheels for the short ride across Redfish Bay. An ocean cruise and an island luau, we'd promised the girls. We didn't mention the "cruise" lasted about six minutes. When we rolled up to the one-story pier-and-beam building, the first thing the girls noticed was the rustic sign.

"THE SHADY BOAT AND LEISURE CLUB," Rachel read. "Is this like a country club or something?"

Pete and Johnny laughed. "It's kind of like a club," I answered. "And kind of like a country. Try to keep an open mind."

We drove to the parking area at the side of the building, and the second thing they noticed was a massive feral hog roasting over an open-pit fire. The skinned monster must have weighed two hundred pounds. The tusks in its hairy head were as long as kitchen knives, and a bright red apple was crammed into its charred mouth.

Uncle Flavius and Zachariah Yates were tending the spit, or rather Zach was turning the crank while Flavius guzzled beer and watched. They both looked up when we climbed out of the car. Zach had on denim jeans, a work shirt, and a straw cowboy hat—the only clothes I'd ever seen him wear, but Flavius was dressed more festively, in baggy swim trunks and possibly the ugliest Hawaiian shirt I'd ever seen—a lurid combination of canoes, palm trees, and hula girls in bright primary colors. The sun had inflamed his freckles and skin to match his bright red hair. He looked right at home standing next to the smoking, smoldering firepit.

Johnny introduced the three girls.

"Pleased to meet you ladies," said Zach, tipping his beat-up Stetson.

Flavius nodded in greeting and took another gulp of beer. "I've been tending this hog for almost eighteen hours," he explained. "But Zachariah is about to ruin it with that gravy he keeps swabbing all over it."

"This sop is gonna make it flavorsome," said Zach. "And what do you mean *you've* been tending this hog? All you been doin' since this mornin' is drinking beer and tellin' me what I been doin' wrong. I'm surprised this hog ain't jumped off the spit and run away, just to get outta earshot."

"Almost eighteen hours," Flavius said solemnly.

"Longest day of my life," muttered Zach.

We climbed the stairs to the building entrance and heard the jukebox music blaring from the inside—"Jungle Nights In Harlem," by Duke Ellington. Just as we reached the porch, Rupert threw open the screen door and opened his big arms to embrace us.

"*Aloha!*" he bellowed. "Welcome to Shady's. I'm Rupert Sweetwater, the Big Kahuna on this itty-bitty island."

I could tell the girls were a little overwhelmed by this bear of a man wearing a grass skirt. The string of oversized conch shells around his neck made him look like a Fiji war chief, and his marble-blue eyes gleamed with manic intensity.

Vita appeared from behind Rupert. "Welcome to our luau," she said, placing silk flower leis around the girls' necks. "I'm Vita, the Big Kahuna's wife." She herded us all inside. "You boys come over here, so I can get you lei'ed up."

As we followed her inside, Carmen grabbed my arm and looked around the room at the bar stools, neon beer signs, and keg taps. A hand-lettered sign warned patrons not to set drinks on the jukebox or the cigarette machine. "I thought you said we were going to a restaurant."

"They serve food, too."

"Oh yeah, the *Flintstones* creature I saw roasting outside."

I spotted my dad talking to Cecil Shoat at the end of the bar. I could hear them arguing about whether roughnecking or shrimping was the more dangerous profession. It was an old argument between them. I was a little alarmed to see a highball glass in front of Dad—Jim Beam and Coke, no doubt. He usually didn't switch to the hard stuff until after dinner.

After Vita fixed me up with my own lei, I took Carmen's hand. "I'm going to introduce you to my dad." *Better to get it over with early,* I thought.

I waited for Dad and Cecil to finish comparing jobsite injuries. Cecil had his grease-stained dungarees pulled up over his knee and was showing off a thick whip-scar that traversed his thigh. I cleared my throat. "Dad, I'd like to introduce you to Carmen Delfín."

He looked at me and then at Carmen, and then back at me again. He rose to greet her. "I didn't know you had a girlfriend, Son." He sounded somewhat surprised, and maybe only a little bit in the bag.

"You've been working a lot. I haven't had a chance to tell you."

"Well, first of all, call me Dubber," he said, offering his hand. "Carmen is it? Like that pretty gypsy girl in the opera?"

She nodded, a smile fixed on her face.

"It's a beautiful name for a beautiful girl." Dad could be pretty charming when he chose to be.

Cecil thrust out his hand, too. "I'm Cecil Shoat. And you can call me Cecil." Carmen swallowed and gave the oil-stained paw a polite shake. There was so much grease under his fingernails it looked like he was wearing nail polish. "I've known Charlie here since he ran around the island in diapers," Cecil began, a big grin spreading across his face. "Of course, back then, whenever he dirtied his nappies, he'd just pull 'em off and walk around buck nekkid."

I groaned. "Thanks, Cecil. That's a great story."

Carmen laughed. "What a wild child you were, Charlie."

"Where is your family from, Carmen?" asked my dad, still scrutinizing my date. I suppose he was expecting her to say Corpus. Maybe Victoria.

"From Cuba."

Dad and Cecil stared at her, expressionless.

"Her father's in the Navy," I quickly added.

"The *U.S.* Navy?" Cecil asked, his eyes narrowed in suspicion.

"Yes, sir," answered Carmen. "He's an American. I have dual citizenship."

That seemed to mollify Dad, somewhat. "Swabbie, huh? Good profession."

"So, uh . . . I told Carmen I'd show her around," I said, anxious to leave before the conversation turned to politics. Lately, Dad had become convinced that the Russians were up to no good in Cuba, and that Castro was in league with both Khrushchev and the Devil. Dad's pessimism about world affairs and life in general became gloomier every year. Johnny and I were concerned, but we had no idea what to do about it. We kinda wished he'd find a girlfriend.

Carmen and I peeled away and saw that the rest of our group was busy visiting with Vita and Rupert, so we decided to sneak out through the back door. "Come on, I'll show you where Pete and Johnny and I stay when we work here."

We walked down the sandy trail towards the bait house and Carmen began giggling. "What?" I asked.

"I was just imagining a naked little boy toddling down this path, not a care in the world."

"And with a dirty bottom. It was hard being a feral child."

At the bait house, Carmen poked around a bit and asked questions about the fish camp operation—what kind of customers came there, what kind of jobs we did. She said that, to her, it seemed interesting, fun even. "Sometimes it seems like I've spent my whole life inside a ballet studio."

We moved to the end of the dock and dangled our feet in the bay, enjoying a fresh breeze blowing off the Gulf, following the progress of the setting sun as it ricocheted off the Aransas Pass water tower and bored into the horizon. A small flotilla of cabbage head jellyfish floated by on the tide.

I asked Carmen what her plans were after high school, a subject I'd been worrying about for several weeks. The fact that she would be graduating when I was only finishing my sophomore year was still hard for me to get my head around. Mostly, I worried that I'd never see her again after the school year ended.

"Of course the great Doña Delfín believes I should think *only* of dance," she said, still steamed at her mom. "She has big plans for my career. It's one of the reasons she doesn't want me to have a boyfriend."

Hearing Carmen refer to me as her boyfriend gave me a little thrill. "I'm a distraction, is that it?"

"Something like that."

"Is that what you want to do? Become a professional dancer?"

She took a deep breath. "I don't know. It's all I've ever thought about doing. The problem is where."

I tried to think of cities that might have a decent ballet company. They would be big, sophisticated cities. Far away cities. Cities unlike Rockport or Corpus Christi.

"My mom's thinking about returning to Cuba, and of course, she expects me to go with her."

"To Cuba? But . . . it's a communist country now. A dictatorship. You told me so yourself." I tried to hide my concern and confusion. I'd for sure never see Carmen again if she moved to Cuba. "Do they even *have* ballet there?"

Carmen didn't answer, so I repeated my question.

"Do you remember Ramón?" she asked.

"The guy at your house? The guy who says he's from Mexico?"

"Well, he's not really from Mexico."

"It didn't seem like it."

"He may live there now, but he's originally from Cuba, and he told my mother that certain people in Cuba want her to direct a national ballet academy in Havana."

"A *national* ballet academy? Who are these people in Cuba? Are they Castro's people?"

"I suppose they are. The state would fund the program, and she would run it."

"So this guy, Ramón . . . he was here in Corpus on business. And he stopped by your house because, by chance, he ran into your mom's brother in some little town in the Cuban countryside. And because he loves ballet, and knows people who love ballet, he also happened to have in his pocket an offer from the Cuban government for your mom to start a national ballet school?"

"I know it sounds crazy."

"It is crazy."

"I know, but the way he explained it seemed to make sense. At any rate, my mom believes him, or wants to, anyway.

"He's a smooth talker, alright."

I remembered Jesse telling me that his wife and daughter had been trapped in Cuba since Castro took over. He said they could still get out, but it would take money to make it happen. The purse from his first prizefight was earmarked for their "freedom" flight over.

"Carmen, the other day, didn't you tell me that Cuba was . . . closed, or something like that?"

"Yes, there's an embargo."

"Right, so if you had to move there, would you be able to leave the country whenever you wanted? I mean, could we—"

"Could we still see each other?"

"Well, yeah. That's exactly what I mean."

Carmen hesitated before speaking. "That's a good question. I don't really know. Ramón said that once the ballet was established, the company would perform in cities around the world." She reached up and brushed a strand of blonde hair out of her face. "Anyway, it doesn't matter. I don't think I wanna go. I'll be eighteen in December and can do whatever I want."

Somehow I doubted she'd told this to her mom or that her mom would even consider it, but I was relieved to hear her say it nonetheless.

"Let's go back to the party," she suggested. "Charlie, please don't say anything about Ramón, or about the dance academy offer. I don't know what my mother's decision is going to be. I hope she decides to stay here, but she may not, you know?"

"Okay, Carmen. Mum's the word."

When we went inside, the cooked pig was laid out on the serving table like a cadaver on a slab. Zach was garnishing it with pineapples, green onions, and parsley, while Rupert sharpened a long carving knife that looked like a pirate's scimitar. Tiki torches were mounted in brackets on the walls, and Flavius was mixing up pitchers of something that involved rum, pineapple juice, and coconut shells with little umbrellas in them.

The guests had gathered around to watch the dissection. One of the Shady's regulars, Peggy Storey, helped Vita and Miz Leona bring out bowls of long-grain rice, cabbage salad, and fresh fruit. Uncle Noble contributed a platter of coconut shrimp, the signature dish in his Corpus Christi ice house.

When the long table was filled, the feast began in earnest. The girls were squeamish about eating at first, daunted by the dismembered pig carcass that dominated the buffet, but once they tried the succulent meat, they went back for seconds. Those who didn't have a coconut to drink out of helped themselves to a tub of cold beer on the bar.

After dinner, Rupert cranked up the jukebox and people began dancing. I even saw Zachariah execute a sprightly jig with my Aunt Vita. At one point, Pete made an effeminate curtsy and pretended to be the guy we'd seen dancing at the ballet studio. Rachel, who'd had several coconuts, laughed and told him he wasn't in good enough shape to dance ballet . . . that it would be too hard for him. Pete had also had a tot or two, and he drew himself up and stated that he was in the best shape of his life, fighting shape, and could dance circles around any swishy guy in tights. The next thing I knew, the girls had challenged us to complete one full ballet session with them and Efrain, the ballet guy. Before Johnny or I could object, Pete had accepted the challenge and the bet was on: if we made it through the dance session in an acceptable manner, the girls would buy us burgers and shakes at the Whataburger. If not, dinner was on us.

All in all, it was a great party. The girls seemed to have a good time, and there was only one fistfight, starring Guess Who, who ran afoul with a random oysterman who'd wandered in. There was always a fistfight when someone tried to joke with Flavius about his name, his height, his red hair, or his temper—take your pick; Flavius would pick a fight with a cardboard box.

When we dropped Carmen off at her house, I insisted on walking her to the door.

"My mom might ambush you on the porch if you do that."

"She'll think less of me if I don't do it," I said.

In the back of my mind, I harbored the foolish hope that one day Doña Delfín would recognize my chivalry and good intentions and maybe, just maybe, approve of my courtship of her daughter. I'd always been an optimist that way. That was the difference between me and my dad. He believed that misery was lurking just around the corner and that the world could blow itself to pieces at any moment. I believed we could all live happily every after. We'll see which one of us is right.

─────

CHAPTER 11

A single light bulb illuminated the entrance to Hunsacker's Gym. It was another Monday and another ungodly pre-dawn workout. In the wake of the Ransom Island luau and the chores Dad gave us the following day, I felt like a wad of chewed-up gum.

Johnny knocked on the door and we waited, watching moths flutter around the bulb cage. A wooden sign sat on the lip of the door-frame: BOXING, it read in block letters, bracketed by the CCPD logo on one side and a graphic of a pair of boxing gloves on the other. Stubby had started locking the front door in the off hours ever since the Miami Chamber of Commerce came to call. He let us in with a cursory grunt and turned on the fluorescent gym lights.

We half sleepwalked to the dressing area to change into our boxing togs. While we folded our street clothes and placed them in wire baskets, we heard the clacking of chalk on the blackboard as Stubby updated the Space Race tally; VOSTOK 3 and VOSTOK 4 had been added to the USSR column.

"They're sending up two at a time now?" Johnny asked.

"Yep."

"Hardly seems fair."

"I'll be sure and tell Khrushchev next time I see 'im." Stubby turned and scrutinized us.

"How much do you weigh?" he asked me.

"I don't know. Maybe one-fifty."

Stubby grunted. "Maybe one forty-five." He squeezed my shoulder like he was testing a cantaloupe for ripeness. "You're filling out. Keep eating, keep lifting weights."

"Yes, sir," I answered. Encouraged, I decided to float an idea I'd been working up the courage to present to him. "Mr. Hunsacker? Do you think I could try and enter the Gloves competition in January? I'll be sixteen before the state tournament rolls around in March, and I figured there's a good chance they'll let me compete."

I figured wrong. Stubby looked up at me irritably, his cigar shifting from one side of his mouth to the other. "Of course not. You're too young. You know the rules." Seeing my disappointment, he eased off a little. "Don't rush it, kid. You're gonna have your time."

"Yes, sir," I mumbled.

"In the meantime, you can help *him* get ready for *his* matches," he jabbed a thumb toward Johnny. "You boys get warm and then glove up. Charlie, I want to see you test your brother in the ring this morning."

As we walked to the gym mat, Johnny gave me a light shove. "What'd you think he'd say, numbnuts? You know how by-the-book he is."

I didn't answer. As improbable as it was, I had hoped Stubby might try and enter me in the tournament, or at least say he'd think about it.

"So, are you going to pout about it . . . *kid?*" Johnny laughed and punched me on the arm. "You heard the man. You need to think about helping the older, more experienced boxers, like me, get ready for their big tournaments. He wants to see you *test* me."

He kept ribbing me as we went through our warm-up and wrapped our hands. I couldn't wait to get into the ring so I could shut him up.

Stubby climbed through the ropes and checked our gloves and headgear. "Okay, boys, today I want to see what kind of shape you're in. Three good rounds at full speed, got it?"

We nodded. "Okay."

He stepped back and yelled, "Box!"

I came at Johnny like a freight train, throwing a series of combinations that he avoided by covering up, and I ended the flurry with a wild haymaker that he barely dodged. When he raised his head, he was grinning at me. I came at him again, and this time I landed a solid left hook that popped his head back. The grin on his face disappeared, and we spent the next two-and-a-half minutes whaling on each other.

We finished the round red-faced and panting. Stubby shook his head. "If you boys think you can go three rounds like that, go right ahead. But my advice is to start boxing instead of brawling."

I noticed Jesse standing ringside, still in his jogging sweats. He ran along Ocean Drive every morning and usually showed up at the gym about halfway through our workout. He pantomimed a slip counter punch move that he'd showed me before. I nodded that I understood.

When Stubby yelled "Box!" to start the second round, Johnny began utilizing his long jab, popping me in the face a number of times. Remembering Jesse's advice, I dipped outside his jab and threw a straight punch to his nose. "Good counter, Charlie," Stubby said. The move worked so well I tried it again a short time later, but this time Johnny blocked it and staggered me with a right cross that knocked me off balance. "Great cross!" shouted Stubby. "That's what happens when you telegraph your counters, Charlie. Mix 'em up!"

We finished the round with a spirited exchange of blows that drew approval from both Stubby and Jesse.

"*Vaya, Flaco!*" I heard Naco Flores yell behind me. Naco usually stopped by the gym on his way to school.

"Okay, boys. Last round," Stubby said. "Don't slow down now. In a real match, this is where you'll win the fight or lose it."

The mention of a "real" boxing match, one that I wouldn't be allowed to participate in until next year, tee'd me off again, and I was determined to take it out on my "soon-to-be-boxing-in-his-second-tournament" brother.

About halfway through the third round, the phone started ringing, and I was dimly aware of Naco running into Stubby's office to answer it, as he often did when Stubby was busy with a boxer. Johnny and I were clinched up in the center of the ring when an ear-splitting explosion ripped through the back wall of the building, spraying window glass across the gym like buckshot. My brother and I instinctively crouched down and covered our faces with our gloves. Stubby and Jesse ducked behind the platform. I literally couldn't imagine what might have happened.

"Naco!" I screamed. I leapt over the ropes and hit the floor rolling, but was up quickly and sprinting for Stubby's office, trying to unlace my gloves with my teeth as I ran. Smoke and plaster dust drifted through the jagged hole in the masonry wall, the grey dawn light filtering in through the haze. I found Naco on the floor with Stubby's heavy metal desk on top of him.

I rushed to his side. "Naco, are you alright?" But it was instantly clear he was anything but. He was unconscious and having trouble breathing. His face and head were bleeding badly. Stubby and Jesse helped me lift the desk off him, and then Stubby checked for a pulse.

"Pulse is okay," said Stubby. "Jesse, run and get the first aid kit."

My ears were still ringing, but I heard Johnny yell to Jesse that he was going to find a phone and call an ambulance. Soon after, while Stubby pressed gauze bandages over Naco's wounds, I heard the wail of sirens.

"What just happened, Mr. Hunsacker?"

He shook his head sadly. "This is my fault."

I waited for him to say more, but he was quiet, the cigar absent from his lips, Naco's head resting on his knees. We stayed with him until the ambulance arrived and the paramedics carried him off on a stretcher.

Afterwards, firemen poked around inside and outside the building, conferring with police and talking into radios. Later, I noticed Harley Radcliff, the cop who'd accompanied Mavis McDevitt to the gym a couple of months back. He was in plain clothes, but the way the uniformed policemen talked to him, I gathered he carried some weight inside the organization. A uniformed cop came by and asked if I felt up to talking to the police detective.

"Sure," I said. Detective Radcliff found me sitting on the floor on the other side of gym. I was holding what street clothes I could locate in the rubble, and my ears still rang from the explosion.

"You hurt?" he asked.

I shook my head no. "I'm okay."

"You and your brother were the first ones here this morning, besides the old man. Did you see anything unusual? Anything suspicious?"

"No."

"Tell me what happened after you got here."

I walked him through our routine up to the point where Naco answered the phone and the north wall got blown off the building. "What caused the explosion?" I asked at the end.

Radcliff peered over to where the uniforms and the firemen were poking aimlessly around the debris. "They're still trying to figure it out . . . but I can tell you what I think about it."

I looked at him inquiringly.

"I think it was dynamite. Ringer on the phone set it off. Lucky the package wasn't inside the office or that kid would have been spaghetti sauce. I think somebody wanted to scare or maybe even cripple the old man, but the kid got to the phone first."

Radcliff took off his fedora and ran his fingers through his hair. "Where was the jig during all this?" he asked. He meant Jesse.

"Feo? I told you. He was watching me spar with my brother."

"Feo?"

"Jesse. In the gym we call him 'Feo.'"

The detective lit a cigarette. "He's kinda got a temper, doesn't he? The way he roughed up the McDevitt kid?"

"He didn't *rough him up*," I protested. "That's not what happened."

"So did Feo leave the building at any time?" Radcliff continued.

"No."

"Did he act surprised when the bomb went off?"

I looked up at him. "He acted like anyone would act when a bomb goes off."

"How was that?"

"He ducked."

Detective Radcliff smirked and took a long drag on his cigarette. "Jesse Martel. *El Rey Feo.* Supposed to be a big-time prizefighter someday. He that good?"

"Everyone seems to think so."

"If he's so good, how come he's got such a small-time manager?"

I didn't know how to answer that, and I wasn't sure what he was driving at. What I did know was that I didn't like the detective. I didn't like his hair, his shifty eyes, or that he was bound up somehow with Karl McDevitt's mother. And I really didn't like how he talked about Jesse.

"He ever mention he wanted a new one?"

"A new what?"

"Manager. Maybe he's got a contract with Hunsacker he'd like to get out of?"

"He never mentioned anything like that to me." *Far from it,* I thought. *Jesse always said Stubby had his back.*

"No? You two don't talk? I thought y'all were friends." He looked at me one last time and then flicked his hand impatiently. "Y'all get outta here."

As he started to walk away, I asked him, "How's Diego?"

He paused and looked back at me. "Who?"

"The kid who was hurt."

"The retard?" he shrugged. "How would I know?" Harley Radcliff flipped his cigarette onto the floor. "He a friend of yours, too?" He laughed and then walked away to talk with one of the firemen.

When Johnny and I were driving to the hospital to check on Naco, we talked about Radcliff.

"The guy's an asshole," said Johnny.

"Yeah. He gives me the creeps. He told me he thought the explosion was caused by a stick of dynamite wired to the phone . . . and that someone was out to get Stubby."

Johnny looked surprised. "Did he ask you a bunch of questions about Jesse?"

"Yep. Like Jesse might've been in on it."

"Shit."

The sun was low and blinding as it climbed above Corpus Christi Bay. I turned away from the harsh light and looked at my brother. "You think those Miami gangsters might've been behind this?"

"That thought crossed my mind."

"Think we should tell Radcliff about them?"

"I don't know," he answered. "I don't trust him. We'll see how Stubby plays it. He may have told the cops about 'em already."

When we got to the hospital, Stubby and Jesse were waiting outside the emergency room.

Jesse stood up. "They wouldn't let us see Naco, but they tol' us he was gonna be okay."

"How bad was he hurt?" asked Johnny.

Stubby answered. "A concussion, a bunch of stitches, a dislocated shoulder. I'm just glad it wasn't worse."

"Did they say what caused the explosion?" I asked him.

"They said it was the water heater."

"Can a water heater do that? Cause that much damage?"

Stubby caught my eye and held it. *No more second-guessing*, the look said. *Not in front of Jesse.* "The cops and the firemen seem to think so. So I guess that's what happened."

A few minutes later, Jesse went upstairs to the restroom—they didn't have a washroom for Negroes on our floor—and I waited until he was out of earshot. "Coach, that police detective told me it might've been dynamite."

"Son," Stubby said firmly, "we were told it was probably that old water heater that blew. And that's the only story you need to repeat."

We waited around another hour or so and then left the hospital. We could tell Stubby felt terrible about what had happened.

"Why doesn't Stubby tell Feo those Florida guys came back and slapped him around?" I said to Johnny when we were in the car. "And that he ran 'em off with a gun?"

"I think he's trying to protect Feo. I think he's worried that if he tells Feo, he might go to Miami just to keep Stubby out of harm's way."

I thought about that for a moment. "Feo has a right to know."

"Stubby's the guy to tell him. Not us."

Neither one of us felt like going to school, so we skipped class and drove to the beach instead. Neither of us spoke. Sometimes the best thing to do is just sit in the sand, turn off the brain, and watch the ocean lap at the shore.

———

CHAPTER 12

September ended well. No one else got blown up. The hole in Hunsacker's Gym had been repaired, or at least covered over with plywood. Naco Flores had mended, more or less, and was back to his bean-balling self, and our football team was 4–0 going into district play. Last Friday we'd steamrolled the Ingleside Mustangs, and people were calling us the stud-ducks of Class AA South Texas football. There was talk around town that this was the Pirates' year to make the state playoffs. To top it off, Carmen was showing every indication that she was my steady girl. It all seemed too good to be true.

When she called on Sunday morning and reminded me that this was the day we'd promised to go through a ballet workout at her mother's studio, I figured, *How hard can it be?*

Pete and Johnny felt the same, and on the way to the studio, we laughed and joked about it. When we arrived, the girls were out front waiting, wearing big step-into-my-parlor smiles. Something about those smiles made me wonder if the joke might be on us, and a whisper of doubt began to form in my smug noggin.

"Where's Nureyev?" I asked. I'd been brushing up on my ballet history at the school library.

"Efrain has been here for two hours already," Carmen answered.

"Doing what?" asked Pete. "Painting his twinkle toes?"

Johnny rolled his eyes. "Y'all just ignore Pete. He has about as much culture as a wombat."

Veronica examined our T-shirts, chinos, and Chuck Taylor high-tops. "I hope you boys brought some other clothes."

I told her we had our boxing gear in the car.

"Go get it," said Carmen, looking around anxiously. "And try to hurry. We're not really supposed to be here."

I was a little apprehensive about sneaking into Doña Delfín's Académie de Danse. "Carmen, are you sure this is a good idea?" I asked.

Rachel groaned. "Don't be a killjoy, *sophomore,* or we'll send you home."

I followed Pete and Johnny to the car to get my bag, a little stung by Rachel's comment.

After we slipped into the building, we saw Efrain in the main studio holding onto a long wooden bar, squatting and rising, down and up. He smiled when he saw us. "Hey, guys. Welcome to the torture chamber."

We changed clothes and waited for the girls to come out. What the hell had Pete gotten us into? Efrain had on tights and we tried mightily not to let our gaze stray too low by accident. We had no idea what to say to him, so we tried to hide our apprehension by horsing around, throwing punches at the mirrored walls, and doing standing broad jumps. Finally, the girls came in dressed to dance, clapping their hands in anticipation. "This is going to be a scream," said Rachel.

"Okay, dancers, over here," Efrain said amiably. "You too, guys." We moved to a wooden rail that Efrain called the *barre.* "Now, watch me and do what I do."

We began doing a series of squats, *plies* he called them. "Keep your feet turned out," he instructed. We continued to hold onto the *barre* while we did a whole bunch of leg lifts: to the front, to the side, backwards; and then a combination of squats plus leg extensions. Efrain told us the names of the movements—*tendus, degages, fondus, développés, battements;* why the French got to name them, I don't know.

He counted out the movements, punctuating the eight counts with a ton of corrections: "Turn out, tuck in, don't arch your back, turn out more from the hip, keep your neck straight, keep the top of your head lifted."

The girls were practically weeping with laughter watching us try to get it right. Boxing was all about the economy of short motions ending in a forceful impact; this was about fluidity and seamless flow. Or at least it was when Efrain and the girls did it. Efrain told us he could spend a month working with us on each individual movement, but his orders were to take us through one full ballet class, and that was what he was going to do. By the time we finished with the *barre,* our thighs were burning and our heads were swimming with unfamiliar words and movements. Literally and physically, we were learning another language.

"That was fun," said Johnny. "How'd we do?"

Rachel and Veronica looked at each other and shook their heads mournfully, as though they had witnessed a dreadful wreck.

Pete acted hurt. "What? We did the exact same thing as y'all."

"Oh, yeah, exactly the same," said Rachel.

I looked at Carmen. "Was it that bad?"

"My mother would have burned her ballet slippers."

"Okay, center *barre,*" Efrain commanded. We moved away from the wall and went through the same movements again, but this time without the benefit of the handrail for balance, which made it considerably harder. It's amazing how many muscles you use just to keep from falling onto your face.

"Good warm-up, guys," said Efrain.

Warm-up?

"Now we're going to combine the moves we worked on at the *barre* and learn some simple combinations. *Adagios* first, then we'll work up to *petite allegros.* If you can still stand, I'll show you a couple of *grand allegros.*"

"What the hell is he talking about?" Pete asked under his breath.

Rachel smiled. "Follow along as best as you can."

Efrain instructed us through some slow moving combinations, the *adagios,* and we thought we were doing pretty well until we looked in the wall mirror and saw ourselves moving alongside the trained dancers. Next to them, we looked like a trio of Frankenstein monsters. Efrain tried his best to correct our form, but his enthusiasm began to lag when he realized how hopeless it was. To his credit, he didn't give up or burst out laughing.

Carmen turned on the record player, and Efrain showed us a *petite allegro* combination. Johnny, Pete, and I gamely tried to follow, our tennis shoes squeaking across the hardwood floor, but we were so awkward that everyone was laughing by the end of the exercise, including us.

Efrain looked at Carmen. "Should we turn it up a notch?"

Carmen smiled. "Definitely."

He instructed us to pair up with the girls and move with him across the floor from one end to the other. "From the corner," he shouted. The piano music was livelier this time, and the combinations were more difficult. As we danced across the floor, Pete began dancing with exaggerated sloppiness. Johnny started doing the Charleston, and I dropped my arms like an orangutan and swung my knuckles in time to the music. We heard the record needle screech across the vinyl as Veronica stopped the music.

"Uh-uh," she said, wagging her finger at us. "You guys have to give one hundred percent or you lose the bet. No clowning around."

"Okay," said Johnny. "No clowning around."

We kept doing the floor routines until we were breathing heavily. It was like wind sprints in football practice, except you had to concentrate on being fluid and graceful. Despite the AC, we were soon dripping with sweat. Fluid and graceful can really take it out of you.

"Not bad, fellows," said Efrain. "One more segment and then it's burger time. Carmen, what do you think? Some big jumps?"

She grinned and put on another record. Efrain looked at us and raised his eyebrows. "You guys ready for this?"

"Let's see what you've got," Pete challenged.

"Okay," said Efrain. "Pay attention." He showed us a combination, one piece at a time. Each part had a fancy name, but to us, they were just hard jumps, harder jumps, and impossible gyrations that sent each of us to the floor at least once when we tried them. On one particular leap, I thought my groin might rip in half. I suppose that, taken individually, the jumps weren't impossible, but there's the aesthetic aspect, too. Our versions were smaller, slower, and sloppier than Efrain's by a long shot. When we tried to put all the moves together into one sequence, I seriously thought we might break something. Evidently, Efrain thought the same thing.

"Let's knock off here, guys."

We may have been in the best shape of our lives, but by the end of the class, we were wiped out. Efrain, on the other hand, seemed to feel fine. He exploded across the floor into a *grand jeté,* appearing weightless and powerful at the same time, and then did a combination of big leaps and turns that defied gravity. Having muscled through the basic mechanics of the moves, we admired Efrain's strength and skill all the more. We did not attempt to follow him.

The next song came on, and the girls perked up. "Do it, Carmen!" Veronica exclaimed.

"Do what?" asked Pete.

"The *pas de deux* from *The Nutcracker*," said Efrain. "I love doing lifts with Carmen."

"What's a lift?"

Without warning, Efrain put his hands on Pete's waist and lifted him high above his head, rotating a full turn in the process. When Pete's feet were back on the floor, he looked at Efrain with astonishment, and maybe a little fear, too. It's damned hard to deadlift a hundred and twelve pounds over your head, flatfooted. Efrain made it look like he was putting on a hat.

We sat and watched Efrain and Carmen perform their *paw-de-doo*. They were completely in sync and completely absorbed in the dance. We were mesmerized.

As we prepared to leave, Rachel patted us on the back. "Congratulations, boys. A few more months of practice and you can join our class for eight-to-ten year olds. Girls, that is."

We left the gym with a new appreciation for ballet. Efrain shook our hands affably and thanked us for putting forth an honest effort. "You guys are good athletes. And I'm not kidding when I say that ballet will make you better football players . . . better boxers, too."

We told him we believed him. And we weren't kidding either. Pete, Johnny, and I each stuck out our hands and congratulated Efrain on an eye-opening experience.

We climbed in our cars and headed to the Whataburger to settle the bet. The girls were willing to foot the bill, since technically, we had completed the class, but we insisted that it was on us, saying the experience was unlike anything we had imagined.

"To men in tights," said Johnny, raising his chocolate milkshake in a toast.

"To men in tights," we rejoined.

Efrain had been a good sport about the whole thing, and I had no doubt he would one day have his name on ballet posters similar to the ones I'd seen in Doña Delfín's living room. Before we left, he pulled a Polaroid camera out of his bag and snapped a group picture of us leaning against the Jeep. He pulled the film square out of the camera and we gathered around and watched our images materialize on the paper—a new-fangled novelty that seemed mysterious, even magical to all of us. Efrain gave the photo to me, and I stashed it in the glove compartment of our wagon.

Pete was in his dad's car and had to get back to his house. Veronica left with Rachel since they both lived in uptown neighborhoods near the country club. Carmen lived the opposite direction, so Johnny and I offered to give her a lift home. When we were a block from her house, Carmen said, "It's probably better that you drop me off here."

Johnny pulled to the curb, and I held the door for her as she got out. "I don't really like being a secret boyfriend," I told her.

She gave me a peck on the cheek. "I know. But it's the only way we can see each other right now."

"Jesse told me what *palurdo* means."

Carmen averted her eyes. "I'm sorry my mother called you that. Anyway, she doesn't speak for me. I'll see you next week, *ballerino*."

I got back in the car, and Johnny and I watched her walk away. "What does *palurdo* mean?" he asked.

"It's Cuban for 'ignorant hillbilly.'"

Johnny grinned. "Ouch."

We waited until Carmen entered the house, and then Johnny put the Jeep in gear. "Wait," I said. "Turn off the car." Right after Carmen went inside, Ramón walked out, followed by Jesse Martel. Johnny saw me stiffen in the seat.

"Who's that with Jesse?"

"His name's Ramón Cruz. Supposedly, he's a friend of the family. He claims he's a Mexican businessman."

"'Claims?'"

"I'll tell you later."

We watched Jesse and Ramón conversing at the curb. Whatever they were talking about, it did not sit well with Jesse, because his body language changed. At one point, Ramón tried to place his arm around Jesse's shoulder, but Jesse brushed it off. Ramón continued speaking, and we saw Jesse's head drop to his chest as he listened, then he looked up angrily and began shaking his head. When Ramón started to say something else, Jesse showed him his palm to shut him up and then walked back into the house.

"What the hell was that about?" asked Johnny as Ramón drove away.

"I don't know. But that guy is bad news. I don't trust him as far as I can throw him."

"Let's follow him." Johnny suggested, putting the Jeep in gear. "What else can you tell me about Mr. Ramón Cruz?"

As we followed Ramón's tan sedan down Ocean Drive, I told my brother about meeting Ramon at the dinner party, and about Carmen's comments later on. "Carmen asked me to keep the dance offer quiet," I said when I'd finished. "I don't think she wants to ruin her mother's chances of running the Cuban ballet program."

Johnny nodded his head thoughtfully. "Why do you think Jesse got so upset back there?"

"Maybe he doesn't want Doña Delfín to leave Corpus, since he lives with her and all."

Johnny shook his head. "Seems like he'd want whatever would be best for her. He could find another place to live. Besides, you know Jesse. He's not a selfish guy."

I agreed.

"But how does this so-called Mexican businessman have the stroke to offer someone the head position of a national arts program?" Johnny mused.

"I think Ramón's lying about being a Mexican businessman. And I think he made up that story about accidentally running into Doña Delfín's brother in Commiguey, or whatever the town is called."

"You know," said Johnny, "I'd bet ol' Castro would love to bring a top-notch prima ballerina to Cuba to kick-start a national ballet program. Add some class to his rough little people's republic? Show the world how sophisticated his brand of socialism can be?" He bobbed his head up and down. "And it's not like he can call up Mrs. Delfín and just invite her over," he continued. "It would take some face-to-face convincing. Besides, I imagine our spies monitor all his calls to the US, anyway."

We both looked at each other, sharing the same thought. "You think that sumbitch Ramón could be a Cuban agent," I asked.

Johnny nodded. "I think he could be, brother. Or at least a messenger for Fidel."

We crossed Harbor Bridge until Ramón turned off the freeway onto an exit ramp that led to North Beach. It had been years since I'd been to the North Beach district, and the last time was on a dare. Once, it had been a place to take the family. Now, nobody went there unless they were down and out, looking for trouble, or cruising for drugs, booze, or loose women. North Beach was *dangerous.*

"Strange place for a globe-trotting international businessman to stay when he's in town, isn't it?" said Johnny.

"But a great place for a spy to hide out." I leaned forward and looked left and right down the side streets as we drove. "Where'd he go? Shit, I think we've lost him."

Johnny's checked his rearview mirror. "Or else he lost us."

"Let's get outta here."

We drove back to Rockport in silence, thrilled, but also troubled by our new theory.

"We don't know for sure if he's a spy," Johnny said as we pulled into our driveway. "Maybe his story's legit. Maybe he drove to North Beach to look for a little action while he was in town."

He had a point, but the notion that he was a secret agent was too exciting to disregard. Over the past few summers, we'd devoured Mickey Spillane and Ian Fleming's James Bond novels, and before that, the crime-and-espionage-fighting exploits of the Hardy Boys. What more did we need to know about spycraft?

"Okay, maybe he's not a spy," I conceded. "But wouldn't it be cool if he was?"

CHAPTER 13

We invited the girls to Rockport to watch us play a game on Friday night, and I'd be lying if I said we didn't want to show off for them. We had a weak opponent in the Cuero Gobblers, so we pretty much had the game in hand midway through the second half.

In the third quarter, I made an interception at midfield and ran it back for a touchdown, and as I crossed the goal line, I leapt into the air and executed a *grand jeté* I thought was worthy of the Bolshoi Ballet. Unfortunately, when I extended my arms, the football slipped from my hand and rolled . . . out . . . of the end zone. It was like a horror movie; I could see it happening in slow motion, but I couldn't do a thing to stop it.

In my mind, the goal line leap was meant to be grace in motion, a tribute to cross-sport training, but in my coach's mind, it was something else entirely. You could've heard him yelling in Galveston.

"Sweetwater! What in *Gawd's* name was that Mickey Mouse crap I just saw on my football field? Do you think you're in the circus? Is my name Barnum and Bailey? Sit your ass on that bench and don't even *look* at me until I say so. Weeping Jesus!"

The referees were conferring on the field, trying to decide if I had crossed the goal line before I did my airborne clown act. They wanted to penalize me, but they couldn't find anything in the rulebook that might apply. In the end, they decided to rule it a touchdown.

My teammates cast sideways glances at me for the rest of the ballgame, probably wondering if I had taken one too many hits in practice, or maybe had been smoking reefer under the bleachers before the game. Johnny walked by and shook his head, trying to keep from laughing. He knelt down in front of me, stabbing his finger in my chest like he was giving me a top-shelf scolding. But what he said in a low, amused voice was, "I'm disappointed in you, man. You didn't point your toes and your line was *way* off."

After the game, and more ass-chewings from the head coach, the assistant coach, the JV coach, and even the trainer, I showered and left the stadium to meet the girls.

"Thanks for the performance, Charlie," said Carmen. "It was hysterical."

"You laughed?"

"What else could we do? Veronica and I both were in stitches."

"We were the only ones, though," Veronica said, smiling. "The Pirates boosters sitting around us didn't know what to make of it, but I don't think they thought it was funny at all."

Pete and Johnny walked up, both with wide grins on their faces.

"I don't know whether to congratulate you for the touchdown, or throw you a bouquet of flowers," Pete joked. "I think you've started a whole new trend in football."

Johnny laughed. "But you've set ballet back by fifty years."

"Hey, where'd Rachel go?" asked Pete, looking around. His pompadour was freshly oiled, and he was wearing a new sport coat. He'd watched the game with the girls and was obviously expecting a big post-game night with his intermittent girlfriend.

Veronica looked at Carmen, who answered. "Sorry, Pete. She couldn't stay. She had to go back to Corpus."

"She's got another date, is that it?"

"You know Rachel, always pushing the limits. She's meeting some guy she said reminds her of Marlon Brando's character in that motorcycle movie, *The Wild One.*"

"What is it about girls and motorcycles?" asked Pete dejectedly. I was pretty sure he'd fallen for Rachel more than he let on.

We all piled into the Jeep and drove the short distance from the high school to downtown Rockport to begin celebrating our gridiron victory. The post-game victory tour up and down South Austin Street was a local tradition. After we'd made the five-block loop around the main drag, receiving honks from a few cars full of Pirates fans, we were right back where we started. The victory cruise had taken exactly four minutes. We sat in the car in silence.

"That was fun," said Veronica. "Are we gonna to do it again?"

Johnny and I squirmed in our seats. Our town had never seemed so small. I cleared my throat and was about to suggest we drop by Johnson's Drug Store for a Coke, when my brother proposed a better option.

"Pete, doesn't your uncle own a dancehall out in the country somewhere?"

"Yeah, near Sinton, but we can't go there, man."

"Why not?"

"'Cause it's a Mexican joint."

"So what? You're a Mexican. Veronica *looks* Mexican, and Carmen *speaks* Mexican."

"*Híjole,* I don't know, man. You and Charlie look about as gringo as Wonder Bread."

"I'll tell you what, when we get there, you run in and ask your uncle if it's okay. If he says yes, great; if not, we'll drive to Corpus and take our lovely dates to Pick's for a soda."

Pete was still shaking his head.

"Come on, man, it's my birthday."

"It's your birthday?" the girls exclaimed. "Fantastic! Come on, Pete, let's take Birthday Boy dancing!"

Johnny's birthday was a week away, but I decided not to say anything.

Pete sighed. "Okay, but let's swing by and pick up Maria first. If my uncle says it's okay to stay, then I'm gonna need a dance partner."

The old whitewashed dancehall sat a quarter mile off the road in a cotton field between Taft and Sinton. The sign on the false front read THE BENITEZ BALLROOM. Dozens of cars and pickups were parked around the building, and we could hear the thumping of a bass and drum inside. Pink and yellow neon ran under the eaves of the low-slung cement-block building. It looked exactly like the kind of place where you might have to buy your own hubcaps back at the end of the night.

"Wait here," said Pete.

"What kind of music are they playing?" asked Carmen. We could hear something that sounded kind of like a waltz, but a lot more peppy and assertive, and with horns.

"*Conjunto,*" said Maria.

Maria laughed a lot and liked to have a good time. She was short, a little on the plump side, and had a pretty face and a dazzling mane of sable hair that reached to her waist.

"Is it like Mexican folk music?"

Maria smiled. "It's Tex-Mex border music. It's not like anything you've ever heard."

Pete came back and stuck his head into the car. "Okay, we're in, but if anybody asks," he looked at me and Johnny, "you two guys are talent scouts for a new record label in Houston." He paused. "Listen. People in here are generally pretty friendly, but don't jack around, okay?"

Johnny rubbed his hands together. "Talent scouts. That's exactly what we are. Come on, girls, let's polka."

The place was jumping when we walked in. Waves of dancers moved around the dance floor, counterclockwise, shuffling to the lively music of *El Conjunto Bernal*. A bajo sexto guitar provided bass rhythm and a melodic counter to a three-row button-accordion lead. The bajo player and the squeezebox man did the singing, in Spanish, mostly. An electric bass and drum set pounded out the backbeat.

We shook hands with Benny Benitez, Pete's uncle, and thanked him for letting us in. "You kids have fun," he said. "And if you want to hold on to your pretty dates, I suggest you take 'em out there on the dance floor *inmediatamente.*"

"*Vámonos!*" said Pete. He grabbed Maria's hand and they skipped out to join a bouncy cumbia that had started up. "Follow me," he shouted. "Maria and I are going to show you some classical dance moves, *Tejano* style."

We inserted ourselves into the scrum of dancers and watched and learned. The girls picked up the moves quickly; it took Johnny and me a little longer. But soon we were laughing, dancing, and sweating along with the crowd. A few cold beers materialized, which helped our dancing immensely.

Occasionally, we sat down to catch our breath, watching the dancers and digging the music. Later, when a second accordion and a third vocalist joined the band, the building could scarcely contain the sound. Word had spread that Johnny and I were big city talent scouts, and rounds of beers kept showing up at our table. Whether anyone actually believed it, I don't know, but the folks there were welcoming all the same.

A little after midnight, we reluctantly left the party so we could get the girls home at a semi-respectable hour. We thanked Benny for his hospitality, tipped our imaginary hats to the band, and told enthusiastic *Conjunto Bernal* fans that, as far as these city-slicker talent scouts were concerned, it was the best dang *conjunto* music we'd ever heard.

———

CHAPTER 14

Monday morning we overslept and arrived at the gym forty-five minutes late. "Stubby's gonna be pissed," I said. "Should we tell him we ran out of gas?"

Johnny shook his head. "Won't make any difference."

My brother was right. Stubby didn't believe in excuses, even if they were caused by acts of God. He'd told us, and every other boxer who had trained at his gym, that he believed in discipline, honesty, pain, and maintaining a positive attitude. But Rule Number One on Stubby's posted list of rules, at the top and all in caps, was NO EXCUSES. We knew we would have to make up the missed time over the course of the week.

"We'll have to be here so early we might as well sleep in the car," I complained.

Johnny raised his fist to knock, but paused when we heard the sound of car tires screeching around the corner. We turned to look and saw a car running without lights, speeding away from us down the unlit street.

Johnny tried the knob, which turned easily. "Why is the door open?"

We looked at each other with apprehension. "It's pretty late," I said. "I bet Feo's already here."

The gym was dark except for Stubby's desk light, but no one was in the office. "Feo? Mr. Hunsacker?" Johnny called.

We heard soft moaning at the back of the gym. The office door was open and light spilled out into the darkness. At first we couldn't see anyone, but when we rounded the boxing ring we saw Jesse kneeling over the body of Stubby Hunsacker. The moaning was coming from Jesse. A low primal sound, like a wounded beast.

Johnny and I approached the two men cautiously, both of us aware that something terrible had happened. When we were close enough, we saw a dark pool of blood puddling on the floor around Stubby's head, which was wet and mashed up on one side. He was lying on his back, his eyes open but unfocused.

"What happened, Feo?" Johnny managed to ask.

Jesse continued to moan, and I saw that his face was wet with tears. I dropped to one knee and put my hand on his shoulder. "Is he dead?"

"Lo mató," he said.

Johnny knelt down and put his ear to Stubby's chest. "I don't hear a heartbeat." When he pressed down on his chest, as we had learned to do in a Red Cross class, blood oozed out of his head wound. I looked away, sickened by the sight.

Jesse made the sign of the cross and then covered his face with his hands, all the while talking in Spanish, either to himself, to Stubby, or to God, I don't know which. *"Lo mató,"* he said again. *"Que Dios me ayude. Lo mató."*

I began crying too. All I could think to do was put my arm around Jesse's big shoulders and shut my eyes. Johnny must have gone to the phone and called for help because the next thing I remember, someone was pulling me away from the body.

The overhead lights came on, and soon after, policemen hustled us away while medics crouched over Stubby. They escorted Jesse into the gym office and closed the door. I recognized Harley Radcliff in there with him. Johnny was taken to a bench by the free weights, and I was directed to a stool near the boxing ring. A cop told me to sit still and wait until an officer could question me. A photographer began snapping pictures of the body and, from where I sat, I could see Stubby's legs protruding beyond the edge of the boxing platform. The heels of his shoes were run down, and there was a hole in one sole. I turned my stool to face the wall and tried to think of nothing.

A little later, a policeman moved in front of me, holding a notepad in his hand. "Hey, kiddo, I need to ask you a few questions. You up to it?"

I nodded yes. It occurred to me I probably should've called my dad, but at that point, I was kind of numb with the shock of it all.

After the cop had written down my name and address and asked about my business at the gym, he said. "Tell me exactly what happened from the moment you arrived."

I told him everything I could remember.

When he finished with me, he sat with Johnny in another part of the gym. I watched them talk until the policeman looked up and caught my eye. He motioned me over. "You boys sit tight. We'll be finished with you soon."

We watched them zip Stubby up in a body bag and haul him out the door like a sack of laundry.

"I don't understand why this happened," I said to Johnny.

"I don't either."

We waited in silence, dumbfounded by what we'd seen.

"Why are they taking so long with Feo?" Johnny asked half an hour later. Radcliff was still questioning him in the office.

"We need to tell that detective about the Miami guys," said Johnny.

"Do you think they murdered Stubby?"

"I don't know."

I thought of the two Miami characters who had visited Stubby, remembered the way they had muscled the old man around. And then the bomb. Then I recalled the car that sped away as we drove up.

"I bet that was them driving away when we pulled up," I said.

Johnny nodded. "I was thinking the same thing."

A few minutes later, Harley Radcliff walked out of the office. Two uniformed policemen went inside and hovered over Jesse, who had on the grey jogging sweats he wore every morning when he showed up at the gym. Radcliff had a few words with the policeman who'd questioned us before, and then he walked over to where we were sitting.

"Morning, boys." I didn't like it that he seemed to be enjoying his job so much. "The officer tells me you saw Jesse standing over Stubby Hunsacker's body when you walked in this morning."

"He was *kneeling* next to him," said Johnny.

"Okay, you saw him kneeling over his dead body."

It sounded terrible when he put it that way, but that was the way it was.

"He also mentioned that Mr. Martel said something to you," Radcliff continued. He stressed the "Mister" sarcastically. "Can you tell me what it was?"

"He was speaking in Spanish," I answered.

"You *habla* a little Spanish, don't ya? Since you two are such good friends? Can't you remember a few words?"

I shook my head.

"Try," he said frostily.

"He said something about *Dios* . . . God, that's the only word I recognized."

"What else?"

"That's all I remember."

Harley Radcliff looked at Johnny. "What about you?"

"He said something *mato,* but I didn't understand it."

The detective wrote that down in his book and looked at me. "That what you heard, too?"

"Yeah, I think he said '*Se mato,*' or something. '*Lo mato,*' that was it. He kept repeating it."

The detective wrote that down too and left to confer with another policeman, this one a Mexican guy. Whatever they talked about, it must have been important, because Radcliff walked purposefully into the office and closed the door behind him. A moment later, I saw a policeman unhook his handcuffs and put them on Jesse. Radcliff leaned in close and said something into Jesse's ear. I could have sworn the detective had a self-satisfied grin on his face.

I stood and turned to a cop standing nearby. "What's going on? Why are they cuffing Jesse?" I ran to the office and threw open the door. "What are y'all doing? Let Feo go!" I was pissed off and scared, and Radcliff must have seen something in my eyes he didn't like.

"Hold him back," Radcliff shouted as they raised Jesse from the chair. Jesse's face was still contorted in grief, and he seemed to be unconcerned about what was happening to him.

Johnny appeared behind me. "What are you doing, Detective?" he yelled. "There's more to tell. You need to know about the Mafia guys that threatened Stubby last month . . . and the car. What about the car? Jesse hasn't done anything wrong, goddamnit!"

"Get control of that one, too," Radcliff ordered. One of the cops shoved Johnny against the wall and held his arm behind his back as they pushed Jesse through the door and escorted him toward the exit.

"Careful," Radcliff cautioned the policemen. "That black monkey's a dangerous one."

After Jesse was out of the building and inside the squad car, the cops let us go. "You kids better settle down unless you wanna go along for the ride."

But Johnny kept pressing. "He didn't do anything wrong. Why did you arrest him?"

"Suspicion of murder," said another policeman. "What's it to you?"

"Jesse Martel didn't kill Stubby," I shouted.

The cop looked at me crossly. "Well, it sure looks that way to us. Sounds like he even confessed."

"What?" we both said at once. "What do you mean, 'confessed'? What did he say?"

The Mexican cop was standing nearby. He turned and looked us over. "He said he killed him. What do you think '*lo mato*' means?"

Johnny and I stared at him, speechless.

———

CHAPTER 15

The steps leading to the entrance of the Nueces County Courthouse and Jail were steep and narrow. Johnny, Pete, and I climbed them slowly, gazing up at the massive columns that buttressed the portico. Above the columns were four tall statues, stern figures in robes—lawmakers and angels, I supposed—staring vacantly into the distance. If the architect's intent was to provoke dread, he'd sure as hell succeeded. The stone building seemed hard and pitiless, uncompromising—a bad place to be if you'd been accused of a capital crime.

Three days had passed since the murder, and we thought Jesse would've been released by now. Not only was he still behind bars, he'd not even had a bond hearing set. When would they realize the terrible mistake they'd made? Didn't they know that Feo idolized Stubby Hunsacker? Once they knew that, there was no way Radcliff and the rest could think Jesse had murdered him, no matter what they might have thought he said at the scene. *It's probably just a paperwork mix up,* we told ourselves.

Walking up to that imposing building, suddenly we were not so sure anymore.

We'd attended Stubby's funeral earlier that day. The service was perfunctory and sparsely attended. We were surprised to learn that Stubby had been a veteran, so there was an obligatory color guard, but that was about all the pomp anyone could muster. The main sounds, besides the preacher-for-hire droning on, was the wind rattling the palm fronds and rustling the live oak trees that shaded the cemetery.

There were a couple of uniformed policemen I recognized from workouts at the gym, and also a few teenage boxers who, like us, had skipped school without permission. The only Hunsacker family member who showed up was a short, rheumy-eyed man who claimed to be Stubby's brother. "Did you boys know he won the Navy Cross?" he asked us, apropos of nothing. "After the war, he wound up in Hollywood. Helped teach Kirk Douglas how to box when Kirk made that movie *Champion*. My brother . . . he was somethin'."

The preacher called Stubby "Isaac." We'd never known his first name. We were sad and a little embarrassed by how little we knew about his family or his life outside the gym, especially considering how big a role he'd played in ours. Dad had called us from his ship-to-shore earlier that day. He'd tried, in his fumbling way, to offer some adult comfort and perspective, the way he thought a dad was supposed to do.

"You boys just have to remember the good things about Mr. Hunsacker," he'd said. "Ashes to ashes, and like that. The Bible says somethin' about it somewhere."

We appreciated the effort, but it didn't make us feel any better.

In the main lobby of the courthouse, a uniformed dispatcher behind a high wooden podium looked at us with curiosity when we approached.

"Help you boys?"

"We've come to see a prisoner," said Johnny.

"That so? We got a mess of 'em. Have one in mind?"

"His name is Jesse Martel."

The officer leaned back in his seat and arched his eyebrows. He nodded his head toward one of the staircases that curved upwards to the second floor. "You'll have to ask about that upstairs. The admitting desk is the first door down the left hallway."

In the admitting office, some cops were drinking coffee and chatting around a long, elevated desk. Nobody we knew from the gym. When they noticed us standing at the door, they grew quiet.

"What can we do for you boys?" said a round-faced man sitting behind the desk. His beard and close-cropped hair seemed to have been arranged on his head like the metal shavings on a Wooly Willy magnetic board game.

"We'd like to see a man you have locked up in your jail," said Johnny. "His name is Jesse Martel." Johnny never seemed to be intimidated by uniforms.

The expressions on the cops' faces hardened, until the round-faced man, the gatekeeper, asked, "Are y'all family?" The rest of the men grinned. One of them laughed out loud.

"No, sir, we're friends of his," Johnny answered.

"Is that right? Well, I'm afraid that won't be possible."

"How come?" I asked, adding "sir" a second later when I noted the sergeant's stripes on his sleeve.

Wooly Willy crooked his finger and motioned us up to the desk. "Boys, your *friend* is in a whole bunch of trouble. And since y'all obviously aren't his lawyers, and are a little on the pale side for blood relations, there ain't no way you're getting upstairs to see the murder suspect."

"Commie murder suspect," one of the cops said under his breath.

The sergeant sighed and pushed a paper pad to the front of the desk, "How 'bout you kids write down your names and contact information, so we know who you are. After that, you can tell me what business you have with our perp."

He held out a pen, but Johnny made no effort to take it. "I'm Johnny Sweetwater," he said. "This is Pete Lopez, and this is my brother, Charlie."

"We're boxers from Hunsacker's Gym," Pete added.

"Friends of Stubby Hunsacker, too, huh?"

"We were at his funeral this morning," answered Pete.

One of the policemen leaned toward us. His breath smelled of cigarettes and beer. "Then why do you want to see the man who bashed his head in? Is this some kind of half-assed lynch mob?" The group of cops looked at us with amusement.

"Jesse Martel didn't kill Mr. Hunsacker," I said, irritated that they were treating this like a joke.

The sergeant scooted his chair back and stood up, frowning. "That's enough. You boys got no business in here. Now git, before I book you for truancy or somethin'."

We headed dejectedly for the door, but I stopped and turned around. "What about bail?"

The bearded sergeant looked up, clearly surprised to see us still there. "Bail? Shit, the judge hasn't even set a hearing. And if he does, you can pretty much forget about your friend bonding out. A nigger kills a white man in Nueces County?" He looked at his cop friends, speaking to them as much as to us. "He'd have a better chance winning a Hy-wayan vacation."

And that, for the moment, was that. We could hear the cops' laughter in the hallway.

—

On Friday night we got our asses whipped by the Robstown Cotton Pickers, a team we were favored to beat by two touchdowns. Between Johnny's interceptions and my dropped passes, I'm surprised our opponents didn't present us with the game ball. As expected, our coach was livid. "What is *wrong* with you two?" he asked us after the game. "What has happened to your give-a-shit?"

We didn't even try to defend ourselves. "No excuses," Stubby would have told us. For the first time in our young lives, football just seemed like a *game.* Anyway, Coach wouldn't have understood or cared that we were down in mouth about the death of a crotchety old gym owner and the arrest of a colored boxer. But lately, we hadn't been able to think of much else.

I called Carmen on Saturday and asked if I could see her. We hadn't had much of an opportunity to talk since Jesse was arrested. She agreed to meet me for lunch at the Black Diamond Oyster Bar in Corpus. I promised Johnny I'd have the Jeep back by dark, washed and with a full tank of gas. He thought he might go fishing, to take his mind off things.

I found a table in the corner of the restaurant, underneath a six-foot plastic marlin. When Carmen walked into the dim dining room, the place seemed to brighten considerably. I still felt a visceral jolt of excitement each time I saw her.

I stood up to greet her, expecting a kiss on the cheek, but she wrapped her arms around me instead, squeezing tightly. "Jesse is in so much trouble," she said with emotion. "What are we going to do?"

"I don't know."

When we sat down, I saw that that her eyes were wet with tears, and I realized how difficult things must have been for her and her mother since Jesse was arrested. Having an accused murderer living under their roof was bound to be something people would ask about.

"It's been terrible, Charlie. The police are treating us like we've done something wrong, like we're criminals. Reporters follow us everywhere, asking awful questions."

"What are they asking?"

She dabbed at her eyes with a napkin. "They ask about our loyalty to the USA, if we'll be sent back to Cuba. Why we let a Negro man live with us in our house, if Jesse is a communist, if *we* are communists."

I was shocked. Johnny and I had been unaware of the hubbub this had caused. It never occurred to me that Carmen and her mother would be targeted like this.

"But those things have nothing to do with . . . anything."

She nodded. "I know. But everyone seems to think they do. Half the dancers at Mother's studio have dropped out because of the negative publicity."

"I'm so sorry." And I was. Corpus was a small town in a lot of ways, and full of busybodies.

A waitress took our order, and afterwards, Carmen and I sat quietly, holding hands. "I know Feo didn't kill Stubby Hunsacker," I said to break the silence.

She squeezed my hand. "Thank you for saying that."

"Have you been to see him since they put him in jail?"

"Once, with my mother. We went after the arraignment. You know they're charging him with first degree murder?"

I nodded and thought back to what the cynical sergeant had told me. "Does he have a good lawyer?" I asked.

"Mother called a few of the big firms in town, but none of them wanted to touch it. The state had to appoint an attorney to defend Jesse."

"What's he like, this attorney?"

She waved her hand contemptuously. "He's a public defender, working for peanuts. I get the feeling he's just going through the motions."

After a pause, I asked her how Jesse was doing.

"He's sad, and he really misses his family. He's afraid he'll never see them again."

Jesse had showed me pictures of his wife, Isabella, and their beautiful baby daughter, who Jesse called Mariposa. His wife was an attractive woman with long dark hair and skin as white as Carmen's. The little girl had Jesse's skin color, and looked about two or three years old. Jesse told me his plan was to bring them to Texas with the money he earned from his first pro fight, but politics were gumming up the works.

"Fighting is simple," he'd told me. "I go out, hit somebody in the head. It's life that is complicated, you know?"

"We tried to go see him at the jail—me, Johnny, Pete—but they just about laughed us out of there. Will you tell him we tried to visit, the next time you see him?"

"Of course. He'll be happy to know that you tried."

Our waitress came around and poured us more iced tea. Carmen took a sip and then looked at me. "Charlie, they'll ask you to testify at the grand jury, you know. Your brother, too."

This hadn't occurred to me, but I suppose it made sense, since Johnny and I were the first ones on the scene that morning, besides Jesse. "Well, we'll tell them he didn't do it. We'll tell 'em that Jesse arrived a few minutes before we did and found Stubby lying on the floor, just like we did."

Carmen gave me a weak smile. "I wish that were enough."

Our platter of fried shrimp arrived, and we dipped them in cocktail sauce and ate a few bites. I reminded Carmen of the two Miami thugs who Stubby had run out of his gym last month. It had to be connected somehow. She said she'd speak to Jesse's lawyer about it. I told her Johnny and I would do the same.

While we were eating, Carmen said, "Charlie, there's something I've been meaning to ask you."

"Shoot."

"When my mom and I were at the police station, one of the policemen mentioned that Jesse said something to you before they arrested him. He implied that it was something incriminating. Do you recall what it was?"

I tensed up a bit, remembering how Harley Radcliff had pressed us to repeat what we'd heard Jesse say over Stubby's bleeding body. "Feo . . . Jesse, didn't actually say anything to *me*. He was just saying it to himself, like a lament or something. He was very upset."

"What were the words?" she asked again.

"They were in Spanish, so I didn't really understand them. He mentioned *Dios*, which I know means God, and then he said *lo mato*, or something like that."

115 | **15**

Carmen looked up quickly. "Was it *lo mato,* or *lo mató?*"

I blinked.

"Which was it?" she insisted. "It's important."

My heart rate accelerated as I struggled to remember. I pictured Jesse bent over Stubby's body, the bloody, mashed-up wound on his head, Jesse moaning and rocking back and forth, repeating his plaintive refrain. "Is there a difference?" I asked weakly.

"Yes, there is a difference," she said, her voice rising. "*lo mato* means, or at least implies 'I killed him.' *Lo mató,* with the accent on the last syllable, means 'They killed him.'"

"I . . . I'm not sure." I suppressed a wave of nausea. "I think I told them the first one."

"Oh, Charlie, please tell me you didn't."

She stared at me in disbelief, and all at once I felt hot, damp, and nauseated. I sprang up and rushed to the bathroom. Hunched over in a filthy stall, retching into the toilet bowl, I cursed myself for being so careless and ignorant. My statement had put Jesse in jail. My flawed recollection of his words, words he uttered over his murdered friend—my murdered friend—had put his life in danger. I'd given the police his confession.

If they electrocuted Jesse Martel for the murder of Stubby Hunsacker, it would be my goddamn fault.

CHAPTER 16

I returned to Rockport and told Johnny about my colossal screw-up. When I finished the story, he walked out to the wooden deck and sat on the porch step, holding his head in his hands.

"Shit. It's my fault too, brother. We both got it wrong."

I sat down next to him, and we glumly looked seaward, watching a flock of screeching seagulls harass a bay shrimper as it chugged home to Fulton Harbor. The frenzy of birds formed a dense white cloud around the boat as the fishermen shook out their nets.

"We've got to do something," I said.

"I know. I'm thinking," Johnny answered.

"We should talk to Jesse's lawyer. Tell him about the Miami guys, and about the explosion, and the car. Tell him we don't speak Spanish for shit."

Johnny nodded. "Yeah, we'll do that for sure, and soon. But I don't think it'll be enough."

"Should we tell the cops?"

Johnny gave a hollow laugh. "Do you think that sleazy detective is gonna listen to us?"

I remembered how pleased Harley Radcliff seemed with himself when he arrested Jesse, and I remembered his "black monkey" comment as they hauled him off to jail. "No, I don't . . . . I wish we could talk to Feo."

Johnny shook his head. "Right now, I don't know how I could face him."

We sat and worried together, and even wondered aloud what our dad might do. He might have been cranky and aloof most of the time, but he was as resourceful as they come when he put his mind to something. But, as usual, he was out in the Gulf, dragging his nets over the seabed like he had a personal vendetta against brown shrimp.

Johnny snapped his fingers. "Uncle Noble," he said. "He was a cop once, and with the military police during the war. I think he's got some juice with the CCPD. Half the police force drinks beer at his ice house."

Uncle Noble's joint had been a favorite of the local constabulary from the minute he plugged in the jukebox and turned on the neon beer signs. Cops loved to tell stories—the more cynical, gruesome, and hilarious, the better—and Noble was a good listener. Plus, his background as an MP made him sort of an honorary member of the brethren.

Johnny stood up and went inside. He spent ten minutes on the phone discussing the situation with our uncle, leaving nothing out. After he hung up, he said, "He probably won't be able to get us an answer until Monday."

"But he thinks we might be able to talk to Feo?"

"He said he'd do his best."

—

Uncle Noble called on Monday morning before we left for school. "The chief says okay, but it can only be one of you at a time."

When Johnny asked how he'd gotten the approval so fast, Uncle Noble told him the chief, Al Pettis, had dropped by the ice house to watch the game on Sunday. "The Cowboys beat the Steelers and the beer was on the house. It put Al in an agreeable mood."

Before our uncle hung up, he made us promise to come by his place to talk to him more about the case. "If the mob had anything to do with Stubby's murder," he said, "you boys had better choose your words carefully and watch your step. Believe me, I know what I'm talking about."

As soon as football practice was over, we drove the thirty miles to the Nueces County Jail. Johnny insisted I see Jesse first. I think he knew how important it was to me. I really wanted to tell Jesse about my screw-up and get it off my chest. I needed to confess.

The guards were closed-mouthed and sullen as they escorted me through the maze of elevators and hallways that led to the lockup section on the sixth floor. They handed me off to another officer, who made me empty my pockets and take off my shoes before he patted me down. When I entered the cellblock, I saw that Jesse was alone in a cell at the end of a hallway. A single barred window high in the cell threw a square of light onto the dingy wall. He was the only inmate in the block.

"You have ten minutes," said the officer.

I heard Jesse's deep laugh even before I saw him. *"Que milagro!"* he said, hopping off a bare metal bed hinged to the wall. "I am so glad to see you, my friend." He thrust his arms through the bars and grabbed my shoulders warmly. "I can' believe they let you in here."

"Hey, I know people," I said, trying to be upbeat. He was smiling, but he clung to me like a drowning man. "How are you, Feo?"

"Ah, well, the food is not quite so good as Doña Delfín's, but they give me a room with a nice view. Other than that . . . ." He shrugged with Latin resignation.

I wasn't too adept at small talk, especially under the circumstances, so I got straight to the point. "Feo, I know you didn't kill Stubby, but who did?"

Jesse released me and rested his elbows on a cross bar. *"Ay, carajo,* I don' know. I really don'." His eyes clouded over, and he stared at the stained concrete floor as if he were back in the gym on that terrible morning, looking down at his friend. "I don' know why anyone would wanna hurt that man."

"Did Stubby tell you some *mafioso* guys came by again?"

"Que?" Jesse straightened up. "What are you talkin' about, Charlie? What guys?"

"It happened last month. About a week before the explosion."

"The fat one with the cigar? The one that came before?"

"Yeah. That one, but this time he brought a friend. Johnny and I came in early and saw them slapping Stubby around inside his office. When we yelled for them to stop, they came after us. It got a little crazy, so Stubby pulled a gun on them and made them leave."

Jesse listened with interest. "What you mean, 'it got a little crazy?'"

"Johnny and I thought we could take 'em. We couldn't."

"So Stubby showed them his little gun? Why didn' I know about this?"

"Stubby told us not to tell you, not to mention it to anyone. He said you had plenty to worry about already, with the fight and everything. He was trying to protect you."

Jesse bowed his head, processing what I had told him. A moment later he looked up. "Santo Traficante," he said quietly.

"Who?"

"He's a *mafioso* boss in Florida. I know a couple a fighters in his camp. They tol' me he wanted to bring me over. Tha' fat guy, the one with the cigar? I thought he might work for Traficante, but I don' mention it to Stubby . . . because I don' want *him* to worry." He laughed bitterly. "We both tryin' to protect each other. Anyway," he puffed his cheeks and blew out a lungful of air, "Traficante is not a man you wanna make angry."

"Well, if those were his guys who visited the gym last month, they weren't too happy when they left. They told us it wasn't over."

Jesse paced back and forth in his cell. "And then the explosion. The police say it was the water heater."

"Yeah, that's what they said. But Johnny and I think it was Traficante's men giving Stubby a little payback for pullin' the gun on 'em. Feo, that morning they arrested you, we tried to tell the cops about the *mafiosos*, but they wouldn't listen. So Johnny and I think we should meet with your lawyer, tell him the whole story. It should help your case, right?"

Jesse stopped pacing and looked at me. "It might, Charlie. Thanks for doin' that."

But the way he said it, it didn't seem like he was very convinced. The jailer stuck his head into the hallway. "Time to wrap it up, kid."

I watched Jesse walk to the window and look up at the sky. "Did they bury Stubby?" he asked.

"The funeral was last Thursday. Most of the boxers from the gym were there. It was a real nice service," I lied.

Jesse mumbled something in Spanish and crossed himself.

When I heard him speak Spanish, the tightness returned to my chest. It was time to tell him about my screw-up with the police. He listened carefully as I recounted what happened and how I'd only realized the extent of my blunder after I'd talked to Carmen. His jaw hardened as I spoke.

"I'm so sorry, Feo. I didn't know."

His faced relaxed again as he walked to the steel door and reached through, placing a massive hand on my shoulder. "It's okay, Charlie. It was an honest mistake. You don' speak Spanish."

"I want to learn, Feo. Maybe you can teach me when you get out?"

"Sure, Charlie," he answered with a faint smile. "And if I don' teach you, then maybe Carmen will do it."

I could tell right then that Jesse Martel believed he would never get out of jail. I could tell he believed he would never breathe free air again. How do you get your head around something like that?

When the jailer came to get me, I embraced Jesse through the bars and promised I'd come back to see him as soon as I could. "Johnny will be up here in a few minutes. We're all pulling for you, Feo," I said as I walked out.

I exited the elevator, glad to be delivered from that hellish place, and found Johnny in the coffee shop. He, and everyone else—cops, lawyers, judges, secretaries, cooks, and waitresses—were huddled together in the restaurant, watching a small black and white TV that sat on a shelf behind the counter. I approached the group uneasily, aware that something important had happened. On the television, President Kennedy was sitting behind a large desk, looking straight into the broadcast camera and talking directly to me and the rest of the American people.

". . . . It shall be the policy of this nation, to regard any nuclear missile, launched from Cuba, against any nation in the Western Hemisphere, as an attack by the Soviet Union on the United States, requiring a full retaliatory response upon the Soviet Union."

I stood next to Johnny and nudged him. "What's going on?"

"The Russians put a bunch of nukes in Cuba," he whispered. "Aimed at us."

I tried to ask more questions but he, and several people near him, told me to keep quiet and listen. The President continued, calling for Khrushchev to abandon his "course of world domination" and "move the world back from the abyss of destruction."

Next he spoke "to the captive people of Cuba," telling them that their leaders had betrayed them and had turned Cuba "into the first Latin American country to become a target for nuclear war."

I was feeling anxious and lightheaded. I'd journeyed into that cavernous hellhole of a jail and returned to a world transformed into something new, frightening, and unrecognizable. "Nuclear war? An 'abyss of destruction?'" It was the stuff of science fiction. I felt as though I'd stepped into an episode of *The Twilight Zone.*

My next thought was of Jesse. Jesse's family was in Cuba, where the President had just painted a big atomic bull's-eye.

Kennedy ended his emergency address by telling us that the cost of freedom was high, but Americans had always paid it. "And one path we shall never choose," he said "is the path of surrender or submission."

After the speech, the crowd sat in stunned silence until somebody announced, to no one in particular, that if the "commie bastards" wanted war, then by God, we'd give it to 'em. This started a belligerent discussion about U.S. nuclear superiority, first strike capabilities, radioactivity, and other crazy stuff.

Johnny looked at me wide-eyed. "Spooky, huh?"

All I could think of to say was, "I was only gone for twelve minutes."

————

CHAPTER 17

Around dawn the next day, I was awakened by a loud clanking noise outside my window. I peered through the porthole above my bed and saw Dad behind the controls of a Caterpillar backhoe excavating our lush green Saint Augustine lawn.

Johnny walked into my room rubbing his eyes. "What the hell's going on?"

"I think Dad's digging a fallout shelter."

Johnny peered out the window. "Lordy, Lordy. What are we gonna do with him, brother?"

We pulled on our clothes and shuffled outside. Dad turned off the machine and looked at us. "If you boys want to sleep through the apocalypse, go right ahead."

It looked like *he* hadn't slept in a week. My guess was that the moment he heard President Kennedy's dire announcement on the ship radio, he hightailed it back to port. How he had already managed to wrangle a backhoe, I didn't know. Like I said, he could be very resourceful when he wanted to be.

"I left a list for each of you boys on the kitchen table," he said without preamble. "Johnny, you take my truck to get batteries, candles, and the lumber I'll need to frame out the inside of this shelter. It's all spelled out on the list. Charlie, you're in charge of food. Take your brother's wagon and get what you can. It's going to be a madhouse at the stores."

Johnny and I stood there in the damp grass and stared at the hole in our yard. Dad already had a storeroom full of emergency supplies in our fortified concrete house—hurricane provisions, he said—but apparently it wasn't enough to get us through the apocalypse.

"Are you two just gonna stand there with your thumbs up your butts? Get moving. I need your help on the shelter as soon as you get back."

Johnny and I loped into the house, grabbed our end-of-the-world supply lists, checked in with our dad once more, and then went on our respective quests. As I drove by Big Todd's Building Supply store, I saw a full parking lot and a throng of people gathered outside the door waiting to get in. Big Todd stood behind the glass watching them uneasily before he unlocked the double doors. In my rearview mirror, I saw Johnny's determined face as he turned Dad's pickup into the store lot.

The grocery was just as crazy. I parked on the side of the road, walked into the crowded store, and went straight to the canned goods aisle. I found slim pickings on the shelves, but stuffed as many tins into my sweatshirt pocket as I could fit: canned beets, tomato paste, canned artichokes, and something labeled Veg-All. I discovered a can of Campbell's Soup that had rolled under a shelf and stuffed that in my sweatshirt too.

After a half hour in the store, searching high and low for supplies, I realized I'd barely dented the long list Dad had given me. He was not going to be happy. As I carried my meager haul to the Jeep, an ear-splitting siren began wailing from nearby. Those of us caught out in the parking lot froze in place and instinctively looked up at the sky, expecting to see . . . I don't know what. The wispy vapor trail of a nuclear missile? A bright flash signaling the bomb's detonation? A monstrous walking tripod from H. G. Well's *War of the Worlds*?

Each school year they made us watch the same corny Civil Defense film, a cartoon narrated by an animated turtle named Bert, who showed us how to "duck-and-cover" if we were caught out in the open and saw the initial flash of a nuclear bomb. This exercise seemed as pointless to me as crawling under my classroom desk in the event of an attack, a drill our school made us practice once a month without fail. All us kids obediently watched the film, and during the drills we tucked up under our desks in little adolescent knots, knowing all the while that if the Big One dropped, we were well and truly fucked.

We'd all seen footage of the nuke tests out in the desert, and we'd seen the photographs of a devastated Hiroshima and Nagasaki, too. Now the bombs were ten times more destructive than the ones that instantly killed a hundred thousand Japanese less than twenty years ago. Before we'd left the house, Dad had told us that Corpus Christi, a major seaport and home to a naval air station as well as several oil refineries, would be a prime target for a Soviet first strike. He told us that in Rockport, we'd probably have a 50–80% chance of survival, as long as we were protected at the time of the blast and protected from the fallout raining down afterwards.

The siren continued to blare, and I considered ducking under a car, but like others caught out in the parking lot, I stood fixed in place. Finally someone ran outside the store shouting that the siren was a drill, it was only a drill. I made brief eye contact with a few terrified townspeople, and then the siren stopped. We all took a deep breath and then did our best to go about our business—rattled, vigilant, and glad to be alive, at least for the moment.

I drove home in a state of grim readiness. For what, I didn't know. I found myself scanning the horizon, halfway expecting to see a bright mushroom cloud rising into the sky, scorching it and everything beneath it. Havana was less than a thousand miles away, about the same distance as Beaumont to El Paso. How long would it take a ballistic missile to cover that measly distance?

As expected, Dad was plenty pissed when we returned with our paltry load of survival rations. We spent the rest of the day helping him frame out a crude refuge that, in the end, felt more like a coyote den than a fallout shelter. Because we'd hit the water table six feet down (we should've known we would), the structure was cramped, low, and soggy, and we had to stoop to keep from banging our heads on the ceiling. After we'd stocked it with supplies, there was scarcely room to sit on the canvas army cots. I'd been in more comfortable deer blinds.

"It's a little tight," Dad observed after we'd finished. "But at least we'll survive."

Once we were out of earshot, Johnny and I told each other we'd take our chances in our cement house, rather than spend a week in that claustrophobic crawl space with our father.

The week dragged on. Television broadcasts and newspapers informed us of the ongoing naval blockade, of Russian vessels being boarded and searched at sea, and of President Kennedy's unflinching resolve as he stared down the godless commie aggressors. At every opportunity, the media reminded us of our civil defense responsibilities. We were shown political maps illustrating the reach of the Cuban-based nuclear arsenal—Rockport was just inside the first circle of their short-range missiles. It was surreal going to class and getting homework assignments that assumed you wouldn't be a glowing charcoal briquette by the same time tomorrow. Just saying "so long" to our friends after school every day took on an ominous meaning.

Johnny and I were surprised that our Friday-night game against the Yoakum Bulldogs proceeded as scheduled. It was still Texas, after all, and not even the Red Menace could eliminate football. The stands were almost empty, and nobody from either team seemed to have his head or heart in the game. The band, majorettes, and cheerleaders didn't even bother showing up. We lost 21–14, but there was little reaction from either side after the final whistle. The Bulldogs trotted off the field and boarded their bus without even showering. In our locker room, the coach muttered something about it being a good game, and then told us to go home to our families.

The following day, our dad found refuge in one of the local bars, apparently deciding he'd rather witness the end of the world with a drink in his hand than pace around the house waiting for the bright flash. Johnny and I elected to drive over to Uncle Noble's Ice House in Corpus.

His tavern was, in fact, a converted ice house, with an L-shaped bar, three aisles of snacks and groceries, and two sets of roll-up garage doors that opened to the street, the better to accommodate the beer drinkers and domino players. Out back, a washer-pitching setup was located next to a brick patio. On football game days, Noble occasionally fired up the 55-gallon drum barbecue pit for burgers or a mess of pulled pork.

In spite of the impending war, the ice house was full of patrons. Noble was behind the bar chatting with some customers when he saw us walk in. He inclined his head toward the back of the building and then hollered to a pretty, if overworked waitress, "Jo Carol, I'm goin' out back for a smoke."

Outside, Noble sat across from us at one of the picnic tables and set three bottles of beer and three bags of Fritos on the table. "The neighbors made a run on my groceries, but I squirreled away some chips . . . you know, for emergencies," he said drily. He popped the cap off the beers and thrust two of them toward us. "Here's to surviving another day."

We tapped bottles and took emphatic gulps. Underage drinking was another one of the many rules the Sweetwater clan ignored. Besides, it was the end of the world, right?

"How's Dubber?" he asked.

"He dug a hole in our front yard," said Johnny.

"A fallout shelter," I added.

"Sounds like something he'd do." Uncle Noble tossed a handful of Fritos into his mouth. "Of course Rupert's reaction to all this was to plan a Day-of-Reckoning party at Shady's. You know *that* place'll be packed."

Uncle Rupert was already famous for his hurricane parties, even though the last storm, Carla, almost turned his beerjoint into a beer-and-rum-soaked ark.

"Your place seems to be pretty popular, too," Johnny noted.

Noble looked through the open back door at the patrons crowded around his bar. "It does, doesn't it?" he said, as if he'd just realized he had a packed house. "I don't know whether people are here because they're *not* worried about a war, or they're here because they are. Anyway, I'm glad to have 'em." He crunched on his chips and looked at us. "I read in the paper y'all lost another game last night."

"'Fraid so," Johnny answered.

"Still got a chance at winning district?"

"Mathematically, I guess we do, but I wouldn't bet on it."

Noble grunted and took a swig of beer. "Seems kind of unimportant, all things considered. Which reminds me, Flavius wants to know if you two are keeping at your boxing training."

It figured. Looming nuclear attack, boxing trainer murdered, our good friend in jail—in Flavius' mind, none of these was a reason not to train. "No," I said. "We haven't really thought about it much."

Noble nodded sympathetically. "Didn't think so. I'll tell him that y'all have been busy, but you're planning to start back soon. Maybe that will keep him off your backs for awhile. Were you able to see Jesse in the county jail?"

"We were," I said. "Or at least I was. Thanks for your help on that. We're gonna try again later this afternoon."

"Everyone seems convinced he did it, you know," said Noble. "You talked to his lawyer about the mob guys?"

"I talked to him on the phone," said Johnny. "He wants to take our deposition, but he didn't seem as excited about the information as I thought he'd be."

"He's probably not sure how credible your story will be in front of a jury."

"What does that mean?" I asked defensively. "We're telling the truth."

"I don't doubt it, nephew, but testimony from Jesse's two friends? And two kids at that? I'm just not sure how much good it'll do. The district attorney's apt to chew you up and spit you out."

"We were friends with Stubby, too, you know," I added, needlessly.

"What about the cops?" Johnny asked. "Aren't they supposed to look into stuff like that?"

Noble took his time fishing a cigarette out of the pack he kept in his shirt pocket. After he lit it, he blew out a plume of smoke. "Lemme tell you boys about the police. Their job isn't to solve cases; their job is to clear cases. Wrap 'em up, give a credible suspect to the D.A., and move along to the next poor SOB in their sights. A colored man standing over a white man's body? That's Christmas, for them. Justice doesn't really enter into the picture."

Johnny cursed under his breath, and I shook my head in disgust.

"Let's talk about those East Coast guys again," Noble suggested.

Johnny and I went through the story from beginning to end, and our uncle listened carefully.

"You say one of the guys' names was Walter?"

"Right. The short guy was Walter," said Johnny.

"Any other distinguishing features about Walter, or the big guy, Walter's associate?"

"Other than the associate was about six-five and strong as an elephant?" I asked. "None that I can think of."

"He had short hair," Johnny added. "Like a flattop."

"Let me ask around," said Noble. "I've got some old MP buddies who moved on to Miami after the war. A couple of them wound up on the police force there. They might know those particular characters."

"Jesse mentioned a guy named Santo Traficante," I suddenly recalled.

Our uncle's dour expression grew even more glum. "That name rings a bell. Not a guy you'd want to meet in a dark alley, or a well-lit one, either. I'll pass it along to my buddies and let you know what they say."

We thanked our uncle and drove to the Nueces County Jail to see Jesse. The guards reluctantly gave us five minutes each. Like most people we'd talked to all week, they seemed sullen and distracted because of the national emergency. I thought Jesse looked very sad, and old beyond his years. It didn't seem right to talk about the missile crisis or about the pending grand jury hearing, so I made small talk and, before I left, promised him I'd look in on Carmen and her mother.

Johnny's visit didn't go much better. "Jesus, that was depressing," he said as we left the courthouse.

"No kidding. I've never seen anybody so low. By the way, I told him we'd drop by Carmen's house to see how everyone's doing."

Johnny shot me a half smile. "That was big of you. Think she'll see you?"

I shrugged. I hadn't spoken to Carmen in a week, and my calls to her had gone unanswered. I assumed she was still angry about my linguistic fuck-up. "Guess we'll see."

It didn't take long to get my answer. Johnny parked across the street and watched me knock on Carmen's front door. Their car was in the driveway, but other than that, the neighborhood was quiet. Evidently, the newspapers were no longer interested in hounding Jesse's relatives, having bigger stories to cover with the apocalypse and all.

I knocked again and was pretty sure I heard footsteps inside the house. After a final knock, I retreated to the car.

"Nobody home?"

"Nobody that wants to see *me*."

"Could be it's just Carmen's mom in there."

"Could be." At least I hoped that was the case. "Let's go home."

—

CHAPTER 18

On Sunday, the crisis abruptly ended. Khrushchev pulled out his missiles in exchange for the US lifting the blockade and agreeing not to invade Cuba. It seemed like a good deal to me, especially for our side.

Around town, some men slapped each other on the back and boasted how we'd sure shown those Ruskies who was boss. Even President Kennedy, who most people in Texas regarded as about half-commie himself, got a few kind words. I was just glad nobody pushed the button that would've started World War III, and, as Johnny wryly noted, ruined our chances of going to the state playoffs.

That afternoon, Johnny elected to stay at the house and finish an English paper he had to turn in the following day. Despite our devil-may-care reputation at school, we were pretty serious about keeping our grades up. Our mother wanted us to have a proper education, and before she died, she made Dad promise he would make it so, even if he had to stand over us with a fence slat. What he didn't expect was that we would embrace the idea so readily on our own. We saw college as a ticket out of our one-horse town and a way to avoid a backbreaking career in the family shrimping business.

I decided to visit Jesse and let him know his family was out of danger, that we were all out of danger. But by the time I got in to see him, he'd already heard the news. I could tell he was relieved.

"It was a very long week," he said. "I'm happy we are still alive."

"I know you were worried for your family."

He opened his hands in acknowledgment. "For my family, for my town . . . for Cuba, for America, for the whole worl', Charlie." He shook his head in dismay. "Who would *not* be affected if the bombs were let loose?"

"Nobody," I said.

"Right, nobody. *Fue una locura* . . . crazy."

It *was* crazy. I thought of the sirens, the drills, the fear in people's eyes as they sleepwalked through the week, continuing to make their plans, but making them quietly, tentatively. What else could we do? For most of us, life went on with strained regularity, with everyone thinking it could end, literally, in a flash.

"What will happen now, Feo? Do you think your wife and baby can come see you?"

"No, I don' think so. My two countries hate each other now more than ever." He went to the window and looked through the bars, as if he were trying to see across the Gulf all the way to Havana. When he turned around he said, "An' I'm afraid I miss my chance to go back to Cuba. I should've taken Ramón's offer."

"Offer?"

Jesse sat down on his bunk. "To box for Cuba. That was why Ramón came to Corpus. Why he visited our house."

"For boxing? I thought it was because of Doña Delfín, and the National Ballet Academy, and all of that."

Jesse raised his head and looked at me. "*El Comandante* cares more about boxing than ballet."

I pictured Fidel, with his bushy beard, cigar, and army fatigues. He didn't seem to me like a patron of the arts. "My brother said it would be good propaganda for Cuba. Ballet, I mean."

"Maybe so, but Fidel is more interested in the propaganda of knocking Yankee imperialist boxers on their asses." He laughed a bitter laugh. "*Coño* . . . . He is thinkin' abou' the Olympics . . . a big international stage where he can wave his flag."

"So the offer to Doña Delfín was a lie?"

"No, I think Ramón is not lying about that. If Alisa goes to Cuba, I thin' she will have her academy."

"He was after you all along, wasn't he?"

Jesse nodded. "He believe that if the only family I have in the USA returns to Cuba, then I will go back, too. He got very angry when I said no. And then *I* got angry when he bring up my wife an' my baby." I watched him clinch and unclench his big hands, his knuckles popping when he made a fist.

"What did he say?"

"He say the governmen' will make it very hard on them if I don' go back."

"That's not fair," I protested.

"No, it's not fair."

"Feo, why *did* you decide to stay here?"

"I don' like bullies, Charlie. An' neither did Mr. Hunsacker." His brows had dipped to form a fierce scowl, but it faded quickly. "An' I suppose I still believed I could bring my family here. We had a plan all worked out. A plane, a pilot . . . we were jus' waitin' for the money from the fight." He looked at me expectantly. "It woulda worked, too."

He waited until I nodded in agreement, and then he sighed deeply. "But then, Stubby, the missiles, an' . . . " He spread his hands to encompass the tiny, clammy cell, the jailhouse bars, and what he regarded as his inevitable fate at the hands of a Texas jury. "An' then this. My wife and I, we wanted our daughter to grow up in America. We coulda had a good life here, Charlie."

Jesse sat down on his bed, pain and misery creasing his face. The jailer walked in rattling his keys at me. "Time's up, kid."

I said goodbye to Jesse, but I don't think he even heard me. After I left the courthouse, I drove around aimlessly, thinking about Ramón's deception and manipulation, and about Jesse's ruined dreams.

Without realizing it, I found myself on Carmen's street. I pulled to the curb in front of her house and sat in the car gathering my courage, determined to see her this time. I *needed* to see her.

After the twentieth knock, Doña Delfín answered the door. "She's not here."

"Then I'll wait."

"She doesn't want to see you."

That flustered me for a moment, but I stood my ground. I refused to believe Carmen would stay mad at me for that long. "Why won't you let me see your daughter, Doña Delfín? I don't understand."

Her expression softened some, and I thought for a moment she was going to tell me something, but she seemed to change her mind. "You are both too young."

"Like you were?"

I could tell this made her angry, but I wouldn't look away.

"Yes, like I was," she said after a pause.

When she started to close the door, I tried a different approach. "I talked to Jesse today."

She paused, her anger fading. "How is he?"

"He misses his family."

She took a deep breath. "His family misses him." For the first time, Doña Delfín looked at me with kind eyes. "Thank you for going by, Charlie. Your visits mean a lot to him."

I wondered if she was going to invite me in, but she didn't. "I will tell my daughter that you came by."

She closed the door, and I stood there awkwardly for a moment.

I looked through the window of the garage and noticed the car was gone—Carmen had probably taken it—so I decided to wait for her. A couple of hours later, the sun set and, up and down the block, porch lights began to switch on, illuminating every front door but Carmen's. Sitting on the dark stoop, I could feel Doña Delfín looking at me now and then through the curtains. Later I heard the television set and the sound of pots and pans rattling in the kitchen as she cooked supper. I was prepared to stay until breakfast if that's what it took.

Another half hour went by, and then a tan sedan pulled up behind my Jeep. Ramón Cruz got out of the car and observed me curiously as he walked up.

"Let me guess. Doña Delfín won't let you in the house. You are a stubborn one, aren't you, kid?"

The sight of Ramón really hacked me off. "What are you doing here, Ra-*món*?" I said, sarcastically. "Or is that even your real name?"

Ramón's eyes sparked for a second, but then a smile appeared under his thick black mustache. He sat down beside me and pulled a cigar out of his coat pocket. "Care for one?"

"No."

I watched him light the cigar, noticing for the first time his rough, calloused hands. "Maybe when you're older," he said, exhaling a cloud of smoke upward. He rolled the long cigar in his fingers and sniffed it approvingly. "*Que rico*. You know, this last week I was reminded how we must savor the pleasures in our lives . . . because it could all be over in a instant."

"Thanks to your commie bosses in Cuba."

"Ah, you think *we* were being provocative?"

"You and your comrades in Moscow."

He looked at me, the haughty smile still on his face. "Doña Delfín was right. You Americans are hopelessly naïve. But dangerous at the same time. Not a good combination."

"You put missiles in our backyard."

"*Your* backyard, *your* playground." Ramón gave a derisive laugh. "That *is* how your country thinks of us, isn't it?"

Ramón puffed on his cigar and shook his head sardonically. "These last two weeks were nothing more than political theater, and you almost blew up the world because of it."

I noticed that Ramón's Mexican accent was gone. The guy spoke better English than I did. Apparently he'd decided I wasn't worth deceiving any longer.

"We didn't start it," I said. I felt like a kid explaining a playground fight to his parents and I hated it.

"No? Maybe you think Cuba was the aggressor? The CIA or their mobster friends have been trying to assassinate our leader for years. Six months ago, they sponsored an invasion. There's no limit to the dirty tricks your government will use to get what it wants."

"Dirty tricks like telling someone you'll hurt his family unless he returns to Cuba?"

Ramón looked at me sharply. "I see you have been talking to Jesse Martel. Well," he shrugged and took a puff of his cigar, "Jesse is out of the game now. He had his chance."

"He didn't kill Stubby Hunsacker. "

"I know he didn't."

That simple, definitive statement took my breath away for a moment.

"If you know he didn't do it, you can help clear his name."

Ramón shook his head "It's too late. An offer was made. Jesse rejected it. Instead of returning to fight for his country, he decided to stay here and fight for money."

"He was loyal to Mr. Hunsacker," I said defensively. "There's nothing wrong with that."

"I suppose loyalty has its virtues, even if it is misplaced. But once his manager was out of the way, loyalty was no longer an issue, was it? Jesse had no reason to stay. But then someone came along and ruined his chances, even giving the police the confession they needed to put him in jail."

I realized he was referring to me, and following that, I realized something else. "Maybe you killed Stubby."

"Maybe I did. I have my loyalties, too."

When I looked at him, he had such a smug look on his face; it really set me off.

"You bastard!" I intended to plant my fist in his ear, but before I could scramble to my feet, he grabbed my wrist with one hand and pinned it to the ground, and then with the other hand seized my throat in a chokehold that compressed my airway so completely I couldn't even gasp.

"Listen to me you little *gallito*," he whispered in my ear. "You're nothing but a little boy with a big mouth. I'm inclined to shut it for you."

He tightened his grip on my throat. With my trachea compressed, I was running out of breath. I was faintly aware of car lights shining on the house and of wheels turning into the driveway. Ramón released my throat but continued holding me down by the wrist. He leaned in close and whispered, *"Viva la revolución."*

About the time Carmen opened the car door, her mother opened the front door to the house. "Doña Delfín!" Ramón said affably. "How nice to see you."

I staggered off the porch toward Carmen, gasping for breath. When she saw the stricken look on my face, she froze in place. "What's wrong, Charlie? Are you okay?"

"Let's go," I said hoarsely. She followed me to my car and climbed into the passenger seat. I could hear her mother calling her from the porch.

As we sped away, Carmen watched me with concern. "Slow down," she said. "You're driving like a lunatic."

I slowed the car and pulled into traffic on Ocean Drive. I could still feel the pressure points where Ramón's fingers had seized my throat.

"Charlie, what on earth were you and Ramón doing when I drove up? It looked like you two were sharing a secret."

"The crazy bastard was trying to strangle me."

Carmen tilted her head, not understanding, and a bit shocked by my outburst. "What are you talking about?"

The story spilled out of me, from the conversation with Jesse in jail, to the confrontation with Ramón at the house. The moment I finished, I realized how disjointed and crazed I must have sounded. A "little boy with a big mouth," as Ramón had put it. Carmen was mostly quiet afterwards, asking a few questions, but asking them in way that made me think she didn't quite believe me.

"Why would I make this up, Carmen?"

"I don't know. I mean, you wouldn't. But . . ." I saw her look at me, "I know how much you want to help Jesse."

"What I told you is true."

"I believe you. Let's back up. Are you sure Ramón didn't mean something else?"

"Yes."

"He was speaking in English?"

"Yes, goddamnit. I understand English." I have to admit, it was a fair question. I'd already demonstrated my ability to misapprehend Castilian.

"Don't get mad at *me*, Charlie. I'm just trying to understand."

I took a deep breath. "I know." I replayed Ramón's words in my head. "He called me a *'gallito.'* That was the only Spanish word he used. I don't know what it means."

A thin smile appeared on Carmen's face, and she scooted next to me in the seat. "Literally, it's a little rooster, but in Cuba it also means 'troublemaker.' It's a name that fits you, Charlie . . . but you are a good troublemaker. You do it for the right reasons." She kissed me on the cheek. "It's one of your best qualities."

We stopped on the T-head and sat on the concrete steps, watching the bay and holding hands. I was still keyed up, the fear and adrenaline taking its time to subside. Carmen sensed my mood and simply sat beside me, quietly.

"Charlie, where were you last week?" she asked later. "I kept expecting you to call me or come by."

"I tried. I even came by your house. I thought maybe you were still mad at me after, you know, after we talked last time."

"No, I *wanted* to see you. Ugh . . . . What a terrible week. Dozens of panicky phone calls with relatives in Cuba—my mom was so flipped out by everything that was happening. Kids and teachers at school looking at me and talking to me in this weird, guarded way. I called you a couple of times, but no one answered."

"I'm sorry, Carmen. Tonight your mom told me you didn't want to see me."

"It's not true." She grabbed my arm and leaned on my shoulder. "Not true at all."

We sat and listened to the water splash against the bulkhead for awhile, and then I drove Carmen back to her house. I saw that Ramón's car was gone. "Carmen, you and your mother need to be careful with Ramón. He's not what he seems. He's a very dangerous man."

"We'll be careful. I promise." She paused before she closed the car door. "Charlie, it's probably best that you stay away from our house for a little while. I'll come to you. When can I see you again?"

"We play West Oso on Friday night; the game's here in Corpus."

"I'll be there to cheer for you."

"We can go out afterwards?"

"I'll look forward to it, Carlito."

———

CHAPTER 19

Uncle Noble called us midweek to tell us he had spoken with his Florida law enforcement friends. "It wasn't Santo Traficante," he said. "The guys that strong-armed you at Hunsacker's gym work for another mob guy, Johnny Roselli, a guy connected with the Chicago syndicate. But he's based outta Miami."

"Chicago? Why are they interested in a Cuban boxer?"

"Almost all the major families had a big stake in Cuba before the revolution—hotels, casinos . . . some of the Cuban boxers, too."

"So you think this Roselli guy could've had Stubby killed?" asked Johnny.

"I don't think so. One of the cops in the organized crime unit said the underworld's interest in Martel dried up a while ago. Probably because your friend Hunsacker was such a pain in the ass. Said they'd written him off and already had new fighters they were bringing up."

Johnny and I both had our ears next to the phone, but I grabbed the receiver when I heard this. "Well, *sure* they're not interested now that he's in jail. But maybe they didn't expect him to get blamed for the murder? Maybe they didn't expect him to show up that morning?"

"I get your point, Charlie, but gangsters can afford to be pragmatists; there's plenty of pigeons out there. When Hunsacker wouldn't bend, and Jesse stood by him, they had other fighters to go after. No need to kill somebody over it. They're smarter than that."

"The two guys we met didn't seem that smart."

"Look, boys," said Noble. "I know y'all want to clear Jesse's name, but I'm telling you, my contacts don't think the mob did it. They seemed pretty sure about it."

"What about the bomb blast?" asked Johnny.

"That probably *was* Roselli's boys, especially since it happened so soon after Hunsacker pulled his gun on 'em. Their way of getting' back at him for embarrassing 'em like he did. But the murder? I don't think so."

I moved my mouth closer to the handset. "Your cop friends at the ice house, what are they saying about Jesse's case?"

We could hear Uncle Noble exhale through the receiver. "You boys know he was indicted by a grand jury on Tuesday? Murder One."

"Yeah, we heard," Johnny answered tonelessly. "They didn't even bother to call us as witnesses."

"They're pushing it through the system pretty fast, that's for sure. I also heard that the public defender they gave Jesse, J.C. Dingwall? The guy's a bum. They say he's undependable and a boozer, to boot. And none of my CCPD buddies in uniform think too highly of the detective who handled the case, either."

"Harley Radcliff," I said.

"Right, Radcliff. Kind of a weasel. He used to come in here sometimes, usually with his wife. I think the last time she threw a drink in his face and left by herself."

"He still married?" asked Johnny, wondering, like I was, if the detective had some side action going with Mavis McDevitt.

"Far as I know, he is."

"Is there any good news, Uncle?" I asked.

"Well, the DA wouldn't mind having a murder weapon, but . . . ."

"But what?"

"They *all* think Jesse Martel is gonna be convicted and probably executed for the crime. Like I told you boys, cops and courts generally take the path of least resistance. Jesse is poor, he's colored, and he's handy. In this part of the country, that's good enough."

Johnny and I winced and then thanked our uncle for his help. After we hung up the phone, Johnny shook his head. "Brother, it's not looking good for Feo."

I paced around the room. "And nobody's *doing* anything."

"What do you think we should do?"

"I don't know. Maybe we should tell someone about Ramón."

"We don't know where he's hiding. We don't even know if he's still in the country. And even if we did, what would we do? Tell that dickhead Radcliff about him? About the possible Cuban spy who sort of suggested he might have killed Stubby . . . before he tried to strangle you?"

"What about the lawyer?" I asked. "Let's tell him."

Johnny shook his head. "We can try, but Dingwall didn't even believe us when we told him about the Mafia guys. He'd think Ramón was just another bullshit story from two kids desperate to get their friend out of jail."

I knew my brother was right, and I kicked the concrete wall of our house in frustration. Johnny began pacing the floor, too, restless, cracking his knuckles. A moment later, he stopped and looked at me expectantly. "Box?"

I nodded in agreement and hurried to the steamer trunk, pulling out two pairs of Hutch boxing gloves, hand-me-downs from our uncle Flavius. I threw a pair to my brother, and we laced them on without speaking, anxious to get to it. It wasn't the first time we'd resorted to this. Dad used to make us do it when he got tired of us scuffling as kids, but then we started fighting each other because we liked it.

On the patio deck, in the fading light, Johnny and I spent the next half hour knocking the living shit out of each other, channeling our pent-up frustration into jabs, body shots, and uppercuts. I think we liked receiving the punishment as much we did dishing it out. We'd slug away for a few minutes, catch our breath, and then go at it again. When it was too dark to see anymore, we went inside, dripping with sweat. At least we'd done *something*, even if it was only to beat on each other.

—

The West Oso Bears hadn't won a game all season, but our coach wasn't taking any chances. He built up the game like it was the Cotton Bowl and let us know, in no uncertain terms, that we were defending not only the honor of Rockport-Fulton High, but pretty much the whole community, as well as the American Way of Life.

I suppose Johnny and I were still carrying around some of the frustration and anger we'd stored up, because we played all-out, recklessly almost, and had exceptional games—flat tore up the gridiron. Before the coach pulled us near the end of the third quarter and emptied the bench, Johnny and I had combined for twenty-eight points and a dozen tackles each. The American Way was safe for another Friday night.

Veronica and Carmen met us at the gate after we showered.

"Were y'all showing off for us, again?" asked Veronica.

"Naw," Johnny answered, "We just wanted to show you how much ballet has improved our football."

Veronica laughed. "We'll be sure and tell Efrain."

I looked around for Rachel. "Did Rachel already leave with Pete?"

Carmen and Veronica shared a glance. "Rachel didn't come tonight," said Carmen. "She said she had other plans. Pete was so disappointed he left at halftime. Don't tell him, but I think there's another guy in the picture."

We decided to go to Snapka's Drive-In over on Weber Road for our victory feast. Johnny rode with Veronica in her car; Carmen and I went in the Jeep. The joint was crawling with high school kids, but we lucked out and found two spaces under the awning where we could park the cars side-by-side. A pretty carhop bounced over and took our orders: Dixie Burgers for Johnny and Veronica, a chili dog for Carmen, and an order of crispy tacos for me, a Snapka's specialty.

I recognized a group of West Oso football players milling around a souped-up roadster a couple of rows down. I could tell by their dirty looks that they recognized us as well. Three of the biggest guys swaggered our way, and I looked over at Johnny for a sign as to how we were going to handle it. I wasn't in the mood for a fistfight, but I knew I wouldn't back down either.

"Hey, guys," Johnny called out amiably from the car window. "What's up?"

They slouched against Veronica's car and stared down at Johnny, trying to look tough. They had the sleeves of their letter jackets pushed halfway up their forearms. It was a West Oso thing.

"Some game tonight, huh?" said Johnny. Veronica shifted a little uncomfortably in her seat.

"Maybe it's time we evened the score a little," said a horse-faced kid with tape across the bridge of his nose.

"Ah, come on, fellas, there's no need for that." He smiled at them like they were his best buddies. "Once baseball season rolls around, you guys know you're gonna hand us our asses. We haven't won a game off West Oso in what? Four years?"

"More like six years," said one of them.

"Okay, six years. I figure y'all will probably take State this year."

The three guys relaxed a little, and their spokesman agreed with Johnny. "We've got a good chance, if we can get past South San Antonio in the quarterfinals."

Johnny nodded thoughtfully. "They're tough alright, but y'all have better pitching this year. I think you'll take 'em."

They continued chatting a few minutes and ended up shaking hands. "Good game tonight, Sweetwater. Y'all kicked our asses but good."

"Guess I can't ask you to take it easy on us when baseball season comes around?" asked Johnny.

"Not a chance," said one of them, smiling.

The three guys looked at Carmen and Veronica approvingly, and then gave me a respectful nod before they walked back to their car. No pretty girls hanging around there, I couldn't help but notice.

"Wow," said Carmen, "That was pretty slick. Your brother should be a diplomat when he grows up."

I didn't disagree. Johnny could charm his way into, or bullshit his way out of, just about anything when he wanted to. It seemed to run in the family.

Our food was delivered and we ate greedily. I quickly finished my tacos and declared that I could by-God eat a couple more. When I looked over at Carmen, she'd already devoured her chili dog, and said that if I was ordering again, she'd have another as well. I noticed a big glob of chili on the front of her blouse.

"You know, for a graceful ballerina, you sure can make a mess of a chili dog."

Carmen laughed. "It's one of the things you love about me."

She was right about that. Carmen was the perfect balance of proper and improper. I knew I'd be heartbroke if she disappeared from my life after graduation. The saddest song on the Top Forty wouldn't be able to touch it.

As though she were reading my mind, she brought up her mother and the Cuban Ballet Academy.

"It really is a chance of a lifetime, Charlie," she said. "Instead of teaching a bunch of bored girls whose mothers *make* them take ballet, she'd have serious students, the best dancers from an entire country, dancers who would work until their feet bled to please the great Doña Delfín."

Though there was respect in Carmen's tone, there was an underlying bitterness, too, and I mentioned this to her.

"It's my mother's dream, not mine."

"If she goes back to Cuba, you know she's going to insist you go with her."

"I know. I haven't decided what I'm going to do yet."

I took a deep breath, losing my appetite for another round of tacos. Carmen was headstrong and independent, but she was no match for her mother. Doña Delfín was more intimidating than any football or boxing coach I'd ever seen, including Stubby Hunsacker. I was surprised no one had named a hurricane after her.

"It's not just the ballet academy, though. It's also because of what happened to Jesse, how they've treated him, how they've treated us. She's come to hate this country, and I can't say I blame her."

"Do *you* hate this country?"

"No," she answered after a thoughtful pause. "But I saw how ugly Americans can be about race and about politics. You can't believe the comments I've heard since Jesse's arrest, and since the crisis with Cuba."

"They don't have racist assholes in Cuba? And how do they treat people with different political views there?" I'm not sure why I was getting defensive. The way Jesse and Carmen and Doña Delfín had been treated made me mad, too.

"Yeah, there are problems. It was a big scandal when Jesse married my aunt. Mixed-race marriages are still frowned upon there. And if you have different political views you'll be jailed or executed. I'm not defending Cuba, Charlie. I'm just disappointed in what I've seen in this country. I guess I expected better."

Our food came and we set the baskets on the seat, neither of us hungry any longer. I glanced over at Johnny and Veronica, who were laughing as they competed to see who could finish their chocolate malt the fastest.

"I'm sorry, Carmen. I want you to stay, that's all."

"I know, *Flaco*." She put her arm around me. "I know."

We both looked up when we heard a motorcycle roar up to the drive-in. Karl McDevitt was driving, and sitting behind him, with her arms around his waist, was Rachel.

"Is that Rachel?" asked Carmen. "That's her mysterious new boyfriend?"

"That guy's trouble," I said. "She shouldn't be going out with him."

"Rachel loves trouble. Or at least she thinks she does."

As Rachel climbed off the motorcycle, Boyd Parker, Karl's only friend it seemed, got out of his own car and walked over to talk to them. While they were loitering in front of the restaurant, Karl surveyed the crowd, scowling at anyone who made eye contact. He saw me and furrowed his brow. But I noticed that when he saw Johnny, he looked away. Maybe Jesse was right. Maybe Karl McDevitt *was* scared of my brother after what happened at the gym.

But he sure wasn't scared of me.

"I should go talk to Rachel," said Carmen.

I started to protest, but I didn't want her to know I was afraid to walk over there with her. Luckily, the situation resolved itself when Rachel climbed back on Karl's bike and the two of them rumbled off down Weber Road.

"When you do talk to her," I said, "tell her her boyfriend is a *mala hierba*."

Carmen looked at me, surprised. "Where did you hear that?"

"From Feo. And I believe him."

CHAPTER 20

On Sunday morning we brought a sack of donuts to the courthouse, figuring that Jesse would be getting plenty tired of prison chow by now.

"What do you kids think this is, the Plaza Hotel?" said the fat sergeant on duty. "There ain't no room service here. Besides, *Mister* Martel is busy right now."

"Busy? Doing what?" I asked.

"Talking to some people."

"Who?"

"That's none of your business, junior."

Johnny pulled a donut out of the sack, took a bite, and pushed the sack towards the cop. "Want a sinker?" he asked. "They're from Shipley's."

The sergeant, who obviously never met a donut he didn't like, eyed the sack with interest. "Don't mind if I do," he said. A couple of other men hanging around the counter watched him reach into the sack.

"Officers?" Johnny asked, holding the donuts out to them. "Get 'em while they're hot." The greasy sack was emptied in no time. Johnny sat down next to me, and we split the last donut.

"So is it Mrs. Delfín and her daughter?" Johnny asked casually. "Is that who Jesse is talking to?"

The sergeant chewed contentedly. "No, somebody else. A couple of guys in suits. They went through the chief, not me."

"So they might be a while," Johnny ventured.

He shrugged. "Who knows? Like I said, this is the chief's deal."

Johnny wiped his hands on the sack and then walked to the trash bin to throw it away. "Must be Jesse's lawyer and one of his clerks," he said.

"J.C. Dingwall?" laughed the sergeant. "On a weekend? I can guarantee you he's out on the golf course this morning. Or sleeping off a bender from last night. Hell, you boys have been in here more than that little ambulance chaser has."

If these "suits" were talking to Jesse without J.C., I wondered what was up. I'd seen enough episodes of *Perry Mason* to know that the accused's lawyer should be present during questioning. Of course, Perry Mason never practiced law in Nueces County.

"Mind if we wait?" Johnny asked.

"Suit yourself," answered the sergeant. After he polished off his donut, he picked up the phone and told somebody we were there.

We sat in the waiting area until the sergeant received a call. "The guard's on his way down to fetch you," he said after he hung up. When we both stood up and walked toward the elevator, he stopped us. "Hey, one at time. You kids oughta know the rules by now."

"You go first," I said to Johnny.

After half an hour of waiting, I wondered if the jailer was easing off the ten-minute visitation limit. Thank God for donuts. Finally, the elevator door opened and the guard stepped out. "You," he said, crooking his finger at me. "Come with me."

"Where's my brother?" I asked.

The guard ignored my question. The elevator stopped on the fourth floor instead of the sixth, and I asked if they'd moved Jesse somewhere else. Still no answer.

As I was led down a dreary, fluorescent-lit corridor of holding rooms, I glimpsed Johnny in one of them, talking to a couple of men in dark grey suits, and guessed they were the ones who'd been talking to Jesse earlier. The guard took me to an empty room with a metal desk and three chairs and instructed me to sit and wait. There was a D-ring welded onto the top of the desk for chaining prisoners; it gave me a bad feeling. About ten minutes later, the two suits came in and closed the door behind them.

One was a young guy, kind of skinny, with a crew cut and a hatchet face. The other one was older and heavier, with wavy, slicked-back hair.

The big guy sat down and regarded me sternly through black-framed eyeglasses. The young one removed his suit coat and placed it over his lap when he sat down, smiling at me like we were old friends.

"Your brother tells me you're a big fan of boxing," he said.

"I guess. Who are you guys?"

"He says you're both in Golden Gloves. Great program. You know Sonny Liston and Cassius Clay were Golden Gloves champions?"

I nodded. Everyone knew that.

"I've heard people say Jesse Martel had the makings of a future champion, too. What do you think?"

I noted the past tense with unease. "Is this about him? About Feo?"

"Oh, yeah, *El Rey Feo*—his ring name. You call him Feo, huh? I guess you two are pretty good friends. The guard says you've been up here to visit him a few times."

"We're friends, yeah."

The older guy sat quietly, a grim expression on his face. The chatty one adjusted himself in his chair. "Don't you think that's a little . . . unusual?"

"What?"

"A young white kid, an older colored man? What's the story there?"

"I don't know what you mean."

"Jesse has a niece, doesn't she? Pretty blonde girl? Is that your angle? Make friends with the girl's uncle, score some points with the family, maybe?"

This guy was starting to get under my skin. "No. Jesse and I train at the same gym."

"Wasn't Isaac Hunsacker your friend, too?"

"You mean Stubby? Yeah."

"That's kinda strange, too, isn't it? You being a friend with Hunsacker and the guy who killed him."

"Feo didn't kill him."

The two men exchanged a look, and then the older guy stood up and his partner followed him outside. I guess, technically, I could have gotten up and walked out myself. But I didn't. Twenty minutes later, they returned.

"Let's talk about Jesse's family," said the man with the crewcut.

I folded my arms. "Until y'all tell me who you are, I'm through talking."

The older guy snorted and shook his head. His associate smiled patiently and leaned forward. "We're with the government, kid. Just answer our questions, and you'll be out of here in no time."

"The government" was a pretty vague term—FBI? Immigration? US Postal Service? I pressed them to be more specific, but they ignored my question and kept asking me about Jesse and about Carmen and Doña Delfín. Although they seemed to know plenty about them already.

"On your visits to their house, did you ever see anyone else there?" asked the younger guy. "Relatives? Friends? Strangers?"

While I pretended to search my memory, I could feel the slick-haired man boring holes through me with his eyes. "Nobody I can recall," I lied. There was something shadowy and covert about these guys, and I felt like the less I told them, the better. At least for the moment.

They asked a few more questions and then rose to go, walking out without saying a word. A couple of minutes later, a deputy came by with Johnny at his side. He escorted us to the elevator and pushed the down button to the lobby floor.

"But we haven't seen Jesse yet," I protested.

"You won't be seeing him today."

"Says who?" asked Johnny.

"Don't push it, kid. I'll follow my orders, and you follow yours, okay?"

On the drive back to Rockport, Johnny and I compared notes.

"You think we should've told them about Ramón and about the *mafiosos*?" I asked.

"Beats me. But since they wouldn't tell me jack about who they were, I didn't feel I owed them anything. Plus, I didn't want to say anything that might be used against Feo."

"Same here. They said they worked for the government."

"Doesn't narrow it down much."

"No it doesn't."

Johnny looked over at me. "Maybe they were with the CIA—real-live, secret agent spooks."

I laughed at the notion. But I didn't dismiss the idea out of hand, either.

CHAPTER 21

We played our last game of the season against the district-leading Aransas Pass Panthers. We already knew we weren't advancing to the regional playoffs, so we played like we had nothing to lose, and surprisingly, we won. In the locker room after the game, Coach thanked us for our dedication and effort and told us that even though we didn't win 'em all that year, we were a fine bunch of Christian athletes and a real special team—one of his all-time favorites. Pretty much the same end-of-season speech Johnny said he'd heard last year. I suspected we'd hear it next year, too.

We showered and migrated over to Pug Greenlee's house, where a mob of students and a keg of beer awaited us. Why Pug's parents thought they could leave town on weekends and entrust their country house to their boy, I'll never know. His parties were so infamous around town that many parents preemptively grounded their kids *before* the parties took place. We tapped the keg, flirted with the girls, and rehashed a season of gridiron ups and downs.

At some point during the beer bash, probably when he walked into the treeline to take a pee, Johnny found a bullfrog, and he hid it under his ballcap for the remainder of the party. Every once in awhile the cap would jump a little on his head, and Johnny would adjust the cap back into place, never acknowledging that it'd moved. I played the straight man, and suggested to anyone who commented that they must be seeing things, or else had had too much to drink.

When the cops finally came to break up the party, people scattered in every direction to keep from getting caught. Johnny and I circled back to where the squad cars were parked and Johnny tossed the bullfrog through the open window of one of the vehicles. "That'll make him jump," he laughed, as we hightailed it back to our Jeep. "The frog *and* the cop."

The next morning, my brother and I were awakened by voices in our house. We found our dad sitting at the kitchen table drinking coffee with Uncle Flavius.

"Hey, whaddaya know, it's the talk of the town," said Dad. "Good game last night. I heard y'all stole one from Aransas Pass."

Johnny and I wandered to the coffee pot and poured ourselves a cup. Dad had probably been at the game—he almost always watched us play when he wasn't out in the Gulf— but for some reason he never let on that he'd been there.

"Are the Pirates headed for the playoffs?" he asked. "Or is that it?"

"Naw, we're done," Johnny answered.

"Oh well, maybe next year."

Uncle Flavius slurped his coffee and scrutinized us with his usual sour expression. "Morning, Uncle," I said cautiously. I could tell he was pissed off about something, and I had a feeling I knew what it was.

"What's good about it?" he growled.

"My brother is here to talk about something besides football," said our dad.

"Bowling?" asked Johnny.

I stifled a grin. "Badminton?"

"Boxing, goddamnit!" Flavius' face looked like it was about to combust. "Yesterday I went by Hunsacker's Gym and found out neither one of you peckerheads has been there in over a month."

"I'm not going back there," I said.

Johnny shook his head. "Me neither."

Flavius glared at me and my brother and then his expression mellowed. "Look, I know what happened there was no picnic for you boys. But sometimes that's just the way the ball bounces, you know? And the best thing to do is get back on that horse. You have to learn to roll with the punches."

Johnny and I waited to see if Flavius had any more empty clichés to offer, but apparently he'd exhausted his inventory.

"We understand what you're saying, Uncle. We just don't want to go back to that gym," said Johnny.

Flavius narrowed his eyes at us, and then an idea struck him. "Then I'll take you somewhere else. Get dressed," he commanded, "and follow me." He drained his coffee cup and rose to leave. "Thanks for breakfast, Dubber." As he walked out the door we heard him yell, "Don't forget your boxing gear."

We stood at the kitchen counter, not quite sure what to do. Our dad chuckled. "Might as well do what he says. Once he gets an idea in his head . . . . Well, you know how he is. There's some warm biscuits in the oven. Grab a couple on your way out."

We followed Flavius to a new place in Corpus called the Baltazar Boxing Gym. It was central city, not far from Hunsacker's place, and surrounded by a neighborhood of shabby shotgun bungalows and a low-slung row of stucco storefronts. The gym itself was a converted auto-parts warehouse. A long, hand-painted sign along the top of the building had the gym name and a picture of a crown with a pair of boxing gloves dangling from it.

In essential respects, it resembled Stubby's; there was the requisite array of equipment—the speed bags along the wall, the heavy bags hanging from the ceiling, skip ropes, free weights, and, of course, the elevated canvas ring. Pictures and posters of boxers and boxing competitions lined the walls. But one notable difference was the floor; it was painted red—a bright crimson red that spilled out into the gym like an oil slick. Johnny and I hesitated before stepping over the threshold.

"What's with the floor?" Johnny asked.

"Red makes you more aggressive," said Flavius. "It's a scientific fact."

Maybe he was right; it certainly helped explain why my red-haired uncle had spent most of his life looking for fights.

"More confident," said a trim, compact man who appeared from the wings, "not necessarily more aggressive." The Mexican man appeared to be in his mid-thirties and carried himself in a way that made me suspect he'd been in the military.

"Same damn thing," our uncle said, testily.

"You must be Flavius Sweetwater," said the man. "I'm Ralph Baltazar."

Uncle Flavius sized up the man and decided not to take offense. "Nice to know you," he said, pumping Ralph's hand. "These are my nephews, Johnny and Charlie."

"I remember seeing you at Stubby's funeral," said Johnny, extending his hand.

"I was there, alright. Mr. Hunsacker did a lot for me. In fact, he helped me start this gym," Ralph looked around the converted warehouse, "even though, technically, he knew it would make us competitors. I respected the man a great deal."

Johnny and I nodded, silently acknowledging, and sharing, Ralph's respect for our former trainer.

"So, you boys are interested in boxing?"

"Damn straight they are," said Flavius. "But they've got some catching up to do." He gave us a disapproving glance. "They've been slacking off for over a month."

I personally didn't think playing varsity football constituted "slacking off," but I wasn't about to speak up.

"Well," said Ralph, "I'd be proud to train 'em if they still want to compete. Unless, of course, you're already handling that role, Mr. Sweetwater."

"I've taught these boys a lot," said Flavius. "But I don't have the time, you know, what with my work in the family business and everything. So, yeah, that'd be okay with me."

To his credit, Ralph Baltazar directed the same question directly to us. "What do you say, guys?"

We looked at each other and nodded. "Sure," said Johnny. "That'd be swell."

Ralph nodded back. "Okay, then." He tilted his head at Flavius and grinned. "You know, your uncle was a heck of a flyweight back in the thirties. 'Riptide' beat 'em all . . . almost."

"Damn right, I did."

"Riptide?" I asked. Johnny and I were both smiling at that one. Flavius had never mentioned his ring name to us.

"What the hell are you boys standing there for?" Flavius said crossly. "Go put on your togs. Did you think this was a social visit?"

"Sure thing, Riptide," said Johnny.

Flavius shot Johnny a dirty look and then turned to Ralph Baltazar, our new trainer. "As you can see, my nephews are a couple of wiseasses. They give you any lip, just smack 'em, okay?"

Later, Ralph declined my uncle's "kind offer" to hang around and assist and thanked him for entrusting him with his nephews. "We'll get along just fine, Mr. Sweetwater," he assured him. After he walked Flavius outside, he took us to the dressing room and assigned us a locker. While we changed, Ralph talked. "You boys are already familiar with the gym rules because I use the same ones Stubby used at his place. Like I said before, he taught me just about everything I know about boxing. He was a hell of guy."

We agreed.

"By the way, if either of you is planning to enter the Gloves competition in January, my gym will be happy to sponsor you. We've got twelve boxers already signed up to compete." He looked at Johnny. "I believe you fought in the welterweight division last year; I remember watching you. It looks like you've put on some muscle since then."

"I've moved up to middleweight now," said Johnny.

"What about you, Charlie?"

"I'm a welterweight."

"He's also fifteen," Johnny added. "Won't be sixteen until March."

Ralph saw the look on my face and pursed his lips. "So the Golden Gloves is out."

"It's a stupid rule," I said.

"But a rule they won't fudge on. How bad do you want an official fight?" asked Ralph.

"Bad."

"Well, I can get you one with the AAU, the Amateur Athletic Union, but you'd have to travel to San Antonio to compete. I've already got two boys going in December, one flyweight and one bantamweight."

"I want to compete. Just tell me what I gotta do."

Ralph held up a finger. "Before we commit to anything," he said, "I'd kind of like to see where we're at, boxing-wise. You'd be fighting in the fifteen/sixteen-year-old division, Charlie, and I wanna make sure you're advanced enough to handle some of the older, bigger boys. I'll look around and see if I can find sparring partners for you two."

"My brother and I spar with each other all the time," said Johnny. "Why don't you put us in the ring together?"

Ralph said okay, and after we'd warmed up, he helped us wrap our hands and put on our gloves. "You boys boxed for Stubby, so you know the drill. Give me two or three good rounds."

We climbed into the ring, and Ralph gave the word. Several boxers wandered over to check us out. Johnny and I were eager to make a good first impression, so we went at each other pretty hard at first. After we'd rested for a minute, Ralph instructed us to slow it down a bit. "Okay, this round pick your punches. Make 'em count. Let's go."

Football had kept us in shape . . . for football, but this was a different kind of conditioning, so we were both pretty winded after three hard rounds. Our month away from the gym had set us back, and we realized we weren't anywhere near fighting shape.

"Well, I have to say," Ralph said at the end, "Stubby and your Uncle Flavius did a good job teaching you two the fundamentals." He began unlacing our gloves. "I like what I saw."

"We learned from our friend, Jesse Martel, too," I said. I don't know why I felt the need to declare my allegiance to Feo. Almost everyone, including Ralph Baltazar, I assumed, figured that he had killed Stubby Hunsacker. I guess I wanted my new trainer to know where I stood on the issue.

Ralph was quiet, deciding how to respond. "One of the finest boxers I've ever had the pleasure of watching," he said before looking up. "So, Charlie, you've got about four weeks to improve your conditioning and get ready for San Antonio. Not much time, but I think it's do-able, don't you?"

I nodded. "I'll make it, Coach."

"And you, Johnny, you've got a couple of months before the Gloves tournament. Are you two ready to go to work?"

We said yes and promised Ralph we'd be there every day after school and on the weekend too.

"I like your fire, but I ask my competitive boxers to take off one day a week. You pick the day. I don't care which it is. The body needs a chance to rejuvenate, you know." He pulled off our gloves and showed us where to hang them after sparring. "Now, follow me and I'll tour you through the club."

As Ralph Baltazar walked us through the workout stations, we greeted several fighters we knew from previous Gloves tournaments, or who had changed gyms after Stubby died. The gym was even more of a mixed bag than Stubby's, with about an equal number of whites, Mexicans, and Negroes, from young teens to full-grown men. Ralph told us that two professional boxers trained there as well, and he pointed out the promotional posters from some of their fights. All in all, it seemed like a pretty good group of guys and a decent gym. Mounted over the door to Ralph's office, I noticed a picture of about a dozen soldiers, confirming my guess that he'd been in the service. The caption read, "Dog Squad, Korea, 1952," and a young, smiling Ralph Baltazar was squatting on his haunches in the very front.

After our workout, we dressed, showered, and were heading out the door when we bumped into Karl McDevitt and his permanent shadow, Boyd Parker.

"Oh, shit," I muttered.

"Well I'll be go-to-hell, Boyd," mouthed Karl. "It's the Stink-water brothers. Please don't tell me Ralph's gonna let those two losers train in our gym."

Boyd, as usual, didn't say a word. He was a weedy, vaguely creepy-looking kid who always seemed to walk or stand a step behind Karl.

"Get used to it, McDevitt," said Johnny. "We'll be here every day, in case you're looking for somebody to spar with."

We brushed past them, and I heard Karl's voice behind us. "You two better watch your step around here. You don't have Stubby and that commie coon to protect you anymore."

I stopped and was about to turn around, but Johnny pushed me forward. "Not now, brother. Not here. It's only our first day."

"By the way," Karl yelled, "y'all sure got a sweet car." We could hear him cackling inside the gym as we exited. "Or had one, anyway."

When we got to the Jeep, we saw a deep scratch in the paint, running the entire length of the wagon. "That son-of-a-bitch keyed our car!" I said.

"He sure as hell did," said Johnny, as he ran his finger across the scarred door panels. He scanned the parking lot, searching for Karl's ride, and then a roguish smile appeared on his face. "Hop in. I've got an idea."

Johnny drove us to a marine supply store near the ship channel.

"You gonna tell me what we're doing?" I asked, as we walked inside.

"Payback, brother man. Payback."

Johnny picked out a stout padlock and had the store cut us ten feet of half-inch galvanized anchor chain. Then he asked to see the boat anchors. "Whaddaya got that's cheap? Used, even?"

We settled on a rusty two hundred-pound "mushroom" anchor the guy found out in the scrap yard. He said he'd give it to us for free if we were strong enough to lug it to our Jeep. Mushroom anchors weren't used much on the Texas coast because they were hard to set in the Gulf's sandy sea bottom and tended to drag, but they were heavy as hell and perfect for our purposes. For an extra six bucks they welded the anchor onto the chain for us.

When we returned to the boxing gym, we parked next to Karl's bike, a chopped-out Triumph Bonneville, and went to work on it. We wrapped the chain through every hole and crevice—through the forks, the spokes, the pipes, around the handlebars—until it resembled a Chicago mob victim, ready for a watery grave. The last few feet of chain were welded fast to the anchor, which sat incongruously on the asphalt next to the bike. We padlocked the loose end of the chain back onto itself and tossed the key down a nearby storm drain. We stood back and admired our work.

"Run aground," said Johnny.

"High and dry," I added.

Satisfied, we peeled out of the parking lot with the radio blaring, singing and dancing "The Loco-motion" along with Little Eva, and imagining Karl's face when he discovered that his chopped-out symbol of freedom, rebellion, and bad-assery had been magically transformed into ballast.

CHAPTER 22

I arranged to see Carmen on Sunday, taking the path of least resistance and using Veronica as a go-between. The girls agreed to meet Johnny and me at the Lawrence Street T-Head on Corpus Christi Bay. We ate lunch at the marina, and then Johnny and Veronica left in her car to catch a movie. Carmen and I strolled along the bayfront promenade, holding hands and enjoying the warm, humid breeze.

We talked about Jesse and about his pending trial, which was scheduled to start at the beginning of the year. Carmen said her mother was so angry about the bias against him that she'd stated she wouldn't set foot inside the courtroom—the *"tribunal illegal"* she called it.

"It's Spanish for 'kangaroo court,'" Carmen added. "Things have been pretty tense at our house. It seems like she's angry at everyone."

"Including me."

Carmen sighed. "It's not you so much. I think it has more to do with what happened between her and my dad."

"She's afraid I'll be that gringo that's going to knock up her daughter and ruin her life?"

"Yeah, pretty much."

We walked in silence for awhile, thinking about our futures. Mine was pretty fuzzy, but I could have spent a big chunk of it just walking along the waterfront with Carmen, holding hands.

"Anyway, my mom's returning to Cuba after the trial. She announced it to the dancers on Friday."

"What happens to the studio?" I asked, trying not to sound upset. If her mom was leaving for Cuba, it seemed to me that Carmen would be going as well, whether she wanted to or not.

"She's selling it to one of her assistants . . . practically giving it away, actually. To a Ukrainian dancer who defected from Russia. Ironic, isn't it?"

"Sure, if you say so."

Carmen squeezed my hand. "Hey, don't be such a sourpuss. Anyway, I think she's going to let me finish high school here in Corpus."

This was very good news. "Where will you live?"

"Veronica's family has offered to take me in until the end of the school term in May. So, after Christmas, we won't have to sneak around anymore, eh?"

"I'm surprised your mom is being so cool about this. I figured she'd be dead set against you staying here."

"She was, and still is. But I fought her pretty hard on it. In fact, I've been a perfect bitch about the whole thing. I reminded her that my eighteenth birthday is next month, and if I wanted to, I could choose to live with my dad. He isn't as bad a guy as my mother makes him out to be, at least as a father."

"Somewhere in Italy, right?"

"Right, and after I graduate, I might still do it. You could come visit me, Charlie. How's your Italian?"

"Almost as good as my Spanish."

"Well, you better get busy, buster."

"Italian and Spanish, I'll get right on it."

"*Buenísimo!* That's your word of the day."

"*Buenísimo!*" I picked her up and swung her around. "You know what?" I said. "I think I'm going to buy you a frozen custard . . . *un gelato custardo.*"

We took the Jeep to Fran's Frozen Custard on South Chaparral and then drove around while we ate our cones.

"Isn't your old boxing gym around here?" Carmen asked.

"Not too far. Why?" I had no desire to see *that* place again, especially on such a splendid afternoon.

"I've been wondering what happened to Diego, that boy who hung out there. The one who was missing an arm."

"I'm not sure what happened to him. I haven't seen him in almost a month."

Carmen licked her custard quietly, thinking, I presumed, about Naco Flores. I felt a pang of guilt. I'd hardly given the kid a second thought since Stubby was killed.

When I glanced at Carmen, she was looking at me. "Should we go see if he's at the gym?"

I was turning the car around before she finished her sentence.

I wasn't prepared for the emotion I felt when we drove up to the old Centennial Building. I had to force myself to get out of the car and go inside. Carmen held my hand tightly, sensing the violence and wrong that had happened there. We walked though the gym, and several boxers I knew nodded in recognition. In the corner, I saw Pete Lopez making the speed bag dance, and I went over to greet him.

"Charlie, *que pasa?*" he said, smiling. "It's great to see you, man. You here to train?"

"No, Carmen and I were in the neighborhood."

She smiled at him and they gave each other a brief *abrazo;* Pete was too sweaty for any prolonged embrace. He gave the bag one last whack and then held it still. "Haven't seen you for awhile, man. What've you Sweetwater boys been up to?"

"Football mostly, but now that the season's over, we've started training again. We moved over to Baltazar's on 19th Street. You should check it out."

"Yeah? I might do that. It's been dead around here since . . . ." he stopped, embarrassed by the inadvertent pun and changed the subject. "Hey, that was some pretty crazy shit happened over the last few weeks, huh?"

There'd been a lot of crazy shit happen to me over the last few weeks, but I assumed Pete was referring to the Missile Crisis.

"Unreal."

Pete saw me surveying the gym, and he followed my gaze. "Seems different, doesn't it? It's not the same since Stubby passed. It's like part of the place died with him, you know?"

I did know. "Who's running it now?"

Pete shrugged. "Some squares from the police department. They don't know beans about boxing." He looked over at Carmen. "How's Feo?"

"*Mas o menos,*" she answered. "So-so," she repeated for my benefit.

"Tell him hello for me. Rachel, too, if you happen to see her."

Carmen said she would, and then she gave me a nudge in the ribs to remind me to ask about Naco.

"Oh, Pete, you haven't seen Naco Flores around here lately, have you?"

Pete shook his head. "He came by every day for awhile, just like he always did, you know? He'd mope around the gym, asking everyone where Stubby was, when he was coming back . . . . It was pretty sad, man." Pete looked up at me. "He asked about you, too, *Flaco.*"

It felt like Pete had hit me in the gut.

"Anyway, the new manager finally kicked him out and told him not to come back. You know how Naco is, throwing those medicine balls around and everything." Pete took an angry whack at the speed bag. "They said Naco was *dangerous,* can you believe it?"

In the office I saw a couple of cops dressed in grey sweats seated around Stubby's desk smoking cigarettes and sipping on soft drinks. The office glass had been replaced, but plywood still covered the area where the explosion blew out the wall. A schedule of the gym's new hours was chalked onto the blackboard. Stubby's Space Race tally had been erased, which really ticked me off for some reason. All of a sudden, I had to get out of there.

"Pete, I'm serious about that other gym," I said. "The trainer there, Ralph Baltazar, he seems like a good egg. You should think about it."

"Okay, Charlie. I will. Hey, Carmen . . . . Is Rachel still going out with Mr. Rebel Without a Clue?"

"She broke up with him," Carmen answered, "but don't waste your time on her. She's never dated anyone more than a couple of months. She's a hopeless *coqueta* . . . a flirt."

Pete smiled thinly. "Yeah, I guess I knew that. But, *dang,* she sure was fun." We turned to leave, but Pete grabbed my arm. "Hey, Charlie? Now that I think about it, a couple of times I'm pretty sure I saw Naco hanging out in the park out back. At least I think it was him. Might be worth checking out."

We left the gym and walked through South Bluff Park. Sure enough, we found Naco sitting on a park bench under a tree, looking at the comic strips in an old newspaper. When he saw me, he jumped up from the bench and put his one arm around me. "Flaco and Naco!" he said idiotically. He gave Carmen a hug too, smiling his bucktoothed smile.

We sat and talked for a while, or rather Carmen conversed with him in Spanish, and I sat there and listened. A couple of times she looked at me with a pained expression on her face.

"What's he saying?" I asked.

She held up her hand for me to be patient, and after another few minutes of talking and pointing, she stood up. "We're giving Diego a ride home," she said. "We're going to meet his mother."

On the way to Diego's house, which was near the ship channel in a rundown neighborhood off Port Avenue, Carmen and Naco continued talking. I'd never heard him jabber so much in my life. He directed us to his house, and we pulled up in front. The shotgun shack was about three missing boards short of a teardown, with a raggedy couch and a partially disassembled outboard motor crowding the small porch. The air stunk of refinery by-products, and beyond the small neighborhood, I could see the crude oil cracking towers and the masts of cargo ships.

Naco walked in straight away, but we stood on the porch and waited for him to get his mom. We heard voices and then footsteps until a woman answered the door. She might have been in her late twenties and even pretty at one time, but hard living had taken a toll. I remembered Pete saying she was an alcoholic. She gathered her house robe around her and peered at us through the screen door.

"Diego is in trouble?" she asked warily.

"No, nothing like that," I answered. "We're friends of his. We just wanted to make sure he got home alright."

The woman looked at us more carefully, and when we didn't leave the porch she asked, "What you want?"

Carmen noted the strong accent and asked her something in Spanish.

"Where are you from?" she asked suspiciously.

"Cuba."

"Humph. Everyone is white in Cuba?"

"No. Are you Diego's mother?"

She nodded and studied us with bleary eyes. A man's voice called out from the back bedroom, demanding to know who she was talking to, goddamnit. When Diego's mother didn't answer, the man staggered out of the room and came to the door, clearly well into his Sunday afternoon bottle.

"Who the hell did you bring to the house?" he yelled at Diego, who shrank back against the wall. The man was white, obviously not Naco's natural father.

"They say they are friends of Diego," said the woman.

The man laughed. "He doesn't have any friends. What the hell do y'all want?"

"We just wanted to see where Diego lived," I answered, a little intimidated by the guy. He looked like a roughneck or a dockworker, with a beer gut and ropy muscles. Through the dirty screen door, I noticed a hardhat sitting on a kitchen table, next to a half-empty bottle of gin and a pack of smokes.

"We were concerned about Diego, that's all," Carmen added.

The mother yelled something in Spanish at her boy and then turned to us. "He no go to school. He no work. I don' know what to do with him."

"You know what to do," said the boyfriend. "Send him to that retard school. Let the state take care of him. Hell, he'd be better off anyway." He looked at the boy. "Hey kid, you want to go to a *special* school? Be around other kids *just like you?*"

"Yes," Naco said.

"What'd I tell you?" he said.

"He say yes to everything," the mother answered with exasperation.

"Diego just got a new job," I said. I'm not sure why I said it. I guess I didn't want to see Naco end up in the mental institution for the rest of his life. I'd heard horror stories about what happens in that place.

"Yeah? Where?" demanded the man.

"Baltazar's Boxing Gym, on 19th Street."

"How much?" asked the mother.

"How much what?"

"How much money?"

"Minimum wage," I lied. "At least thirty hours a week."

Naco's mother and her boyfriend looked at each other. I could see their greedy minds calculating the boy's earnings and converting them into booze and cigarettes.

"When does he start?" she asked.

"Supposed to start today. The owner of the gym sent us over because he needed an address to fill out the paperwork. Diego couldn't remember it."

"Figures," sneered the boyfriend. He turned and walked back into the kitchen, wondering aloud why anyone would hire a one-armed spic retard.

The mother looked at Carmen and asked her something in Spanish. Carmen nodded and crossed herself. "Yes, he is telling the truth," she answered.

The mother motioned for her son to go with us, and practically pushed him out the door. "When does he bring some money?" she asked.

"We'll be sure and ask," I answered. I couldn't wait to leave that wretched place.

As we drove away, with Naco in the backseat wondering what the hell was happening, Carmen looked over at me. "I sure hope this works, Charlie."

"Me too. Especially considering I made it up on the spot."

Thankfully, my gut impression about Ralph Baltazar proved to be correct. After we'd explained Naco's situation, Ralph agreed to hire the boy part time: sweeping floors, wiping down the weights and weight benches, and putting away equipment. He even said he'd pay part of Naco's salary off the books, so the kid could buy some new shoes or maybe an ice cream cone once in awhile. "Stubby told me about this boy, and about his crummy home life," he said. "Kids like him need all the help they can get."

I couldn't have agreed more. Ralph thanked us and said he'd make sure Naco knew how to get home on his own.

Carmen scooted next to me in the car and put her head on my shoulder as we drove back to the T-Head to meet Veronica and my brother. "I'll bet Stubby Hunsacker is smiling down on you right now . . . after what you did."

"It was your idea, Carmen. I should've checked on the kid weeks ago. But it's a nice thought."

I tried to remember if I'd ever seen Stubby smile in the four years I'd known him and concluded that I hadn't. Stubby's character benchmarks were simple and Spartan. He didn't reward good behavior; he expected it. His highest form of praise was a brief nod and a grunt . . . and that was dispensed rarely. But whenever he gave it, it had meant more to me than a whole cheering section.

―――――

CHAPTER 23

When Johnny and I went to visit Jesse late that afternoon, we didn't even make it to the elevator before we were intercepted by our two new friends from the "government." They put us in an interrogation room and sat us down at a table. The shabby, linoleum-floored room, with its beat-up furniture and flat overhead lighting suited them—like they spent lots of time in such rooms.

The older man, the one with the Brylcreem hair and horn-rimmed glasses, looked even crankier than before. The younger one tried to look angry, too, but it came off more as if we'd just hurt his feelings.

"You boys kind of jacked us around the last time we talked," said the young one. "Why is that?"

Johnny and I were silent.

He pulled a small notebook out of his pocket, consulted a page, and then looked up at me. "Charlie, you're really in with Jesse's family. Even have dinner at their house now and then."

"Just the one time."

"Any interesting dinner guests?"

I knew right then that this was about Ramón Cruz. "A guy was there who claimed he was from Mexico, but later I found out he was from Cuba."

"He told you that at the dinner party? That he was Cuban?"

"No, he told me that another time."

"So you've had multiple meetings with this fellow. You just said you only saw him once. Which is it?" He tried to give me a hard-case stare but couldn't quite pull it off.

Johnny leaned forward. "He said he only had dinner at Carmen's house once. Who are you guys, anyway?" he asked, looking at the older man, who scowled at my brother with paternal condescension, trying to browbeat him into submission. But Johnny didn't bully easily, and he stared right back at him.

"So, what's this Cuban's name?" the young one asked me.

"Ramón," I answered. "He said his name was Ramón Cruz."

The man scribbled the name in his notepad. "And do you have any idea why this Ramón would be interested in your girlfriend's family?"

I remembered Carmen asking me not to say anything that might jeopardize her mother's chance at having her own dance academy in Cuba, but something told me these two guys weren't interested in that. "He said he was a ballet fan," I answered.

The young guy laughed. "Ballet. Sure, that's what it was." He walked around the table and stood directly behind me, his hands bearing down on my shoulders. "Let's try again."

"This is bullshit," said Johnny. "How about let's be straight with each other? You guys are some sort of government spooks chasing Cuban spies, right? Maybe if you told us who you were and what you wanted, this would go faster. Trying to glare us to death isn't gonna work very well."

The older guy nodded at his partner. "Okay," said the younger one, "let's say you're right. Now, let's *do* talk about Ramón. Was he over at Jesse's house often?"

"At least three times, that I know of," I said, wondering how much I should trust the two agents. They noted my hesitation.

"Listen, kid, if you know anything or anybody that could be considered a threat to the safety and security of the United States of America, it's your patriotic duty to tell us."

I'd always thought of myself as patriotic, when I thought about it at all, which was seldom. Ramón was in this country under false pretenses and clearly up to no good. But at the same time, I was worried about the fallout for Carmen, and for Jesse and Doña Delfín if I said too much. I looked at Johnny, and he shrugged.

"Might as well," he said. "It being our patriotic duty and all."

I took a deep breath and told them everything I knew about Ramón: the dinner conversation at Carmen's house, the ballet offer for Doña Delfín, the argument he'd had with Jesse on their front lawn, the assault on the porch step. Johnny added a few details when he could. To my relief, the agents seemed completely uninterested in Doña Delfín and the ballet academy offer and stayed on the relationship between Ramón and Jesse Martel. They asked me about my jailhouse conversations with Jesse and perked up when I mentioned that Ramón tried to make a deal with him for his return to Cuba.

"What was Jesse's answer?"

"He told him to take a hike."

The two men were paying close attention now. "Why?" continued the young one. "He would rejoin his family. He'd become a national sports hero. He'd probably become one of Fidel's best friends."

"He didn't liked it when Ramón brought Feo's family into it. Told him they'd make it hard on his wife and daughter if he didn't return to Cuba."

"Seems like that'd convince him right there."

"Feo doesn't like being pushed around."

"Or maybe Martel rejected it because he was holding out for a better deal. Maybe he wanted money in return for giving up his pro career."

I shook my head angrily. "No. That was never it."

"Look," said Johnny. "Jesse wanted to live here, he wanted to work here, and he wanted to raise his family here."

"Yet he left them in Cuba while he came here to get rich as a prize fighter."

"He left before the revolution," said Johnny. "He was going to bring his wife and daughter here with the money he earned from his first pro fight. I heard people make it out all the time."

"Not if Castro's secret police know they're flight risks. I wouldn't be surprised if Martel's relatives haven't been locked up already. Those fanatics will do anything to get what they want."

I remembered Ramón saying the same thing about the Americans.

Johnny fidgeted in his chair. I could tell he was getting frustrated. "Why are you guys asking us these stupid questions? The big question, the only question, is who killed Stubby Hunsacker? We know it wasn't Feo."

"Does Jesse talk much about his family?" asked the agent, ignoring my brother's question. "Does he act like he misses them?"

But Johnny wasn't so easily redirected. "Shit, of course he misses them, what do you think? Why don't we talk about the Florida mob?" he said. "Why aren't you investigating those guys?"

"The Florida mob? For what?" asked the agent.

"For Stubby Hunsacker's murder." Johnny told them about the incident with the two goons at the gym and the explosion a week later. Their reaction was odd. They barely listened to his story and didn't take any notes, even when Johnny mentioned Santo Traficante and John Roselli.

After Johnny finished talking, the agent simply said, "It wasn't them."

"But how do you—"

"It wasn't them," he said again. "They're on our side."

I didn't understand what he meant—how could the Mafia be on the same side as our government?—but evidently Johnny *did* understand.

"You mean, they're *against* Castro."

The young agent looked exasperated, and when he turned to his dour associate, the older man spoke for the first time.

"Yeah, they're against Castro, son, and they're against Communism. Now, let's cut the crap. You might have noticed that two weeks ago we almost went to war with Russia. And what we're trying to determine is where this Cuban boxer's loyalties lie. He's a celebrity in some circles. That makes him a person of interest to us."

Johnny and I looked at each other, both of us baffled. "His loyalties?" said Johnny. "Mister, I don't see that any of that matters. Commie or not, in two months Jesse is going on trial for murder, and unless we find out who killed Stubby Hunsacker, he's finished."

"I think Ramón Cruz is the guy you ought to be questioning," I said.

The hatchet-faced agent looked up quickly. "Do you know where he is?" When I didn't answer right away he added, "You have a choice to make, kid. If you *do* know, and decide to keep jerking us off, you'll be aiding an enemy of your country—which is a felony, just so you know."

The old guy leaned forward and looked directly at me. "Also known as treason, son."

Even though I had no idea where Ramón was and couldn't think of anything I'd said or done that would've helped him, these guys were beginning to scare me. I could feel sweat running down my armpits as the two agents watched me.

Johnny broke the silence. "We don't know where he is. And my guess is, you don't either. Must be embarrassing to have to learn about a Cuban secret agent operating under your noses from a couple of teenagers, huh?"

Abruptly the older agent scooted back his chair. "Balls," he said. "We're wasting our time with these smart-mouth kids, Larry. Get 'em out of here."

Larry stood up and motioned for us to follow him out the door. We walked down the corridor scratching our heads. On the way to the elevator, he handed us a mostly blank business card with a telephone number on it. "You be sure and call this number if you find out anything that can help us."

"Right," said Johnny, taking the card and stuffing it into his back pocket. "And you guys be sure and call us when you find out who really killed Stubby Hunsacker."

"Oh, we'll find somebody," Larry answered.

Outside the courthouse, I asked Johnny what he thought the agents—whoever they worked for—were after. "The courts are going to give Feo the death penalty unless things change before January, and all those clowns want to know is whether he's pro-American or pro-Castro? I don't get it."

"I don't either," said Johnny. "Gotta be a bigger picture. There's something going on we can't see."

CHAPTER 24

When we walked into the gym on Friday after school, the place was buzzing about Cassius Clay knocking out Archie Moore, the reigning light heavyweight, the night before in Los Angeles. Clay had called the knockout round before the fight, something he was in the habit of doing. As we headed to change, all the young fighters in the gym were bouncing around, trying to mimic Clay's floating, dancing style.

"Personally, I think he's a smartass," said Ralph Baltazar, "but he's got all the tools." Ralph looked a little sad. He'd seen Moore come up.

Ralph worked us hard during our first week at his gym, and we found that he was instructive and knowledgeable about the sport. He may not have had Stubby's experience, but he made up for it with communication skills that made our old trainer seem like the Sphinx by comparison.

For a new gym, Baltazar's had attracted a solid bunch of boxers. It helped that Ralph had been a popular local fighter in the 1950s; his name and photo were featured on some of the fight posters tacked to the walls. He'd been a fan favorite at the Friday night fights in the Municipal Auditorium. They'd called him "Battlin' Baltazar, the Tex-Mex Tornado." Promoters love that shit. Several times during that first week, we saw him glove up and spar with some of his boxers, and we could tell he still had skills.

My brother and I got along great with the guys, and our standing in the gym went up considerably when we convinced Pete Lopez to come over. Our reputation had also been boosted by the early Christmas present we'd given Karl McDevitt. It had been a week ago, and everyone was still laughing about it. Karl brought people together; everyone in the gym thought he was a dick.

Thankfully, we hadn't run into him yet, but I knew that he wouldn't be one to forgive and forget. Witnesses said he went berserk when he discovered his anchor-wrapped Triumph in the parking lot. I just hoped I wasn't alone the next time I saw him.

After our workout, Johnny, Pete, and I discussed our plans for the weekend.

"The girls are rehearsing for the *Nutcracker* ballet performances they'll be doing in December," I said, "and Carmen said they'd be in the studio most of the weekend."

"What about Rachel?" asked Pete.

"Since we're speaking of nutcrackers," Johnny added, deadpan.

Pete reached up and thumped his ear. "Screw you, white boy."

I smiled. "I don't know, Pete. I'm not even sure she's dancing anymore."

Pete nodded his head sullenly. He couldn't seem to let her go.

After a short discussion, we decided we'd meet up the next morning at the Horace Caldwell Pier with our surfboards and our fishing tackle. We wanted to be prepared for whichever option offered the most promise. Surfing or fishing. Some choices you look forward to making.

—

Late that night, I was awakened by the urgent ringing of the telephone, which clanged around our echo chamber of a house like a bell clapper. Dad was shrimping again, so I stumbled into the living room and picked up the receiver.

"Charlie? Rachel's been hurt." Carmen's voice was ragged, scared. I leaned against our kitchen counter while she gave a halting and disjointed account of what had happened. Before hanging up, I agreed to meet her at the hospital in Corpus as soon as I could get there.

"It'll be okay," I told her, "Rachel will be okay." When I hung up the phone, Johnny was standing beside me. "How bad?"

"Bad. She's still in the emergency room at Spohn Hospital."

"Car wreck?"

I shook my head. "Somebody beat her up. A group of guys found her in the old cemetery near the courthouse and ran to an all-night café to call for help. Carmen said she and Veronica haven't been able to see her yet, and no one will give them any details."

We were silent as we drove to the hospital in Corpus, thinking about what had happened to Rachel. It had must have been brutal if she was still in the emergency room.

We found the girls in the waiting area. Carmen ran over and put her arms around me. "Who would do such a thing, Charlie?"

I looked around the waiting room and saw that most of the wooden chairs and worn plaid couches were filled with friends from Rachel's high school, along with members of her family. Cops stood around smoking cigarettes, discussing the usual Friday-night carnage, I gathered. The high schoolers looked distinctly out of place.

Carmen and Veronica pushed us outside and into the hallway before they updated us on Rachel's status. "We finally got a nurse to talk to us," said Veronica. "She's going to make it, but she's lost a lot of blood."

Johnny asked what happened.

Veronica looked away, but Carmen spoke up. "She's bleeding internally, from having something . . . shoved inside her." I must have looked confused so she spelled it out. "She was raped by a stick or a broom handle or something like it. It damaged her insides." Her voice was shaking.

I felt both sickened and enraged. I couldn't believe someone could do something so awful to another human being. It was a brutal assault. But it was also a theft, a humiliation, and an obliteration of this girl's dignity. I wanted to lash out at something, put my fist through the wall.

As usual, Johnny seemed to read my mind. "Easy, little brother." He put a firm hand on my shoulder and moved the conversation to safer ground, asking the girls how Rachel's family was doing.

"It's weird," Veronica answered. "They aren't talking about what *really* happened to her. The mother keeps saying her daughter was mugged, and she's going to be fine."

"They're ashamed to say she was raped," Carmen added more bluntly. "When I came out and said it, they both looked at me like I was deranged."

"Do the cops know who did it?" I asked.

"I don't think so," Veronica answered.

Feeling the need to do something, do anything to help out, Johnny and I offered to get the girls some coffee from the café down the street. Speaking for myself, I wanted to get the hell out of there.

My memories of Cristus Spohn Hospital were hazy, but sufficiently disturbing that I avoided going there unless I absolutely had to. I was five years old when my mom got cancer, and to my young mind, all I knew was that she was healthy, vibrant, and beautiful when she checked into the hospital for "treatment," and then, over the next six weeks I watched these things stripped away from her until finally one day, everyone began talking about her in the past tense. Just the smell of the place made me sad and angry.

We ran into Pete outside the hospital entrance. "Any change?" he asked with concern.

"She's still in the emergency room," Johnny answered. "Did you just get here?"

"No, man. I got here right after they brought her in. I was gettin' the lowdown from some of my friends . . . some of the vatos who found her."

"What'd they say, Pete? Your friends."

"They said it was bad, man. Said she was all cut up and her clothes were scattered around like they got tore off by a wild animal or something."

"Did they see who did it?" Johnny asked.

"They didn't see nobody. And they don't know how long she'd been there when they came by. Two guys stayed with her in the cemetery while the other three ran to get help."

"Why was Rachel in the graveyard?" I asked, trying to puzzle it out. "Or your friends?"

Pete shot me a dirty look. "You sound like the fucking cops. They asked the same thing, like maybe Rachel was asking for it by being where she was, and maybe it was my friends who done this to her. *Cabrones.*" He kicked at a pebble on the sidewalk. In his anger and frustration, Pete was resorting to barrio street lingo I'd never heard him use before.

"Then why would your friends run straight to the nearest telephone and call an ambulance?" asked Johnny.

Pete looked up quickly. "Exactly!"

"Or stay with Rachel until help arrived?" I added.

"No shit! But it sure took the *pinche* police a long time to figure that out. They just let 'em go about an hour ago. Not so much as a fucking thank you for what they done. You know, she could've bled to death if they hadn't found her when they did."

We nodded in agreement. Finally, Johnny asked the question. "Pete, do you know if she might have been out with you-know-who tonight?"

Pete's eyes narrowed. "I don't know yet, but I'll kill that fucker if it was him that did this to her." He paused and took a breath. "If she *was* with him, she didn't tell nobody about it. I thought they'd broke up, but Rachel . . . she's unpredictable, you know? She could've met up with him somewhere."

"Could've," said Johnny. "Where's her car?"

"I don't know."

"Do the girls know?"

"I was going to ask them about it, but . . . ." Pete looked away. "Some cop made me leave the waiting room before they arrived."

I looked at him. "Why?"

He kicked the ground. "The dude said Rachel's family didn't want me hanging around."

At first I didn't understand, but then realized it was because Pete was Mexican. "That's bullshit," I protested.

Johnny placed his hands on our backs and propelled us down the sidewalk. "Let's get that coffee for the girls . . . then we'll see if we can find Rachel's car."

As we walked to the café, I could feel the wind shifting to the north. I felt tired to the bone. But at least we were doing *something*.

The waitresses who served us were just finishing up their shift, but before they removed their aprons they poured our coffees and recounted with melodramatic gusto their version of the night's drama: the three boys running into the restaurant pleading for someone to call an ambulance, the wailing sirens, and then the cops carrying the "Mezkins" off to the police station.

"I tell ya, when those boys first come in here they were scared as the dickens," said one of the waitresses.

"Like they'd seen a ghost in that graveyard," said the other, shaking her head. "After they called for the ambulance, Lorraine told 'em they'd better call the cops, too."

Lorraine nodded. "I didn't want the police gettin' the wrong idea about those boys, ya know? But it didn't make no difference."

"They hauled 'em in all the same," said the other waitress.

Lorraine cast a glance at Pete, and then, in a low voice, said to me and Johnny, "They were *helping*, you understand. Being Good Samaritans." Then she turned to Pete and repeated for his benefit, "Really trying to help," as if she were giving him a great gift by pointing this out.

It was an innocent enough gesture, even well intentioned, and I suppose the woman was proud of herself for recognizing the boys' valiant actions, proud of herself for acknowledging and praising these *good* Mexicans, as opposed to all those *other* Mexicans. But from Pete's perspective, it had to sting. Maybe he was used to hearing these patronizing reactions from white people whenever he acted like any decent person would act. Still, it pissed me off, and I was about to say something when Johnny stepped in front of me and handed me two Styrofoam cups of coffee.

"Stay focused," he said.

Back at the hospital, when we informed the girls that we were going to search for Rachel's car, they insisted on going with us.

As we cruised down Ocean Drive, we made a list of all the likely haunts: Snapka's, Pick's, the dance studio, the Center and the Ritz theaters, the Thunderbird Drive-In Theater, Lichtenstein's Department Store, the Black Diamond Oyster Bar, the Gulf Skating Rink, the High-Hat Drive-In. We even went by Buccaneer Stadium and the high school gym.

"Does anyone know where Karl McDevitt lives?" asked Pete.

None of us did.

Back at the hospital, the head nurse told us that Rachel's condition was stable and they had moved her into the intensive care unit. But per her parents' request, visiting restrictions still applied; no one but immediate family was allowed to see her. By then, all of us were edgy and exhausted, and it seemed like a good time to take a break. Johnny and I decided to go home.

As we drove over the tall hump of the Harbor Bridge, I gazed down at the North Beach neighborhood below. It looked gloomy and pitiful and dark. Very different from the view on the other side of the high bridge, where the shimmering lights of Corpus—The Sparkling City by the Sea—formed a bright crescent along the edge of the bay. North Beach was a narrow peninsula with crushed shell streets and block after block of dilapidated buildings with flat tarpaper roofs.

Once it had been a popular tourist destination, full of boisterous vacationers, stevedores, and sailors, along with local well-to-do families.

Billboards promoted it as Texas's own Coney Island, "the Playground of the South." I had vivid childhood memories of the long fishing pier, the saltwater swimming pool with its high-diving board, and next to it, the Surf Bath House, where you could rinse off in a fresh-water shower after swimming, and then order an ice cream float from the soda fountain.

I loved walking through the colorful, light-filled amusement park with my folks—both of them then—taking rides on the roller coaster, the Tilt-A-Whirl, and the carousel. You could see clear to Mustang Island from the top of the Ferris wheel.

Later, when we were a little older, Johnny and I would save up the money we earned working on Ransom Island and then blow most of it playing the penny arcades and viewing the lurid sideshow attractions. How can you *not* go see the Dog-Faced Boy or The Human Caterpillar?

Uncle Rupert insists that he met his first wife at the big dance pavilion that extended out into the bay. And Noble tells the story about how he and his brothers cut the ropes on a circus tent and collapsed it around a rough bunch of carnies in retribution for them beating up Flavius, who no doubt picked the fight in the first place.

But North Beach had changed since then. The carnival and amusement park went broke after the causeway was constructed, and a few years later, when the pivoting Bascule Bridge was replaced by the high-arch Harbor Bridge, people and cars began to hurry past the area as if it were a drunk passed out on the street. You could stare as you went by, but you sure didn't want to stop. A year after the Harbor Bridge was completed, Hurricane Carla took out the piers, the promenade, and most of the beachside restaurants. Now only a few greasy spoons, pawn shops, dollar-a-day flophouses, and a handful of windowless bars remained—bars off the beaten path, bars that people went to when they didn't want to be seen, or found.

"Johnny?"

"What, brother man?"

"Do you think Rachel would've been crazy enough to duck into one of those North Beach joints?"

He eased his foot off the accelerator, thinking about it, and then zipped over to catch the last North Beach exit before the Nueces Bay Causeway. "It's worth a shot," he answered. "And, yeah, I think she's crazy enough."

It was way past closing time, but the joints were open and serving liquor when Johnny and I wandered into the first one on the strip.

Painted-over windows. A beat-up wooden door with an opaque, port-hole-sized window. No "Open" or "Welcome" sign that I could see.

In the dimly-lit interior, several quiet couples huddled at their tables, kissing and clinging to each other. A cluster of card players was seated at another table, enveloped in a cloud of cigarette smoke. Hank Williams played on the jukebox, sounding as mournful as the collection of humanity before us looked. As we approached the bar, a couple of down-and-out types on neighboring stools looked up from their drinks.

"Hey, Clarence," said one of them. "You serving kids in here now?"

The bartender lowered the newspaper he was reading. "The hell y'all doin' in here?" he asked us.

"Maybe they're sellin' Boy Scout cookies," said one of the drunks.

"We're looking for a girl," Johnny explained.

Clarence narrowed his eyes at us. "This is a bar, not a cathouse."

"She's a friend of ours. Goes to Miller High."

"Look, kid, does this look like a malt shop to you?"

"No, sir," Johnny answered. "But this girl was a little . . . lost tonight, if you know what I mean. We're just making sure she didn't come in here. By mistake, of course."

Clarence leaned over the bar. He was fat and smelled like cigars. "Nobody comes here by mistake," he growled. "Except maybe you little shits. Y'all scram, before you damage our reputation."

The drunks at the bar snorted and guffawed at that one, and Johnny and I turned and left.

"Nice place," said Johnny when we were outside. "I hope we didn't catch the clap off the doorknob."

The patrons of the next two bars were about as helpful as the first one, and even more depressing. I remembered the Polaroid photo I'd stashed in the glove box of the car, the one Efrain had taken, and we took it in with us to the all-nite cafés and hotel lobbies we visited next. Most of the people we talked to had the same response. Why would a pretty South-Side princess like that ever set foot in North Beach in the first place? Was she nuts? Look around you.

The stars had disappeared, and the sky was lightening by the time we reached the end of Surfside Boulevard. There we found the tattoo joint run by a guy named "Bill the Beachcomber." He was the closest thing North Beach had to a celebrity, thanks to his international clientele of sailors and dockworkers. Even I'd stuck my head in the door when North Beach was in its heyday.

When we walked in, Bill was etching an extravagant floral design on a broad-backed Mexican man. "I'll be closing after this customer," said Bill. "But you boys can come back this evening."

"Do you ever put tattoos on women?" asked Johnny. I was a little shocked at the notion, but Rachel might consider it if someone planted the idea in her head or else dared her to do it.

"It's rare," said Bill, without looking up from his work. "But I've done it before."

"Do you remember doing one recently for *this* girl?" Johnny held out the photo and pointed to Rachel, who stood smiling next to Pete, her arm around his shoulders.

The beefy Hispanic fellow craned his head around to look at the photo, too. "She goes out with Mexicans?" he asked. "How 'bout you give me her number?"

Johnny ignored the man and kept watching Bill.

"Haven't seen her," he said. "I think I'd remember a girl like that if she came in."

Johnny put the photo in his pocket and sighed.

"She missing or something?" he asked.

"Not exactly, but we're trying to figure out where she went last night."

Bill glanced up and nodded knowingly. "I see. Well, sorry I can't help you boys."

While Johnny was talking, I surveyed the photos of body tattoos Bill had crafted over the years: dragons, devils, mermaids, eagles, anchors. And the names of myriad girlfriends.

"Have you recently tattooed a name, 'Rachel,' on anybody?" I asked.

Bill looked up again. "Rachel the girl in that picture?"

I nodded.

He clicked off his etching tool and rolled back his stool. "That's enough for this session, Lucho. After this heals up, we'll work on it some more . . . in about three weeks or so."

Bill used antiseptic to clean the inflamed area of skin where he'd been working on a cascade of thorns and roses that covered most of Lucho's back. A bandage was applied, and the big Mexican put on his shirt and ambled outside into the dreary morning, but not before asking for Rachel's phone number one last time.

Bill spoke to us while he put away his tools. "I don't normally remember the names I put on my customers. In fact, I usually try to talk 'em out of it, knowing how unpredictable love can be." He chuckled to himself. "But I remember that name, 'Rachel'. The skin had barely healed on this fellow's arm, when he came back asking me to take it off."

"Tall guy? Fit. About twenty-something years old?" asked Johnny. "Kind of an asshole?"

"He rides a motorcycle," I added.

Bill nodded. "Sounds like the guy."

"When did this happen?" asked Johnny. "When did he ask you to remove the name?"

"It was just a couple of days ago, and boy, did he throw a fit when I told him I didn't do tattoo removal. Rough surgery, that. Basically, you have to sand the skin down to the quick. Hurts like a mother. Anyway, I thought I was going to have to use a sap on the guy to get him out of my studio."

"Did he mention why he was in such a hurry to remove the name?" I asked.

"We didn't have a conversation about it, but it was pretty clear he and this girl had had a falling out."

Before we left, Bill the Beachcomber asked if either of us was interested in getting a tattoo. For a moment I imagined how the name *Carmen* might look stenciled across my shoulder, but I recalled Bill's comment about love's unpredictability, and I let the thought go.

CHAPTER 25

Johnny and I purchased another bag of donuts before going to the jailhouse on Sunday morning.

"Well, if it isn't the Katzenjammer Kids," said the desk sergeant. "Y'all here to see your favorite convict?"

Johnny plopped the bag of sinkers on the desk. "Yes, sir. If you'll allow it."

"Well, you're out of luck. Those two Yankee spooks said to keep you boys away from their prisoner." The sergeant opened the bag and peeked inside, selecting a chocolate covered donut and eyeing it thoughtfully. "Can you believe they said that? *Their prisoner?* Like we worked for them. It kind of rubbed us the wrong way, you know?"

We stood silently in front of the sergeant, waiting for him to conclude his conversation with the donut.

"Well, the hell with them. Nueces County signs my paycheck, not the Feds." He took a big bite out of the pastry and picked up the phone. "Clem? Got a couple of boys here to see Martel . . . . Yeah, just let 'em both go up. Screw those assholes."

While we waited for Clem to come down on the elevator, Johnny asked the sergeant if they had any suspects for the assault at the Old Bayview Cemetery.

"Did you know that girl?" he asked.

"She's a friend of ours."

"We don't know who done it yet, but we'll run the sumbitch to ground."

"Can she identify the guy who did it?" I asked.

He shook his head. "Naw, the officer who caught the call said she didn't remember a thing." The sergeant looked at us sympathetically. "She's lucky to be alive, you know. I got a daughter near her age."

The elevator dinged, and Clem told us to follow him up.

"Your uncle owns the ice house on McArdle Road?" he said after the door closed. When we said yes, he nodded in approval. "Swell joint."

Johnny took advantage of the opening and asked Clem if *he* knew anything about Rachel's assault. He told us the same thing as the sergeant. They were working on it.

Unsatisfied with the stock response, I went ahead and started naming names. "I hope you guys questioned her crazy ex-boyfriend, Karl McDevitt. They recently broke up, and he was pretty hot about it."

Clem looked at me sharply and then relaxed. "Look, you didn't hear it from me, but we talked to him already. In fact, he came in here voluntarily, or rather, he came in with his mom." He shook his head, "What a piece a work *she* is. Anyway, yesterday morning the two of 'em showed up at the station and told us they'd heard what happened and that Karl had nothing to do with it. She said she just wanted to prove her son was innocent before we started hassling him. It was kinda weird."

"How'd she prove it?" asked Johnny.

"Apparently, her boy was at a movie on Friday night."

"And y'all believed him?" I said.

Clem shrugged. "He had the ticket stub to prove it and a witness saying he was there."

"Boyd Parker, he's the witness?"

"Right. Kid's name was Parker."

Shit, I thought. Boyd would set fire to his own ass if Karl told him to.

The elevator opened and we walked with Clem down the drab corridor, while he told us how Mavis McDevitt "raised ten kinds of hell" inside the station. "She said we had no right to pick on her son just because some rich girl got beat up. Kept insisting that the Parker kid drove him straight home after the movie, and then he went to bed. Said she'd sue the city if we didn't stop harassing them."

"Harassing? But y'all hadn't even accused him of anything," said Johnny.

"Didn't matter to that woman." He shook his head. "Reminds me of my ex-wife. Anyway, she was convinced we had it in for her boy. And said so pretty loud. She was about to get her ass run in on a disorderly charge, and would've, too, if it hadn't been for Radcliff."

"Harley Radcliff? The detective?"

"Yeah," said Clem, his thin mouth turning down. "Not my favorite guy, but he showed up and managed to get the woman chilled out and off the premises before she got her own self booked."

Johnny and I looked at each other. This was the second time Radcliff had helped out Mavis McDevitt.

We were handed off to the cellblock officer who would frisk us before we entered Jesse's cellblock, but before Clem walked away, Johnny asked him one more question:

"What movie?"

"Say again?"

"What movie did Karl say he went to?"

"Oh, it was *Lawrence of Arabia*."

In the cellblock, Jesse's elation at seeing us turned to sadness when we told him about Rachel. I asked him if something like that could happen to a girl in Cuba.

"There are bad people everywhere, Charlie. *Siempre ha sido, y siempre lo será*. Always been, always will be."

Our conversation turned to boxing, and Jesse said he was glad we'd started training again.

"Maybe tha's why you don' come by to see me lately, eh?" he joked. "You are too busy gettin' in shape."

"It wasn't that, Feo," I answered. "A couple of guys who said they work for the government hijacked us the last two times we tried to see you."

"Ah, so you have met my new friends from the CIA?"

So it really was *the CIA*, I thought. We'd only been half joking about it.

"They asked us a million questions about you and your family," said Johnny. "And when they found out Charlie had met Ramón, well, then they really got excited."

"They know he came here for you," I said. "And I told them about how he threatened to harm your family if you didn't go back to Cuba. I hope it's okay I told them that, Feo."

"It's okay, Charlie." Jesse bobbed his head, puzzling something out. "It's funny, you know? Those guys keep talkin' to me like they *want* me to return and box for Cuba, like there is a chance I can leave this jail and go back there."

"We noticed that too," said Johnny. "It's like they know who murdered Stubby but won't say who it is, unless . . . ." He grabbed the bars and looked at Jesse. "Unless they want you to go back to Cuba and spy for them. Is that it, Feo?"

Jesse paced back and forth in his cell. "They didn' actually *ask* me that, but . . . ."

The idea scared me. The CIA didn't give a shit what happened to Jesse or to his family. They'd already implied they knew he was innocent, yet they were willing to let him rot in jail or go to the chair if he didn't work for them. Was this the way America did business these days? I wondered what Mrs. Audain, my ninth-grade civics teacher, would have thought.

"What would happen if Castro found out you were spying for the CIA?" I asked.

"I am sure *El Comandante* would do what he does to all spies."

"What?"

"He would stand me up against a wall and shoot me."

Jesse saw the look on my face and a deep laugh rumbled from his chest. "There is a saying in Spanish . . . *Estoy entre la espada y la pared.*"

"What does it mean?"

"Literally, it says I am between the sword and the wall. But what it really means is that, either way, I'm fucked."

The block warden opened the door and jangled his keys. "Okay, boys. Time's up."

"What do we do, Feo?" I asked.

"I don' know, Charlie; I don' know."

When we were outside the building, I repeated the question to Johnny, adding, "We've got to do something, or Jesse is going to die." In the movies, it would have sounded melodramatic. But standing there on the courthouse steps, it hit us full force. This was really happening.

My brother agreed. "We have to find out who killed Stubby."

———

CHAPTER 26

Dad proposed Johnny and I kick off the Thanksgiving break by helping him do some work on his shrimp boat. Dad had never been a big holiday nut, and after Mom died he seemed to lose interest almost entirely. For Christmas last year, we ate TV dinners in front of the tube and then changed out a bilge pump on the *Ramrod*.

It was a cold, drizzly morning, and we squatted on the Fulton Harbor pier mending Dad's trawl nets and fantasizing about the exciting lives we would live once we got the hell out of Rockport-Fulton. We'd pretty much made up our minds that when we finished high school, our futures would not involve shrimp, shrimping, or commercial fishing, in any way.

But our career paths were still a little murky.

"I see myself as a diplomat," Johnny mused. "A globe-trotting ambassador for truth, justice, and the American way."

"You know you'd be taking orders from the President, right? Or possibly some asshole from the CIA?"

"Then why don't *you* become President? I'll help you get elected, and then I'll become your closest advisor. You can be Jack and I'll be Bobby.

"Naw. I never pictured myself as a politician. But I *am* going to live in another country. Spain, Argentina . . . somewhere semi-exotic. Somewhere with old churches and nice beaches. A volcano'd be nice, too."

"And do what?"

"Doesn't matter. Be a philosopher, maybe. But I'll learn to speak Spanish, and I'll become an expert on the customs, the food, the fishing . . . and the girls, of course. I'll go native."

"Sounds like a good plan. Maybe you could work on a Mexican shrimp boat. What's the Spanish word for 'trawl net'?"

I plucked a rotten cigar fish out of the net webbing and threw it at my brother. He was getting ready to throw it back when we spied Uncle Noble walking up the pier. He was wearing a Navy surplus pea jacket with the collar turned up around his sallow face. Smoke from his cigarette trailed behind him.

"Morning, *Tío*," I said, amiably.

When he didn't smile back, I knew something was wrong. He cast a disapproving glance at us. "Did you boys know that your pal Pete Lopez was arrested for burglary last night?" Our uncle wasn't big on chit-chat.

Dad came out of the wheelhouse, where he'd been fiddling with a new depth finder. "Morning, brother. What's this about a burglary?"

"Pete Lopez got himself arrested for breaking into a house in Corpus." Noble turned back to us. "You boys wouldn't know anything about that, would you?"

We continued to stare at him with disbelief.

Dad looked at us sternly. "What the hell have y'all been up to in Corpus? I'll sell that car of yours in a New York minute if I find out you or your friends are getting into trouble over there."

"Dad, we're not," I said. "And neither is Pete."

The two of them looked at me, waiting for me to elaborate, but I didn't know anything about it. I just knew it didn't make any sense.

"Pete's pretty much a Boy Scout," said Johnny, as much to himself as to them. "He'd be the last person to do something like this. How'd you hear about it, Uncle?"

Noble shook out another cigarette and lit it with his lighter. "I heard about it from a couple of cops at the café this morning. They were laughing about the crazy woman lived in the house that was robbed. She was there when the cops nabbed him. Said she wanted 'em to shoot the perp first and ask questions later. Anyway, I didn't give it any thought until they mentioned the kid's name."

"Whose house?" I asked, a possible explanation starting to form in my head.

"McDevitt was the last name, I believe," said Noble.

Shit. I could have guessed.

Dad saw my expression and realized there was a dimension to the conversation that he was missing. "Isn't McDevitt that kid you two boys got tangled up with last summer?"

Johnny nodded. "He was going out with a girl Pete is sweet on. Rachel Worthington."

"The girl that was attacked last week?" asked Noble. "Is that what this is about? Does Pete suspect the McDevitt kid had something to do with *that*?" His long face got even longer.

"Dad?" asked Johnny. "Mind if we go call Pete's house?"

"Go ahead. But get your asses back right after. These nets aren't gonna mend themselves, you know."

I followed my brother to a restaurant near the harbor and stood by as he called Pete's house. No one answered, so he called the boxing gym to see if Ralph Baltazar knew anything about it. Ralph pretty much lived at the place, even on holidays, and barrio news usually reached the gym faster than anywhere else.

Ralph did, in fact, know something about it, and while he talked, Johnny listened, occasionally putting his hand over the receiver to repeat what Ralph was saying. "Pete was arrested, but he bailed out . . . . The judge allowed him to go to Harlingen with his family . . . . They're spending Thanksgiving down there with some of the Lopez clan . . . . But he has to be back in town Monday to meet with the judge."

"Ask Ralph if anything happened between Pete and Karl yesterday."

Johnny nodded and asked the question. After he hung up, he looked at me. "He said Karl came by yesterday afternoon. Pete was there too, working out, but Ralph doesn't remember seeing them cross paths. He really doesn't know what the hell prompted Pete to do what he did."

And neither did we.

We returned to the shrimp boat and finished repairing the nets. Noble had already left; we would see him later at Rupert and Vita's restaurant on Ransom Island, where the Sweetwater clan held their traditional Thanksgiving feast. At least someone in the family celebrated the holidays. I had invited Carmen, but she and her mom were spending the weekend with Veronica and her family at their ranch near Freer.

"Before we drive over to Shady's," said Dad, "I need one of you boys to climb out on the outrigger and unkink the starboard stabilizer chain. It got hung up on the last trip."

"Charlie has the best balance," Johnny said quickly, before I could nominate him first.

Dad lowered the outrigger and I climbed out to the end on all fours. It took a lot of prying with a screwdriver and four or five good whacks with a rubber hammer to straighten out the chain, but soon it was fixed and the stabilizer was ready for its next voyage to the Gulf. The drizzle had increased, and the footing was slick, but the bay was pretty calm that morning. So to show my brother and my dad how agile I truly was, I stood upright and began walking down the outrigger beam like one of Ringling Bros.'s finest daredevils.

Dad and Johnny watched with amusement, when suddenly, Johnny's eyes widened and he pointed to a patch of sky behind me. "Jesus Christ, Dad! What the hell is that?"

Johnny's outcry and my dad's astonished expression made me turn and look at . . . absolutely nothing. I lost my balance and, gravity being gravity, had no choice but to fall into the harbor. I distinctly heard my father and my brother laughing as I went into the chill gray water.

They helped me onto the pier, stifling their grins and deliberately keeping silent, which was way worse than hearing them rib me about it.

When we got to the parking lot, Dad put his arm around my soggy shoulder. "I'll tell you what, son. We'll head on over to Rupe's in my truck, and you can take the Jeep back to the house and change clothes. We'll catch up with you later at Shady's."

Johnny dangled the keys in front of me, and I snatched them from his hand. "Asshole."

"Sorry, brother. But I needed something to cheer me up. I'm much obliged to you."

Aransas Bay is cold as hell in late November, so when I got to the house, I jumped into the shower and stood for a long while under a hot stream of water, wondering and worrying about Pete Lopez. Crazy little Mexican. What was he up to? If he was there to confront Karl, it was the wrong time and place to do it. Karl likely would have killed him and then claimed self-defense. And God knows what would've happened if Mavis McDevitt caught him inside her house. She probably kept a sawed-off shotgun and an axe in her broom closet. Next to a shovel and a bag of lime.

I went to my bedroom and hurried to dress, still chilled from the unplanned dip in the bay. Through my little window, I saw it was overcast, and it smelled like it was getting ready to rain. Our house, with its concrete walls and tiny porthole windows, was as cold and dreary as an Alcatraz cellblock. As I walked through the living room, I noticed, or sensed, something not right—something out of place. Out of the corner of my eye, I thought I saw a figure seated in a chair on the far side of the room, but it was too dark to be sure.

"Happy Thanksgiving, Charlie."

Ramón fuckin' Cruz.

I mustered as much bravado as I could manage. "It was," I said, my voice pitched a little higher than I would've liked. I figured he had a gun pointed at me, and I wondered if I could make it to the door before he shot me.

"Relax, amigo. I'm not here to hurt you."

Even though I couldn't see his face, I could tell the son-of-a-bitch was smiling. I saw the line of white teeth under his bandido moustache. He'd scared the piss out of me, which probably made his day.

"What do you want?" I asked.

"I want to talk about our friend, Jesse Martel."

I moved toward the lamp, but Ramón told me to leave it off. "It's better like this," he said.

"In the shadows."

I heard him laugh. "Yes, in the shadows. You're a clever boy, Charlie. I have to admit I like you, even though you've been a big pain in my ass since I came to this god-forsaken place."

"Then why don't you go back to Cuba?"

"I plan to, very soon. But first I want to propose something to you."

I found a chair and sat down tentatively.

"Good boy," he said, like he'd speak to an obedient pet. "Now, do you think you can pay attention for a few minutes?"

When I said yes, he began. "The way I see it, Charlie, Mr. Martel has three options in front of him. Let me help you with one of them." He held up a finger. "Your friends from the CIA have been trying to convince Jesse he should go back to Cuba and spy for your government. And in return, they are promising to smuggle him and his family to the US . . . at some unspecified time in the future." He waved his hand around contemptuously. "A promise I doubt they intend to keep."

I wasn't sure how he knew all this, but I decided it was safer not to ask.

"Of course, if he tries to spy for them, we will execute him and then send his family to prison."

My eyes had adjusted to the darkness, and I noticed for the first time that he wasn't holding a gun. I guess he figured he didn't need one, and sadly for me, he was probably right. He held up another finger.

"And then there is the second option," he continued. "Where Jesse Martel declines the kind offer from your government and takes his chances with your Texas justice system. A violent black man, from Castro's Cuba, discovered at the murder scene with blood on his hands? And on top of that, there is his confession. '*Lo mato.*'"

"That's not what he said."

"No, but it's what *you* told the policeman he said."

I saw a match flair and rise to the tip of a cigar. Ramón raised his eyes and watched me until the cigar began to glow. "You really should learn Spanish, Charlie. It is such a beautiful language. The language of Cervantes and Neruda. At any rate, your friend will be found guilty, and most likely put to death by, what method do you use here? The electric chair, no?"

"Your firing squads are better?" I asked.

Ramón's white teeth flashed at me from the shadows. "Either way, Jesse would be executed, either by my government or by yours."

"What's the third option?"

"Ah, now you are interested? *Bueno*, let's discuss it. The third option is that Jesse lies to the CIA." He paused for effect. "He tells them he *will* spy for them if they send him back to Cuba. But when he returns there, to his homeland, he forgets all about the CIA. He rejoins his family, and he begins boxing for *la República de Cuba*. Your Rey Feo will probably become a national hero, and will live a long and happy life *with* his family."

I let this sink in. "There's something I don't understand."

"Now is the time to ask."

"Jesse is accused of a capital crime. How is he going to get out of jail? You said yourself a jury will probably convict him."

"Yes, I did. But if the CIA believes he will help them, that he will be their spy, they will see to it that he gets out of jail *before* the trial begins."

I had trouble believing this. "Can they do that?"

The cigar pulsated as Ramón drew in smoke. "They simply need to find a suitable replacement for Jesse."

"How? Do they have a new suspect?"

"It doesn't matter, one will be provided for them."

I recalled hearing the CIA agent at the jail saying something similar, that they would "find somebody."

"There is a negotiation taking place between our governments," Ramón continued, "that will likely result in a prisoner exchange. Actually, the deal is better described as a ransom, being offered by your government, in exchange for the invaders we captured in the Bay of Pigs disaster. As it happens, Jesse Martel is one of the bargaining chips in this negotiation. The murder charge is an inconvenience, but one your federal friends will deal with."

"Do *you* know who murdered Stubby?" I asked. "The last time I asked you, you made me think that you did it."

"I didn't do it," Ramón said flatly.

Outside the door, I could hear the rain, having arrived at last, falling onto the porch deck. "Why are you telling me all this? I'm not sure what you want from me."

"I want you to communicate these options to Jesse. You have access. He respects you, and he listens to you. He needs to know that if he attempts to spy for the CIA, he will be put to death for his troubles.

"And, he needs to understand that it is okay with us to *tell* the CIA he is willing to spy for them. Once he is released from jail and returns home . . . well, then he can tell your government to go fuck itself. But I need *you* to let him know that the Cuban negotiators will play along with this fabrication, this life-saving deception, until he is safely in Cuba. Obviously, I can't deliver this message to him, but you can."

I shifted in my chair, thinking it over. As much as I mistrusted Ramón, his proposal made sense. It was the best, and maybe the only, way to free Jesse. If I did nothing, he would be executed for a crime he didn't commit. A crime I'd mistakenly helped hang around his neck.

But on the other hand . . . by helping Ramón, and by extension Fidel Castro and the communists, I would be aiding and abetting the enemy. I'd become, for a fact, what the two government spooks had warned me about—a traitor to my country.

So be it.

"Okay," I said. "I'll do it."

I stood up to leave, terrified of my decision and anxious to get away from the devious bastard sitting in my living room. But Ramón wasn't finished.

"Sit down," he commanded.

I sat back down.

"There is one more thing. When the police announce their new murder suspect, you need to keep your mouth shut. If you interfere, it could undermine the whole negotiation."

"Why would I interfere? Do you know who the suspect is?"

"Remember, this deal is happening *at the highest levels* of our respective governments. And it will save Jesse's life."

"Who is the suspect, Ramón?"

"I don't know, and it doesn't matter. I'm sure they'll find someone . . . convenient. All that matters is whether or not you'll help Jesse."

I took a deep breath. "I said I would do it."

Ramón rose from his chair and pointed his cigar at me. "Don't fuck this up, Charlie."

He walked by me and put his hand on the doorknob. "By the way, when you communicate this plan to Jesse, I would suggest a written note."

When I gave him a puzzled look, he cupped his ear. "The walls in the jail have ears."

"You mean bugged? That's crazy."

Ramón laughed. "Last year your CIA friends tried to send a box of exploding cigars to Comrade Castro. Now, *that's crazy*." He opened the door and glanced back at me. "Enjoy your turkey."

———

CHAPTER 27

I drove to Ransom Island in a jittery funk, wondering if Ramón Cruz was really that clever, wondering if I could trust him, wondering *why* I should trust him. I reminded myself that he was, after all, an enemy spy.

The CIA suits had said that it was my "duty" to inform them about any threat to the safety and security of the USA. The "or else" went unspoken. A fleeting image of prison passed through my mind—me standing in a chow line or chopping brush on a road gang with a bunch of guys who looked like Karl McDevitt.

Screw those guys, I said to myself. I was pretty sure the CIA would be more than happy to sacrifice Jesse in order gain a small victory, however remote the chance of success. It wasn't a case of good guys and bad guys, but bad guys and worse guys.

I arrived at the landing and waited for the ferry. Through my rain-splattered windshield, I watched the awkward vessel rumble toward the pier and gracelessly bang into the mooring bumpers. My car was the only vehicle going to, or coming from, Ransom Island, and when the drawbridge dropped onto the landing, the ferry attendant waved me on without even bothering to rise from his chair. I felt more like I was going to a funeral than a Thanksgiving feast. I had never felt so lonely.

Fortunately, Shady's didn't care about my problems. A cluster of automobiles nosed up against the railroad-tie parking barriers that fronted the building, and the chatter, laughter, and aromas I encountered when I pushed through the double doors resurrected my spirits and my appetite.

How could they not? Rupert and Vita had a "too much ain't enough" attitude about Thanksgiving, and there was never any telling who would show up for turkey and fixings at the old bar and grill. In the big room, a long table was filled with noisy guests who formed a cross-section of the Texas coast: roughnecks and other itinerant blue-collar workers, various and sundry fishermen, a uniformed Ethiopian ship captain and his first mate, and even a couple of characters who I'm pretty sure were hobos who had wandered over from the Aransas Pass train station. Rupert saw me at the door and waved me in.

"Hey everybody, this is my nephew Charlie," he boomed over the racket. "He's a little late because he insisted on *swimming* over from Rockport."

The table of revelers erupted in laughter. Apparently, the story about my unplanned dip in the bay had made the rounds. Rupert came over and draped his Popeye-sized arm around my shoulders. "Go fill your plate and find a spot at the table, son. And be sure to sample a piece of Vita's sweetbread and oyster pie. Everybody's scared to try it, and I think it's hurtin' her feelings."

As I shuffled toward the makeshift buffet line at the bar, I caught Johnny's eye. He popped up from the table and joined me.

"What's going on, brother man? You're acting weird. I've seen Egyptian mummies that looked happier."

"Let's go out on the deck." I had never been able to bluff my brother, so I didn't bother trying.

We slipped out the back door and leaned against the railing on the lee side of the building, out of the drizzle, where I carefully described the encounter with Ramón Cruz. Truthfully, I was glad to have the opportunity to repeat Ramón's proposal. It was important that I remember every detail. Jesse's life was at stake and, if I could believe Ramón, in my hands.

Johnny listened carefully until I was through. "You told him you'd do it? That you'd try to convince Jesse to lie to the CIA?"

I nodded slowly, worried for a moment that my brother disapproved and that I'd made a terrible mistake. But after a pause, Johnny nodded too.

"It sounds crazy, but it might just work . . . . Besides, it's the only plan we've got right now. That always helps simplify things."

"That's the way I saw it."

"Do you have any idea who this new suspect might be?"

"Not a clue."

Johnny sighed. "Me neither." Before we went back inside, he punched me on the arm, "You did good, little brother, for a guy who's not me."

"Will you help me?"

"Of course I will" He grinned at me. "What do you think I am, a traitor?"

I smiled weakly, and then followed Johnny inside, turning my attention to the buffet that Rupert, Vita, and Miz Leona had laid out. Because I'd arrived late, the good stuff had been pretty well picked over. Vita's sweetbread and oyster pie had barely been touched. Johnny saw me hesitate in front of the platter.

"I had some earlier. It's not terrible."

"I don't even know what a sweetbread is."

"Don't ask. Zach told me, and I don't want to spoil your appetite."

I filled my plate with food and found an open spot at the table between Giddyup Dodson and a fishing guide from Seadrift named Crumley. When I sat down, the two men were discussing how a Russian nuclear bomb attack would affect the fishing in Redfish Bay.

"There'd be nothing left to catch," Crumley insisted. "Everything would be dead."

Giddyup forked a piece of pumpkin pie into his mouth and shook his head. "Naw, I disagree. Let's figure the blast would be on the other side of Corpus Christi Bay, at the naval base. That's about twenty miles from here. With twelve feet of water over 'em, the fish would be fine."

"Now that's just stupid. Have you ever seen what happens when you dynamite a stock pond?" asked the fishing guide, polishing off a can of Falstaff beer and placing it next to a half-dozen empties. "I'll *tell* you what happens. Ever' single fish goes belly-up. Turtles and frogs too."

"A bay is a hell of a lot bigger than a pond," said Giddyup.

"And a nuke is a hell of a lot bigger than a stick of dynamite," answered Crumley.

Giddyup Dodson put down his own beer and turned to me. "What do you think, Charlie?" All of a sudden, I was the voice of reason. God help us.

I shrugged. "Even if the fish survived, I wouldn't want to eat 'em."

The two men agreed.

"They'd be radioactivated, that's for sure. Sumbitches'd glow in the dark."

"Probably mutate into something ugly and enormous."

"Like those gigantic ants did in *Them!*"

"I hate those guys."

I discovered I'd forgotten my knife and fork, so I picked up my plate and headed back to the buffet. As educational as the table discussion might have been, I just wasn't in the mood for it, so I grabbed the utensils and sidled around behind the bar. A bead curtain covered the entrance to the tiny office that Rupert and Vita used to do the books. The space was narrow, but it provided a quiet refuge for me to eat my Thanksgiving dinner.

As I picked at my food, I studied a large nautical map that was tacked to the wall, occasionally stealing glances at the Jackson Dredging Services calendar mounted beside it. The calendar was still turned to August, either because Rupert had forgotten to advance the pages, or, more likely, because he fancied the graphic illustration of the topless brunette that waved at him from the picture as she held a three-foot spanner. The pretty woman smiled and waved at me, too. August seemed like such a long time ago.

I thought back to that first meeting with Carmen. That seemed forever ago, as well. The crush I'd had on her seemed to have deepened since then. Ripened, somehow, into something more than a fifteen-year old's infatuation with a pretty girl.

The beaded curtain rustled and Vita appeared, breaking my reverie.

"I see you're admiring Rupert's fine art collection," she said, raising an eyebrow.

I blushed a little and it dawned on me that the model on the calendar bore more than a passing resemblance to Vita in her younger days. She'd always been a looker. "There wasn't any room at the big table," I lied.

Vita smiled. "I think you just didn't want me to see you *not* eat my sweetbread and oyster pie. I brought that recipe with me from Arnaud's in New Orleans, but it's clearly wasted on you heathens."

I gamely took a bite of her pie; it was much better than I would have thought. "It's very good, Aunt Vita."

She let out a musical laugh and put her hand on my shoulder. "You're a real gentleman, Charlie. No wonder the girls like you so much. I tell you what," she continued. "I'll bring you a slice of dessert pie before Cecil Shoat inhales the lot of them. Rhubarb, pecan, or pumpkin?" she asked.

"Pecan."

"I'll be right back."

She returned with two slices of pie, and we ate them together in the quiet little office. Outside, the party was ratcheting up to new levels of clamor, but back here, I was glad for the silence. Vita was a formidable inquisitor when she wanted to be, but she also sensed when it was best to lay off.

"Thanks for not making me join the party."

"I can tell you've got a lot on your mind, Charlie."

I gave her a brave smile. "And thanks for the pie."

Vita arched her eyebrows. "For the sweetbread and oyster pie?"

"Sure, that one too. Tell Mr. Arnaud many thanks."

———

CHAPTER 28

Johnny and I went to the jail on Friday morning. We'd stayed up late the night before, working out how best to communicate Ramón's message to Feo. In case the jail cell was bugged, we decided to risk a written note, as Ramón had suggested. Johnny would use one transport method; I would use another.

I don't know whether it was the all-powerful sack of donuts, or if the desk sergeant was still pissed because the big-shot federal agents were treating him and his fellow cops like the help, but thankfully, he agreed to let us visit Jesse again, but only one of us at a time, like it'd been before. As per our plan, I went up first.

The guard handed me off to the cellblock officer, and we got to the part where I emptied my pockets and the officer frisked me. I hoped my nervousness wasn't too apparent. He examined my wallet and handed it back, and then picked up the pack of gum I'd brought along.

"You like clove gum?" I asked.

The guard took a sniff, turned up his nose, and handed me back the package. "Naw. I'm a Doublemint man."

I unwrapped a piece and folded it into my mouth, and then pulled out another stick and gestured toward the metal door. "Mind if I give him one?"

The guard paused a moment, and then shrugged. "What do I care?"

He ushered me into the cellblock, told me I had the usual ten minutes, and then locked the door behind me. Jesse was lying on his metal bed, curled up under his blanket. I was a little surprised he wasn't waiting to greet me. On previous visits, he seemed to know I was coming even before the guard stuck his key in the heavy cellblock door.

"Feo? It's me, Charlie."

Jesse stirred but made no effort to get up. I wondered if he was ill.

"Are you okay, Feo?" I walked up to the bars of his cell. "Jesse?"

The springs on the bed creaked, and Jesse rolled over and looked at me, his face barely visible in the dim light.

"Are you okay?" I asked again. "Are you sick?"

He sat up slowly and shook his head. "No, I am not sick." He moved his feet to the floor and sat on the edge of the bed. I waited for him to stand up, but he continued to sit, staring listlessly between his feet at the stained concrete floor.

I shivered. It was cold and damp inside the cellblock, and I wondered if the grim surroundings had finally got to him. They sure as hell would me. I felt a weight growing in my chest. Jesse had been locked up alone in this depressing cell for over six weeks and was facing the prospect of spending the rest of his short life on Death Row—for a crime he didn't commit.

Had he already told the agents to go to hell? That he *wouldn't* spy against the country where he was born? Had he decided that the risk of getting caught was too great? Not just for him, but for his family as well?

"You are still between the sword and the wall?" I asked.

Jesse looked up and smiled weakly. "*Entre la espada y la pared. Seguro,* Charlie."

"What kind of food did they bring you for your Thanksgiving dinner?"

"I think it was turkey, but I don' know for sure. It was chopped up an' put on a piece of toast."

"My uncle told me that guys in the army call that dish 'shit on a shingle.'" He either didn't hear my little joke, or chose to ignore it.

He lifted his head and sighed. "Do you know what today is, Charlie?"

"Uh, November 23rd?"

"Is my daughter's birthday. She makes four years today."

Now I better understood the reason for Jesse's sadness, and as much as I wanted to respect his mood, I needed to get him off his cot and close to the bars so I could pass him the note. I didn't have a lot of time.

"Feo . . . I need your help on something. I'm competing in the AAU boxing tournament in San Antonio in a couple of weeks, and Ralph Baltazar, the trainer over at Baltazar Gym, he suggested I talk to you. Ralph said there's a fighter I could be facing in my weight class that's almost eight inches shorter than me. I've never fought anybody that short." The truth was, I had no idea who I'd be fighting in San Antonio, but I hoped the subject of boxing would shake Jesse out of his gloom.

Jesse was silent, but he lifted his head. I could tell he was paying attention.

"Ralph says I'll have to use my jab to keep away from him, otherwise he'll kill me inside. But . . . what if he does get inside? What if he gets me on the ropes or hemmed into a corner? How do I defend myself?"

Jesse looked up. "Ralph tol' you to talk to me?"

"Yes," I lied.

"But why?"

"Because you're the best."

The change of subject seemed to prod him out of his funk. He stood up and began to pace back and forth. Then he stopped and looked at me. "Well, okay. Ralph is right. That *tipo bajito* will definitely try an' get inside. An' if he's any good, he'll do it aggressively, takin' several blows to get to you. He'll aim for your chin an' try to punish you with the body blows. Use your jab to hold him off, Charlie, like Ralph said, and don' be afraid to plant your lead foot, eh? . . . . That way you hol' your position and it give your punches more force."

Jesse crouched in a boxer stance and threw a few phantom punches, as if he were imagining himself in the ring with an opponent. "Mix it up," he said. "He'll be expectin' the jab, so throw the right hand sometime."

"But what if he does get inside?" Me, thinking, *Get over here, dammit.*

"If he gets close and you can' get away . . . then get even closer."

"Get *closer?*"

"Use your body to smother him, man. Lean on him, clinch him, plant your hips an' hang on him. He will get tired very quickly if you do this. And he will get frustrated." Jesse nodded to himself, seeing it in his mind.

While Jesse talked, I removed the gum wrapper and shoved it through the bars so he could see it. "That's very good advice, Feo."

He looked at the paper curiously, and then he looked at me. I put a finger to my lips to make sure he didn't say anything, and then I touched my ear and pointed to the corners of the cellblock. Jesse seemed to understand, and he took the paper and studied the message I'd written on the wrapper. I hoped to hell it was legible, and that he got what we were trying to communicate.

There's not a lot of room on a chewing gum wrapper, and Johnny and I wrote multiple drafts and went through several packs of gum before we felt we got it right. We burned the incriminating drafts afterward, something we remembered from one of the Hardy Boys adventures we'd read.

As Jesse read the note, I tried to think of conversation to fill the silence. "I'll remember those moves when I go to San Antonio, Feo. Of course, I might not get very far in the tournament. I could draw a tall skinny guy like me . . . and be eliminated in the first bout." Jesse ignored me as he read and reread the note.

When he finished, he raised his head, his eyes shining with hope. I held out the unwrapped stick of gum and smiled at him. "Here, have some gum." He put the gum in his mouth and started chewing. "I wish you could be there to watch me, Feo. I wish Stubby could be there too."

He handed back the wrapper, grinning. "I think maybe Stubby would be proud of you, Charlie."

"I hope so, Feo."

I had just stuffed the gum wrapper into my pants when the metal door opened and the guard walked in. "Sorry, kid. Your time's up."

As I walked out, I heard Jesse's voice behind me. "Good luck on your boxing, Charlie. I will always be thinkin' of you. And what you tol' me."

His comment had the sound of a final goodbye, so I turned around and waved at him. "I'll never forget you, Feo."

When I passed Johnny in the waiting area, he was momentarily confused by the tears in my eyes. "It's okay," I said under my breath.

"You sure?" he asked.

"He got it. Let's get the hell out of here."

Johnny nodded and reached into his pocket and said in a loud voice, "Why don't you put some gas in the car, brother? And this time, put in more than a dollar's worth."

He pushed the keys into my hand and walked onto the elevator with Officer Clem, who was chuckling at my brother's last comment.

"My kid does the same thing. I ask him to fill the tank and he'll put in a quart of gas and try to coast home, the little cheapskate."

Johnny shrugged. "At a thirty cents a gallon, can you blame him?"

I hurried out of the room and opened my hand as I descended the stairs to the lobby. Wadded up next to the keys, I saw the other note we had made for Jesse, the one that Johnny had hidden inside the band of his underwear. He had pulled it out of his pants and palmed it when he retrieved his keys, figuring why take the risk when the first note had been successfully delivered? My big brother could be pretty clever when he put his mind to it. He'd make a good spy.

———

CHAPTER 29

A warped and wavering finger pier jutted out into the bay behind our house. Hurricane Carla had done a number on it, stripping much of its planking and leaving wide gaps in the walkway. Other sections listed drunkenly toward the water. But the square dock at the pier's terminus had survived relatively intact, and if you were agile enough to navigate the hundred and fifty-foot passage, it provided a stable platform for fishing, beer drinking, and, occasionally, schoolwork.

When we absolutely had to study, Johnny and I preferred to hit the books outdoors, and our overwater dock was just the place to do it, weather permitting. This day, it did. The cold front that had sullied Thanksgiving Day with rain had pushed through, and the sky was flawless sapphire. The water in the bay had turned, as it does in late fall, and you could see six feet to the muddy bottom.

Sometimes, like today, studying al fresco was a necessity. It was almost impossible to concentrate inside the house when Dad was home. When he wasn't at the harbor working on one of his boats, he would hunker down in front of the television with a cooler of beer and a sack of unshelled peanuts, and then, all day long, he'd stare at the tube, with the volume blaring. He'd switch it on in the morning and sit there in his Barcalounger until midnight, when the networks concluded their broadcast and switched to white noise and the Indian-head test pattern they put on the screen. Didn't much matter what was on, from soap operas to pro wrestling. He said the distraction of the TV kept him from getting in trouble when he wasn't working, but I think he was just lonely; he never watched TV when Mom was alive.

It was late afternoon, and my brother and I sat across from each other on the dock, our backs against creosote pilings, open textbooks resting on our laps. Since we were already on the water, we figured we might as well wet a line while we studied, especially on such a fine autumn day. An improvised PVC rod holder clamped to the dock held our rods, and for the moment, our fishing lines were slack and expectant, waiting for something to take the dead shrimp we'd cast into the bay.

I was wrestling with math formulas and seriously considering chunking my textbook into the bay, when a formation of pintails whooshed by. I watched the ducks fly off toward Saint Jo and then looked over at my brother. "Did you *really* learn these stupid trig functions last year, or did you cheat on your test?"

"I memorized them."

"Bullshit."

"Ask me one."

"Okay. Um, let's see . . . . How about the ratios of the sides of a right triangle?"

Johnny closed his eyes and concentrated. "Sine equals opposite over hypotenuse; cosine equals adjacent over hypotenuse; tangent equals opposite over adjacent." He opened one eye. "Am I right?"

I checked my book. "You actually *memorized* that?"

"There's a trick you can use. Simple mnemonics."

I knew the word, but had never thought to use it in conversation. My brother was rapidly becoming insufferable. "That's never worked for me."

"I promise you this one will. You know Shelly Bendorf?"

"Yeah, so?" Shelly was a shy, bookish girl who played cello in the school orchestra. She had recently blossomed into a beautiful young woman but still didn't realize how pretty she was, even if others, including us, had.

"And, of course, you know Ozzie Richards."

Ozzie played right guard on our football team—a big, strapping kid who would sweat like a hippo when he exerted himself. Nobody wanted to be anywhere near him, his locker, or his foul smelling gear after a game or a workout "What's that have to do with—"

"Okay, so remember this: 'Shelly can tell Ozzie has a hard-on always.'"

I stared at my brother.

"Sine, Cosine, Tangent," he continued. "Shelly, Can, Tell—"

I visualized the equation alongside the lewd image of my two classmates.

$$\text{SINE} = \text{OPPOSITE} / \text{HYPOTENUSE}$$
$$(\text{SHELLY}) \quad\quad (\text{OZZIE}) \quad\quad (\text{HAS})$$

$$\text{COSINE} = \text{ADJACENT} / \text{HYPOTENUSE}$$
$$(\text{CAN}) \quad\quad (\text{A}) \quad\quad (\text{HARD})$$

$$\text{TANGENT} = \text{OPPOSITE} / \text{ADJACENT}$$
$$(\text{TELL}) \quad\quad (\text{ON}) \quad\quad (\text{ALWAYS})$$

How could I not remember the equation now? I'd probably have to avert my eyes each time I walked by either Ozzie or Shelly, for fear of staring at his crotch or blushing at her imaginary fixation with Ozzie's "hypotenuse opposite."

The drag on my reel clicked tentatively, and I glanced at the rod tip. When it bent again I picked up the rod, set the hook, and began reeling in. The drag was set pretty low, but the fish, whatever it was, didn't put up much of a fight at first. Then it seemed to realize it was hooked and took off.

Johnny listened to the line spool out as the fish ran. "Drum?"

"Don't think so. Not big enough."

The fish fought a little more and then let itself be dragged in, like it was saying, *The hell with it.* It wasn't much of an adrenaline rush, and felt kind of like I was reeling in a waterlogged boot. As I pulled the fish up to the dock, we heard our dad yelling at us from the house and saw him motioning for us to come in. Johnny waved back and then stood up.

I hoisted the fish out of the water, and it landed with a splat on the wooden platform.

"Why, looky there, Huck," said Johnny. "You caught yourself a toad-fish. Kiss it and maybe it'll turn into Carmen."

We examined the mucousy, muddy-brown fish that croaked and grunted at our feet. I half expected it to hop away like its namesake. It had a fist-shaped head and a tremendous, toothy mouth that chomped angrily at the shank of the fishhook. I carefully freed the hook and kicked the creature back into the water.

Johnny gathered his books and fishing gear and then bumped me with his shoulder. "Last one to the house is a slimy toadfish."

Remembering my Thanksgiving Day dip in Fulton Harbor, I took my sweet time negotiating the tricky pier back to shore.

When I hopped onto the bulkhead, Dad looked past Johnny and glared at me. "Maybe your brother knows something about it," he said hotly.

"About what?" I asked.

Johnny turned to me. "Uncle Noble called and said one of his police cronies told him they were looking at a new suspect for Stubby's murder. Dad thinks it might be Pete."

I shook my head. "No way. It can't be Pete."

Ramon's statement about the cops finding a "new murder suspect" instantly came to mind. Had Jesse decided to follow through with Ramón's plan? Had the CIA boys struck a deal with him already? My head was spinning.

"You didn't think Pete would break into a house, either, did you?" said Dad. "But he sure as hell did."

"Did Uncle Noble mention Pete's name?" Johnny asked.

"He didn't say a name, but he said it was a Mexican fella."

"That describes about half of Corpus," I said.

"Well, the cop told Noble they haven't picked the suspect up yet, but whoever he is, he better be no amigo of yours. Like I said before, if I find out you boys are hanging around with a bunch of police characters in Corpus, I'm taking away your truck and hiring you two out to the RYSKO shipyards to work for wages."

It was Dad's usual threat.

He rubbed his chin and his frustration seemed to ebb. "I admit it's hard to believe. Pete's always seemed like a good kid." His eyes narrowed again. "But from what I've been reading in the *Caller-Times* lately, it sounds like South Bluff has gone straight to the dogs. A 'crime-ridden ghetto,' they say. And that gym of yours is right smack in the middle of it. Hell of a place for you boys to be going every afternoon."

"It's not like that," said Johnny. "And the new gym—"

Dad held up his hand and sighed. "I know, I know. I guess I don't believe a word of it anyway. Bunch of self-serving assholes trying to sell papers or get re-elected." He paused and then looked solemnly at both of us. "I just hope you boys aren't in over your heads."

I glanced at my brother and could tell he was hoping the same thing.

CHAPTER 30

I hardly slept on Sunday night. In one of my dreams I was a one-man firing squad, and Jesse and Pete were blindfolded and lined up against the wall, side by side—I had one bullet and had to choose which friend to shoot. And I had better choose quick because there was a gun pointed at my head as well.

The hell with that.

After school on Monday, which I stumbled through in a daze, Johnny and I drove straight to Pete's house. Nobody was home, so we went to Baltazar's for our workout. Even though my mind was elsewhere, I still had a boxing tournament coming up in less than two weeks, and I had no intention of pulling out or being embarrassed. I'd waited a long time for a sanctioned fight and would do my best to be ready.

When we walked into the gym, we were astonished and greatly relieved to see Pete Lopez in the ring sparring with Ralph Baltazar. We suited up and waited impatiently as Ralph schooled Pete through the session. Naco Flores joined us ringside to watch.

After they finished sparring, we helped Pete pull off his gloves and unwrap his hands. He hardly seemed winded, and he sure didn't seem worried.

"Hey, Naco," said Johnny. "Here's a dime. Why don't you go buy yourself a Coke?" As soon as Naco ran off, we threw about a dozen questions at Pete at once.

"Hold your horses, boys," he answered, lifting his hands as if to deflect punches, "and I'll tell you what happened."

Pete admitted that Detective Radcliff had caught him red-handed at the McDevitt house. "He rolled right up in that unmarked car of his while I was hanging half out the window; Karl's mom was with him in the car. It surprised the hell out of all of us. I took off running, and the son-of-a-bitch chased me down and pulled his gun. Threatened to shoot me if I didn't stop . . . so I did. I believe he'd have done it, too."

"You're lucky he didn't," I said. "You probably wouldn't be the first Mexican he's put down."

Pete wiped his face with a towel. "No shit. Karl's mom was sure yelling for Radcliff to shoot me. Even after he'd cuffed me and we were waiting for a squad car to take me to the police station, she was *still* begging him to rough me up . . . the crazy witch."

"What the hell was Radcliff doing with Karl's mom?" I asked.

Pete gave a fatalistic shrug. "Who knows, man? Maybe they're gettin' it on, as scary as that sounds. Personally, I'd rather put my dick in a blender."

"Was Karl there?" asked Johnny.

"Never saw him. Anyway, my lawyer said that since this was my first offense, I'd probably just get probation. The judge didn't seem all that wound up about it, either, considering I didn't take anything. But my ass is sure in a wringer at home."

Johnny leaned forward. "Have the police mentioned anything *else* they might charge you with, Pete?"

Pete looked surprised. "No, why would they?"

We told him what Uncle Noble had heard, and Pete looked hurt. "It figures. If you need a fall guy, arrest a Mexican. One's as good as the next."

Pete had a right to be pissed. It made us mad too, that such a thing was even possible, as we knew it was.

"So, Pete," Johnny began after a pause, "what the hell *were* you doing in Karl's house that night?"

Pete glanced around to make sure he wouldn't be overheard. "Remember last week, you told me Karl said he was at a movie the night Rachel was hurt?"

"Yeah. It was *Lawrence of Arabia*."

"Right, *Lawrence of Arabia*. That movie was his alibi." He leaned in closer. "Well, he never saw it."

"How do you know that?" asked Johnny.

"The other day I was working out on the heavy bag," he nodded toward the white, sand-filled bags suspended from rafters near the free weights, "and some of the guys that were lifting started talking about the movie. One guy is spotting Karl on the bench press, egging him on to do a couple more reps at the end of his set, you know? And the guy mentions the line that the Lawrence character, Peter O'Toole, says to his buddies when he's putting the lit match out with his fingers."

"The trick is not minding that it hurts," I said, remembering the line.

"Exactly, that one. Well, Karl tells him he doesn't have a clue what he's talking about, and when the guy tries to explain it, Karl tells him to can it, 'cause he wouldn't waste time on a movie like that, anyway . . . . So it got me to thinking."

"Okay, so Karl's alibi was a lie," said Johnny. "He lies all the time. But what did you expect to find in his house?"

Pete looked away self-consciously. "Something of hers."

"Something of Rachel's?" I asked.

Pete nodded. "One of my uncles did a stretch at a TDC unit in Hidalgo County. He said a lot of rapists like to keep things from the girls they . . . attack. Kind of like a trophy or something. She had a necklace she wore—one that I gave her. Carmen said it was missing." Pete sighed. "So anyway, after the workout I followed him home to find out where he lived."

"And then you broke into his house," said Johnny. "Did you find anything?"

"Nothin' that would connect him to the rape. But I found somethin' else." Pete looked at each of us pointedly. "I found Stubby's autographed Joe Louis photo, still in the frame; he had it in a box under his bed."

"The bastard," I said. "I figured it might have been Karl that trashed the gym office. He did it to get back at Stubby for kicking him out."

Pete nodded. "Kinda what I figured, too. There was other stuff in the box that he probably stole."

"Like what?" Johnny asked.

"I didn't have much time. Radcliff and McDevitt's mom drove up right after I found the box. And I only had a little flashlight to see with. But there was a switchblade, a pair of sunglasses, and other random stuff in there: a couple of girlie magazines, some smokes and cigarette lighters, and oh, that funny-looking bulldog statue that Stubby used to keep on his desk."

Johnny and I looked at one another. The bulldog had to have been stolen after the Joe Louis photograph; we'd seen one of the mob guys holding the hefty cast iron paperweight when we'd surprised them at the gym. Stubby's office had been vandalized three weeks earlier. I started to say something, but Ralph Baltazar walked up.

"Was Pete giving you details about his little screw-up last week?"

Johnny looked up at Ralph, still thinking about what Pete had said. "Uh, yeah, that's exactly what he was doing."

"And did he tell you he's learned his lesson? That nothing like that is ever gonna happen again?"

Johnny nodded. "Yep, that's what he told us."

"Do you guys think he learned his lesson?"

We both nodded.

"Well, me, too. He gave me his word on it." Ralph placed a heavy hand on Pete's shoulder. "Right, Lopez?"

"Yessir, Coach," Pete mumbled.

"That's what I thought."

For whatever reason, Ralph decided to personally take us through our training session, so my brother and I had no opportunity to confer about Pete's discovery. But over the next couple of hours, every time I threw a shadow punch, hit the mitts, or pounded the heavy bag, I imagined my fists turning Karl McDevitt's face into chop suey. If Karl had the bulldog, it means he probably broke into Stubby's office again, and I couldn't help but think it was the morning Stubby was murdered. I remained preoccupied the whole workout, including during my sparring session with Ralph.

"Come on, Charlie. Pay attention!" he kept repeating, and he made a point to ring my chimes every time my attention strayed.

After the workout, Pete jumped into the car with us and we dropped by Spohn to see how Rachel was coming along. Pete had visited the hospital every day since the attack, whether he was able to see Rachel or not. At first, her parents wouldn't allow him into her room, but eventually they relented when Rachel began to ask for him.

Carmen and Veronica were there as well, and we all stood around Rachel's bed and made small talk. She was hooked up to tubes and monitors, and her face was still covered in bandages, so it seemed weird to gossip about school and other trivial stuff while she just lay there, sometimes giving us a weak smile, but usually expressionless. Nobody ever mentioned the thing that had happened to her. I was uncomfortable as hell.

It was also eating me up inside that I couldn't tell Carmen about the high stakes parley going on between Cuba and the US—possibly resulting in a deal that could set Jesse free. I wanted to tell her about Ramón's cynical plan, and about the message I'd delivered to Jesse in his jail cell. But Johnny and I agreed it was best to keep it quiet. For now, at least. The situation was just too delicate, too fluid . . . not to mention that our actions could maybe land us in Leavenworth.

As we left, I gave Carmen a hug and told her that Rachel was lucky to have such swell girlfriends.

Pete was pretty worked up after we left the hospital, and he asked if we would cruise through Karl's neighborhood. "I wanna show you where that motherfucker lives."

Ocean Drive it was not. Dusty chinaberry trees drooped dispiritedly over cracked sidewalks, and several of the houses had sofas or washing machines on the front porch. Bar ditches full of stagnant water swarmed with mosquitos, even in November.

"That's his room there," said Pete as we drove slowly by his house. His bedroom was a converted garage attached to the side of a small, boxy bungalow with peeling paint. A curtain parted in the main house, and we saw Mavis McDevitt's face appear in the front window, peering out into the gathering evening.

"Hi, Mom," said Johnny, speeding up. Pete crossed himself and muttered a Spanish curse.

"Do you think she saw us?" I asked.

Johnny shrugged. "Who cares?'"

Next stop was Pick's Drive-In to grab some supper. The three of us chewed in silence until we had polished off our burgers.

"Just because the paperweight was under Karl's bed doesn't mean he killed him," Pete offered as he sipped on his Coke.

Johnny nodded. "I suppose he could've picked it up after the explosion. I mean, the whole damn wall was blown off. He could've wandered over to check out the damage, found it on the ground, and just picked it up. Stubby and Jesse didn't start patching the wall until late the next day."

Pete began shaking his head. "No, I saw the thing in Stubby's office *after* the explosion."

"You sure about that?" I asked.

"Yeah, I'm sure. Stubby called me in a couple of times to talk about me going pro after I graduated. And that ugly-ass dog was sittin' right there on the corner of his desk, like it always did."

Johnny wadded up his hamburger wrapper and tossed it onto the side tray that fastened to the car window. "I don't get why Karl would sneak into the gym again. There was nothing left to steal. When Stubby kicked him out, he was plenty pissed, sure, but . . . I kinda figured that was the end of it after Karl came in with his mom and that asshole detective."

"And then came back a few days later and trashed the office," I added.

"Maybe he just likes tearing shit up," said Johnny.

"He probably broke in that second time because Stubby kicked him out a second time," said Pete.

"What do you mean?" asked Johnny. "You saying Karl got kicked out *again?*" This was news to us.

"Yeah, about six or seven weeks ago. He walked in one Saturday afternoon and started lifting weights, like nothing had happened. You guys weren't there that weekend. I think you had a road game or something."

"What did Stubby do?" I asked.

Pete laughed. "He went off like one of those rockets he was always keeping track of, what do you think? And Karl acted like a dickhead again. He told Stubby he could go straight to hell. Called him every name in the book."

"When did this happen?" Johnny asked. "What was the date?"

"Umm, let's see. It was the first weekend in October. Like I said, you guys were out of town. I just forgot to tell you about it the next time I saw you."

I looked at Johnny. "The week before Stubby was killed."

"You think he'd go that far?" asked Johnny. "Kill Stubby? Just because he was pissed off about getting kicked out of the gym a couple of times?"

Pete stopped chewing. "Fuck, yeah, he'd go that far."

"Could be he broke in and meant to vandalize the place again," I said. "And Stubby walked in and surprised him."

Johnny nodded. "Could be."

"Remember that car that we heard peeling away from the gym that morning?" I asked. "Are we sure it couldn't have been a motorcycle?"

"Karl's motorcycle?"

"Yeah."

"I'm pretty sure it was a car."

I drummed my fingers on the dashboard. "You think we should take this to the police?"

"No, not with Radcliff on the case. And so far, the only evidence we think we have is in that box under Karl's bed, which Pete could've planted there."

"What?! I didn't plant anything. Screw you, *cabrón*."

"Keep your shirt on, Pete. We know that. I'm just saying it's something Karl could easily accuse you of. And the cops, or a jury, or whoever, would probably believe it. Especially since you were the one caught climbing out of Karl's bedroom window."

"*Chingao*," Pete muttered in frustration.

Johnny sighed. "We need to think this through before we do anything, guys. Could be this 'new suspect' Uncle Noble heard about has already confessed to the murder. If that's happened, we don't have to do anything. The case will be closed."

"And Jesse will be set free," I added hopefully.

"That, too."

"Even if someone else confesses," Pete said solemnly, "I still believe Karl is guilty. I think he killed Stubby, and I think he hurt Rachel. I think the bastard should be locked up and they should throw away the key. He's no damn good, I tell you. Rotten to the core. He's a . . . a menace to society."

Johnny and I couldn't help but laugh at Pete's speech. His face reddened, and Johnny patted him on the knee. "Sorry, Pete. We thought for a second you were auditioning for a role in *Dragnet*." In unison, we began humming the theme song: "Dum-ti-dum-dum/ Dum-ti-dum-dum-DAAA."

"Fuck you guys."

Johnny handed his tray to the Pick's carhop. "Don't get the wrong idea, amigo. We agree with you. We think Karl's guilty, too. Only question is, of what?" He turned the ignition and looked back at me, "Well, brother man . . . whadaya say we take Señor Sergeant Friday back to the precinct?" He hooted with laughter. "'Menace to society.'"

"Dum-ti-dum-dum." I couldn't help myself.

CHAPTER 31

We'd no sooner walked in the door of the gym the next day, when Ralph Baltazar called us into his office. We could tell by the look on his face that something was wrong. "What's up?" I asked.

Ralph closed the door and nodded at a pair of metal folding chairs in front of his cluttered desk. "Sit down, guys."

Johnny and I eased hesitantly into the chairs.

"I got a call from the district attorney's office today, telling me the cops arrested Diego Flores. I guess he gave them my name."

"Arrested Naco?" I leaned forward. "For what?"

Ralph cleared his throat. "He's been charged with killing Stubby Hunsacker."

"What? Bullshit! No way he killed Stubby. I mean . . . no way."

"The man also said . . ." Ralph continued slowly, "that Flores confessed."

Johnny began shaking his head. "Naw, that's not right. That can't be right."

"Hell no, it's not right," I said, pacing around the office. "It's ridiculous. If they had asked him if he shot Abraham Lincoln, he would've said yes to that, too. They can't be serious."

"Apparently, they are. The assistant DA I talked to said that, because of Diego's age and his, uh, disability, the kid most likely won't stand trial. Said the judge will probably call a competency hearing and recommend they institutionalize him. Going home's not an option."

Johnny scooted his chair closer to the table. "Ralph, do you really believe Naco is capable of murdering someone? That a fourteen-year-old one-armed kid with the I.Q. of a third grader bashed Stubby Hunsacker over the head and left him to die?"

Ralph shook his head sadly. "No, of course I don't."

"No. It's crazy. They're desperate, and they're sacrificing Naco because they have to find a new suspect."

"Why would they have to find a new suspect?" asked Ralph.

Johnny backpedaled. "I'm just saying Naco is an easy target. Easier to convict, I guess."

"Because he can't defend himself," I said. "Whatever's going on, it's a cruddy deal all the way around."

"Except for Jesse Martel, maybe," Ralph added.

Johnny and I traded knowing glances. So this was how the CIA boys had decided to play it. They'd found their scapegoat to take Jesse's place. A defenseless kid who would spend the rest of his life inside a loony bin so they could play their spy vs. spy games against Castro.

A blizzard of thoughts swirled through my head: Where did that leave Jesse? Was there any way to get Naco off the hook without jeopardizing Jesse's shot at freedom? Now I realized why Ramón had made such a big deal about me promising to keep quiet when the new suspect was named. Did he know it would be Naco? Suddenly, I was sick to death of all the double-dealing and subterfuge. I hated all those spook bastards, and I hated the games they played.

". . . the guy from the DA's office told me to keep it quiet," Ralph was saying. "For some reason, they want this under the radar for now. Maybe they're planning to have a press conference at some point, what the hell do I know? He only called me because Diego works . . . worked for me here at the gym. And I'm telling you two because y'all had a special relationship with the kid . . . especially you, Charlie."

I had barely been listening, but the mention of my name brought my attention back around. "Where's Naco now?" I asked.

"He's being held at the juvie detention center until they figure out what to do with him." Ralph stood up and regarded us sympathetically. "Look, if you guys want to skip the workout today, it's up to you."

Johnny and I thanked him and then wandered outside in a daze. "What a fucked-up mess," said Johnny. "But it's happening just like Ramón said it would."

"I hate it," I said. "You know what we have to do, don't you?"

My brother looked at me and nodded slowly. "Karl McDevitt."

"We've got to prove he did it." I picked up an oyster shell from the parking lot and slung it at an abandoned warehouse across the street. It clanged loudly against the tin siding. "Any ideas?"

"Not at the moment."

We cruised over to the harbor and sat on the stone steps, tossing potato chips to the seagulls and thrashing out ideas on how we could nail Karl's sorry ass to the wall, but nothing sensible presented itself. Eventually, for lack of anything better to do, we drove by Karl's house. Maybe he'd come running outside and confess.

We parked a block away and waited about an hour, but the house seemed vacant. A couple of cars pulled into neighboring driveways, and some kids on bikes wheeled by, but the McDevitt house remained locked and unassailable. I didn't think it was possible for a house to look guilty, but it certainly seemed that way to me. I imagined the box under Karl's bed, the autographed photo of Joe Louis and the bulldog paperweight hiding inside it, waiting to be revealed. As a teenager, I was used to feeling semi-powerless in a grown-up world, but this was a whole new level of frustration. Johnny and I drove home in silence.

Each night that week, after our boxing workout, we swung down Karl's street on our way home. Three times we saw Boyd Parker's beat-up Chevy on the curb, and twice we saw Harley Radcliff's unmarked police car parked in the driveway—a monkey-shit brown Ford Fairlane with a whip antenna and a floodlight mounted on the driver's side.

"I thought Uncle Noble said Radcliff was married," said Johnny.

"He did. You think he's got something going with Karl's mom, like Pete said?"

"Jeez, I don't know. Makes my brain hurt just to think about it."

We weren't sure why we continued these pointless drive-bys. What could we hope to learn? I guess we were just frustrated by the unfairness of it all. The way we saw it, two innocent people were behind bars, and the son-of-a-bitch who probably killed Stubby and raped Rachel was still walking free.

CHAPTER 32

On Saturday night I had a proper date with Carmen Delfín. Sport coat. Fresh haircut. A new pair of penny loafers that pinched my feet. The whole nine yards. I insisted on picking her up at her house.

"My mother will be there," she cautioned.

"I *want* her to be there. I want to talk to her."

I arrived at the house with a bouquet of store-bought flowers. I wanted to show Doña Delfín that I was not wholly without manners. She'd made it clear she didn't want me in the picture, but I was determined to change her mind.

Before I knocked, I turned around to take in the magnificent sunset. I wondered if Jesse could see the brilliant colors from his jail cell, or if Naco's room, wherever it was, even had a window. I wondered if Carmen and her mother knew about Naco's arrest, or Jesse's possible release.

I pushed away these thoughts and made myself focus on the "speech" I'd prepared for Doña Delfín. Carmen opened the door and greeted me with a smile. "Lovely flowers, Charlie."

"For you and your mother. The best blooms Rexall Drugs had to offer."

"You are such a lady killer."

"We'll see if your mom thinks so." I took a deep breath and stepped across the threshold into the tiled vestibule.

While Carmen went to the kitchen to find a vase for the flowers, I took note of the packing boxes scattered around the living room. The pictures, photos, and paintings had been removed from the walls, and even the rugs had been rolled up and pushed behind the sofa.

"Sorry about the mess," said Carmen when she returned from the kitchen.

"I thought she wasn't leaving until after the first of the year."

"She moved up her timetable. She leaves in a week."

"She's leaving before she knows the outcome of Feo's . . . situation?"

"Jesse insisted. He said he would rather she be there to support Isabella, Jesse's wife, than be here."

Doña Delfín walked into the room and regarded me coolly.

"Hello, Doña Delfín. It's nice to see you. Congratulations on your new job."

"So my daughter has told you?" She cast a sideways glance at Carmen.

"She said it was the opportunity of a lifetime," I added.

She gave a cursory nod. "Yes. I am anxious to get started. There is much work to do."

"Look, Mamá," said Carmen. "Charlie brought us flowers."

Her eyes rested on the dozen long stemmed roses I clutched in my hand, a thoughtful, almost sad expression on her face. "They are very nice," she said quietly.

I decided that this was as good a time as any to deliver my speech. I cleared my throat. "Doña Delfín, before you return to Cuba, there is something I want to say."

Carmen's mother raised her head and eyed me suspiciously.

"What I want to say . . . is that I've never met anyone as beautiful, or as interesting, or as wonderful as Carmen. I know you disapprove of me, and I'm sorry if I've done anything to offend you, but I've got strong feelings for your daughter, and I want you to know I plan to continue seeing her. That is, if she'll let me." I glanced at Carmen, who watched my presentation with surprise and, I hoped, some admiration. I couldn't read her mother's face at all. "And I promise you that I'll treat her with respect and be a gentleman at all times."

I stopped and there was an awkward silence. It was by far the longest sustained piece of verbiage I'd ever delivered.

"You have my word on it, Doña Delfín," I added.

"Are you finished?"

"Yes. I, um, I just wanted to tell you this before you left town. And I guess I wanted your permission to keep seeing your daughter."

"And what would you do if I *didn't* give my permission?"

I was silent, but I held her gaze. I was gonna keep seeing Carmen whether her mother approved or not.

Doña Delfín sighed and walked past me, as if she realized it was time to fold a losing hand. "I suppose it doesn't matter. My daughter will do as she pleases, no matter what I say. She is so very headstrong," she added for Carmen's benefit.

"I inherited that quality from you, Mamá."

"True," Doña Delfín conceded. "I guess I just don't want you . . . ." She stopped short and took a deep breath.

"Don't worry," said Carmen. "I won't disappoint you. And neither will Charlie."

Doña Delfín's face softened, and she held her daughter's chin affectionately. "I know you won't, *mi querida*. And I don't think he will either. At least he had the courage to speak to me in person." She looked at me more closely. "Besides, you gave me your word, didn't you, Mr. Sweetwater? That's a very serious obligation in our culture."

"Yes, ma'am," I answered. "It is in mine, too."

"*Bien*," said Doña Delfín, signaling the end of the conversation. "You two kids have a good time tonight." She presented us with a rare smile.

Carmen kissed her mom on both cheeks and gave her a hug. "*Gracias, Mamá. Te amo.*"

"I love you, too," she replied.

In the car, Carmen scooted close to me and gave me a kiss, as well. "Not bad, Carlito. My mother is warming up to you."

"One week before she leaves."

"You will still have chances to impress her. If not here, maybe in Cuba."

This hint at a possible future with Carmen and her family was thrilling to think about. For a moment, I imagined myself sitting in an outdoor café in Havana—an older, wiser, and more cosmopolitan me—drinking beer and smoking hand-rolled Cuban cigars, conversing happily and fluently in Spanish with Carmen, Jesse, Doña Delfín, and other family members. Somewhere, a flamenco guitar would be playing. Maybe by then, Castro and JFK would have made up and become fishing buddies. Just maybe.

"I would like to visit Cuba some day," I said.

She smiled. "We'll go together. It's a date."

We had dinner at the Ship Ahoy restaurant on the bay. White table-cloths and jacketed waiters gave the place a swanky feel, even though the fried shrimp couldn't touch my Uncle Rupert's recipe. I waited until the dishes had been cleared before I mentioned how frustrated I was by Naco Flores's arrest. I suppose I thought this would have been old news to Carmen by now—he had been taken into custody five days ago—but I was wrong. The DA had kept it under the radar, alright.

Carmen was shocked and saddened by the news, and then, like I had done, began to wonder where that left Jesse.

"You haven't heard anything new from his lawyer?" I asked.

"He certainly hasn't mentioned *this*. The only thing new is that they won't let me or my mother inside the jail to see Jesse any longer." Carmen's eyes began to blink rapidly, something she did when she was working out a problem in her head. "I'm confused, Charlie. If they know Jesse is innocent, why don't they release him? And Diego Flores?" She looked at me across the table. "He couldn't have killed Mr. Hunsacker, could he?"

"Not in a million years."

"Then what is going on? Why are they trying to pin this on that poor boy?"

My eyes must have betrayed something because Carmen reached across the table and grabbed both my hands. "Charlie. What's going on? Tell me. Please."

If I was serious about having Carmen in my life, and me being in hers, I couldn't hide something like this from her. Besides, I'd been dying to tell her all week. "Okay," I said. "But not here."

I paid the check and drove the car to the T-Head on Peoples Street, parking in front of the marina. A small cold front had arrived, and most of the sailboats looked buttoned-up and abandoned, their rigging clanging against the metal masts in the cold north wind. I took off my sport coat and draped it around Carmen's shoulders.

I told Carmen about Ramón and the risky scheme he'd devised for Jesse and about my part in delivering the jailhouse message. I told her about Pete and his discovery in Karl's bedroom and our suspicions about Karl.

Carmen listened closely and asked questions as I talked. By the end of the story, she had gone through the same thought process I had. And she'd landed in the same place. Stuck.

"You did the right thing delivering that note, Charlie," she said after a long pause.

"I sure as hell hope so."

A new Cadillac pulled out of the Yacht Club parking lot and drove by us before it turned onto Ocean Drive. Noticing the Worthington dealer tags around the license plate, I asked about Rachel.

"Has she remembered anything about what happened?"

Carmen shook her head. "She says no. And probably it's the truth. She's a black-out drunk when she gets going."

"But before she passed out, where was she? Who was she with?"

Carmen shifted in her seat and faced me. "You know those rich daddy's boys who hang around the Yacht Club?" She motioned toward the club where the Caddy had been parked. "She's been running with them off and on for years."

"You've mentioned them before."

"Well, I found out Rachel was with them on one of those fancy boats the night it happened. They were having a party and everyone was drinking. When Rachel passed out, a couple of the guys put her in her car and left her there."

"Just left her in her car? Unconscious?"

Carmen frowned. "When I found out who, I confronted them about it. They said they thought somebody was going to drive her home."

"Somebody *else*."

"Right."

"What assholes. Where was her car?"

Carmen pointed below us to the parking area at the end of the T-Head. "Right down there."

"The one place we forgot to look that night."

Carmen nodded. "Her car was still there the next day. But I can't figure out how she ended up at the cemetery."

We were silent for a moment, studying the parking lot, trying to imagine what might have happened. My mind immediately turned to Karl. Apparently, Carmen's did, too.

"Do you think Karl did this, Charlie?"

"I don't know. But it wouldn't surprise me to find out he did."

So if the bastard *did* do it, how do we prove it?" There was an edge in Carmen's voice I hadn't heard before.

"I don't know. We're working on it."

"Good," she said forcefully. "Just be careful, Charlie. If he could do something that horrible to Rachel, and to Mr. Hunsacker . . . ." Her voice trailed off. "I never imagined people like that existed. He's a—"

"A *mala yierba*?"

"Yes. The worst kind."

CHAPTER 33

By the time the AAU boxing tournament rolled around in mid-December, I was ready. Or at least I thought I was. I'd trained hard in the two weeks leading up to it, and though Ralph Baltazar said he would have liked another month or so to work with me, he figured I was ready enough.

"You've had a lot of distractions to deal with this fall, Charlie, but you should be okay this weekend if you stay focused." He whacked me on the back a couple of times and grinned. "It's like Stubby always told me, 'You just gotta hurt them faster than they can hurt you.'"

Christmas was only ten days away but, honest to God, it was the last thing on my mind. Even my attempt at buying Carmen a Christmas present had been a disaster. When I'd visited Rockport's only women's clothing store, I became so confused by the clerk's suggestions of scarves, gloves, and handbags, that I ended up going to the record store where I bought her a bossa nova LP by Stan Getz, which, when we opened our presents early, it turned out she already had. What's worse, she presented me with an authentic pair of bongo drums from Havana, which was probably the coolest gift I'd ever received.

On Friday afternoon, the other boxers and I piled into Ralph's car and drove to San Antonio. Ralph checked us into a place called The

Ranch Motel near Brackenridge Park, where we dropped our bags and then headed straight for the arena. Elimination rounds began that afternoon. Carmen was busy with the *Nutcracker* performances back in Corpus, but Johnny and Pete were coming later that evening to watch the fights and support their gym.

The tournament was held in the Bexar County Coliseum, a big domed structure east of the river. The coliseum also hosted rodeos, stock shows, Mexican wrestling, and music concerts. Ralph said he saw Elvis Presley rock the house there in 1956. "That crazy guy could stick and jab, sure enough," Ralph said. "But his footwork was terrible."

Even though boxing was a big deal in San Antonio, it didn't look like this amateur tournament was going to draw a lot of fans. We passed through the entrance ramp and stopped to stare at the boxing ring, which seemed tiny and isolated out in the center of the coliseum floor, surrounded by maybe a dozen rows of folding chairs. A few people milled around, but otherwise, the place was empty.

"Dressing rooms are over there," said Ralph, pointing to one of the tunnels at floor level. "You guys take a seat and relax for a little while. I'm gonna go find out your weigh-in times."

The two fighters I'd travelled with were as nervous as I was—it was their first fight, too—and we fidgeted in our seats until Ralph returned. He pointed a finger to the kid at my right.

"Sanchez, your bout starts at six-thirty. Johnston, yours is at seven. Weigh-in takes place right outside the locker room a half hour before your fight." He looked down at his clipboard. "I don't recognize the names of your opponents. You'll just have to size 'em up in the ring."

"Charlie," he looked over at me. "You've drawn a southpaw from Floresville. I've seen this kid fight before. He's no slouch. You're gonna have to be sharp tonight. Eight-fifteen is your time slot."

I'd rather have drawn an earlier slot and gotten it over with. Less time for the yips to set in, and I could enjoy watching the other matches. In the hours leading up to my fight, I was so jumpy I could barely hold a thought in my head. Johnny and Pete showed up when I was completing my warm-up.

Pete threw a couple of phantom punches at me. "Hey, Sweet Dreams. Your first fight, man. How do you feel?"

"Nervous."

"Ahh, it's just butterflies, man. Ain't no big deal. Once that bell rings, they'll go away."

Johnny checked my hand wraps and the laces on my boxing boots. "He's right, brother. I'm sure Ralph's already told you this, but stick to the fundamentals. Box this guy, don't try to kill him."

"He's a southpaw."

"A lefty, huh?" Johnny shrugged. "It'll be awkward at first, but you'll figure him out."

I glanced over at my opponent, who was warming up nearby—a white kid with a bull neck and thick wrists. He looked like he'd been pitching hay bales all his life. He'd been trying to stare me down since we'd weighed in together.

Pete noticed him glaring at me, and slapped the back of my head. "Don't look away when he does that, Charlie. Show that chump you're not scared of him."

A judge walked over and checked my hand wraps. "Okay, son. Time to get your gloves." He indicated a table where a guy smoking a cigar dispensed the boxing gloves. "Ten minutes till your bout."

Ralph gave me last-minute instructions in a low voice as he laced me up. "Use this first round to find your opponent's weaknesses. Throw feeler jabs, establish your reach, put your gloves on the guy, okay? And keep moving. You have to conserve your energy in the first round, but don't be too passive. Judges don't like passive fighters. Throw a combination, move away. Stick and move, stick and move, three-punch combo, stick and move. But walk when you're moving. Don't be hopping around or backpedaling out there."

I nodded. "Okay, I got it."

"Here, don't forget your mouthpiece."

When I climbed through the ropes and stepped into the ring, my mind went blank as an empty chalkboard, and every instruction I'd just been given was instantly forgotten. Across the ring, the Floresville southpaw bounced on the balls of his feet and pounded his gloves together. He was still scowling at me like I'd insulted his mother and kicked his dog. I was dimly aware that Ralph was still talking into my ear.

" . . . and for God's sake, Charlie, don't forget to breathe."

"Breathe?" I asked. Suddenly I realized I'd been holding my breath. I closed my eyes and inhaled about half an acre of oxygen.

"Yes, breathe, for Christ's sake. Your breathing sets the pace. Keep it steady. Charlie, are you listening to me?"

Truth was, I wasn't listening to anything. Not the crowd, which had grown considerably since we'd arrived, not my trainer, not even the sound of my pounding heart. It was as if a firecracker had exploded next to my ears, filling my head with a low, white-noise hum.

I noticed the referee motioning me out into the center of the ring. I stood in front of my ill-tempered opponent while the ref issued some instructions. I touched gloves with the other boxer, the bell rang, and it was on.

I don't remember much about the first minute, except that I was terrified and we kept stepping on each other's lead foot. My arms and legs felt like spaghetti, and I was sure I was flailing around like a drunkard. Finally the guy connected with a solid right cross that sent me reeling backwards.

I think that punch woke me up.

He'd delivered a clear shot to my jaw, and although it rattled my teeth, I realized *I was still standing*. I was still standing. My own brother had hit me a lot harder than that. After that punch, everything seemed to come into focus. Now I could hear Ralph's instructions from the corner.

"Breathe, Charlie. Breathe! Watch out for that cross."

As the round progressed, I settled a bit and found a comfortable rhythm. I also began to notice a few flaws in the other fighter's pattern, and it occurred to me for the first time that I could beat this hayshaker.

After the first round bell, Ralph gave me a squirt of water and massaged my neck. "A little shaky at the start, Charlie, but you picked it up. This next round you need to score some points. Get in there and hit the guy, but don't let your guard down while you're doing it. Let him know that *you're* the big dog now. He'll take notice, and so will the judges."

The second round went by fast, and both of us got in our share of punches. His badass glare had gone away, and I knew he was thinking now that he might not win the fight after all. At the end of the round, I connected on a quick series of jabs and right hands that sent *him* staggering backwards. I heard a roar of approval from the crowd . . . and I *liked* it.

The third round was an out-and-out brawl, and neither one of us wanted to give an inch. We must've thrown over a hundred punches each, and each of us landed a good percentage of them. By the end of the fight, we were both spent. My arms felt like boiled shoelaces. The crowd cheered appreciatively; nothing revs up a boxing fan like two guys standing toe-to-toe and beating the snot out of each other.

I won the fight by a slight margin, and the Floresville southpaw dropped his glare and congratulated me with a handshake and a smile. "Nice fight, Sweetwater. Let's do it again sometime."

Ralph was smiling as well. "Nobody forgets their first fight, Charlie. And that was a dandy. Both of you really mixed it up out there."

With sweat dripping into my eyes and my chest heaving, I looked back at my opponent. "He seems to be taking it pretty well."

"Amateur boxing is all about good sportsmanship and fair play, kid. I'm sure Stubby drilled that into your head."

Stubby had. I remembered again his list of "rules" posted around the gym. Half of them had to do with respect for yourself, and the other half, respect for the gym and for others. "I wish he could've been here tonight," I said, suddenly emotional.

Ralph smiled. "Aw, I expect he watched the fight." He pointed upward. "From The Big Ringside. If he were here, he'd have been real proud of you for fighting the way you did, and then he would've busted your chops for entering a tournament after he told you not to."

"You knew about that?"

Ralph chuckled. "Yeah, he mentioned you'd asked him about the Gloves tournament. But you see, I did the same thing when I was your age. Stubby wanted me to wait until I was sixteen, too, so of course I snuck over to Houston to fight in an unsanctioned tournament, using my cousin's club sponsorship to get in. Stubby found out about it, though, and I had to clean the bathroom in that stinky old Centennial Building every day for three months."

Johnny and Pete walked up and slapped me on the back. "Well done, brother man," said Johnny, grinning broadly. "You did good. Although I was a little worried about you at first. You kinda sleep-walked through the first part of round one. Looked like you were hug-dancing with Carmen."

"Like a deer in headlights, man," Pete laughed. "But you came around after he knocked the crap out of you, didn't you?"

"It got my attention."

"That's what it takes sometimes," Johnny agreed. "Hey, we're gonna stay and watch some more fights while you shower. We'll do a scouting report for you."

As I walked to the dressing room, I passed the next pair of fighters. One was a rangy Negro kid, and the second was a short, tough-looking Mexican with a Zorro mustache and a Jesus tattoo on his shoulder. I turned and watched them walk toward the ring. The Mexican had a swagger to him and acted like he was taking a stroll in the park, which I could tell made the colored kid nervous as hell.

As I was putting on my street clothes, yakking with some of the other boxers, including the Floresville southpaw, I heard the crowd erupt.

"I wonder what that's about?" asked one of the fighters.

We found out a few minutes later when two men dragged the semi-conscious black kid into the room and sat him down on the massage table. One of the men, a tournament doctor I assumed, took a penlight and examined the boy's eyes.

"He'll be alright," he pronounced. "Just got his bell rung, that's all. I don't think I've ever seen a knock-out happen that early in a fight."

I left as quickly as I could and found Johnny and Pete. "What just happened?" I asked.

"Holy shit!" said Pete, his eyes wide. "That Mexican took the black kid out in *ten seconds*. It's like he had a brick in his glove, man. Brutal. You better hope you don't draw *that* guy tomorrow night. He's a welterweight . . . like you, *vato.*"

"Do you know who he is?" I asked. Pete had boxed in a lot of tournaments and knew pretty much all the good Texas boxers.

"No, man. First time I've seen him."

Johnny studied the fight program. "Name's Mata, and it says here he's from El Paso."

"Maybe that's why I don't know him," said Pete. "El Paso's a million miles from everywhere, except Juarez, and most of their tournaments are local, anyway."

"Was it a lucky punch?" I asked hopefully.

Johnny shook his head. "Uh-uh. This guy knew what he was doing. He zeroed in and . . . *bam!* The colored kid was out. Never knew what hit him."

———

After the fights, Pete and Johnny left to go stay with one of Pete's relatives. Pete had a big family and they seemed to be scattered all over the state. Ralph drove me and the other two boxers back to the motel, and all four of us crammed into one room. Later, as we ate fried chicken at Earl Abel's restaurant a few blocks away, Ralph broke down each of our fights and made suggestions for improvements. Manny Sanchez had advanced, like me, but Bret Johnston had been beaten by a lightning-quick kid from Seguin. His right eye had already started to blue up underneath.

Before we went to bed, Ralph told me not to worry about my draw the following day, but climbing into the ring with that Mexican with the horseshoe in his glove was all I could think about.

I did not sleep well.

———

CHAPTER 34

The next morning, we spent a couple of hours watching the animals at the Brackenridge zoo. Ralph said it would help us relax, but it didn't. And then, like good card-carrying Texans, we made the obligatory pilgrimage to the Alamo, which I'd never seen. It looked just as tiny as everybody said, perched in the shadow of a giant Joske's department store. The place was mobbed with tourists; one of the curio clerks told us that crowds had really picked up after the John Wayne film a couple of years back.

Then it was on to the Coliseum to find out our draws and fight times.

I drew the El Paso boxer, of course, and my fight was scheduled for seven o'clock that evening. Johnston and Sanchez avoided me the rest of the day, leaving me alone with my black thoughts.

Pete and Johnny wandered into the Coliseum an hour and a half before my fight, just as I was beginning my warm-up routine. Their eyes were red and puffy, like they'd painted the town the night before.

"You guys look like shit."

"Who'd you draw, Charlie?" asked Pete straight away, ignoring my comment.

"Who do you think? Guillermo Mata, from El Paso."

Pete and Johnny looked at each other. "That's what we were afraid of," said Pete.

"What's the problem?" They were making me more nervous than I already was. "He some kind of Mexican superman or something?"

"I'll tell you what's he not," Johnny answered. "He's not an amateur boxer."

"What?"

Pete quickly laid out the story: the night before, he and Johnny had gone with some of Pete's relatives to a riverside bar called the Esquire Tavern to drink beer and listen to music. They saw Mata there with a big group of friends. "He was pretty blotto, man, buying drinks for everybody—"

"*Buying* drinks?"

"Oh, he's old enough, lemme tell you. Twenty-one, at least. Probably closer to twenty-two."

"But how could he be—"

Johnny put his hand on my shoulder. "The guy you're fighting isn't Guillermo Mata. It's his cousin, Fernando Mata, and he's from Juarez, not El Paso."

"Yeah, and get this," Pete continued. "He's been fighting on the pro circuit in Chihuahua for at least a couple of years."

I held up my hand to stop them. "Wait a minute. I'm fighting a professional boxer? What's he doing here? How'd he even enter the tournament?"

Pete shrugged. "Claimed to be his younger cousin, I guess. Lied about his age."

"What about the boxing club that sponsored him?"

"It's in El Paso. Who knows? Probably a relative that owns it."

"Fuck."

"They were all laughing about it at the bar last night," Pete continued. "And our group was sitting close enough to hear 'em. Of course, your gringo brother couldn't understand a word, since they were talking in Spanish."

"What else did they say?"

"Apparently the Mata clan is in San Antonio for a wedding—last night was the bachelor party—and when they found out about the tournament, they figured what the hell? They'd play a little trick on the locals while they were here and have some fun, too. They've been making side bets on how long it'll take Fernando to knock out his opponents."

I sat still and tried to think. "Should we tell Ralph?"

Pete squirmed. "I don't know, man. It would be our word against theirs. Ralph wouldn't be too happy to find out we were out drinking in a bar last night. Besides, those Mata boys seem like a pretty rough bunch. I'm not sure we want to start trouble with 'em."

"Well, I'll tell you what *I'm* sure of. I'm sure I don't want to fight a professional boxer who is almost as old as Feo."

"You can withdraw," Johnny suggested.

I could tell by the way he looked at me that he wouldn't withdraw if he were in my shoes. It would be a chickenshit thing to do. I shook my head. "No, I'll fight him."

Johnny smiled. "What's the worst that could happen?"

"Right," Pete agreed. "Maybe you can hang with him a couple of rounds. The ref will stop the fight if it looks like you're gettin' hurt."

"Right," I repeated. But in my mind, all I could see was that Negro kid they dragged into the dressing room the night before, his eyes glazed, his head rolling around on his shoulders, trying to understand what the hell just happened to him.

I sleepwalked through my warm-up routine and watched the big Coliseum clock like a condemned man counting down to midnight. At the pre-fight weigh-in, Mata was sullen and uncommunicative. I could smell last night's booze on his breath and in his sweat. He may have been the one with a hangover, but I was the one who made two trips to the toilet stall to throw up. Ralph was waiting for me outside.

"You okay, Charlie? You seem even more nervous than last night."

"I'm okay," I lied.

"Look, this guy is tough, but he's not invincible. Remember what we talked about and you'll do fine."

The final moments leading up to the match were a blur, but when the bell finally dinged, there was nothing left to do but come out fighting. The problem was, I'd seemed to have forgotten how. All I could do was cover up, backpedal, and clinch during the first couple of minutes. It got so bad the ref even called me over and told me I'd better show him something quick or he'd stop the fight.

When I did step up to show him something, planting my foot and throwing a few jabs and combos, Mata came back at me with so many unanswered punches that the ref was forced to give me a standing eight count. Seconds before the end of the round, I narrowly avoided a couple of massive right crosses that Mata threw at me—the bastard was clearly going for another first-round KO. He lunged at me so aggressively with a final roundhouse punch that he almost fell on his face when I dodged it.

Ralph was not happy. "What the hell are you doing, Charlie? You look like you're terrified of this guy. He's almost six inches shorter than you. Stick him with your jab. Use those long arms to hit the guy."

I sat on my stool and tried to listen. I was almost panting I was so scared.

Ralph stood in front of me, blocking my view of the other corner. "Deep breaths Charlie. You're off the rails right now, but you can get back on track. Breathe. That's better. Listen, go out there and *box* this guy. He's not as sharp as he was yesterday. He's vulnerable. I don't know what he did last night, but I can smell the sour booze in his sweat from here. Keep throwing punches at him. I don't care if they don't hurt him. I don't care if they even land. Just keep busy. The change in rhythm will surprise the guy, and you might just remember that you know how to box."

I looked at Ralph and nodded. "Okay." I recalled what Johnny had said: *What's the worst that could happen?*

I tried my best to follow Ralph's instructions, and at first Mata did seem confused by the change in pace. Instead of backing away, I was moving in, moving sideways, circling around him, throwing punches the whole time. The blows seemed to annoy him more than anything else, and I could tell they weren't having much effect. During the last minute, Mata started stalking me, looking for the knockout again. But this time I wasn't backing away, which gave him multiple opportunities to get inside and pound me with a barrage of blows—so many, in fact, the referee was forced to give me another standing eight-count.

"You alright, son?" he asked, holding my gloves and examining my eyes—one of which was puffing up nicely. Behind my mouthpiece, at least one of my teeth seemed to be sort of wandering around in its socket.

"Yes, sir. Just getting warmed up."

He looked at me dubiously and let me continue. Somehow I managed to survive the round. Somehow I was still alive.

Ralph raised his eyebrows when I retreated to my corner. "This guy's fast and he's strong, and to be honest with you, he looks a lot older than sixteen. You wanna go another round with him? I'll under-stand if you don't."

"I got nowhere else to be, Coach."

"Okay, just keep using the same strategy—keep moving and keep swinging. But fair warning, the ref is gonna stop the fight if Mata keeps punishing you like he did at the end there. And if he doesn't stop it, I sure as hell will."

I'm sure Ralph meant well and didn't want to see me get hurt, but I gotta say, it was a pretty lousy pep talk.

As the seconds ticked down before the final round began, I wondered what Jesse would do to this guy. He'd beat the shit out of him, that's what he'd do. He'd give the cocky bastard some of his own medicine. Thinking of Jesse, I remembered the advice he'd given me during my last visit to the jail when I'd asked him how to fight a shorter opponent: *"If he gets close and you can't get away, then get even closer."*

The bell rang to start the third and final round, so I popped up and went after Mata again. For every punch I landed, he landed two. I don't know for sure if he felt mine, but I sure as hell felt his. I didn't want the ref to stop the fight, so I decided to give Jesse's strategy a shot. *Okay, Feo, I thought. This one's for you.*

The next time Mata slipped inside my jab, I lowered my head, stepped up, and hit him four times in the midsection. The ref separated us and warned me not to lower my head or he'd penalize me. Mata came at me again and I moved into him. We hammered each other at close range, but at that distance, none of the blows had much effect—his or mine. He tried to shove me off and I grabbed his arms, pulling him with me. He cursed in frustration.

The ref stepped in, pushed us apart, and signaled for us to begin again. Each time Mata powered past my long-range punches, I stepped inside, close to him, almost belly to belly, and began pounding his ribs, throwing short uppercuts to his chin, and sometimes reaching over and giving him an overhand smack to the side of his head. A couple of times, I rested my forearms on his shoulders and leaned on him, with all my weight, like Feo told me. Mata pushed me off angrily and looked to the referee for a foul. But the ref only motioned for us to continue.

It went on like this, and I suppose it was pretty boring from the audience's perspective—they wanted to see another knockout—but I didn't care. I just wanted to go the distance with this son-of-a-bitch. Screw him and his knockout bets.

Getting desperate, Mata began to talk into my ear when we got tangled up. "Come on white boy. Why you fightin' like a little girl? Why you wanna dance instead of fight, huh? *Cabrón?* He stank of sweat, hair oil, and last night's booze.

I heard Ralph yell from the corner. "One more minute!"

Mata must have heard it, too, because he bellowed in frustration and pushed me off him with all his strength. As I was going backwards, I delivered a strong right cross that caught him square on the nose. He snuffed a small bubble of blood back into his nostril before the referee could see it, and then came at me like a wild man. For the next thirty seconds I did my best to duck and cover up, until he finally stopped wailing on me. When he stepped back to recharge, I moved in on him again, accidentally stepping on his right foot.

That did it. A murderous expression crossed his face, and he cocked back his right hand and delivered a low blow to my family jewels that sent me straight to the canvas.

Despite the groin guard I wore, the punch sent a sharp, almost unbearable pain down through my legs and up into my kidneys and abdomen. The pain was so intense I couldn't breathe, couldn't see, and damn sure couldn't stand. My legs turned to water and down I went. It was all I could do to keep from throwing my guts up.

Resting on all fours, I was dimly aware of the commotion a few feet away. I could hear the referee yelling at Mata, and Mata yelling back at him. Did the ref just say that he was disqualified?

From my prone position, I managed to draw a breath, and then I blinked my eyes until they came back into focus. I planted one foot on the mat and put a hand on my knee for balance. The crowd was screaming and jeering in Spanish and English, and I think I heard Ralph yelling at the ref to "throw the bum out." I glanced down at my boxing trunks and searched around me to make sure my balls weren't splattered across the mat. Slowly, the pain started to ebb, and I raised my head.

Mata was pointing at me, yelling that it wasn't a low blow, and that I was faking, that I was throwing the fight. But the referee was adamant. Mata was disqualified, and I was damned glad of it. A two-year pro beating up on novices. Screw him. He was a cheater and a dirty fighter.

Mata shook off the ref and made like he was walking back to his corner, but he circled around and edged up next to me, instead. "Suck my dick, *maricón,*" he sneered.

I know I should have kept my head and let the comment slide. He'd already been kicked out of the tournament, and technically, I had won the fight. But I didn't let the comment slide. I couldn't. I lost my temper.

In one fluid motion, I exploded upwards and threw a full-out haymaker at the Mexican's head. I saw a flash of surprise in Mata's eyes as his head popped backwards, and then I saw him stagger, swoon, and tumble to the canvas.

The referee looked at me disbelievingly. "Son, are you *crazy?*" He made a dramatic disqualification gesture and yelled for me to get my ass to my corner. He wanted both boxers out of his ring, now! Mata's crew crawled through the ropes to help their felled fighter. The ref had to hold a couple of them back to keep them from charging me.

Ralph jumped in and hustled me to my corner. He looked at me with wide, unbelieving eyes. "Jesus Christ, Charlie. Why did you do that?"

I shook my head and opened my gloves in resignation. I didn't know what to say. Neither did anyone else. There was no excuse for it.

The fight was recorded in the AAU books as a "no-contest." A double disqualification.

So much for good sportsmanship.

Since Sanchez had lost his match as well, the Baltazar Boxing Gym contingent was done. But instead of watching the rest of the tournament, Ralph herded us into his station wagon and headed for home, not even giving me time to change into my street clothes. He was pissed and I couldn't blame him. I'd betrayed the ideals he'd tried to instill in me. But sometimes you just have to say "Fuck it" and lower the boom.

Nobody said a word on the long drive back to Corpus Christi.

CHAPTER 35

Ralph was still plenty steamed when I showed up at the gym on Tuesday afternoon. He called Johnny and me into his office, and I figured I'd either be kicked out of the program or handed a toothbrush and a bucket and told to get to work on the bathroom.

"I'm still not happy with the way you handled yourself in the ring, Charlie. It was bush league. You could've fought for the tournament title on Sunday, but instead, you lost your temper. Stubby would've been ashamed of you."

That really stung. "I'm sorry, Coach. I just lost it there at the end."

"You couldn't wait to test yourself in a sanctioned fight, remember? And when the time came, you blew it." Ralph leaned back in his chair and exhaled, the disappointed expression fading. "Anyway, I can't say I blame you *too* much for reacting the way you did. That was a deliberate low blow . . . a sucker punch if I ever saw one. Had to have hurt like hell."

"It hurt like hell."

"Just so you know, I found out about Mata."

Johnny and I swapped glances.

"Somebody from one of the other boxing programs finally recognized him and put two and two together." Ralph shook his head. "It was a dangerous stunt they pulled, putting a pro in the ring with a novice six years his junior. You could've been hurt a lot worse, Charlie, or even crippled. I hope they never let that Mexican kid fight in this country again. And that El Paso boxing club that sponsored him? They oughta lose their AAU membership. I'd shut 'em down if it was up to me. But all things considered," Ralph leaned forward in his chair, "you did alright, Charlie, right up 'till that last punch. Anyway, that's not the only reason I called y'all in here."

Johnny looked surprised. "No?"

"I was able to visit Diego at the State School this morning. You remember I told you the judge put him there while his case makes its way through the system?"

"Is he okay?" asked Johnny.

"I guess. He doesn't understand why they won't let him leave. Doesn't have a clue why he's even there. He's been there two weeks already, and his own fucking parents haven't darkened the door of the place." Ralph paused a beat. It was a measure of his frustration that he'd sworn so violently, something he hardly ever did.

"A caseworker visited his house to find out why, and his mom and her worthless boyfriend said they were glad to be rid of him. Anyway, he thought I'd come to pick him up and take him to the gym so he could do his chores. Started packing his bag, thinking we were leaving together. Jesus. It took me half an hour to convince him it wasn't gonna happen."

"Do you think they'll ever let him out?"

"I don't know, Charlie. I asked 'em that, and they said, as per court orders, he was not allowed to leave the premises, period. They've got the place locked down like a prison. It even feels like a prison." Ralph shook his head sadly. "Even if they find him innocent of the murder charge, they act like he's in that institution to stay."

"You mean he'll be in there forever?" I couldn't believe it.

"I asked if the courts would ever reconsider, and at least let me bring him to the gym for a few hours a day, you know? Give him a chance to push the broom a little. He just moves the dust around, but boy, does he ever love doin' that."

Ralph paused, and we recalled how Naco would follow the push broom around the gym like it was a dog on a leash; never going in a straight line, and with an irregular tempo that made it seem like the broom decided when and where to go.

"He'd be supervised of course, kind of like a work-release program, and I'd be his guardian, or whatever. But anyway . . . " Ralph exhaled loudly, "they said it was too early to talk about that kind of thing."

"How'd he seem?" I asked.

"Sad. Confused. It broke my heart to see it."

It broke my heart, too.

——

After our workout, we drove to Veronica's house to pick up the girls. Carmen had been sharing a bedroom with Veronica since Doña Delfín's return to Cuba. We elected to go to Snapka's. It had become our go-to hangout in Corpus.

At the drive-in, Johnny recounted my inglorious boxing exploits to the girls, and the story had them in stitches. Especially the part about me getting punched in the nuts.

I followed up Johnny's tale with Ralph's news about Naco Flores, and the good feelings instantly evaporated. Carmen and Veronica became quiet and pensive.

"Way to go, Charlie," said Johnny, under his breath.

"Sorry, y'all."

It's okay," said Carmen. "I'm glad you told us."

I figured since I'd already rained on everybody's parade, I might as well ask about Jesse.

"I talked to his lawyer again this morning," said Carmen, "and he isn't even sure Jesse is in the county jail. He hasn't seen him in a couple of days, and thinks maybe they've transferred him."

I wondered if the CIA had shipped Jesse back to Cuba, but it didn't seem likely. Prisoners didn't just disappear. Johnny must have been thinking the same thing.

"They can't move Jesse without telling his lawyer, can they?" he asked.

Carmen shook her head. "Not in this country, they can't. Not legally, anyway. The lawyer's been trying to move his complaint up the ladder, but he's not making much progress. His inquiries keep hitting a wall."

"We'll talk to our Uncle Noble," I said. "That ice house of his is like a cop clubhouse. Maybe he can find out what's going on."

I noticed Johnny wasn't listening to the conversation but was concentrating on something outside the car. I followed his line of sight and saw Boyd Parker's Chevy Bel Air parked in a drive-in stall on the other end of the parking lot.

"Is Karl with him?" I asked.

"No, just Boyd." Johnny turned to Veronica and Carmen. "Would you girls excuse us for a couple of minutes while we go talk to somebody?"

Veronica spotted the car. "You mean Boyd Parker?"

"You know him?" asked Johnny.

"Not really. I know he moved here last year from I don't know where. Would've been a senior this year if he hadn't dropped out of school last spring. I only know him because I work in the admin office during homeroom. The vice principal was always having to call his mom 'cause he skipped school a lot."

"What's he like?" I asked.

Veronica shrugged. "Shy. Not too bright. As far as I know, he didn't hang out with anyone at school. Wasn't in any club or on any of the teams. No girlfriend, surprise, surprise. Even ate lunch by himself."

"Haven't we seen him with Karl McDevitt a few times?" asked Carmen.

"Yep," said Johnny. "And that's why Charlie and I are going over to visit with him."

When we approached the Chevy, Boyd's eyes widened, and he fidgeted with his keys like he was thinking he might skeedaddle.

"Relax, Boyd," said my brother. "We just wanna talk."

Johnny put his forearms on the driver window and leaned down, his head almost inside the car. I climbed into the passenger seat. Boyd shifted nervously.

"What do you guys want?"

"How's your buddy Karl?" Johnny asked.

"He ain't my buddy."

"No? We see you two together all the time. Seems like y'all are best pals."

"Attached at the hip, almost," I added.

Johnny nodded. "Always driving around in *your* car. Were you his chauffeur?"

"I don't do that anymore. He got his bike fixed."

Johnny looked puzzled. "What happened to it?"

"He wrecked it. I gave him a few rides while it was being repaired, so what?"

"How'd he wreck it?" I asked.

"The bike? He wiped out on Port Avenue."

"Ah, that's too bad."

Boyd swiveled his head from Johnny to me. "He blames you two guys for that, by the way."

"Us?" Johnny laughed.

"It was right after y'all chained it up. He left the gym looking for you as soon as he untangled his bike, peeling out like a bat outta hell. Lost control and laid it over."

"I guess he shouldn't have keyed our car," I said.

Boyd put his hands on the steering wheel and looked straight ahead. "Look, I have to go."

"You afraid Karl will find out you're talking to us?" Johnny asked. "You scared of him?"

Boyd looked at Johnny. "Hell, yeah I am. You guys ought to be scared of him, too."

"Naw, he's all talk. He just *thinks* he's a badass."

Boyd's eyes flickered in fear; Johnny and I both noticed it.

Johnny changed the subject. "That's a long time to repair a bike."

"It took him a while to earn the dough to fix it."

"Did he really *earn* it?" I asked, "or did he steal wallets or break into houses?"

"Or boxing gyms," Johnny added.

Boyd tried not to react but did a poor job of it.

Johnny kept pushing. "Probably pretty handy for him to have a friend with a car, so he could haul off all that loot. But the stuff you stole from Hunsacker's gym didn't have much value, did it?"

"I don't know what y'all are talking about."

"Yeah, you do. Look, Boyd, we'd kind of like to talk to Karl. Where do you think we might find him?"

"You know where his house is. I seen you drive by."

"Yeah, but that mean ol' detective is always hanging around there. He doesn't much like us. Imagine that."

"I really gotta go," Boyd pleaded. He made like he was taking a sip from his Coke, but there was nothing but ice in the cup, and the straw made a hollow sound when he sucked on it. "What the hell do you guys want from me?"

"We're just shootin' the shit, Boyd," Johnny answered casually. "What I wonder, though, is what *Karl* wants from you? Why is he looking for you?"

Boyd looked up, anxious. "Who told you that?"

Johnny nodded toward the carhops. "They did. Told us he came around earlier and asked if they'd seen you. Wanted to know where he could find you."

I knew Johnny was making this up as he went along. But, of course, Boyd didn't.

"He say why?"

"No. But they did say he was acting strange, panicky like. Kind of gave 'em the creeps."

He let Boyd ponder for a moment. A motorcycle sped down Weber Road, and Boyd looked up quickly at his rear view mirror.

Johnny turned his head and watched the motorcycle pass by. "Don't worry. It's not him." He leaned in and spoke in a low, urgent voice, a different voice than before. "Boyd, listen to me. You *know* why he's looking for you. The cops are on to him, man. They found some stuff under his bed that links him to Stubby's murder and also to the attack on Rachel Worthington. Karl's runnin' scared, man . . . and he's desperate."

Johnny said it so softly, I wondered if Boyd even heard him.

Boyd's grip tightened around the steering wheel. "You're full of shit, Sweetwater."

"No? An autographed Joe Louis photograph, a cast iron paperweight, a necklace that belonged to Rachel. Sound familiar? That bulldog still had some of Stubby's blood on it. The cops came by Baltazar's this afternoon and asked me and Charlie to confirm that the picture and the paperweight belonged to Stubby. And earlier today, the Worthington family identified the necklace. It's just a matter of time before they find Karl and arrest him."

Boyd's face turned white.

"What's weird is why Karl is driving around looking for you, when he should be hiding from the law. You think maybe he's going to ask you to lie for him again? Tell the cops y'all were at another movie? Holding hands, maybe?"

Boyd fumbled with his keys and started the ignition. "I gotta go."

Johnny reached over and turned off the car. "Or maybe he wants to make sure you don't talk at all."

"I mean it. I *gotta go.*"

"Where to, Boyd? Where can you go that he won't find you?"

Johnny's story had had its effect, and now I was certain that Boyd had been involved in the crimes. It was written all over his face.

"You knew all along, didn't you?" I blurted. "You son-of-a-bitch, you were in on it. That was your car we heard speeding away from the gym that morning." I turned toward him, meaning to grab the little weasel by the neck, but Johnny shot me a look that told me to back off and shut the hell up. I bottled up my temper and let Johnny continue. As usual, he was way ahead of me.

Johnny directed Boyd's attention away from me. "Look over here, Boyd. Listen to me; this next part is important. The way I figure it, Karl is gonna do one of two things. If they catch him quick, and interrogate him, he'll point the finger at you . . . he'll say *you* did those horrible things. He'll peddle your ass for a nickle and you know it."

Boyd stared straight ahead, and Johnny continued talking, low and calm. "And if they can't find him right away, if he slips the police . . . he's gonna come after you, isn't he? You're the only eyewitness, the only person who knows he committed those crimes. You don't want him coming after you, do you, Boyd?"

Boyd bowed his head. "But I didn't hurt nobody," he whispered. "It was Karl. It was all Karl."

"I know, Boyd," said Johnny, patting his shoulder sympathetically. "We know what he's like."

"No, you don't. The guy's crazy. Cruel. Meaner than anyone I've ever seen. The things he *does* to people. It's . . . ." Boyd stopped and looked at Johnny with panic in his eyes. "What do I do?"

"You beat Karl to the punch, that's what you do. You tell the cops everything."

Boyd began shaking his head. "He'll kill me. I can't—"

"Boyd, *you are gonna get caught*. But if *you* go to them, before they catch Karl—"

"Or before Karl catches you," I added.

"If you do that . . ." Johnny continued, "you can save yourself. And make Karl pay."

"But Radcliff . . . he's screwing Karl's mom. That woman's got him wrapped around her finger. He'll protect Karl." He looked up at the rearview mirror again. "I am so fucked."

"Don't worry about Radcliff. I know someone who can help you."

"Who? Where?"

"My uncle. He has a joint near here. And believe me, it's the last place Karl McDevitt would think to go."

Boyd nodded meekly, wiping away tears.

Johnny came around and opened the passenger door. Before he climbed into Boyd's car, he put his head near mine. "Take the girls home and meet me at Noble's place. I'll ride over there with Boyd."

Boyd was ready to spill everything. Noble would know how to make it count. I said okay and fast-walked back to the Jeep.

The girls could tell something was up.

"You and your brother are trying to get Boyd Parker to talk, aren't you?" said Carmen.

I nodded. "It's working, too. Johnny made up some stuff that scared the shit out of him. He's ready to rat out his friend."

Veronica's eyes widened, and then narrowed in anger. "So Karl *did* do it."

"Looks that way. Johnny and Boyd are driving to my Uncle Noble's bar now. I'm supposed to meet them there." I hesitated a beat. "It'd probably be better if, um—"

"You can drop us off at Veronica's on your way over," Carmen said, quickly grasping the situation. "I agree it's better if we're not there. You can fill us in later."

At Veronica's house, Carmen leaned into the Jeep before I drove off. "Karl's a monster, Charlie. You need to remember that. And be careful."

———

CHAPTER 36

When I pulled into Noble's Ice House, my headlights sliced across the backyard patio and briefly captured Boyd and Johnny, sitting side-by-side on top of a picnic table. As usual, a couple of prowl cars were parked out front, their off-duty custodians inside sipping suds and playing dominoes. They paid no attention to me as I walked through the bar to the back. When I pushed through the screen door, Noble stepped out of the shadows and stopped me on the porch.

"Let 'em talk, Charlie," he said in a low voice.

"Jesus, you scared me," I whispered.

"The kid's spillin' his guts over there. I called a federal marshal to come get him; he's on his way over."

"Is this marshal the right guy?"

"Yeah, it's in his jurisdiction, and he's as straight as they come. We go way back."

Johnny and Boyd were dark silhouettes on the unlit patio. While Boyd talked, his quiet confession punctuated with broken sobs, Johnny sat beside him, his arms crossed, listening. He offered no comfort.

A few minutes later, we heard car wheels crunching across the oyster shell parking lot. Noble and I went inside and were met by a gigantic man wearing a badge pinned to a crisp white shirt. It took me a few seconds, but I finally recognized him—Red Burton, a good friend of my Uncle Rupert's and former sheriff of San Patricio County.

I'd heard he left Aransas Pass and moved to Los Angeles a few years back, and then returned to Texas after his wife divorced him. He'd recently been appointed district U.S. marshal for South Texas.

He and Noble shook hands and spoke briefly, voices muted. He looked at me and smiled. "Hey, Charlie. Been a long time."

Red was a frequent visitor to Ransom Island when I was a kid. At six foot four inches tall, he seemed like a giant back then, but he'd grown even bigger since. He'd bulked up, and I bet he weighed close to three hundred pounds. A lot of it was fat, but it was *hard* fat, if that makes any sense.

"So you think this kid witnessed a murder?"

"Yes, sir. We think he was with a local thug named Karl McDevitt when Karl killed Stubby Hunsacker, the boxing gym owner. He also might know what happened to a friend of ours, Rachel Worthington. She was assaulted and beaten within an inch of her life."

He looked through the back door. "I heard about both of those. He tellin' your brother about it now?"

"Yes, sir."

"Why do you think he's so talkative all of a sudden?"

"He's scared to death of Karl McDevitt. We, uh, kinda made up a story about Karl being out to get him."

The lawman looked at me with a wry expression. "Looks like it worked."

I saw Johnny motioning me over.

"Go on," the marshal told me.

At the picnic table, Johnny stood up and offered me his seat. "Why don't you sit with Boyd for a minute while I go get us something to drink." He tried to keep his voice relaxed, but I could tell he was rattled.

"Sure," I answered. Boyd sat with his elbows on his knees and didn't look up. I didn't want to say the wrong thing, so I kept my mouth shut. Boyd was silent, too. He seemed wrung out and defeated, but if he decided to jump up and run, I was ready to tackle him and stand on his neck to keep him from getting away. Behind me, I could hear Johnny quietly bringing the marshal up to speed.

Boyd was submissive when Red handcuffed him and put him in the squad car. I think the kid was glad to get it all off his chest. Before the marshal left, he asked my brother and me to follow him to the federal courthouse on Lower Broadway. On the drive there, Johnny recounted Boyd's confession. He sounded tired. Some things will wear your ass out just to hear about them.

Even though I was only fifteen, I wasn't totally wet behind the ears. Hanging around the shrimp docks and around my uncles' bars, I'd seen some tough hombres and some pretty scary badasses. But I wasn't prepared for the kind of twisted shit that Boyd said Karl McDevitt had done. If all of it was true, Karl was far more dangerous than I'd ever suspected. And far worse.

Johnny hated repeating Boyd's confessions as much as I hated hearing them.

Stubby's murder happened much like we'd suspected. Karl was plenty pissed about getting run out of the gym a second time, so he had Boyd Parker drive him there so he could, as he put it, "wreck" the place again. Boyd waited down the street in his car while Karl jimmied the front door lock and went in. When Stubby showed up unexpectedly, Karl hid in the office and bashed him over the head with the cast iron bulldog as soon as he stepped through the door. And then he kept hitting him until he was sure he was dead. Boyd said Karl laughed about it afterwards, saying "the old bastard couldn't go the distance with Karl 'The Bulldog' McDevitt."

As for Rachel Worthington, Boyd and Karl were cruising around drinking beer when they discovered Rachel in the T-Head parking lot, passed out in her car. They dumped her in the trunk of Boyd's Chevy and drove to the Bayview Cemetery nearby, where Boyd stood watch while Karl ravaged her and then left her for dead. Boyd said the assault was so violent and sadistic that it didn't seem real to him while it was happening. Before they left her broken body in the graveyard, Karl ripped the necklace off Rachel's neck because "the bitch owed it to him for jilting him."

Those were the two crimes we knew about. Boyd said there were others, too.

Karl told Boyd that he'd "set on" three other women before Rachel—two itinerant prostitutes and a runaway; girls he'd found in North Beach and who wouldn't be missed.

According to Karl, he'd raped and strangled one girl, and then left her tied to a mesquite tree in a backcountry slough near Rincon Bayou. Another girl he tortured by squirting half a tube of Ben-Gay heat rub up inside of her, "until she screamed like a stuck pig." Boyd shook his head. "But she wasn't making no more noise when he come back to the car. I know Karl did somethin' to shut her up. Somethin' bad."

Johnny told me he almost quit listening right there. But there was more.

Boyd also recounted how Karl had taken him to an overgrown field near the ship channel and showed him a woman's body that was bloating badly in the August heat. He told Boyd he'd beat the girl senseless and then strangled her with a tire iron because she'd tried to steal money out of his wallet after they'd had sex. He said that that's what happened to people who tried to cross him. Boyd said he never forgot it.

Karl seemed to get as big a kick talking about his crimes as he did committing them. And Boyd Parker—friendless, submissive, horrified but also impressed by Karl's tough guy act—was a perfect audience. Karl bragged that he'd killed a wino in North Beach after the man supposedly peed on his motorcycle tire. And Boyd said Karl was pretty sure he'd killed a night watchman during a burglary attempt at a railyard warehouse.

"Do you think it's all true?" I asked.

"I think Karl told him those things, yeah. And if half of them are true—hell if *any* of them is true, I hope they strap the bastard to the electric chair and fry his ass."

I felt the same way.

Before the marshal took Boyd away, he asked Johnny and me to wait in the admitting office until he came back down. We waited there for four hours. We imagined Marshal Burton and some of his deputies standing over Boyd in one of the interrogation rooms, Boyd singing like an opera diva.

When Red Burton finally came for us, daylight wasn't too far off. The marshal looked tired as he took us upstairs to his office. He poured us each a cup of coffee, and one for himself, and then asked me and Johnny to repeat everything Boyd had told us that day. It took awhile.

He checked his notes frequently as we talked. When we'd finished, he leaned back in his chair, put his boots on the desk, and rubbed his eyes. Light was beginning to show through the windows.

"The story's consistent, that's for sure." He pulled a couple of business cards out of his wallet and handed them to us. "I may call you if I have any more questions, and y'all be sure and call me if you think of anything else that might be useful." He leaned back in his chair and eyed us approvingly. "You boys did good."

"What happens next?" asked Johnny.

"Well, we find Karl McDevitt and arrest his sorry ass."

He shook his head and chuckled. "Those Keystone Kops in Corpus are gonna be *pissed*. Having to see a third guy busted for the same murder is downright embarrassing."

Johnny nodded. "Is Boyd Parker's testimony gonna be enough?"

"It's a hell of a start. But that's not all we have. While we were questioning the Parker kid, I stepped out for a minute and woke up a judge. I'd already heard enough to ask him for a search warrant for the suspect's house. My deputies have already been there and come back."

"Was the box still under Karl's bed?" I asked.

"How'd you know about that?" asked the marshal.

"Boyd told us about it," said Johnny without hesitation.

I bit my lip and agreed with my brother. "Right, Boyd mentioned it." No need to complicate matters by bringing Pete's B&E into the story.

The sheriff eyed us for a beat and then continued. "Anyway, somebody had moved the evidence by the time we got there, but when we searched the backyard, my guys noticed a fresh patch of dirt and found it right quick. The box was so full of incriminating material they said they almost expected it to have an evidence tag attached to it, with the case number and date already filled in."

"I bet Mavis McDevitt was happy to see your boys digging up her oleander bushes," said Johnny.

Marshal Burton shook his head. "They finally had to confine her in one of the squad cars. Said she had some mouth on her . . . my Lord. When Frank Hamer blew away Bonnie and Clyde, he said he 'hated to bust a cap on a lady.' But I don't believe he'd have felt the same about Mavis McDevitt."

"Does she know where he is?" asked Johnny.

"It didn't seem like it. But she probably wouldn't say if she did. The way she tells it, her son's an Eagle Scout. Never so much as spit on the sidewalk. But the APB has already been issued. We'll find him soon enough."

"What about Harley Radcliff?" I asked.

Red raised an eyebrow. "The CCPD detective?"

"He's been spending a lot of time with Karl's mom. I think they have a . . . thing, you know?"

The marshal added a couple of notes to his legal pad.

Johnny rotated his Styrofoam cup and watched the steam rising off the coffee. "Marshal, do you think Karl did all those things? Do you think he was telling Boyd the truth?"

"That'll be up to a grand jury to decide. And it can go a million ways, depending on how strong a case the DA thinks he can make. Boyd's a minor in the eyes of the law; I don't know how much weight the jurors will give his story. And Karl's mother will alibi his ass up one side and down the other." Red slurped the last of his coffee. "But that's not my department, thank God. I just catch 'em; I don't have to cook 'em.

"The good thing is, there's enough evidence to arrest him for Hunsacker's murder, and for what he did to that Worthington girl. The other accusations will require a whole lot of police work before any more charges can be added. Again, not my department." The marshal leaned toward us. "But if you want my opinion—and that's all it is . . . my opinion—I think you boys helped us identify a genuine cut-throat killer . . . a real psychopath. Karl McDevitt was just getting a taste for it, too. I believe he'd have kept doing it until he was killed or caught."

"You haven't caught him yet," said Johnny.

Red Burton gave a weary smile. "Aw, hell. That's why I make the big bucks."

CHAPTER 37

Three days passed, and they still hadn't caught Karl McDevitt. I was afraid he'd done what many Texas outlaws had done over the past century—hightailed it to Mexico. Johnny was more optimistic.

"He's too cocky for that. And he thinks he's smarter than the cops."

At any rate, there was nothing we could do about it.

School was out for the Christmas holidays, and Dad was on his way back from the Gulf. So except for some chores around the house and a couple of hours training at the gym, my brother and I were free to do as we pleased. Determined not to let Dad scrooge up the holiday, we dug up and re-potted a small palmetto bush and decorated it with Christmas lights and tinsel. We put Dad's present, a new Shakespeare fishing reel, under the "tree." When a strong cold front brought some respectable waves to Port Aransas, Johnny, Pete, and I strapped our boards to the top of the wagon and headed for the beach. We picked up Carmen and Veronica on the way.

Carmen was all smiles when she climbed into the back seat with me. I couldn't help but smile back. "Why are you so happy today?"

She waited until Veronica was in the car. "Good news."

"Yeah? Lay it on us," said Johnny.

"Jesse has been released. My mom called me last night and said they'd be sending him home on Saturday."

Johnny and I were elated.

"It's about time," he said.

"Is it home, Corpus Christi, or home, Cuba?" I asked. "And who's 'they'?"

"Home Cuba. Havana. Jesse said some government men signed him out last week. Apparently he's been in Miami for over a week, but they wouldn't let him notify anyone until yesterday."

"That's really great news," Pete agreed. "But, Cuba . . . . Is that where he wants to be?"

Carmen thought about it for a moment. "Yes, I think it is. He wanted to be with his family. This was the only way."

The only way—but what might it cost him if he wound up as a chew toy caught between Ramón's secret police and the CIA? But I knew Jesse didn't have much choice in the matter, and I agreed with Carmen. After all that had happened, Cuba was probably his best chance at a happy life, despite the political complications.

But part of me was sad that I wouldn't see him at the gym anymore, and maybe not ever again. The news of his release brought back a cascade of memories . . . good memories, but painful, too: Jesse's beautiful boxing technique, his famous smile, his friendship, Stubby and his smelly old gym, Naco Flores. It would never be like it was before. Everything had changed.

As we headed down Ocean Drive toward the causeway, Veronica instructed Johnny to turn into the driveway of one of the big mansions fronting the bay.

"Is this Rachel's house?" he asked.

Pete looked up quickly. "It sure is. Is she going with us?"

"If it's okay with you guys," Veronica answered. "She's not a hundred percent well yet, but her parents agreed that some fresh air would do her good."

"Heck, yeah, it'll do her some good," said Pete.

If Pete had a tail, it would've been wagging like mad.

Rachel presented us with a cautious smile when she climbed into the car. "Hi ya, guys."

The scars on her face were healing, and I couldn't help but notice she walked with a slight limp, moving in sort of a wary, tentative fashion. It seemed like something was still broken inside her.

Pete smiled and reached for her hand. "Lemme help you," he said. She hesitated a moment, and then took it and eased painfully into the back seat.

On the way to Mustang Island, we carried on about this and that: about the recent movies we'd seen, about the latest Chubby Checker twist song on the radio, and about the *Nutcracker* shows that Carmen and Veronica had been dancing in the past few weeks. We talked about anything except what had happened to Rachel. Johnny finally brought it up in a roundabout way.

"Rachel, we're really glad to see that you're doing better. We've all been pulling for you."

She smiled wanly, nodded in acknowledgment, and then turned to look out the window at the choppy bay below the causeway. The car was quiet for awhile.

We parked near Bob Hall Pier, and while the girls unfolded a blanket to sit on, Johnny and I squeezed into our neoprene vests and unstrapped our surfboards. Pete chose to sit with Rachel and watch from the beach. I noticed he'd removed his jacket and put it around Rachel's shoulders. He'd been treating her with kid gloves ever since she got into the car with us.

We gave a thumbs up to the girls and plunged headlong into the surf.

The waves weren't huge by West Coast standards, but they were plenty fun for us. On one ride, Johnny disappeared into a barrel for a few long seconds and emerged from the other end with his arms held high, fists pumping in celebration. My big moment came when I fell off the tip of a gnarly curl and plowed headfirst into the surf. The wave broke on top of me, grinding me into a sand bar, and when I staggered to my feet, my swimsuit was wrapped around my ankles. That performance got more far more claps and whistles than Johnny's barrel ride. I turned around in the shallow swash and mooned my admirers.

Before sunset, we stowed our boards and changed into our clothes. Pete bought us a round of hot coffees at the snack bar, and we walked out to the end of the pier. Fishermen wrapped in Army surplus blankets, Coast Guard peacoats, and flannel-lined hunting jackets sat in folding chairs along the rail of the 1,200-foot pier, sipping from thermoses or beer cans, monitoring their corks that bobbed in the surf below. Many of them would fish all night, hoping to hook a bull red, a king, or maybe a big shark. None of them said anything about our daring surfboard feats. Fishermen thought surfers were a pain in the ass.

We sipped from our Styrofoam cups, enjoying the chilly northeast wind in our faces. Pete sidled up to Johnny and gave him an elbow nudge, nodding towards Rachel. She hadn't done much talking and now she was leaning on the pier railing, inhaling the vapor from her coffee and starting out at the Gulf. Her shoulders seemed to slump.

"I think we should go now," he said.

Johnny nodded and rounded us up for the trip back.

When we pulled up in front of Rachel's house, Carmen and Veronica climbed out of the car and walked their friend to the front door.

Carmen broke away and came back. "Charlie, I think we're going to stay here awhile. You don't mind, do you?"

"No, of course not. She could probably use a couple of girlfriends right now. It's been a great afternoon, Carmen. Thanks for sharing the news about Jesse."

Carmen smiled up at me. "I'm so glad I know you, Charlie."

Right then, I had never been happier.

Pete, however, was in a different frame of mind. On the drive back to his neighborhood, he asked us to pass by Karl McDevitt's house once again. He glared at the nondescript little bungalow as we rolled by. "I hope the marshal shoots that motherfucker in the dick when he catches him."

We invited Pete to join us for supper, but he declined. "I wouldn't be very good company. I'll catch you guys later."

Johnny and I ate at the Eat-A-Bite—ham steak for me, a chopped steak for my brother—and speculated on Jesse Martel's future.

"I'd like to see the look on those CIA boys' faces when Feo tells them to shove their spy plan up their asses," said Johnny.

"I just hope Ramón and his bosses honor their part of the agreement and leave him alone. Feo's been jerked around enough."

"That's for sure. Everyone wanted a piece of him."

"Everyone except Stubby."

"Everyone except Stubby," Johnny repeated.

"You think Feo will ever come back here?"

"He'd have to defect to do it. And he sure as hell won't leave Cuba without his family again."

"Wouldn't it be fun someday to sit with Feo on the seawall in Havana, laughing about Stubby and drinking . . . what do they drink anyway?"

"Rum," Johnny said definitively. "And lots of it."

"Yeah, rum. We could do it, too, if the damn politicians would get out of the way."

Johnny raised his coffee cup and smiled. "Next year, in Havana."

A waitress wearing a Santa Claus cap dropped off our check. As we paid at the counter, I picked up a Goodart's Peanut Patty. "Should we take one of these over to Pete?" Pete had a real weakness for the pink, sugar-coated delicacy shaped like the state of Texas. "Maybe it'll cheer him up."

"Naw, it wouldn't be right to take just one. We'd have to buy one for everyone in the family." He looked at the box under the glass-topped counter. "And I don't think they have enough." Pete had two brothers, four sisters, and I think at least one set of grandparents living in his house. The place looked like the dang Mexican consulate, especially on the holidays.

A gust of cold wind hit us when we walked outside, so we zipped our jackets and stuffed our hands into our pockets. I hustled to catch up with my brother. "Why do you think it's taking them so long to catch him?"

"Karl? I don't know. Could be he's holing up somewhere. With a friend, maybe."

"I don't think he has any friends. Except Boyd Parker."

"Naw, Boyd was more like his pet dog or something."

"That dog took a piece out of Karl's ass in the end, though, didn't he?"

"That he did."

We started the wagon and meandered through downtown, headed for home. Lichtenstein's Department store on Chaparral Street was lit up with Christmas lights and still buzzing with shoppers, but the streets emptied out as we made our way to the Harbor Bridge. The courthouse, municipal buildings, and even the shipyard were buttoned up tight. Despite the holiday season, the city seemed a little forlorn to me.

On the north side of Harbor Bridge, Johnny slowed and took the North Beach exit. I looked at him for an explanation.

"I just thought of someone who might know if Karl has any friends."

"Who?"

"Bill the Beachcomber."

It seemed like a long shot, but Karl did favor his tattoos, and we knew he'd been to Bill's before. The tattoo parlor was located under the bridge, at the south end of North Beach, so to get there, we had to cruise by the shady-looking businesses that fronted the street. There were hardly any windows on the bars—most joints only had a door, an exterior light, and maybe an awning—and some didn't even have signs. But despite the blank fronts, quite a few cars and motorcycles were parked haphazardly around the buildings, suggesting plenty of action inside. Christmas cheer, however, seemed in short supply.

"Looks like the kind of neighborhood Karl would come to," I said.

Johnny shook his head. "Too good for him."

Bill the Beachcomber's tattoo parlor doubled as a curio shop, where customers could buy a corny T-shirt to cover up their ill-considered tattoo once they sobered up. Bill was locking the front door of his shop when we parked and walked up.

"You two again," he said placidly.

"Yes, sir," Johnny answered. "Sorry to bother you so late."

Bill chuckled. "It's early for North Beach. I was getting ready to close for the holidays. You boys here for a tattoo? I offer a discount for the first one. Got a topless mermaid sittin' on a reindeer that's real popular this time of year."

"We're looking for someone."

"Yeah? Same fella? The one with the girlfriend problems?"

"Yes, sir. Same one. And now the cops are after him, too."

Bill paused on his porch and pulled out a cigarette paper and some tobacco. "What'd he do?"

"The guy killed our boxing trainer," I said.

"And almost killed that girl whose name you tattooed on his arm," Johnny added.

Bill rolled his makings into a neat cylinder, licked it shut, and then fired it up. The hand holding the lighter had a Hawaiian sunset tattooed across the back of it. "Why are you boys involved? Police get paid for this sort of work."

"Just playing a hunch," I said, feeling slightly ridiculous after I'd said it. It sounded like I'd stolen the line from a Hardy Boys story, which I had.

Bill the Beachcomber looked at us through his black-frame eyeglasses, mildly amused. "This guy struck me as a pretty rough customer when he came here to get inked. Not someone a couple of high school kids would wanna tangle with."

"We've tangled with him before," said Johnny.

"This guy you're looking for, he rode a Triumph, didn't he?"

"He did," Johnny answered.

Bill nodded briefly and looked down the street. "Well, last time he was in here, he might have asked about a local motorcycle club that formed not long ago, the Koastal Kronks. Wanted me to put the club's emblem on his arm . . . got a little pissy when I told him he'd have to be accepted into the club first. Anyway, they like to hang out at a place called Blackbeard's. It's on this street, just a few blocks thataway." He nodded his head to the north. "It ain't no malt shop, boys. And the cops won't come running, either."

"Thanks, mister," said Johnny, stepping forward and offering his hand.

Bill the Beachcomber's other hand was tattooed down to the knuckles with a blue spider web design. He shook my brother's hand and grinned. "Offer still stands for that first tattoo. Jack London said 'Show me a man with a tattoo, and I'll show you a man with an interesting past.'"

"I'm not sure I want to be that interesting," Johnny replied.

"Merry Christmas, Bill," I said in parting.

"Merry Christmas." He ground out his cigarette and tossed it away. The cold north wind swept the glowing fragments down Surfside Boulevard. "You boys be careful."

———

CHAPTER 38

There was nothing striking about Blackbeard's, except maybe the long line of choppers parked out front. We counted nine Harleys, an Ariel Cyclone, and two Triumphs, neither of which was Karl's. The cars and motorcycles looked ghostly under the mercury vapor streetlight.

Bikers were a new thing on the coast. We'd seen them rumbling up and down Hwy. 35 from time to time, flying wedges of semi-outlaws wearing greasy denim, leather vests, and expressions of vague menace. They never seemed headed to anywhere in particular.

"Are we gonna be this stupid?" I asked.

Johnny looked at me, thinking it over. "We might look a little young."

He said "we," but I knew he meant me. "Didn't we go in there before? When we were looking for Rachel?"

"I can't remember. All these places kind of run together."

"Well, I'm not scared," I said, even though I was.

"I believe you," he said, even though he didn't.

"You think one of the Koastal Kronks has seen him?"

"How bad do we want to know?"

Johnny continued to watch the dive bar. Dirty fluorescents under the awning smeared the side of the building with bluish light, and I could hear a jukebox throbbing inside. "I have a better idea," he said.

He put the car in gear and drove across the street to a parking lot, pulling in between a trailered jon boat and a junked delivery truck. I was working up the courage to step out of the car when Johnny sat back and stretched his arm across the back of the seat.

"Relax, brother. Let's sit here for awhile and see who comes by. We've got nothing better to do. Tree's up, presents are wrapped, and Santa won't come around 'til Christmas Eve."

"Fine by me." I put a foot up on the dash and tried not to look too relieved.

For having such a notorious reputation, not much seemed to happen at Blackbeard's, at least not outside the building. We watched a burly guy walk out with a cheap looking girl on his arm; he drove her away in a rusty Oldsmobile. A mangy dog trotted by, stopping to pee on a trashcan. A guy who was definitely not Cary Grant came out and drunkenly pissed on the same trashcan as the dog. The jukebox continued to growl and grind.

Mostly I watched bugs flutter around the streetlamp and thought of the North Beach of my childhood. The Ferris wheel had stood no more than fifty yards from where we sat. I remember riding it one time with my mom, and at the top of the wheel's rotation the wind snatched the cotton candy cone from my hand. We both laughed as we watched it sail over the people and noise and light of the amusement park.

At some point, I fell asleep in the car, because Johnny had to nudge me awake.

"Hey, check it out."

A dingy brown Ford rolled to a stop at the perimeter of the bar's parking lot, just out of the pool of dirty blue fluorescence, and turned off its headlights. The driver stayed in the car. I noticed the buggy whip antenna and spotlight mounted by the driver's-side rearview window. "Is that Radcliff's Fairlane?" I asked.

"Sure looks like it."

We slid down further in the seat.

"You think he's looking for Karl, too?"

"Yeah, but *why* is he looking for him?"

I thought about that a minute. Inside the dark Fairlane I saw a match flare and touch the end of a cigarette, briefly illuminating Detective Radcliff's droopy face. "Seems like he would bring back-up if someone tipped him off that Karl was here."

"It would if he was planning to arrest him."

"Why else would he be here?"

"I don't know. Let's hide and watch."

It suddenly occurred to me that our surfboards were still strapped to the top of our station wagon. We might as well have been in a Good Humor ice cream truck as far as being inconspicuous went. "You think he can see us over here?"

"We're pretty far away. Anyway, it's too late to do anything about it."

Over the next half hour, an assortment of Blackbeard's customers came and went, paying no attention to the unmarked cop car or to our surfmobile across the street. Around midnight, a Triumph motorcycle rumbled into view from the north. Karl McDevitt had on his leather jacket, but he'd added a WWII aviator helmet and goggles to his getup, no doubt to disguise his wanted face. A suitcase was strapped to the back of his bike. Johnny and I held our breath.

Karl circled the parking lot and pulled in next to Radcliff's sedan. We could see the two of them talking to each other. Karl stayed on his bike, and Radcliff never left his car. After a short conversation, Radcliff handed Karl a leather satchel through the window.

"What the hell's going on?" I whispered.

"If I had to guess, I'd say our detective friend is helping Karl get away."

Karl opened the bag and pulled out an envelope full of what appeared to be cash, by the way he thumbed through it.

"I'd bet you're right. Shit. What do you wanna bet Radcliff is doing this for Karl's mom?"

Johnny nodded. "I'd bet you're right, too."

"All for a piece of ass?"

"Maybe. Maybe she's blackmailing him, threatening to tell Radcliff's wife that her husband's a cheatin' sumbitch. Could be he just wants Karl out of there so he and Karl's mom can play house. Who the hell knows?"

Karl slung the satchel strap over his head and positioned it near his chest, bandolier style. Radcliff tossed his cigarette and rolled up the car window. Karl gave the detective a short wave, put his bike in gear, and then headed toward the highway. At the same time, Radcliff started his car and took off in the opposite direction.

I looked at Johnny. "Karl's gonna get away. What do we do?"

"I don't know. We can follow him. At least until we see which way he's going. When we know that, we'll stop at the first phone booth we find and call Marshal Burton."

"We're pretty obvious with those boards on top."

"No time to take 'em off. I'll stay far enough back that he won't notice us."

"Okay . . . . What's the worst that could happen?"

Johnny flashed me a quick smile and started the car. "The Sweetwater family motto."

Two short blocks in front of us, we spotted Karl driving north, parallel to the bridge. As soon as he reached an on-ramp, he hopped onto the long causeway that crossed Nueces Bay. The small town of Portland was on the other side, followed by Gregory, Aransas Pass, and then Rockport.

I wondered briefly if he might be heading straight to our house, looking for payback. There was no telling what his crazy-ass mom had put in his get-away bag. Probably a Bowie knife, a pistol, and a couple of hand grenades. Maybe a bazooka. I pushed aside a surge of fear and focused on Karl's motorcycle in the distance.

Even though it was past midnight, there was enough traffic on the road that we were able to keep a car or two between us and Karl's Triumph, but still stay close enough to keep him in sight.

"If he's going to Houston, he'll have to pass through Rockport and Fulton," I said. "We can call the marshal from there. They might be able to catch him on the Copano Bridge when he crosses Aransas Bay."

Johnny nodded. "If he can get the local cops to scramble fast enough."

But Karl had another route in mind. As soon as he crossed the causeway into Portland, he turned off and began backtracking to the southwest on a farm to market road.

"Dammit," said Johnny. "I bet Radcliff warned him to keep off the main roads. There's no telling where he's going. This is gonna be tricky."

The country roads that crisscrossed the Gulf Coast farm belt were not heavily traveled and were mostly used by farmers to haul their crops to market. Johnny had to hang way back so Karl wouldn't realize he had a tail. He also had to push the Jeep wagon pretty hard to keep the single red taillight from Karl's Triumph in view. About halfway to Taft, we spotted multiple taillights in the distance. When we were close enough, we saw they belonged to a big cotton trailer and the tractor that pulled it. The rig was hogging three quarters of the road.

"Can you pass it?" I asked.

"I don't know. There's hardly any shoulder."

The tractor chugged slowly down the road. The wire-mesh trailer was piled high with winter cotton, heading for the nearest gin. Karl had raced right by it, and was surely speeding north as fast as he could go. If we waited much longer, Karl would get away. I shot a worried look at Johnny.

"Here goes nothin'," he said, slashing to the left of the trailer and fishtailing in the soft dirt alongside the road. I think the car's left wheels rolled down a plowed cotton furrow for ten to twenty yards. Finally, the car wheels found pavement again and we sped ahead of the tractor.

Johnny leaned forward, peering through the windshield. "I don't see him."

I searched the darkness beyond the headlights, but I couldn't see anything, either. A few miles down the road, we passed the bright lights of a cotton gin, which was working around the clock during harvest. Cotton wagons, empty and full, were lined up around the gin, and the air was hazy with dust from the ginning machines. Cotton lint blew across the highway and blanketed the stripped fields like snow.

Johnny floored the accelerator, and we plunged headlong down the dark road. Soon a soft glow glimmered on the horizon.

"We're screwed if he beat us to Taft," said Johnny.

Taft was a tiny town, but there were four or five roads spoking off the main street. "We'll just have to guess which road he took."

"Or we call the marshal and let him know Karl's last known location."

"That makes more sense," I agreed.

A moment later, I noticed Johnny's eyes alternating between the rearview mirror and the road ahead. "Somebody's coming up behind us."

I turned around and saw a single headlight approaching. "Jesus, he's hauling ass. You think it's him?"

Johnny slowed to a normal speed. "Guess we'll find out."

I watched the light bear down on our Jeep until it was directly behind us, blinding us. The motorcycle slowed briefly then juked to the left, coming up alongside our car. Karl turned his head toward us, a fierce frown beneath his goggles. Johnny and I frowned back.

His right hand left the handlebar and disappeared into his jacket. Johnny and I both spotted the pistol the moment he pulled it out.

"Get down!" Johnny shouted.

A shot shattered the driver window and Johnny stomped on the brakes, throwing me into the dash. When I raised my head, I saw the back end of one of the surfboards pivot around to the front of the car, and then, as Johnny hurried to turn the car around, the board broke loose and tumbled into a roadside ditch.

"Are you okay?" I yelled.

Johnny floored the accelerator again. I reached up and turned on the dome light.

"Is that blood on your face? Were you hit?"

Johnny rubbed his face with his hand and looked at his palm. "They're just glass cuts. What about you?"

"I'm fine," I answered, although my heart was beating like mad. "How'd he sneak up on us like that?"

"Probably hid behind a cotton trailer back at that gin." We were both screaming to be heard over the wind that howled through the shattered window.

I turned around and watched the road. Soon the headlight was coming for us again, coming at us like a guided missile. "He's behind us again. What do we do?"

Johnny glanced at the mirror. "We can't outrun him in this old jalopy."

"Maybe we can keep him behind us," I shouted. "Keep him from pulling alongside." I couldn't dispel the image of Karl's crazed face as he fired point blank into our car.

"He can shoot through the back window, too."

"Right . . . . Think we can make it to Portland before he catches us? Maybe we'll see a cop there."

Johnny shook his head. "No way we'll make it."

We were probably going eighty miles an hour, but the headlight behind us seemed to have our car in its grasp, like a tractor beam, pulling us toward it.

"I've got an idea," Johnny yelled. "Switch places with me."

Before I could ask him to explain, he'd taken his foot off the gas and was scooting over. "Grab the wheel!"

I grabbed the wheel and climbed over him, punching the gas again. I anxiously watched the rearview mirror while Johnny rolled down the passenger window and climbed halfway outside.

"What the hell?" I yelled. "He's gonna shoot you."

Johnny pulled his head back into the car. "Slow down to sixty."

"But he'll catch us."

"He's gonna catch us anyway. Just keep him behind us."

Johnny pulled out his pocketknife, opened the blade, and then climbed so far out the window he was standing on the seat. I swerved from side to side, trying to keep Karl from pulling alongside us, but also mindful that Johnny was hanging out the window. *What the hell was he doing up there?* In the mirror, I saw Karl's Triumph settle into our draft, and then, through the glare of his headlight, I watched him reach into his pocket for the handgun.

The muzzle flashed when he fired. Instinctively, I pressed the accelerator. The back window exploded when Karl fired again. "Johnny!" I yelled. "Come back inside! Dammit, what are you doing?"

I found out soon enough, although it took me a moment to realize what I was seeing. In the mirror my eye caught a flash of white as he cut the surfboard lose. Then I saw the motorcycle headlight jump crazily from side to side and then flicker out. A spray of sparks enveloped the bike as the machine went down, skidding across the pavement, a whirligig of metal, leather, and flesh. The airborne surfboard bounced off the road, spiraled away, and disappeared into the darkness. A second later, Karl and his bike disappeared, too.

Johnny climbed back inside as I slowed the Jeep and then stopped in the middle of the road. Both of us were breathing heavily.

"Turn around and let's see if he's alive," said Johnny.

I couldn't imagine any way that he was, but as calmly as I could, I made a three-point turn on the narrow road and drove back to the crash site. Chunks of fiberglass surfboard were scattered across the pavement and alongside the road. We had to swerve around a big piece resting on the center stripe. Curlicues of stinking black rubber striped the road.

"Where's the bike?" I asked.

We got out of the Jeep and searched the area illuminated by our headlights.

"He went off the road here," said Johnny, pointing to scrape marks on the asphalt, and to deep grooves and divots in the dirt shoulder. "Point the headlights thisaway, out into the field."

I ran to the Jeep and pulled it around as Johnny had asked, and then I joined him in the search. It didn't take long for us to find the motorcycle. It was half buried in a drainage ditch that lined the field, the hot metal still crackling as it cooled. In the stripped field, random wads of dirty cotton hung on the otherwise barren plant stalks. We found Karl's body ten yards in, sprawled across a couple of plough troughs.

Nothing quite prepares you for seeing a mangled body. I'd seen pictures of them in the gory driver's-ed movies they made us watch in school, the ones with titles like *Red Asphalt* and *The Last Prom*. But it's different when you walk up on a real one: the broken limbs, the twisted, unnatural contortions, the disfigured face, the open, unseeing eyes. The surfboard, probably the fin, had sheared off the top of Karl's head. Johnny and I stood over the body, the idling of our car the only sound in the night.

"Why don't you drive on to Portland and call the marshal," he said. "I'll stay here until you get back."

I looked at my brother in disbelief.

"The police might arrive before you get back. It'll be easier for them to find the wreck if I flag them down."

Had I been braver, I would've volunteered to stay, and I would've insisted that Johnny drive to town to report the accident. After all, he was the one who risked his life by crawling around on the roof of the car to cut loose the surfboard. But what if he'd said yes? The truth was, I couldn't wait to get away from that bloody field. Sitting alone on that dark road with a dead body —especially Karl's—would have been too much.

I drove to town as fast as I dared, and when I returned, Johnny was sitting cross-legged on the narrow road shoulder. He'd fished a pack of cigarettes out of Karl's busted-open suitcase and was puffing on one. I'd never seen him smoke before.

"Am I glad to see you," he said.

He didn't have to explain why.

Soon we heard sirens in the distance, and shortly after, saw the flashing lights. A Sinton unit was first on the scene, but by the end of the hour, it seemed like half the state's police force was there.

A medic cleaned up Johnny's cuts, and we waited for Marshal Burton before we gave our statements. We didn't have to wait long. The marshal listened, made a few notes, and after we'd told him everything, he stuffed the notepad in his pocket. "You boys have had a long night. Do you think you can make it home on your own? I'd drive you myself, but I have some internal police business I've got to take care of."

We knew he was referring to Harley Radcliff.

"We're fine," Johnny answered.

"You sure? I can have a deputy drive you."

We told him we'd make our own way.

Neither of us spoke as we drove back to Rockport, and we welcomed the cold, clean air that blew through the open car.

———

CHAPTER 39

Our dad was waiting for us when we got home; somehow he'd already heard the news. He wasn't yet fifty, but for the first time he looked old to me. I expect we had something to do with it. He questioned us about what happened six ways to Sunday, but there wasn't any coherent way to explain that my big brother had basically decapitated a guy with a surfboard.

"Why is it every time I take the boat out, you boys put yourselves in some kind of jam? What the hell were you thinking, chasing a lunatic like that?"

Johnny and I sat side by side on the couch, trying our best to look repentant, but mostly we just wanted to sleep.

"Do y'all think you're some kind of teenage vigilantes? You think you're bulletproof but I'm here to tell you you're not. You could've been killed on that road." He paced back and forth in front of us. "Christ almighty! When Red called I couldn't believe what I was hearing."

We tried to pay attention to Dad's rant, but we were having trouble focusing. I think I might have even dozed off. We both looked up when we noticed he wasn't talking anymore. He was staring at us and shaking his head.

"Y'all get to bed," he said wearily. "We're all tired. I'm just glad you're okay."

My brother and I slept until late in the afternoon. That evening, Dad fixed us dinner, and the three of us watched *Ed Sullivan* and *Bonanza* on the television while we ate. After that, Johnny and I sacked out for another twelve hours. We still felt foggy and sluggish on Sunday morning, so we packed our workout bags and told Dad we were heading to the gym.

"Unless you're coming back here after the workout, you better pack a sport coat, a clean shirt, and a tie," he said, "'cause we're going to the ballet this evening."

We stopped at the door. *Say what?*

"Carmen called this morning while you two were snoozing. She invited us all to the *Nutcracker* tonight: Rupert and Vita, Noble, Flavius . . . the whole clan. Even Zach's going. We've got front row tickets for the six o'clock show."

He grinned at the surprised looks on our faces. He'd been a long time between smiles lately. "Don't ever let anyone tell you the Sweetwaters ain't got no culture."

———

When we walked into the gym, we saw Naco pushing a dust mop across the red concrete floor.

"Naco and Flaco!" he shouted when he saw me.

Ralph Baltazar saw our astonished expressions and waved us into his office, a smile on his face. "Bet you didn't expect to see him here, did you? Considering the new developments in the Hunsacker case, the judge cut Diego loose, or cut him some slack, anyway. He'll still be a ward of the state school, at least until he's eighteen, but they've dropped the charges against him. They also agreed to bring him by here every morning, and then pick him up in the afternoon."

"What about his folks?" Johnny asked.

Ralph made a face like he'd tasted something awful. "They were at the hearing, but it was mainly to make sure they weren't gonna be out any money."

The bitter look vanished as he watched Diego follow his dust mop around the gym floor. "You know, I've spent a little more time at that school they stuck him in, and it's not as bad as I first thought. They've put Diego in a different wing, and he's kinda getting used to it. To tell you the truth, it's probably the best place for him to be right now."

We supposed that Ralph was probably right. Where else was the kid gonna go?

"Hey, you two heard about Karl McDevitt?" asked Ralph.

Johnny pursed his lips and nodded. "Yeah, we heard."

"It looks like he ate it out on some farm-to-market road outside of town. Hell of a wreck, from what I heard."

"Is that so?" Johnny replied. I guess my brother didn't want to be known as the guy who punched psycho-killer Karl McDevitt's ticket. I didn't blame him. That kind of notoriety wouldn't do him or me any good. We'd told Pete about it, and then made him swear to the Holy Mother Mary, the Virgin of Guadalupe, and St. Nicholas, patron saint of boxers, not to tell a soul. He solemnly agreed, but asked us to repeat the part about the bike wreck several times. He seemed to get some kind of grim satisfaction from imagining Karl's death. As for Karl, I was ready to forget the son-of-a-bitch ever existed, although I knew I never would.

It felt good to work up a sweat at the gym. The more I hit the heavy bag, skipped the rope, and hopped around boxing my shadow, the better I felt. The cold front had blown itself out, and it had warmed up considerably. Ralph raised the big overhead door, which opened to the sunny side of the street. Christmas music drifted in from somewhere.

As we were finishing up, Carmen and Veronica walked into the gym. All training came to an abrupt halt, and around two-dozen heads turned to stare. The girls were dressed in their Sunday best. Fitted skirts that ended above the knee. Heels. A red blouse for Carmen that managed to flatter every curve, and a blue sweater for Veronica, which did her a lot of favors as well. Barring Kim Novak and Liz Taylor popping up, we had a lock on the two prettiest girls in town.

After showering and changing, we met them at the entrance. "I hope you two aren't wearing those outfits to the ballet tonight," said Carmen, looking us over. I had on battered khakis stained with marine motor oil, and my letter jacket over a white T-shirt. Johnny, that elegant bastard, favored Levis ripped at one knee, a sweatshirt that read "Port Aransas Tarpon Rodeo," and a UT Longhorns baseball cap.

"Too casual?" Johnny asked.

Veronica laughed. "When I'm on stage, I can see every person in the first row. I'd probably fall down laughing."

Pete walked out of the dressing room wearing a shiny new suit. Rachel had invited him to sit with her and her family at the performance, and he looked as spiffy as El Catrín, the dapper gentlemen in the Mexican bingo game we sometimes played with him at Shady's.

Johnny stepped back in mock surprise. "Dang, Pete, is that you?"

"You clowns try not to embarrass me tonight, okay?" He straightened the knot in his necktie. "And don't forget, I'll be watching you from above in my VIP box seat."

"Ha!" Johnny laughed. "I won't make any promises. Carmen invited the whole Sweetwater clan."

I looked at Carmen. "You sure did."

"I didn't think you'd mind. Are you angry that I invited them?"

"No, not at all. Just surprised. My family's used to a different type of dancing, that's all."

Carmen laughed. "I know. I jitterbugged with your dad and all three of your uncles last time we were at Shady's. But your father seemed very excited when I talked to him on the phone, and he was very gracious."

"Well, thank you. But that many Sweetwaters under one roof can be . . . memorable. Anyway, I'm sure the show will be spectacular. What's your part again? Some kind of fairy queen deal?"

"I'm the Sugar Plum Fairy." She struck a regal pose that reminded me of Doña Delfín.

"She'll be dancing with Efrain," said Veronica. "A marvelous *pas de deux*."

"I've seen it before, remember?"

"Oh, that's right," laughed Carmen. "In my mother's studio." She grabbed both my hands and squeezed. "By the way, she called today and told me Jesse arrived in Cuba. Our two countries agreed to some kind of exchange. Castro is sending around a thousand Bay of Pigs prisoners to Miami, and Kennedy is giving Cuba a bunch of food and drugs and stuff."

"And he's giving them Jesse," I said.

Carmen heard the disappointment in my voice. "Mother said he cried when he saw his wife and daughter. He wants to be with them, Charlie. He'll be happy with them."

I couldn't argue with that. In that moment, I knew I'd made the right decision.

Carmen and Veronica gave us each a kiss on the cheek before they left, drawing shouts and wolf-whistles from our fellow boxers.

Johnny and I grabbed our gym bags to leave, but we paused when we noticed Stubby's list of rules posted on the wall near the gym exit. Ralph must have taken the sign from the Centennial Building. Out of respect for my former boxing coach, I read the hand-painted placard one more time, when, out of nowhere, a medicine ball slammed into the side of my head and knocked me to the concrete. Through watery eyes, I saw Naco Flores trot over and scoop up the ball with his supersonic arm. When I finally gathered myself and looked up, I realized he was standing over me, grinning like a bandit.

"Flaco and Naco," he whispered.

———

CHAPTER 40: EPILOGUE

Jesse Martel won his first gold medal at the 1964 Tokyo Olympics, after he KO'd Józev Gorski with a perfect left hook in the third round. The blow connected with Józev's jaw and sent his mouthpiece flying deep into the ringside stands. While his opponent sprawled on the canvas, a concerned Jesse knelt beside him, even trying to help the stupefied Polack to his feet when he finally regained consciousness.

The victory marked the beginning of Cuba's domination of international amateur boxing that continues to this day.

Jesse would hang two more Olympic golds around his neck before he retired, and he would be responsible for dozens more after Castro put him in charge of Cuba's National Boxing team. *El Comandante* touted Jesse as the "Pride of Socialism," but his many fans remember him as "The Black Pearl of the Antilles." He was, and still is, a Cuban national hero.

Of course, Jesse will always be "Feo" to me, the nickname he acquired at Stubby Hunsacker's gym. I'm convinced he would have been a world champion if he'd gone pro, his name mentioned along with other legendary middleweights such as Joe Gans, Sugar Ray Robinson, and Roberto Duran. I still watch grainy videos of his ring victories—his sturdy trunk and powerful chest supported on skinny legs, always moving, advancing on his opponents with controlled aggression, ducking and bobbing, throwing lightning-quick jabs and counterpunches. He was a classic boxer-puncher, always well prepared, and always in superb condition. I see a little bit of Jesse in every boxer that Cuba produces. I suppose he'll always be a part of me, too, even though I hung up the gloves years ago.

For much of that tension-wracked fall of 1962, I'd let myself imagine that Carmen would be a permanent part of my life. I imagined . . . . Hell, I don't know what I imagined. Maybe that she'd be dancing onstage at Lincoln Center in New York while I finished the Great American Novel in our Greenwich Village walk-up. Or maybe something else. You can imagine a lot of things when you're fifteen.

What I couldn't imagine was that Doña Delfín would at last prevail on her daughter to emigrate back to the mother country to help train the next generation of Cuban ballerinas. Carmen had always been torn between loyalties to her two homes, and when she finally chose, I was out of the picture for good. Life's a funny old dog, as Uncle Rupert used to say.

Sometimes, when I'm night fishing off the end of my pier on Rattlesnake Point or when I'm out in the Gulf sitting alone in the wheelhouse of my shrimp boat on a late night trawl, I'll look across those miles of dark water and wonder what she's doing and what might have been.

And I picture her—a solitary girl, her dark blonde hair swirling around a fine-boned face, floating like smoke across a stage. Forever young, always dancing, and always alone.

END

ABOUT THE AUTHOR

Miles Arceneaux is the *nom de plume* of Texas-based writers Brent Douglass, John T. Davis, and James R. Dennis. Miles was born many years ago as this group of friends began a collectively-written story that ultimately became the popular mystery novel *Thin Slice of Life* (2012), followed by *La Salle's Ghost* (2013) and *Ransom Island* (2014). *North Beach* is the fourth in this series of salty Gulf Coast mystery-thrillers.